I knew there could be nothing beyond this. My last picture showed a row of men, Papa among them, on their feet behind a table holding the remains of their pig dinner, jugs, and bones; and damnation on their faces and on the tent wall near their heads, like smoke, the crooked shadow of Harvey skewering Hornette. The picture was partly accidental: I was photographing a sorry cry.

Yet I was calm. Pictures are supposed to reflect the photographer's mood, but nothing could have been further from my somber mood than this frenzy. Though I had caught my breath more than once, the only sound I made was the barely audible click of my Speed Graphic's blink.

I had never felt more alone. I had found what I was looking for; and what Hornette had said was true—it was indescribable. The speaker heaves images around, his telling simplifies the truth until simplicity makes it a lie: words are toys. But my camera saw it all, and my photographs were memory. With equipment far clumsier than words, my trap for available light, I could portray what was unspeakable. And now I had the ultimate picture, a vision of hell.

Also by Paul Theroux
Published by Ballantine Books:

GIRLS AT PLAY
SAINT JACK
THE BLACK HOUSE
THE FAMILY ARSENAL
THE CONSUL'S FILE

Nonfiction:
THE GREAT RAILWAY BAZAAR:
BY TRAIN THROUGH ASIA

Picture Palace

a novel by

Paul Theroux

BALLANTINE BOOKS • NEW YORK

Library of Congress Catalog Card Number: 77-18725

ISBN 0-345-28042-3

This edition published by arrangement with
Houghton Mifflin Company

Printed in Canada

First Ballantine Books Edition: November 1978
First U.S. Edition: May 1979

To Anne

From the first moment I handled my lens with a tender ardor, and it has become to be as a living thing, with a voice and memory and creative vigor.

—Julia Margaret Cameron,
"Annals of My Glass-house"

Part One

Part One

[1]

Camera Obscura

ALL DAY LONG I had been thinking that I had grounds for believing I was an original. A beautiful day.

Now the light was failing, and the old house had that late-evening fatigue that followed a scorcher, a kind of thirst aggravated by crickets: groans from the woodwork and all the closets astir. Beyond the windmill the moon on white fenceposts made tracks to the shore of the Sound. The rest of the Cape was dark, yet I would not have been anywhere else. Blind love? It was an old feeling in me. It made me a photographer.

Some people thought I began in the wet-plate days. No — and I did not invent the camera, though a fair number of admirers told me I was the first to make it work properly, not only with *Boogie-Men,* my early negative prints, *Pigga, Negro Swimming to a Raft,* and *Blind Child with Dead Bat,* but in the simpler *Clamdiggers: Wellfleet* and the very steamy sequence of the Lamar Carney Pig Dinner. *Firebug, Fidel at Harvard,* and my portrait of Ché Guevara were part of the folklore. As for your favorite, *Twenty-two White Horses* — that received more attention than it deserved: it is seldom one's best work that brings one fame. But I was still proud of *Orthodox Jewish Boys, Cummings in Provincetown, Refugees, Danang,* and *Marilyn.*

"I've never seen Marilyn like that before," a critic once said to me.

"That's not Marilyn," I said. "It's a picture."

There were many more. Where was I? A barnacle named Frank Fusco told me that laid end to end in a retrospective they would tell my complete story.

I said, "Just because I happen to be a photographer, it doesn't mean I have to make an exhibition of myself."

"I want to hang your pictures," said Fusco.

"Hang them!" I threw open the windmill, my picture palace. "Hang them until they're dead!"

I was posturing; I still believed in my pictures. And what a posture! Your Walter Mitty dreams of heroism and great deeds. This is not odd, but most heroes and doers I have known dreamed of being Walter Mittys — puzzled benumbed souls with sore teeth and eyeglasses, shuffling through the house in carpet slippers to take a leak. "What's all the fuss about?" says the American creative genius. "I'm just a farmer."

For over fifty years I was a world-famous photographer, but being a woman was regarded as something of a freak. "A credit to her sex," the patronizing critic often said, calling attention to my tits, which they promptly put in the wringer of art criticism.

But art should require no instrument but memory, the pleasurable fear of hunching in a dark room and feeling the day's hot beauty lingering in the house. No photograph could do justice to these aromas. And gin and solitude — drawing the cork and decanting the clear liquid and tasting it to hear the ghosts wake in the walls. A camera was, after all, a room.

As a photographer I considered my camera indistinguishable from my eye. It was my Third Eye, as close-fitting as a jeweler's loupe, almost corporeal. My life was in my pictures. With so many loyal subjects it was easy for me to believe that I was a queen.

Frank had begun to forage in the windmill for the Maude Coffin Pratt Retrospective. I had no reason to discourage him. It was not until I tried to do Graham Greene in London that I had doubts about the whole shooting-match.

[2]

May We Hang You?

IT WAS something of a struggle, getting away from Grand Island (which is not an island, but a "neck" — a South Yarmouth sandbar in Nantucket Sound). No one wanted me to go: afraid I'll croak, barf on my shoes, faint on the plane, get lost, disgrace myself — that sort of elderly caper. My eye! Of course no one admitted it. They said, "Watch out, Maude — he's got a reputation," laying it on thick with that leering insincerity the younger set uses on old ladies. They want to keep us indoors, so they get flirtatious and start the canoodling routine. They are supposedly flattering me by treating me like a fairy's mother, one of those grasping disappointed women who like to be kissed and winked at and warned that they might be in for a little unwanted boom-boom.

I said sharply, "Listen, I don't think a seventy-year-old has much left to fear, do you?"

"Sure, *he's* all right, but what about you, sugar?"

Nudge, nudge; you can't win. They're really saying: Forget it, stay home, frig around with your old prints, leave everything to us; your career is ours now. Kind of a denunciation, and it peeved me.

It was about this time that Frank Fusco came up to the Cape from New York and asked me would I consider a Maude Pratt Retrospective and let him use my "archives," as he called the crates of photographs in my windmill. May we hang you?

I could not refuse. I do not enter that windmill.

And Frank was eager. A tetchy too-skinny bachelor, thirty-odd, Frank seemed to me one of those barnacles of the arts who is more tenacious than any practitioner. He called himself variously a collator or curator or an archivist, but I knew he would flourish tight against my decayed timbers, prove himself my benefactor and show me the value of my bulk. As unobtrusive as a thief and with the same ability to conceal the fidget in his gestures, he was helpful, secretive, unreadable, at my service and irritating in a way that helped me think straight.

"Why bother?" he said when I told him I had been asked to photograph Greene. But I thought: Why not? The Greene portrait could be the last one in the exhibition, a celebrated artist, my own vintage. It would be a fitting end to my career. I could then quietly die — or as Papa said, "leave the building" — with the certainty that I was really done.

The story was that Greene would only consent to a portrait if someone like me did it, a point of view I could well understand, since I would only consent to do a portrait of someone like him. The photographer at the frontier of her profession poses no problems to the distinguished subject — no danger, no indignity; nor does the beginner, who doesn't mind being bullied and condescended to. I know: it was for this reason that, at a fairly young age, I was able to photograph Alfred Stieglitz. But somewhere in between are the ones we've learned to avoid, the hookers and fame-suckers of the trade who want to take you over. Photographers are the worst — they want to marry you, move in, flush your achievement down the tube or gobble you up. The young lady chronicling with her camera is out for blood; young men, too. And they're not attracted by the work. It's the cult of personality they want to glom onto. It's a free country: *Why can't I be you?* At my age, I find them an annoyance rather than a threat, but I felt in all modesty that Mr. Greene needed me.

Frank was opposed to my going. He narrowed his

eyes at the windmill and said, "I could use your help in there."

"Not on your tintype," I said.

"And I don't think you should be traveling." He shook his head and made a cringing appeal, a funny little pitying noise at the back of his throat that meant *at your age.* "I mean, to Yerp."

"You don't think I'm up to it?" *Yerp!*

"I didn't say that," he said hoarsely, backing away. "It just seems kind of, um, precipitate."

"Whip it out," I said.

He blinked.

"That's how all good pictures get taken, Frank. Whip it out when no one's looking. I'm a pioneer of the straight approach. You should know that. Pull down vanity and start blazing away. Velocity. The high-speed method — forget your Stieglitzes and your Strands and all your other failed painters. Snatch up your Speed Graphic and shoot from the hip." I was moving around the room, hunched like a cowboy that hears a rattler. I jerked my hands: "Bam! Bam! Bam! Like that. I was the first photographer to shoot ten rolls of film on one face — never mind whose. But remember, nuance is everything. As soon as your subject remembers he's got a face you've lost your picture."

"Fine, fine," said Frank, trying to get me to simmer down, treating me like a "ree-tard." "But what about the retrospective?"

"This is for the retrospective, you cluck. My last picture. Can't you see it, hanging near the exit, eight by five, a blow-up of Greene? It'll round it off, send them away smiling."

"True," he said.

But it jolly well isn't, I thought. Frank gave me his funereal expression. Your curator, your archivist: they're undertakers. And I had sensed these morbid intimations ever since he came to suggest mounting a retrospective. It was taxidermy, the artist and her work laid dustily out like a museum turkey stuffed with dead grass and old newspapers.

I said, "I don't aim to stop living just for this precious retrospective."

He went silent.

"Anyway, I've always wanted to meet Greene," I said. "I almost did on that Cuba trip, when I did Ernest. Forget the banana skins and make it literary. Our man in Havana — what a picture that would have been!"

"You might not get a seat," said Frank. "It's a weekend — those planes are always full."

I showed him my confirmed ticket and made a saucy face.

"You won't get dinner, you know," he said, his last gasp of opposition, warning me about starving to death the way my old tutor Miss Dromgoole used to. "They're puddlejumpers. They don't serve anything to eat on those flights."

"I'll stop at The Pancake Man on the way and grab a bite. Maybe do a picture of some waffles while I'm at it."

Frank shook his head, and I knew he was worrying about my dignity. The Pancake Man — how can she! He favored a phony English place in Hyannis run by a Greek, with a menu full of mistakes in French: the American reverence for broken-down foreigners and expensive cuisine. He said—it was his last challenge —"What'll you do with your car?"

"Park it," I said crisply.

"You'll run into traffic on Twenty-eight."

"Then I'll sit there and listen to the radio," I said. "One of life's unacknowledged pleasures, Frank. Listening to the car radio in heavy traffic is nearly as good as watching TV in bed."

He was still hedging, but I thought: He's not worried about me at all — he's worried about himself. He's half my age and twice my size and he can't drive, he can't cook, he can't hold his liquor, and he wouldn't say shit if he stepped in it. If I stick around he's okay;

if I go he has to look after himself and he doesn't know how. So much for my welfare. Thanks, fella.

He pretended to be busy while I packed my suitcase and my peep-show. At five I said, "Want some pancakes?"

"How will I get back?" he whined.

I gave him a kiss and thought: Starve, you bugger. He smiled, then he looked thoughtful, concentrated hard, and farted.

"What will you say to Greene?"

"I'll wing it."

On the way to the airport I stopped at The Pancake Man and had a huge plate of blueberry flapjacks with whipped butter and maple syrup. Halfway through I picked up the menu, rolled it into a tube and peered through it: the melting pat of butter was bright and monumental, a great soft raft — the eye is so easily duped. Then I dropped this tube and went on eating, and as I yanched my way through the flapjacks I thought: Look thy last on all things lovely.

A Rotarian

TO GET TO YERP from this part of Cape Cod you take a whiteknuckler with Smilin' Jack at the controls from Hyannis Airport through sea-fog to Logan Airport in Boston. It was a Friday in June and the plane was full. I was jammed next to a character who objected (by meaningfully shifting his legs) to my hand luggage. Off to see her grandchildren, he was thinking. It didn't occur to him that the little old lady was going to London England to photograph Graham Greene. He was sort of kicking and trampling to make room for his feet. I reached down and took my Speed Graphic out from under his moving feet. I loaded it in my lap.

"Nice camera," he said. "Take care of it."

"You took the words out of my mouth."

Waste of a good camera, he was thinking. Snapshots of her grandchildren. Give her an Instamatic; she wouldn't know the difference. He's a Rotarian, stinking with resentment.

"Bumpy," I said. Why quarrel? The plane was pitching up and down and I thought I would calm him. "It's always bumpy. We'll be on the ground in a minute."

"I've been on this flight before," he said, trying to put me in my place.

The pilot's voice came over the loudspeaker: *I'd like to apologize for this aircraft. You might have noticed that it's a little smaller than our usual one —*

10

"I thought it was a bit tight," said the Rotarian, and shimmied in his seat.

"It's a Fokker," I said.

He looked sideways at me.

"Like the one in the joke. General Patton told it to me. About the airman describing a dog-fight — how he shot down this Fokker and that Fokker. His pal looks a bit embarrassed and says to some ladies present that a Fokker is a type of German plane. Heard it?"

"Not that I remember."

" 'No,' says the airman, 'these fokkers were Messerschmitts.' "

The Rotarian looked anxiously out the window.

I sat back and lit up a cigarette and when he faced me again I offered him one. "Care for a choke?"

"I gave them up," he said, with a kind of desperate pride.

"I suppose I should," I said, and coughed, as I always do when I talk about smoking.

He said, "You'd be doing yourself a big favor."

"I'm not in any danger," I said. "At my age."

"Maybe not."

I could tell he didn't want to talk, which irked me. I wanted to tell him who I was, where I was going, why I had this Speed Graphic in my lap. I had prefaced my joke by saying "General Patton told it to me," but that hadn't knocked his socks off. Granted he was only about thirty, but he might have seen the movie. Somehow, I had the idea that he disiked me, and I couldn't bear that. I wanted to cheer him up, so I could have the satisfaction of him thinking: Hey, she's not as dumb as she looks!

"The truth is," I said, as the FASTEN SEATBELTS sign came on, "the truth is, us old folks get treated like mushrooms."

"Really?" He gave me that sideways glance again: She's bats.

"Right. We're kept in the dark and every so often someone dumps shit on us."

He started to laugh as we landed at Logan, and I thought: We made it! I raised my camera and snapped his mirthful face.

"Have a good day," he said.

"You too."

[4]

Yerp

THE LONDON FLIGHT wasn't leaving until eleven. I checked my suitcase, then went upstairs, swinging my camera. It was an amateur's dream: stupendously high ceiling, mostly lighted air, Laszlo Moholy-Nagy girders, some Walker Evans signboards, Paul Strand peasants waiting for the Alitalia flight, Arthur Penn stewardesses, Harry Callahan white areas, and tiny travelers dozing on their bags as in a Minor White manifestation. Shoot down from the catwalk, title it *Departure Lounge,* and turn pro on the strength of your ironic insight into the static crappiness of modern living. But it looked wonderful to me, and though I could have spent a week doing tight close-ups of a nosegay of cigarette butts sprouting from the sand in a magnificent ashtray — ready-made "Pratts" — I spotted a lunch counter and plopped myself down. Move over, Fatso, we've got a live one.

The waitress in the fluffy cap and calico "Puritan" frock looked up from a five-gallon jar of mustard, and I did her, wham, wham, before she could blink. I couldn't decide whether to have a fishwich or a pizza, so I had a cheeseburger and thought about London. It was exciting to have an assignment, a problem to solve, and no one breathing down my neck. This was life, the camera part of my anatomy, a glimmer in my guts that helped me see. It was June, I'd be staying at the Ritz — what could be cushier? Yerp! I remembered what

13

Frank had said about my going, how he had tried to invent reasons for my staying home. Admit it, he was saying, you're dead; and in the retrospective — a word I was already beginning to hate — I saw my obituary in pictures. I found myself loathing Frank for his interest in my work and dreading what my pictures would add up to. This thought affected my digestion: grumbling ruins one's taste buds. I concentrated on London. I would be there a week — a long time between cheeseburgers. I laughed out loud and ordered another one.

"What's the flick?" I asked two hours later as I handed over my boarding pass to the man at the gate.

"We don't show in-flight movies at night," he said. He winked. "But I'll do my best to keep you entertained.

I said, "Act your age, buster, or I'll call a cop."

The plane was less than half full. I had three seats to myself and, after take-off, got a pillow and blanket and curled up. I had a bad case of heartburn — all that food — but I was dead tired. The last thing I heard was the pilot giving our altitude and saying that in an hour or so we would be flying over Gander, Newfoundland. And we had, he said, a good tailwind. I woke up in a red dawn that was spilling across a snowy sea of clouds, the kind of arctic meringue that wins photo competitions for its drifts of utter harmlessness, impenetrably stylish in soft focus. I rejected it for a clumsy shot up the aisle, forty-five elbows and an infant hanging on the curtain to First Class, like a child face down in a deep well.

And the next I knew I was in an English taxi, rattling through London traffic, narrow streets, and wooden signs, a damp summer smell of flowers, cut grass and gasoline in the air, and everyone rather pale but looking fairly well dressed in second-hand clothes. It was a bright morning, with the night's residue of rain still hissing against the tires, and the blue sky stuck on the windowpanes of houses that were otherwise spikes and black bricks.

The people on the sidewalks had that mysteriously purposeful attitude of pedestrians in foreign cities, a hint of destination in their stride. I wondered briefly why they weren't on vacation like me; it was as if they were only pretending to be busy. Mine was the traveler's envy: regretful that I didn't belong here like them and finding an unreality in their manic motion.

But the rest looked grand to me and gave me a new pair of eyes that found a rosy symmetry in the red bus passing between the red pillar box and the red telephone booth, a wonderful Bill Brandt nun unfurling in a gust of wind at Hyde Park Corner, and a splendid glow of anticipation — sunlight in the taxi and a vagrant aroma of breakfast cooking — as we raced down Piccadilly. I had the sense of being a dignitary, of momentarily believing in my fame. But that is every traveler's conceit, the self-importance of flying that dazzles the most ordinary stick-in-the-mud tourist into feeling she's a swan.

"Carry your bag, madam?" It was the doorman at the Ritz in his footman's get-up. I almost laughed. I never hear a foreign accent without thinking, *Come off it!* They're doing it on purpose. They could talk like me if they really wanted to.

Inside, I signed the register and the desk clerk handed me an envelope. Spidery handwriting, flimsy notepaper, almost oriental script, very tiny brushstrokes saying, *I shall be in the downstairs bar at 6. Please join me for a drink if you're free. Graham Greene.*

Greene

THE RITZ BAR was empty, quiet, but crazed with decoration. I tried to get a fix on it. It was white, with a
Bischof gleam, gold-trimmed mirrors that repeated its
Edwardian flourishes of filigree and cigar-wrappers,
frosty statuettes, velvet, and the illusion of crystal in
etched glass. The chocolate box of a whore's boudoir.
I guessed I would have to lie on my belly to get the
shot I wanted, but then I noticed in all that tedious
gilt a man behind the bar polishing a goblet. He wore
a white dinner jacket and was bald; his head shone. I
saw at once how the crown of his skull gathered the
whole room and miniaturized it, and he wore it like a
map pasted to his dome. Shoot him nodding and you've
got a vintage Weegee.

"A very good evening to you, madam."

I thought: You're kidding! I said, "A large gin and
tonic."

"Kew," he said, and handed it over.

"You're welcome," I said. I expected him to take a
swing at me, but he only picked up another goblet and
continued his polishing. What a head! It made the
wide-angle lens obsolete. But I didn't have the heart to
do him. In fact, since arriving in London I had begun
to feel winded and wheezy, a shortness of breath and
a sort of tingling in my fingers and toes I put down to
heartburn and jet-lag.

Greene entered the bar at six sharp, a tall man in a
dark blue suit, slightly crumpled, with an impressive

head and a rather large brooding jaw. I almost fainted:
it was my brother Orlando, a dead ringer. Ollie had
grown old in my mind like this. Greene's face, made
handsome by fatigue, had a sagging summer redness.
He could have passed for a clergyman — he had that
same assured carriage, the bored pitying lips, the gen-
tle look of someone who has just stopped praying. And
yet there was about his look of piety an aspect of raf-
fishness; about his distinguished bearing an air of anonymity; and whether it was caution or breeding, a
slight unease in his hands. Like someone out of uniform, I thought, a general without his medals, a bishop
who's left his robes upstairs, a happy man not quite
succeeding at a scowling disguise. His hair was white,
suggesting baldness at a distance, and while none of
his features was remarkable, together they created an
extraordinary effect of unshakable dignity, the courtly
ferocity you see in very old lions.

And something else, the metaphysical doohickey
fame had printed lightly on his face — a mastery of
form. One look told me he had no boss, no rivals, no
enemies, no deadlines, no hates; not a grumbler, not a
taker of orders. He was free: murder to photograph.

He said, "Miss Pratt?"

A neutral accent, hardly English, with a slight gar-
gle, a glottal stop that turned my name into *Pgatt*.

"Mister Greene," I said.

"So glad you could make it."

We went to a corner table and talked inconsequen-
tially, and it was there, while I was yattering, that I
noticed his eyes. They were pale blue and depthless,
with a curious icy light that made me think of a creature who can see in the dark — the more so because
they were also the intimidating eyes of a blind man,
with a hypnotist's unblinking blue. His magic was in
his eyes, but coldly blazing they gave away nothing but
this warning of indestructible certainty. When he stared
at me I felt as if it were no use confessing — he knew
my secrets. This inspired in me a sense of overwhelm-
ing hopelessness. Nothing I could tell him would be of

the slightest interest to him: he'd heard it before, he'd been there, he'd done it, he'd known. I was extremely frightened: I had never expected to see Orlando again or to feel so naked.

I said, "How did you happen to get my name?"

"I knew it," said Greene. Of course. Then he added, "I've followed your work with enormous interest."

"The feeling's mutual."

"I particularly like your portrait of Evelyn Waugh."

"That's a story," I said. "I was in London. Joe Ackerley said Waugh was at the Dorchester, so I wrote him a note saying how much I enjoyed his books and that I wanted to do him. A reply comes, but it's not addressed to me. It's to *Mister* Pratt and it says something like, 'We have laws in this country restraining women from writing importuning letters to strange men. You should have a word with your wife' — that kind of thing. Pretty funny all the same."

Greene nodded. "I imagine your husband was rather annoyed."

"There was no Mister Pratt," I said. "There still isn't."

Greene looked at me closely, perhaps wondering if I was going to bare my soul.

I said, "But I kept after Waugh and later on he agreed. He liked the picture, too, asked for more prints. It made him look baronial, lord of the manor — it's full of sunshine and cigar smoke. And, God, that suit! I think it was made out of a horse blanket."

"One of the best writers we've ever had," said Greene. "I saw him from time to time, mostly in the Fifties." He thought a moment, and moved his glass of sherry to his lips but didn't drink. "I was in and out of Vietnam then. You've been there, of course. I found your pictures of those refugees very moving."

"The refugees were me," I said. "Just more raggedy, that's all. I couldn't find the pictures I wanted, so I went up to Hué, but they gave me a lot of flak and wouldn't let me leave town. The military started leaning on me. They didn't care about winning the war —

they wanted to keep it going. I felt like a refugee myself, with my bum hanging out and getting kicked around. That's why the pictures were good. I could identify with those people. Oh, I know what they say — 'How can she do it to those poor so-and-so's!' But, really, they were all versions of me. Unfortunately."

"Did you have a pipe?"

"Pardon?"

"Opium," said Greene.

"Lord no."

"They ought to legalize it for people our age," he said. "Once, in Hanoi, I was in an opium place. They didn't know me. They put me in a corner and made a few pipes for me, and just as I was dropping off to sleep I looked up and saw a shelf with several of my books on it. French translations. When I woke up I was alone. I took them down and signed them."

"Then what did you do?"

"I put them back on the shelf and went away. No one saw me, and I never went back. It's a very pleasant memory."

"A photographer doesn't have those satisfactions."

"What about your picture of Ché Guevara?"

"Oh, that," I said. "I've seen it so many times I've forgotten I took it. I never get a by-line on it. It's become part of the folklore."

"Some of us remember."

It is this photograph of Ché that was on the posters, with the Prince Valiant hair and the beret, his face upturned like a saint on an ikon. I regretted it almost as soon as I saw it swimming into focus under the enlarger. It flattered him and simplified his face into an expression of suffering idealism. I had made him seem better than he was. It was the beginning of his myth, a deception people took for truth because it was a photograph. But I knew how photography lied and mistook light for fact. I got Ché on a good day. Luck, nothing more.

"Pagan saints," I said. "That's what I used to specialize in. They seemed right for the age, the best kind of hero, the embattled loser. The angel with the human smell, the innocent, the do-gooder, the outsider, the perfect stranger. I was a great underdogger. They saw things no one else did, or at least I thought so then."

Greene said, "Only the outsider sees. You have to be a stranger to write about any situation."

"Debs," I said.

"Debs?" He frowned. "I didn't think that was your line at all."

"Eugene V. Debs, the reformer," I said. "I did him."

"That's right," said Greene, but he had begun to smile.

"Ernesto wasn't a grumbler," I said. "That's what I liked about him. Raúl was something else."

"When were you in Cuba?"

"Was it 'fifty-nine? I forget. I know it was August. I had wanted to go ever since Walker Evans took his sleazy pictures of those rotting houses. I mentioned this in an interview and the next thing I know I'm awarded the José Martì Scholarship to study God-knows-what at Havana U. Naturally I turned it down."

"But you went."

"With bells on. I had a grand time. I did Ernesto and I don't know how many tractors, and the Joe Palooka of American literature, Mister Hemingway."

"I met Fidel," said Greene. There was just a hint of boasting in it.

I said, "I owe him a letter."

"Interesting chap."

"I did him, too, but he wasn't terribly pleased with it. He wanted me to do him with his arms outstretched, like Christ of the Andes, puffing a two-dollar cigar. No thank you. The one I did of him at Harvard is the best of the bunch — the hairy messiah bellowing at all those fresh-faced kids. Available light, lots of Old Testament drama."

Greene started to laugh. He had a splendid shoulder-shaking laugh, very infectious. It made his face redder, and he touched the back of his hand to his lips when he did it, like a small boy sneaking a giggle. Then he signaled to the waiter and said, "The same again."

"Isn't that Cuban jungle something?" I said.

"Yes, I liked traveling in Cuba," he said. "It could be rough, but not as rough as Africa." He put his hand to his lips again and laughed. "Do you know Jacqueline Bisset?"

"I don't think I've done her, no."

"An actress, very pretty. François Truffaut brought her down to Antibes last year. I gave them dinner and afterwards I began talking about Africa. She was interested that I'd been all over Liberia. 'But you stayed in good hotels?' she said. I explained that there weren't any hotels in the Liberian jungle. 'But you found restaurants?' she said. 'No,' I said, 'no restaurants at all.' This threw her a bit, but then she pressed me quite hard on everything else — the drinking water, the people, the weather, the wild animals and whatnot. Finally, she asked me about my car. I told her I didn't have a car. A bus, maybe? No, I said, no bus. She looked at me, then said, 'Ah, I see how you are traveling — auto-stop!' "

"Pardon?"

"Hitchhiking."

"Bumming rides?"

"That's it — she thought I was hitchhiking through the Liberian jungle in 1935!" He laughed again. "I had to tell her there weren't any roads. She was astonished."

"Say no more. I know the type."

"But very pretty. You ought really to do her sometime."

"I did a series of pretty faces," I said. "My idea was to go to out of the way places and get shots of raving beauties, who didn't know they were pretty. I did hundreds — farm girls, cashiers, housewives, girls lugging firewood, scullions, schoolgirls. A girl at a gas station, another one at a cosmetics counter in Filene's Basement."

"One sees them in the most unlikely places."

"These were heartbreaking. Afterwards, everyone said I'd posed them. But that was just it—the girls didn't have the slightest idea of why I was taking their pictures. Most of them were too poor to own mirrors. One was a knockout — a Spanish girl squatting with her skirt hiked up to her waist, sort of pouting, her bare bottom near her ankles. What a peach — there was a beautiful line cupping her bum and curving up her thigh to her knee. She didn't see me. And another one, a Chinese girl in Hong Kong I did after that Vietnam jaunt — long black hair, skin like porcelain, one of these willowy oriental bodies. She was plucking a chicken in a back alley in Kowloon, a tragic beauty with that half-starved holiness that fashion models make a mockery of. I weep when I think of it. That's partly because" — I leaned forward and whispered — "I've never told anyone this before — she was blind."

"You've done other blind people," said Greene. "I've seen them exhibited."

"When I was very young," I said slowly, trying to evade what was a fact. "I'm ashamed of it now. But the faces of the blind are never false — they are utterly naked. It was the only way I could practice my close-ups. They had no idea of what I was doing — that was the worst of it. But they had this amazing light, the whole face illuminated in beautiful repose. They're such strange pictures. I can't bear to look at them these days. I was blind myself. However, let's not go into that."

But as I described the pictures to Greene I saw that he had this same look on his own face, a blind man's luminous stare and that scarifying scrutiny in his features, his head cocked slightly to one side like a sightless witness listening for mistakes.

"I understand," he said.

"I'll be glad to show you the others," I said. "The pretty faces. You'll cry your eyes out."

"There were some lovely girls in Haiti," he said. "Many were prostitutes. Oh, I remember one night. I was with that couple I called the Smiths in my book. I

said they were vegetarians. They weren't, but they
were Americans. He was a fairly good artist. He could
sketch pictures on the spot. We were at that bar I described in my book — the brothel. He picked one out
and drew her picture, a terribly good likeness. All the
girls came over to admire it." Greene paused to sip at
his sherry, then he said, "She was a very attractive
girl. If the Smiths hadn't been there I would have dated
her myself."

It seemed a rather old-fashioned way of putting it
— "dating" a hooker; but there was a lot of respectful
admiration in his tone, none of the contempt one
usually associates with the whore-hopper.

"Dated her," I said. "You mean a little boom-
boom?"

"Jig-jig," he said. "But it comes to the same thing."

I laughed and said, "I really must be going."

"Have another drink," said Greene.

"Next time," I said. I had lost count of my gins,
but I knew that as soon as I remembered how many
I'd had I'd be drunk.

"Will you join me for dinner? I thought I might go
across the street to Bentley's. That is, if you like fish."

I was tired, my bones ached, I felt woozy and I
knew I was half pickled. I attributed all of this to my
sudden transfer from Grand Island to London. But I
also had a creeping sense of inertia, the slow alarm
of sickness turning me into a piece of meat. I knew
I should go to bed, but I wanted to have dinner with
Greene for my picture's sake. I recognized his invita-
tion as sincere. It was an English sequence: they invite
you for a drink; if you're a dead loss they have a previous engagement; if not, you're invited to dinner. I
was pleased that he hadn't flunked me.

I said, "Lead the way."

Greene went to settle the bill and ring the restaurant
while I tapped a kidney in the ladies room. I met him
outside the bar and said, "Bentley's — isn't that where
your short story takes place?"

"Which one is that?"

" 'The Invisible Japanese Gentlemen.' "

He looked a bit blank, as if he'd forgotten the story, then put on a remembering squint and said, "Oh, yes."

"One of my favorites," I said. We left the Ritz and crossed Piccadilly in the dusty mellow light that hung like lace curtains in the evening sky. Greene towered over me and I had that secure sense of protection that short people feel in the presence of much taller ones. He held my arm and steered me gallantly to Swallow Street. I knew the story well. The couple dining at Bentley's are discussing their plans: their marriage, her book. She's a bright young thing and believes her publisher's flattery — believes that she has remarkable powers of observation. Her fiancé is hopelessly in love with her, but after the meal, when he comments on the eight Japanese that have just left the restaurant, she says, "What Japanese?" and claims he doesn't love her.

I heard the waitresses muttering "Mister Greene" as we were shown to our table. Greene said, "I know what I'm having." He passed me the menu.

He began talking about trips he intended to take: Portugal, Hungary, Panama; and I wondered whether he had people joshing him and trying to persuade him to stay home. Did he have to listen to the sort of guff I had to endure? I guessed he did, even if he didn't have a Frank. I had the feeling of being with a kindred spirit, a fellow sufferer, who was completely alone, who had only his work and who, after seventy years, woke up each morning to start afresh, regarding everything he had done as more or less a failure, an inaccurate rendering of his vision, a betrayal. But I also saw how different we were: he was in his work — I wasn't in mine. And perhaps he was thinking, "This boring little old lady only believes in right and wrong — I believe in good and evil." We were of different countries, and so our ages could never be the same. In the two hours that had passed since I had first seen Orlando in him, Greene had become more and more himself, more the complicated stranger in the fourth dimension that confounds the photograph.

"London's not what it was," he was saying. "Just around the corner one used to see tarts walking up and down. It was better then — they were all over Bayswater."

"I did some of them."

"So did I," said Greene, and passed his hand across his face as if stopping a blush. "When I was at university I used to go down to Soho, have a meal in a nice little French restaurant, a half-bottle of wine, then get myself a tart. That was very pleasant."

I didn't feel I could add anything to this.

He said, "Soho's all porno shops now. It's not erotic art. I find it brutal — there's no tenderness in it."

"It's garbage," I said. "But there's an argument in its favor."

"What's that?"

"It works," I said.

"I wouldn't know," said Greene. "I haven't seen any pornography since they legalized it."

I laughed: it was so like him. And I was annoyed that I couldn't catch that contradiction on his face. He was surprising, funny, alert, alive, a real comedian, wise and droll. Knowing that I was going to meet him for a portrait I had been faced with the dilemma that plagued me every time I set out to do someone. Against my will, I created a picture in my head beforehand and tried to imagine the shot I wanted. I had seen Greene in a bar, seedier than the one in the Ritz, a slightly angled shot with only his face in focus, and the rest — his long body, his reflective posture — dim and slightly blurred: the novelist more real than his surroundings, special and yet part of that world.

Then I saw him in the flesh, his sad heavy face, his severe mouth, his blind man's eyes, and I thought: No, a close-up with a hand on his chin — he had a watchmaker's fine hands. But his laugh changed my mind, and it struck me that it was impossible. I couldn't do him. Any portrait would freeze him, fix him, give him an eternal image, like Ché looking skyward or that tubby talk-show bore everyone forgives because he was once Truman Capote, brooding under a shock of scraped-down hair.

Once, I might have taken my picture and gone, and in the printing seen his whole history in his face, past and future. Tonight, I knew despair. Photography wasn't an art, it was a craft, like making baskets. Error, the essential wrinkle in the fiber of art, was inexcusable in a craft. I had seen too much in Greene for me to be satisfied with a picture.

I said, "I think I ought to tell you that this is my last picture. I'm going to wind it up. Call it a day."

"Whatever for?"

"I'm too old to travel, for one thing."

"Which Frenchman said, 'Travel is the saddest of the pleasures'?"

"It gave me eyes."

"I understand that well enough," said Greene. "Not long ago I saw an item in a newspaper about Kim Philby."

"Always wanted to do him," I said.

"I worked for him during the war in British Intelligence. Anyway, in this item Kim said what he wanted to do more than anything else was split a bottle of wine with Graham Greene and talk over old times. I fired off a cable saying that I would meet him anywhere he named if he supplied the wine. I felt like traveling — it's as you say, an awakening. Kim cabled back, very nicely, he was busy. Some other time. I was sorry. I was quite looking forward to the trip."

"As soon as I leave home my eyes start working. I can see! It's like music — I don't really listen to it, but I can think straight while it's playing. It starts things going in my head."

Greene was listening carefully, with his fingers poised like a pianist's on the edge of the table.

"But there's something else," I said. "They're thinking of getting up a retrospective — fifty years' accumulation of pictures! I have a fella digging them out.

It was his idea. I don't dare look at them — I know what they'll add up to."

"Oh?" he said, and started to smile, as if he knew what I was going to say next.

"Nothing," I said in a whisper, "nothing. They're failures, every last one of them."

"The long defeat of doing nothing well," he said, and sounded as if he was quoting. But he was still smiling. "Does that surprise you?"

"Goddamit, yes!" I said. "I don't want to be famous for something I've failed at."

"It's all failure," he said, speaking a bit too easily for my liking, as if he'd said it before and was getting so bored with it he suspected it of being untrue. Perhaps he saw my scepticism. He added, "Why else would you have started again so many times?"

I said I saw his point, but that I expected more than that from all those years of work. It was a bit late in the day to talk so easily about failure, I said, and it was obnoxious to me to realize that while I thought I had been truthful I had only been deceiving myself. I said I felt like an old fool and the worst of it was that no one else knew, and that was a sadness.

While I had been talking the food arrived. Novelists, I knew, ate what they wrote about; Greene had lemon sole and a cold bottle of Muscadet. Before he started he leaned over and took my hand gently in his. He had long fragile hands, like beautiful gloves, and a pale green ring. He held on and said, "May I ask why you're taking my picture?"

"I wanted to, and you agreed," I said nervously. "It will complete the exhibition."

"What makes you think that?"

I wanted to say a hundred things. Because we're both as old as the hills. Because you've lived a charmed life, as I have. Because no one wanted me to come to London. Because you've known what it is to be rich, famous, and misunderstood. Because anyone but me would violate you. Because you're alone, blind, betrayed, vain. Because you're happy. Because we're equals. Because you look like my poor dead brother.

"Because," I said — *because people will see my face on yours* — "it's the next best thing to taking my own picture."

I was grateful to him for not laughing at this. He said, "I'm afraid you're wrong. Deceived again, Miss Pratt. You're an original."

I said that was all very well but that I still couldn't do a self-portrait.

"Of course you can — you have," he said. "Your self-portrait will be this retrospective, not one picture, but thousands, all those photographs."

"That's what they say. I know all old people are Monday morning quarterbacks, but I also know the life I've had, and it ain't them pictures."

"No?"

"No, sir. It's all the pictures I never took. It's the circumstances."

He put his fingertips together thoughtfully, like a man preparing to pray.

"When I did Cocteau, know what he said to me? He said, 'Ja swee san doot le poet le plew incanoe et le plew celebra.' And I know goddamned well what he meant, pardon my French." I took a few mouthfuls of fish. "When I take your picture, I'm sorry, but it's not going to be you. All I can shoot is your face. If I took my own picture that's all mine would be, an old lady, looking for a house to haunt."

"With a camera," he said.

"Pardon?"

"I said, if you did your self-portrait with a camera."

"What else would I use — a monkey wrench?"

"You could do a book," he said, and dipped his prayerful hands at me as if pronouncing a blessing.

I said, "What do I know about that?"

"The less you know, the better," he said. "You have forgotten memories. What you forget becomes the compost of the imagination."

"My mulch-pile of memories."

He smiled.

"Renounce photography, the gentleman says."

"Exactly." He said it with perfect priestlike certainty.

He made it seem so simple. It was as if he had led me through a cluttered palace of regrets, from room to shadowy room, climbing stairs and kicking carpets, and when we reached the end of the darkened corridor I'd feared most he'd thrown open a door I hadn't seen and shown me air and light and empty space: hope.

"All you have to do," he said, and now he turned, "is open your eyes."

He was staring in the direction of the door.

I saw eight Japanese gentlemen gliding noiselessly in. They wore dark suits, they were small and had that deft, precisely tuned, transistorized movement. They took their places around the large table in the center of the room and sat down.

Greene said, "There's my Japanese!"

"I see them! I see them!" I said. They were angels embodying the urgent proof that I write and remember. They were Greene's own magic trick, eight creaseless Japanese conjured from thin air and seated muttering their gum-chewing language. So the evening had gone from salutation to reminiscence, subtle, solemn, funny, coincidental, and here it paused a valediction, to show my Speed Graphic as more futile than an eyeball, a box of peepstones that could only falsify this two hours. Any picture I took of Greene would be flat as a pancake. I knew that now; but I could begin again.

Greene was reddening and laughing that rich laugh, as if he was amazed by his own success, by how perfectly his trick had worked.

I said, "No one will believe this."

And, by a professional reflex, saw my angle: Greene in Bentley's; his other half on the wall mirror; the sacrificial fish staring up at him; the half-drunk bottle of wine; Greene's face animated by laughter, all his features working at once, creating light; and in the background, just visible, his triumph, the circle of Japanese, their tiny heads and neatly plastered hair. The perfect photograph pausing in a gong of light, the artist at the foreground of his own creation: Greene by Pratt.

There were tears in my eyes as I found the right f-stop and raised my Speed Graphic. I was humbled, just another crafty witness giving permanence to her piece of luck.

Greene reached over — he had very long arms — and touched the instrument. It went cold in my hands. I lowered it.

"No," he said. "Don't spoil it."

"Please."

He said, "Let this be your first memory."

"I want to do you," I said. There were tears rolling down my cheeks, but I didn't care.

"Don't you see? You've already done me."

I still held the camera in my hand. I had looped the strap over my neck. I weighed the camera, wondering what to do with it. I could barely get my breath.

"Do put it away," said Greene.

I let it drop. It jerked my head forward. I said, "I want to tell you about my brother."

"Later," he said. "Tomorrow."

In the Ritz lobby he kissed me good night. I went upstairs, and as soon as I opened the door the floor gave way under me, the ceiling caved in, and I was rolling over and over, down a long bumpy slope, dragging my heart behind me. Still tumbling I yanked the phone down by its cord and gasped into it.

Days later, a British doctor said to me, "You're a jolly lucky girl," but what I clung to was what Greene had said in the restaurant: *Let this be your first memory.*

[6]

My Last Picture

SADNESS is ramshackle, but mourning is formal, such a buttoned-up ritual of shuffling and whispers that I wished on arrival that I hadn't cabled Frank about my spot of bother at the Ritz. Wheeled from the little plane across the Hyannis runway and looking towards the terminal with its silly WELCOME sign, I saw ten of the gloomiest creatures I had ever laid eyes on. I felt like a latecomer to my own funeral, and it struck me that at my advanced age every acquaintance is a prospective mourner. They're sticking around to bury you. That's their secret; but you're not supposed to know.

The irritating aspect of a mourner is the look of satisfaction. He is not ghoulish enough to be glad, just bursting with relief — that weird self-congratulation over being spared. They had warned me that I might snuff it, but a warning is the cheapest form of abuse: it was still ringing in my ears. And their expressions proved it. *I told you so* is one of the most gleeful expressions in the language, and yet no one actually says it in so many words. It is a cautioning wobble of the head, a suppressed smirk, the fish-lips of reproof and a hectoring silence.

Well, I wasn't dead, which was even better from their point of view, because the story was that I had a massive heart seizure (and I could hear them saying, " — all those waffles"). This was a lesson to me; I'd listen to them from now on; I wouldn't be so fractious. But the advantage was mine. I didn't like being treated like a stiff; however, since everyone knew that I'd croaked in London there was nothing they could decently refuse me.

"Here I am," I said. "The Dong with the Luminous Nose."

Frank gave me a kiss and introduced me to the other mourners — neighbors, well-wishers, shutterbugs, characters I scarcely knew. They were all trying to buck me up and at the same time were touching me and peering into my face as if attempting to discover whether I had learned my lesson. In my anger I mentally named them: Grippo, Saliva, Shuffles, the Beeny sisters, Bushrag, Cootie, Prickett, and Munt; and Frank, who had been Thunderbum to me ever since his farty farewell. Naming them was like portraiture and made me feel better.

I said, "I feel like a pizza."

Prickett grunted, but Frank said, "She's the boss" and helped me out of the wheelchair the airline had provided.

"Look," said Shuffles, "a Garry Winogrand." He pointed to the pathetic wheelchair stenciled *New England Airways*.

At the Leaning Tower of Pizza I drew out the envelope I had carried from London and put it on my lap.

"What's that, sugar?" asked the hairy one I thought of as Bushrag. He was wearing army gear — flak jacket, khaki shirt, combat boots, everything but the medals. Dressed as a soldier in the insincere fashion this racket considered stylish. He wouldn't have been able to fight his way out of a pay toilet.

But he had risked fragging me with the question the rest of them had wanted to ask. I pretended I didn't understand. I sipped my Shasta.

"That," he said, jabbing with his finger, "down there."

"Don't point that thing at me. There's a nail on the end of it."

Cootie snorted, and Grippo — who had nearly

broken my hand to show me how glad he was to meet me (quite a problem there: I've never trusted hand-squashers) — Grippo said, "In the folder."

"What folder?"

"Looks like a picture, Miss Pratt," said Munt. Another untrustworthy one. It was his dark basted-looking skin: the vanity of the sunbather. I could almost hear him saying, *I think I'll go work on my tan.*

"Sure does." This from Saliva, smacking his lips.

I picked up the envelope. "This? You wouldn't be interested in this."

Bushrag said, "Yeah, but what is it?"

"Souvenir from London," I said. "Just a picture."

"I'd be very interested," said Frank, putting on his studious Thunderbum expression.

"Came out with fur on it," I said.

Bushrag nodded. "Flaky. Sometimes they're the best kind."

"It wasn't deliberate," I said.

"What's the difference?"

"Pretty big," I said. "I've never held with your blurry photographers. Some characters have lenses that cost three grand, maybe more. They shoot their cuffs, then exhibit them and call them — what? — mood pieces, fragments, dream-sequence, textures, or some nonsense like that. They don't know what they're doing. That's fatal — they're fogbound Guggenheim art."

"Maude's right," said Frank, and in a matter of seconds they were all agreeing with him, fueling my argument so strenuously I couldn't get a word in. They were making off-the-wall generalizations and over-stating everything I had said. Running dogs, wagging their tails at me. It is the worst danger of fame: everyone agrees with you, even when you're wrong. But maybe, I thought, they were doing it because I had come unstuck in London, and that made me feel like a bigger dope.

"You can spot the phonies," I managed to put in.

"Untitled — that's a cry for help. All my pictures have titles."

"What's the name of that one, then?" asked Cootie, indicating the one on my lap.

"This?" I fussed and delayed until they were all listening, then I said, "This here's a portrait of me. I'm thinking of calling it *Maude Pratt.* You might give it another name."

"I thought you didn't allow anyone to take your picture," said one of the Beeny sisters, pushing her moon-dog face at me. "So you could preserve your anonymity kind of."

"I've preserved it long enough."

"It's really you?" said Shuffles.

Grippo said, "Hey, that's historic."

Frank said, "But why?"

"I don't need it no more."

"Don't need it?" Frank's eyes grew tiny in disbelief. "But you said all photographers needed it."

"I ain't a photographer no more," I said. I detached a wedge of pizza and took a bite.

No one was eating. They were staring at me.

Frank shoved his plate aside with the back of his hand. He wanted a little drama. He said, "Maude!"

"Your pizza's getting cold," I said.

"I'd really like to see that picture," he said in a small voice.

"You don't want to see this."

"No, I sincerely would. It's something for the museum. I've got the ear of the guy in Acquisitions."

"Don't bend it on my account. Like I said, this picture's got fur on it."

"We'd still pay."

"For this?"

"Sure. Give us world reproduction rights and your worries are over."

"Frank, do I have worries?"

He winced. "We paid a lot for those Diane Arbus pictures."

"That freak show," I said. "Poor gal needed her engine tuned."

The smaller of the Beeny sisters said, "Her pictures were really strange. I mean, tragic."

"Quite the reverse," I said. "Arbus is all comedy, or at least farce. She was like Weegee. She thought those people looked funny. Now get off the pot."

"I didn't want to start a discussion about Diane Arbus," said Frank. "I was just trying to give you an example of what we pay."

"You haven't mentioned a price," I said.

Frank said, "In the neighborhood of a grand."

"Two is a figure I could live with."

"We'd have to see the picture first."

"I'll make a deal with you," I said. "I told you I ain't a photographer no more. If you promise not to ask me why, you can have this picture free."

Frank said, "Let's have a look at it."

"That's against the rules. But I'll describe it to you."

"Shoot."

"It's got a lot going for it," I said. "Depth of field, symmetry, a kind of brooding cosmic quality. Texture-wise, it's grainy understatement, with ominous shadows, like an untitled by Ralph Eugene Meatyard or one of your Wynn Bullock fern studies with a pair of knockers. My heart's in this, sort of caged in and qualified somewhat by your absence of natural light. It works as an architectonic model —"

I went on in this vein, generally giving him back the critical bull-sugar his sort have been haunting me with for fifty years, the jabber about conceptualizing the vagrant image, redefining the semiology of the foreground and cannibalizing the eye. Quack, quack: I was enjoying myself and he was absolutely lapping it up.

He said, "Okay, say no more — it's a deal."

"You lucky stiff," I said, handing him the envelope.

He was trembling as he tore open the flap, and he looked for a moment as if he was preparing to eat it. Then he pulled it out: my chest x-ray.

He went very quiet. The others leaned over to see what it was. A couple of them were on the point of guffawing. I heard a snort.

Frank said, "That's not funny."

"Then why am I laughing?" I said.

Bushrag said, "That's outasight — it really is an x-ray!"

"Sure it is," I said. "Frame it, call it *Fragments* — no one'll know the difference." Bushrag was laughing; the rest of them were looking at me as if I had gone off my head, that mourner's expression of mingled grief and joy. I said, "It'll win a prize."

Frank said, "You're pulling my leg. You haven't given up photography. You're not feeling too hot — am I right?"

"Listen, doctor," I said. "Have you heard the one about the scientist and the frog? No? Well, there was this scientist. He wanted to find out what happened when you cut a frog's legs off, right? He cuts off the hind legs and says, 'Jump!' Frog sort of lurches forward. He cuts off one of the front legs and says 'Jump!' Frog drags himself an inch or so. Then the scientist cuts off the remaining front leg and says 'Jump!' Nothing happens. He shouts it again. The frog just blinks and sits there."

"Of course —"

"Wait a sec," I said. "So what does the scientist do? He's working for a big foundation — he's got to produce a report or his Guggenheim won't be renewed. He's a researcher, isn't he? The National Endowment for the Arts just bought him a Cadillac so he won't defect to the Russians. He takes out his notebook and writes, 'If you cut the limbs off a frog you make him deaf.' Get it? Okay, the joke's over. Now take me home. I've had a long day."

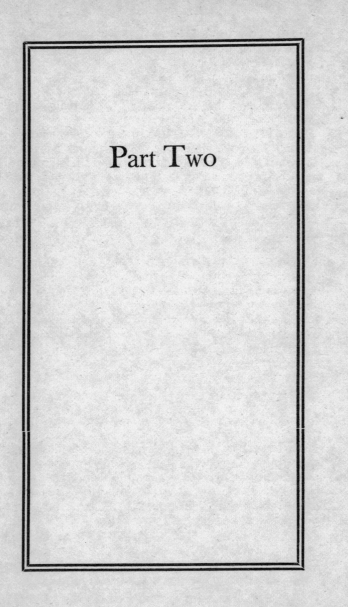

Part Two

Part Two

My First Picture

So, now that I had renounced photography for good, the first thing I wanted to get off my chest was my camera. As any damned fool can see, a photographer does not appear in her own pictures except as a dim and occasional reflection — even the greatest one is no more than a gleam in her subject's eye. It is common enough among painters to do self-portraits, and there is certainly no shortage of writers who put themselves into their books — the most notorious example being your modern writer who can't describe anyone else, which makes it pretty easy for biographers but holy hell for the rest of us.

It is not the cinch it seems for a photographer to take her own picture, and though it is technically feasible in an age when the amateur shutterbug can shoot halitosis in pitch dark, it is seldom done because — unless you have arms like an ape — it entails rigging the camera and then panting into position, a hectic business like a rather exhausting form of suicide. The results usually bear this out in panicky grins and mad staring eyes. Karsh of Ottawa has been content to remain a fancy signature on his clients' lapels, and until I met Mr. Greene, so was I. But I didn't have that thing around my neck anymore, and it seemed high time I considered a memoir. At my age I suspected that it would have the apologetic self-regard of an obituary, but still, wasn't writing the best form of ventilation?

The last picture in this retrospective had to be my own.

Picasso (who loved being photographed stark naked) told me that the surest sign of an artist's poverty was his self-portrait, and I think he meant the spiritual kind —blubbing into a mirror and not knowing which side you're on. But looking back over seventy years I saw nothing but wealth and luck and fame. I was not alone in thinking that, though my heart was not always in it, my career had been absolutely triumphant.

My heart was another story. The truth was that of all the people I had ever done, and that includes all your heavies, your Picassos, your Hemingways, your Phil Rizuttos, your T. S. Eliots and E. V. Debses — of all these people, I liked my brother Orlando best. Take D. H. Lawrence. He hated having his picture done, and no wonder. He had a tiny head, a high voice, and reddish whiskers of the sort that crackers call "jeezly." I found him a most unattractive man who, because he thought he was dynamite sexually, taught me something about the artist's imagination. The rest of us are healthy; it's the wounded who take to art: no one wins more races than the cripple in his sleep.

And — to move on — of all the places I had ever seen, this part of the Cape was my favorite, where the pizza joints, pancake parlors, the nautical saloons— all plastic and leatherette — and the drive-in hamburger stands, flanked by salt marsh and pine woods, face the brimming ocean. Orlando was dead, rest his soul, but I often thought of him as I sped along Route 28 in my new Chevy, with the radio going, marveling at how downright frytastic everything looked, this blend of honky-tonk and brooding, swallowing sea — it was pure Pratt, a vindication of vulgarity. I saw the sunset on the Sound through the hole in a giant Styrofoam donut ("Ho-Made Koffee 'n' Krullers") and I wanted to holler, "What's wrong with that!" and to Orlando in Valhalla, "How am I doing!" These were not questions. In the car, tailgating some retired gent who'd

come down here in his orange pants and polka-dot
shirt and straw fedora to Wrinkle City to check into
some beaverboard condominium until there was room
in one of our "colonial-style" funeral parlors — tailgating that liniment freak, I had a kind of bottomless rev-
erie about having had the best life anyone could want
and how little it showed in the pictures I started to take
when, according to Frank, I was eleven.

It was a summer afternoon in 1917.

My father hung upside down in the little lozenge of
glass; my mother's chair was stuck in a canopy of
flowers where my beautiful brother Orlando's toes
were planted, and he had his arm around my little
sister Phoebe's butterball waist as if he was holding on
for dear life and didn't want to fall. I had stood them
on their heads, but nothing dropped out of their pockets, and I saw at once that they looked even ritzier
this way, like angels or Egyptians reflected in an un-
disturbed pool, wreathed in sunlight from below that
showed the sleepless assurance of their wealth. In this
reversal, their Yankee chins protruded like hatchets,
our white house balanced on its weathervane, our
windmill on its sails, and our trees depended massively,
showing all their apples — with its foliage sprawling
downwards the gnarled plum tree was transformed into
a bird-eating spider. My new perspective offered me
details: Orlando's reckless embrace, the dog's ball
with munch-marks on it glued to a sky of grass; the
cellar door, my cast-off sweater lightly defying gravity,
and the long stripe of my summer shadow narrowing
toward my brother, so that between his feet my little
head lay, at the top end of my distorted body, like a
lover begging for mercy, a sudden monster.

Gulls flew on their backs, the horizon floated on a
cushion of air, and that vapor of glittering winks in the
distance was Nantucket Sound. I had never seen
anything like it. I was enchanted. Until then, I had
been too ashamed to stare — in my family it wasn't
done. But now I could take my time and watch the dog
sliding into focus like a fly crossing a ceiling, and see

the great trick of light magnetizing my family by their feet into miraculous yoga postures.

That was when I noticed the tentative darkness near my father's head, and the more I watched it the further this shadow spread, moving like night from the left-hand corner. The blur hooded them as if for a hanging, four victims awaiting the noose of forgetfulness to tighten the drawstrings and complete the drop: memory's gallows of nameless martyrs with its expressive foreground of unrelated objects, the ball, the sweater, all those feet, and finally only the windmill. Come back!

"I can't see!" I cried.

"Get that thumb of yours off the viewfinder, Maude," said Papa calmly.

I did not look up. I experimented with my thumb and stared at the glass lozenge on the edge of my Brownie. My family reappeared, laughing. But upside down their mockery didn't matter. They swayed as if they were about to be dislodged, the laughter shaking them out of their pompous practiced attitudes and giving them life.

I snapped the picture. I had caught a decisive moment of the past in my mousetrap. I held it in my hands, in that rinky-dink camera (everything further than eight feet was in focus), and I rejoiced.

The best pictures are seldom good pictures. This was the one I always started with when freeloaders like Bushrag and Grippo came out to see me. They had cameras slung around their necks, and their shoulder-bags were crammed with equipment. They wanted to see my work. I offered them the first look I ever had of my own family, and I waited until they saw what I did that hot afternoon.

But they crowded me, they looked over my shoulder and did not see anything. To them I was an antique, like the lobster pots and cranberry scoops they found in West Barnstable and took home to varnish and venerate. They were rediscovering me; it was a big favor — wasn't I lucky? Each one treated me as if

he'd invented me and would show me his Count
Esterhazy shots, lingering too long on the ones he
wanted me to admire, saying, "This one's pretty incredible — I do some pretty incredible things," a dazzling
derivative sunset that was pure vomit, and inevitable
park bench, a dead squirrel, a wino. Another whose
love of cement and rivets surpassed Berenice Abbott's,
would heave his tonnage of New York at me. There
would be the shooter of tropical slums, his pictures telling me nothing more than that he had the air fare to
Caracas: the one with the most expensive equipment
always seemed to concentrate on starving natives — I
could tell the price of a camera by the rags in a picture.
Jostling for my attention they would have my head
spinning with their fisheye lenses or nauseate me with
mood pieces they'd developed in their own bathwater.
The girls would be, as they put it, "into freaks, because
it represents how I feel as a woman." They came to
see me and they did all the talking, pretending an
interest in me to invite my admiration for them, the
kind of coy blackmailing flattery that is a hungering
for praise. I looked at their work. It may not have
been tragedy but it certainly was murder. They were
like amateur assassins whose parents gave them a gun
for Christmas: they brought me their victims. I told
them: A camera isn't a toy, remember that. I didn't
add that it is, but just more dangerous than other toys.

"Your pictures," I said, "are works of subversion.
Are you proud of that?"

Sure, sure, they said. They had shown me theirs;
now they were itching to see mine: my Pig Dinner
sequence, my *Faces of Fiction,* my crying series, my
pictures of empty rooms, my Hollywood shots, *Firebug,
Stieglitz, Slaughter, the Piano Tuner, Huxley,* my
blacks — I was the first to exhibit them: no one had
ever seen them before.

The album was on my lap. There were others in the
windmill, stacked to the ceiling, and trunks full of
contact sheets. But I refused to go in there. My freckled hands remained on this old family photograph, that

summer day I saw upside down through my Kodak
Brownie. They did not want to look. They made the
mistake all young people do when visiting the very
old: we're easy game, we're deaf to sarcasm and can't
see them wink. They made funny faces behind my
back: you can needle an oldster! They talked too loud
and nudged each other and didn't think I knew they
were being insincere. As if I had never seen them before! Still, I wanted them to see this picture, my clumsy
lyric stuck on the first page of my first album. I said
nothing until they began to bounce on the sofa in
impatience: How long is the old girl going to take? No
one said she was a fucken ree-tard!

These believers in the immortality of the photograph
wanted to deal with my life in a single afternoon. They
could not even pronounce Niépce. They were eaten
up with haste. It was their conceit: their speed, the
speed of light.

They had all the equipment — what was the problem? These faddists of high contrast and golf-ball grain
could shoot fly spit, the smell of an onion, sunspots, a
virus picking its nose, bazooka shells bursting out of
gun muzzles, indigestion, a fart in a mitten. With their
motor-driven cameras — a lens for every occasion —
they could do it underwater, with mirrors, twenty
thousand feet over Rangoon. That shotgun was no
shotgun; it was a Hasselblad with a telescopic lens on
a shoulder rest, "for combat situations," as the kid said,
and it really did look lethal. And what of that Japanese capsule, the size of a tranquilizer, with a tiny
pinhole eye? It was a camera so small you could swallow it at noon and photograph your breakfast.

I brushed these trinkets aside. I didn't tell them I
used a box camera until 1923, a folding camera until
1938 and only then broke down and bought a Speed
Graphic for Florida. Instead, I said a few words on
man the picture-maker — erect, sketching his fears
on a cave wall — which left man the tool-maker on all
fours, hunched over a nut he was bludgeoning with a
rock some fool scientist would enshrine. The mind is

made of pictures, I said, not words; thought is pictorial, the eye is all art, get the picture? And, sure, sure, they said — saying no meant saying why. They were in a big hurry to see *Twenty-two White Horses* and my contacts of Ché Guevara and my blacks. Never mind Orlando and Phoebe or myself when young. They didn't have time for that. They took pictures hanging by their ankles, their light meters could detect glowworms in the next county. And at this point they were haywire with curiosity.

"Mind if we turn the page, Miss Pratt?"

I jolly well did mind. My hand held it down. There was that windmill with its narrow window. They wouldn't understand me unless they looked in and saw what I saw.

Impudently, they reached. I didn't say *Patience, children* or *Oh, no, you don't*. I didn't slap them — they would probably have hit me back. The old person who blows her top all of a sudden has been furious for years — I said what I had to and hoped they would see. "Shit and derision!"

[8]

Orlando

BUT even if they had slobbered over every blessed picture in the place they would not have understood, for Frank was in the windmill doing that very thing, and not a day passed without his dragging some forgotten shot to the room that had become my camera obscura and screwing up his face and saying, "What's this one all about?" It helped me remember the pictures I never took, or if I did, the ones I never showed anyone.

I feared that the Maude Coffin Pratt Retrospective, scheduled to open in New York in November, would give little idea of the woman I was or the times I had. I was behind the camera, cheating, not in front of it. I hinted to Frank that I wanted to write something and he humored me with "Might be just the ticket — something short and personal for the catalogue — paragraph or so about your life."

Fuck your catalogue, I thought. A life is too messy and random to be summarized so neatly. It gets out of hand, it haunts, it sprawls beyond the periphery of a single picture, casting shadows every which way. I needed a little latitude if I was going to do complete justice to my life, which I felt had been happy on the whole and fairly interesting if not remarkable. The picture palace on the lawn held half the story, but the mind had its own picture palace, much grander, like a mad queen's extravagance — not the museum show of pictorial fossils — room after room of memory's live ghosts and events only now detectable and surprising revelations behind each creaking door. It was necessary to pass through these chilly bedchambers and along the corridors and climb blindly to the tower of imagination above its ramparts to look down and comprehend the spin of its whole design. My life mattered more than my work, but my work gave no hint of this.

The trouble with cameras is that people see them a mile away and they get self-conscious and sneeze out their souls and put on that numbed guilty expression and act as if you are going to shoot them dead. Or worse, they pose like dummies and show their teeth: even your bare-assed savage knows how to say cheese. As a photographer I was embarrassed to be caught with that contraption in my mitts, like an elderly pervert, a distinguished old lady with my skirt around my neck frightening children at play. Later, I was proud of the way I could conceal my intention and, long before the Japanese produced their tiny instruments, I could disguise my camera — as a shoe box or a handbag or as a ridiculous hat that people gaped at, not knowing that I was recording their curious squints. *Orthodox Jewish Boys,* a small group of dark-eyed youngsters with beanies and sidecurls — some critics found them a bizarre evocation of alienated Americans ignoring the squalor of downtown Brooklyn and looking skyward toward Jehovah — are just some curious kids looking at my hat.

I was anonymous, I made no sound, I never got in the way of my pictures. I wanted the viewer to drown among the images without thinking of me. The whole of my craft went into making it easy for the blinking public; I then withdrew and removed all traces of myself, so that the viewer could believe the discovery to be his. Only after studying it for a long time should the viewer realize that in my early picture, *Negro Swimming to a Raft,* the man is handcuffed and the raft too small and frail to bear his weight; then the rainclouds become apparent, the futility of the swim, the desper-

ate motion in the swift current of the Mystic River —
there is the municipal signboard lettered small on the
far bank (I took this picture in West Medford in 1927;
the convict, one Cecil Jerome, was quickly recaptured). People have seen this photograph and thought
they invented its importance; it was a personal victory
for them, they felt responsible for it, the details were
theirs, and I didn't blame them. Thereafter, everything
they saw was new: I had given them my eyes.

It worked—no one knew me. My exhibitions were
occasions for people to think about themselves as they
might, during a concert of classical music, remember a
compliment or rehearse their marriage, think of everything but the piece being played. And, as I say,
people liked themselves a bit better after seeing my
photographs. They saw their lives flash before them:
for minutes they drowned in my pictures.

I knew this queer experience. It used to interest me,
looking at a picture or a sheet of contact prints, to lose
the image and see my own reflection staring back.
In something beautiful I saw this pining double exposure. The light would glance on my loaf-like face and
print it on the glossy paper, and no matter how hard
I tried I could not regain the original image that lay
beneath it. The pliable paper was a funhouse mirror
of stammering light in which I shimmered and
drooped, now softening sadly, now jumping into splinters to be gathered a moment later into a sheaf of
features. I lost my nose, I watched my cheeks ex-
plode, I was lobotomized by a chance blade of light
that flicked away the front of my head. It was not the
ordinary frenzy for reassurance that people usually
seek in mirrors — indeed, I didn't want to see my
face. But there it was, as ineradicable as the reflected
image one gets on the window of a train late at night
when, hoping for a clue to how far one has traveled,
one looks out and sees one's own kisser staring inquis-
itively in. That rather haunted face peered from many
of the pictures I developed; it wouldn't slide off, I

could not shake it loose, and it was, maddeningly, not a pretty face.

My face, more than anything else, made me career-minded. In those days, attractive girls waited for Mr. Right, and ugly ones, if they had any sense, looked for a job. I was stamped with imperfection. My face was lopsided and when I was tired it looked even worse. I wished I could detach it like a mask; I scrutinized it in the mornings for changes and tried out expressions that made me look less hideous. But I knew with a woe that showed in every feature that this was the face I had to push through the world.

I was a fastidious slob, attentive and yet with such a profound dread of failure that my efforts to be neat produced only disorder and private pain. I was not horrible enough to be frightening, nor plain enough to be invisible, but homely and obvious, the sort of child visitors attempt to compliment by saying, "I'll bet she's good with her hands." It was one of these patronizing people who gave me my first camera: "You'll have hours of fun with that!" If you didn't have looks you had to have a knack, and somehow I earned the reputation — so many physically unattractive people do — of having a good heart. It was conventional flattery; no one ever accused me of being vain and none of my parents' friends treated me like a child. Ugliness itself was like maturity: I looked like an adult at eleven, one of those big serious things whose plainness is taken for intelligence; the ugly child so often looks forty. I was marked.

The upshot of this was a very strange little girl. It made me secretive and pious, and kind of holy cow, and — it is not unusual — it gave me a taste for perfection. I had a precocious grasp of bright symmetries. I loved what was beautiful; I knew I was not. The artist is a packhorse and frequently looks like one, but his eye is responsive and accurate. It was not that I knew what I was; more important, I knew what I was not. I understood fairly early the depressions of our cook, Frenise, and how they must have been caused by a knowledge not that she was black but that she wasn't white.

Frenise returned that understanding. "Just like us," she would say, and at first I wondered who she meant by *us:* blacks? cooks? women? Frenise did the chickens. Near the chicken coop there was a shed where the grain was kept in a barrel. It had a lid, but the lid was usually ajar so the grain would not go moldy. Rats could climb into this barrel, but we didn't discover this until one day a rat had eaten so much it was too fat to climb out. That day Frenise screeched when she leaned over to take a scoop of it. I heard her and ran to the shed.

"Shet," she said, "there's a fat black old rat in there. Bidge can't do nothing — too swole up." She made a kissing sound and I heard the purr of Phoebe's Angora cat, a fluffy white creature with a bell on its collar so he wouldn't eat the robins.

"Just like us," said Frenise. "Faa." She gathered the cat in her arms and stroking it to settle it she turned and poured this length of white fur into the grain barrel. She clapped the lid on and shook her head. There was a thump, the tinkle of a bell, a skidding like grain being sluiced in a bucket, and then only the bell.

Then, Frenise (who played a dime lottery every week she called "The Bug" and said "shet" more times than anyone I have ever known) lifted the lid off the barrel and took out the gasping cat. Its white fur was splashed with blood and one ear was slightly torn. She dropped it and stamped her slippered foot and then reached in again; and when I saw what was attached to that undamaged tail — all those bites on rag and bone, making it look like a chewed radish — I heard Frenise say, "Just like us" and knew she was including me. She saw in me the spitting image of her black self. It is an early picture: me and Frenise and the bitten rat. We carried it to a flowerbed and buried it together.

That night I was chased in a dream. I escaped, I lost my tail, and a bigger blacker Frenise hovered over me and yapped, "You look better that way, Maudie."

People often asked me why it was that my first exhibition of photographs was composed mainly of black portraits, Negroes (as they used to be known) in every human attitude. I used to say, "Because they're so pretty" (this was reported in hayseed language, "Because they're a whole lot purtier than white folks"). It was partly true.

My family was kind. Frenise toughened me with her profanity ("shet," "bidge," and "faa"), they courted me with their sorrow; so they competed with her and made me their madonna. I was not suited to the role, but the weak never choose, and the madonna is made in childhood. They were generous and uncritical, protective, anxious to please me and prompt with their attention. I understood their adoring eyes to mean that I was blessed in some extraordinary way, singled out for their encouragement and praise, and did not guess, not for the longest time, that they did this purely because they thought I was ugly as a monkey.

They magnified my homeliness, so they exaggerated their pity. Children adore being pitied; I mistook it for love, I snuggled up to it and purred and thought they were kissing me when in fact they were trying to lick my wounds. "Her real love," Mama said, "is her camera." Their protective attitude isolated me, and this state of affairs made me look upon my brother and sister as my only friends. I came to depend on them in a way that is known best to people passionately in love. They aroused in me all the instincts of a mistress—jealousy, possessiveness, spite, greed. Pity is uncertain; it has none of love's terrible demand, it asks nothing, it gives nothing, it casts a feeble light on one's defects. I suppose I recognized that uncertainty; it wore me down, it didn't feed me, it made me tricky, a plotting adult at the age of eleven. I came to fear the thought of separation our growing-up would bring — we'd be forced apart, I'd be alone. My father was kindest. I had his face: he took the blame.

Papa loved music — he said it oiled the springs in his mind (which was why he had a season ticket to the opera, though he called it "the uproar"). One April — a Boston April: sunflecks on wet streets — he took Orlando and me to a children's concert at Symphony Hall, and he left us there in the balcony while he ducked out to do some shopping. Out of pure high spirits we ran to the exit when he was gone and after a few heavy doors which I held open for little Orlando we found ourselves on a fire escape, clinging to the rail and looking down — not far, two or three floors. I was in a long dress and Orlando in his sailor suit. We laughed and listened to the rumble of street noise booming in the alley. I cannot remember why we did it, or what we expected to see. Large drops of rain tumbled through sunlight and glittered whole on Orlando's hair.

There was a scrape of feet on the walls, a man walking down the alley. He heard us laughing and looked up, and stared and smiled. Then, I could not have put his thoughts into words, but somehow I knew that if there had only been one of us he would have passed on. He lingered below us. Instinct told him we were brother and sister, not a single image but a double creature, a pair fleetingly but profoundly glimpsed: a dream of love, charming and indivisible. I read his thoughts and saw he was blessing us with his envious approval. We had made his day, he had changed our lives. I took Orlando's hand, drew him to me and kissed his cheek. The stranger was delighted; he watched us until the music knocking on the firedoor called us in. Afterward, I knew he would root for us in his dreams, and dream continually, and as long as he dreamed of us I would love Orlando. If I could assign a date for the beginning of my loving Orlando it would be that afternoon in April, when I saw consent in that stranger's eyes.

I never wanted a pony. Orlando did. I asked for it so that he would want me, and when I got it he did. I could have had anything; I wanted Orlando. And that

was how I learned the difference between love and
pity. Pity was easy, but love seemed a kind of confusion that made the lover both cannibal and mission-
ary, touched with every emotion except doubt. I loved
him, I knew I would be blind without him. He had
grace; he was blameless because he was beautiful; he
was my missing half, whom I did not in the least
resemble. It is not odd that I associate love with childhood. Lovers are always children, because love is
ignorant risk-taking — a stifling illusion of the unat-
tainable, most passionate at its most impossible and
nonexistent otherwise. I never once remembered what
he was, I knew only what I wanted him to be, because together, in Orlando and me, I saw perfection:
body and soul.

It was another summer — easy for me to prettify with
fragrant detail after so long, but memory willfully
erases grandeur and sorts what is left: the leather
smell of the rumble seat, the cushion stitches, the
cloud of dust we raised. Orlando sat between Phoebe
and me as we jounced down Great Gammon Road,
off to Hyannis and Papa's sailboat. Orlando's face was
shining with pleasure. He was happy; I wanted to be
happy. He was handsome; I coveted that. Having him
I could have everything, and it was as if the bargain
had been sealed. I was sure of it when he put one
arm around me tenderly — his other he threw around
Phoebe — his trust resting lightly on my shoulder. It
was a certainty. He could not refuse me, nor would I
share him.

I remembered nothing of the sail itself, and my photograph of the afternoon showed Orlando and Phoebe
in wet clinging bathing suits. Perhaps they swam, perhaps I crouched under my sun hat: some photographs
say very little.

That night I could not sleep. I was fourteen and had
my own room — pictures everywhere, curling edges,
stuck to the walls, several albums already filled. The
child's bedroom is a forcing-house of longings, and

there were mine, scattered around and on view, an early intimation of the artist's magpie mind evident in the clutter, my refusal to discard the mountain of trifles my hobby had produced for me. I lay in bed and thought of Orlando and drew inspiration from my pictures: I knew what I had to do.

I crept out of bed and down the darkened hall, then stood inhaling varnish. The house seemed, as it did on dark nights when I was awake and clammy, as if it were going to fall down. I could hear its frantic crickets, the abrupt groanings of its floors, its beams warning me with grunts. At night it seemed empty and unsupported, and now it trembled under my prowling feet as if a phantom occupant was hurrying away. The floor had tilted like a ramp, tipping me forward on my errand. I expected to hear the splintery sigh of woodwork, a little shake, and the whole place on my head in furious collapse. Yet it held: a miracle.

Orlando's door was open a crack, and showed more darkness. I rapped twice; I didn't speak.

He did, instantly, in a clear voice: "I thought you changed your mind."

I entered. He was nowhere. I heard him breathe from the bed, a sound that lit him like a lamp, and I could feel his warmth from where I stood. The darkness that hid him made me small and noisy. I shuffled across the room, my nightgown going *floop-floop,* and got into bed. I felt for him, searched the cool sandwich of sheets with my hand. He wasn't there.

"Over here, silly."

And then I saw his shadowy outline in a chair just beyond the bed. So he was up! No wonder he sounded so wide-awake! He had been waiting for me.

He sprang into my lap. I caught him with my knees and he hugged me gently, steadying my plump damp arms with a caress and saying, "How do you like this?"

I kissed him. He sniffed and sighed.

"Maude?"

Fumbling in my terror I said, "I was afraid of the dark."

He yanked the light on and we reacted to the brightness that splashed our faces, making wincing masks, squinting as if we had soap in our eyes and trying to swallow the light.

He said, "Let's play cards."

I thought it was a euphemism for a better game and was aroused. But he meant what he said: he was innocent, in rumpled pajamas, just eight years old.

The moths watched us at the screens where they clung, and at dawn, when they shriveled and shut, deadening themselves for the day, and the birds racketed beneath the window, I took myself back to my room. I thought: I will kill anyone who takes Orlando away from me.

It was an easy vow. A family, if it is large and well-connected, is like a religion. It serves the same purpose — to bewitch the believer with joy and offer him salvation; it consoles, it enchants, it purifies. It is roomy seclusion, a kind of sanctified kinship, as much faith as anyone needs. Many religions attempt, unsuccessfully, to be families, but ours worked: on Grand Island we were fenced in from marauding infidels. We had money, space, a prospect of the sea, and like other Cape Codders we were ancestor-worshippers. We had our own reverences and secrets; we were safe: house, windmill, paddock, orchard, shoreline, jetty, pumphouse, well, summer kitchen, winter parlor, greenhouse, and a private road sign-posted Do Not Trespass.

We had staked out our territory and we were so secure we seldom ventured to the frontiers. This suggests a savage tribe, hemmed in by menacing jungle; but it was not that — not a small and haunted hand-to-mouth society we'd established — but something much greater, a nearly limitless world of possibility which Papa ruled with kindly intensity. We believed in the pattern we saw; we tried to please each other; we distrusted everyone else. It was a feast. And it was easy for me to turn these loyalties into desire and not want anything to change; to want it all to last forever just the way it was; easy for the passionate virgin I was to see no harm in saying to Phoebe, "When I grow up I want to marry Orlando."

By the time I recognized my love for Orlando it was too late to do anything about it. But I knew several things: that I would not allow myself to be thwarted; that once I had him there would be nothing left to achieve. So I made my desire a sin because only what was denied me would continue to make me clamor for it. Until then, I had had everything I had ever wanted. It seemed crucial not to have Orlando too soon: the taboo was necessary — it starved me for him and enlivened me with that same hunger.

It was then, by chance, that I learned the value of a camera, how it attracts, persuades, and animates. "Her real love," Mama had said. I used it on him; I did him all the ways one can do. Orlando was delighted to pose for me, and perhaps he knew that I regarded the camera as my abstracted soul seeking fulfillment. The lens is uncritical; it doesn't make the pictures that desire does, and so the activity itself was my excuse to stay a decent distance from him and yet have him all to myself.

Here he is in the garden in his white suit and boater, showing under the straw lid the jut and nibble of his profile; there, grinning from the window of the summer kitchen with jam on his mouth; making a mouse of his bicep; standing on his head, his flannel cuffs at his knees; streaming with surf in his bathing suit — a set of striped long johns in which his penis showed like a hitchhiker's fist; clamming, with his trousers rolled up; fooling at the windmill, with his legs crossed and his hands under his head, whistling; doing cartwheels in the twilight; lowering his head and peering innocently into my box.

Frank brought me some of these pictures — not all. Where were the others? It was a question Orlando stopped asking. Not lost — I remembered them clearly enough, I could peruse them in the dark, shuffle them like a pack of cards and play them to recreate the past as solitaire. But most did not exist. Again, I had denied myself, for though I took hundreds of them, and fussed over each shot — "a little to the left," "come forward," "smile," "hold it" — often when I trained the camera on Orlando I didn't have any film in it. I wanted more than his picture. The camera was only a stratagem to charm him, a trick that was to turn me into an observer of chance, one of life's on-lookers. My instinct told me that a photograph — of which I already had many — only diminished the subject and made it into a trifle. It was something snatched (how apt the term "picture-taking" was!) that afterward seemed much smaller, almost worth-less, a feeble duplicate of what I wanted. Photography was in its infancy and so was he.

No film: my confidence trick. He looked at me more sweetly through the lens. Why spoil it with a photograph? I didn't want his brown blur in an al-bum. I loved him and I wanted to sleep with him.

I could see no point in anything else in the world, certainly none in taking pictures. I used the camera to get close to him, but I knew that as soon as we were lovers I would take that empty apparatus and drown it in the deepest part of Nantucket Sound.

Going downstairs to Frank after raking over the past I felt awkward, as if I had done some shameful thing alone. Photography had been a companionable if fruitless deception, but this reminiscence seemed so embarrassing when I stopped, as if I had been la-boring to uncover some muddy secret, groping for the past on all fours, blundering around in the dark. Already I knew that my retrospective was not his re-trospective. He had pictures; I was flying by the seat of my pants. After a morning of it, verifying the pictures he brought me by remembering how inac-curately they portrayed me, I wanted to re-enter the

present, just to prove that I existed. I half expected
Frank to accuse me with, "What have *you* been
up to?"

He did not say a word. I felt like a jackass. Did
he see me?

"Hi toots!" I was falsely hearty and wondered if
he noticed.

Frank looked up, surprised with handfuls of my
photos. His jacket was off, sleeves rolled up, all business. He was shuffling around, thinking with his
feet, and there on the parlor carpet like a leaf-
storm his latest batch from the windmill. He did not
have the slightest idea who I was and what, apart
from those damned pictures, I had done.

"Anything more you wanted to see?"

"Not at the moment. I just came down for a whizz."

He recoiled at my vulgarity, then smacked his lips
at an old photo and said, "We'll lick it into shape."

Not the slightest idea.

"Sure will."

"Say, Maude, what's this all about?"

And my heart almost stopped. Orlando? Had Frank
guessed what I had just disclosed to myself, the sentence I had discovered in the picture palace of my
memory: *I loved him and I wanted to sleep with
him?* No. It was a rear view, an old shot, the back
of a head. It might have been a weasel.

[9]

A Retreat

MY FATHER WAS a broker. I was afraid of the word; it suggested damage, like something he did with a pick and shovel, or a sledgehammer — certainly a destructive job. Whatever it was, he sometimes did it in New York, saying "Abyssinia!" and setting off for his "orifice" and now and then including a visit to the "uproar." In New York he knew some folks ("good scouts" — Papa's highest praise) called the Seltzers who, being publishers, knew everyone. They gave parties where, so Papa said, you might meet people like Scott Fitzgerald and Bunny Wilson and ones even more famous than they at the time, whose names might ring some bells now but don't open any doors, such as Franklin P. Adams. When I told my father I was going to New York he said, "Then you must stay with the Seltzers," and I was too naive to guess that what he really wanted was for them to keep an eye on me. I was seventeen, still a passionate virgin, had never been to the city and did not know what to drink. Beer made me throw up, and I hated the smell of my parents' whisky lips when they kissed me, as they did at my bedtime. My usual tipple was a glass of expensive burgundy mixed with ginger ale, but even that gave me cramps and dizziness and made me want to lie down. Orlando used to say, "You're a cheap date, Maude."

But I was no one's date, least of all Orlando's, and he was the reason I went to New York. We had spent the summer of 1923 together on the Cape, which had thrown me into confusion. All that winter and spring I had been there with my mother and Phoebe, studying with Miss Dromgoole, the Anglo-Irish tutor Papa had hired to prepare Phoebe and me for the girls' school in Switzerland. Orlando was at boarding school — Andover — and I had not seen him for months. When he wasn't around, which was more than half the year, I could believe that I was imagining it, that feeling of having a sleek animal in me gnawing my guts so hard I couldn't breathe. In June I felt the creature tear around inside me. The three of us swam, Ollie beat us at croquet, we bicycled over to Hyannisport to help Papa with his boat; and I wanted to tell him about this hungering thing within me. But instead of telling him, I pretended I was angry — to provoke his sympathy, so that he would put his arm around me and ask me what was eating me. Yet I knew I could not tell him the real reason, because that would have been to obligate him with our secret. The next move had to be his.

It was a tormenting summer. The Cape heat had needles of chill in it, the whine of the grasshoppers fiddling in the sun was like the sharp teeth of the wakened thing in me chewing at my resolve; and at night the bullfrogs and crickets insisted I stay awake. Twice I went to Orlando's room, but I hesitated at his door and listened to his sleepy snorts. And I saw it all ending, slipping from focus, the family traipsing off in different directions, the order broken up, our faith dispersed. I had been with them too long to think that it would ever be better for me elsewhere. I knew that I was happy and I wanted it to last. Papa and Mama spoke of going on a cruise or to their friend Carney's in Florida; Orlando was already talking about Harvard. Phoebe of Switzerland. I hated hearing people making plans that did not include me. I felt sure that if I wouldn't be happy neither would they, and we could save ourselves by sticking together. One of the consolations of selfishness is that you actually believe you're doing other people a favor.

"How's my photographer?" Orlando said.

I didn't dare say.

"Let's see some pictures," said Papa.

I wouldn't show him.

Phoebe said, "Do me in my new dress, Maude."

I thought: Not on your life, sister.

Mama, seeing me unhappy, bought me a folding camera.

But my picture-taking was too much of a reminder of my remoteness for me to pursue it with them, and I didn't want them to think that I could content myself so easily that way. I would not photograph them. It was then, out of pure spite, that I did my first pictures of the blind: the child holding the bat, blind old Mrs. Conklin the chain smoker, who, clawing at her scalp, had once set her own hair on fire; Slaughter, the piano tuner, and one of Frenise's squiffy-eyed nieces named Verna, from Martha's Vineyard. It was outrageous, I was ashamed of the pictures, I had the prints. I knew I had done it only for the distraction, and I remember Mrs. Conklin demanding suddenly from her darkness, "What are you doing, child?"

One hot day in August I went out to the orchard behind the windmill and sat under a tree to fret. It was damp there, a dark green moisture on the thickness of uncut grass. In rage and frustration I jumped up and pulled on a branch and shook down thirty apples. They hammered from the limb, dropping plumply with skin-splitting plops and I could taste their bitter bruises in the air after they fell. Then I saw Orlando's face rising from the tall grass near the windmill. It was, all at once, blank, curious, defensive, drained of color, and when he stood up I could see the grass stains on his trousers.

"What's wrong, cookie?" he asked gently and squatted and tumbled to his knees.

I was too startled at first to tell him why I was in such a state. But I calmed down. I decided to tell him

the truth, to say, *You're the only person I'll ever love*
— it was the perfect place, secluded and smelling of
smashed apples and dusty flowers. The lush place itself was my excuse; and there was that rumpus in my
vitals.

"Ollie, you're the only —"

I heard a noise and looked up to see if the windmill was turning. The sails were anchored, but sometimes they broke loose and spun all night. Today
there was no feel of wind, only the silken rustle of its
sound.

"Did you hear something?" I said, worried that we'd
be caught alone, discovered like plotters and perhaps
accused.

This took seconds. I saw Phoebe in her white dress
spring up out of the grass and toss her hair and take a
dance step toward us.

"It's only me," she said.

Orlando said, "It was Maude — fooling with the
tree."

Snap: Orlando kneeling innocently on his grass
stains with a slash of sunlight on his face and a kind
of eagerness in his eyes; and behind him — Pre-
Raphaelite, like the paintings Millais did from Rupert
Potter photographs — Phoebe in the dress that gave
her a moth's fragile wing-sleeves, a brittle sprite fluttering over him as if she was learning to fly and about
to droop on his wrist in exhaustion. Two pretty creatures wondering who I was, and in the foreground a
mass of fallen apples like the windfalls on the morning after a storm, with white reflections printed on
their upturned sides, and the birds' mad tweeching and
the sawing of insects' teeth and the wind in the
boughs and leaves that made a sound like surf.

Phoebe said, "We couldn't find you anywhere,
Maude."

I smelled a rich odor of apples and summer, bees
and blossoms and tomato vines and the fish and salt of
the sea, maddening and hurtful.

At dinner that night Orlando said, "If I were you,

know what I'd do? I'd take my camera to New York
City." He touched my hand and set a growl going in
me. "Yes, I would."

The next day I went and stayed with those people,
the Seltzers.

New York then was stink and noise, the dung of dray
horses steaming in the sunlight and dogcarts jumping
on the cobbles, Irish families, all woolens and shoes,
toting patched bundles and pausing in the reek of beer
to turn their white faces toward the fumes of the
harshly honking cars. Half the city seemed to live in
the street, jostling among the fruit and cats for room.
Orlando had ordered me here: I wondered if this descent was a retreat. I had never been so close to such
loud strangers — screwballs, swill-pails, fancy signs
— and it amazed me to think that I had the same
right they did to stare.

I took pictures — bad blundering work that I recall
with great tenderness, because I was overwhelmed by
the crowds and wanted to photograph those trembling
smells, that rapid movement, the laughter of picnickers
in Battery Park, the early-morning stables. I tried and
turned it into blurs, the kind of crudity that saddened
me at the time but later, as memorable imprecision,
fed me keenly each vivid line: the ice man in the rubber cape kneeling over a tombstone of frost and divid-
ing it into bricks with the needle-point of his stiletto —
the chips flying into his face; the men in aprons
mounding sawdust with pushbrooms and the woman
screaming "Waldo!" at a weeping child. The sun struck
the signs SALOON and WOLFPITS FURRIERS and filled
the street with smoldering paint; the trolley cars rattled and sounded their gongs at corners; and I fought
to photograph the oddness of it — the mucky gutters,
the woman smoking a cigarette, an urchin whacking
a ball with a stave, the Chinese grocery, the horses
munching out of the trim canvas buckets that fitted
their faces like masks. I did not feel I was alone; I
believed that the whole world squinted with me

through my camera's lens and that I could call up a
stallion from a clumsy hoofprint.

And yet I was alone. I got unexpected strength
from this — being able to cover huge distances because there was no one with me. If I went far enough
I would get the picture I wanted. Even then I didn't
take the view that one opened one's eyes and there
was one's masterpiece: that goddamned tree. That was
the consolation of laziness (*Just look out your own
window,* the photography handbooks said). It had to
be more than that, a quest which after great exertion
and occasional luck brought me without sight of my
shot; the next few steps composed the picture. My
photographs were miles away. I stalked them and saw
at the moment of discovery how temporary they were,
and how the instant I snapped them they changed and
vanished like smoke, or ceased to sing, like a lark in a
snare. The life of a picture was that stinging second:
there was nothing more.

I was sad over Orlando and had the sad person's
dull stamina, a cranky concentration, as I went about
harvesting these split-second. One picture showed a
huddled family on Mott Street, horses and clutter,
Chinese characters splashed down a wall and a window
of skinny stretched chickens; but what I remembered
best was a song and the smell of frying and the ache
of my swollen feet and how Orlando had said, "Don't
forget to come back." These failures, so irksome then,
gave me back the past. I could enter these pictures and
start drowning and relive my life.

The back of that head Frank had showed me; it had
a face.

It was after I returned from one of these exhausting
outings that Mrs. Seltzer opened the front door and
said in a hostess's obliquely warning way — as much
for the people inside as for me — "We've got company, Maude."

I looked beyond her and saw six or seven people
arguing furiously. "— They're just prostitutes," one
man was saying at the top of his voice.

Mrs. Seltzer said, "Watch your language."

She steered me inside and she introduced me to everyone so fast I just heard my own name six times and didn't catch anyone else's. I was glad to sit down in a corner — I didn't want to stick out and be noticed. Besides the Seltzers there were four men and one plump woman who kept her feet flat on the floor and didn't say a word or even smile. She reminded me of a throbbing potato. And the small dark whiskery man who had been practically screaming turned to me and said in an accent I could not quite place, "What do you do, lass?"

They had been having tea. This activity stopped with a sudden swelling pause and the room became big and still. Everyone looked at me. I looked at my knotted fingers. I didn't know what to say.

Mr. Seltzer said, "Maude's a photographer."

And saved me.

"Are thee?" said the weasel-faced man, passing his hand across his beard.

"Yes. I'm a photographer."

You become what others call you, and this was my baptism. Magic: everyone relaxed. From that moment I understood the access a photographer has, the kind of gate-crashing courage the instrument granted. It was like having a title — make way for the queen; and I didn't even have to show them my pictures. Here I was, seventeen, ignorant, a virgin, not pretty, "a cheap date." But the statement worked a miracle and changed me, because *I am a photographer* implied *You are my subject*. It was much more a novelty then than now. Although photography had been rattling along for a century, cameras were still considered mysterious contraptions and photographers a little suspect in their poaching on the Cubists. Indeed, there was a whole raft of photographers in New York at the time — Stieglitz was only one of them — who were madly signaling their belief that they had killed painting dead with their arsenal of cameras. Photography was new; it was like comedy, it hadn't been tainted by criticism, it was naive chemistry — leather bellows, smelly bottles, wobbly tripods — done in the dark. It was trying to replace painting by imitating it, so photographs looked freckled and corpselike, soft-focus poses that might have been painters' instant fossils. The New York notion (which I did not share) was that pictures were made, not found. I had Orlando to thank for my philosophy of the direct approach: I never created pictures — I took them. But, for my supposedly chemical creativity, the people in the room looked at me with curiosity and affection, a kind of friendly trust that made me feel I belonged. It was so simple! Mr. Seltzer had said it, but I believed it, and so in myself, and stopped doubting. Orlando had been right to send me here.

But the dark man said in his high-pitched voice, "Then where's your bloody camera?"

There was laughter. I said, "It's right out front in the hall, where I left it."

"Take my picture," said the man and showed me his yellow teeth.

"No," said the plump woman, throbbing at him. "Leave the child alone."

"What am I doing here?" said the man. His voice was shrill and complaining. "I don't like it! I don't want to be here!"

I knew he must be someone famous because no one contradicted him or told him to shut his trap. He was being rude, but the silence seemed to say, "It's just his way — he's always like that." The rest of the people resumed chatting about books, while the little man looked at me hard. His ears were purple, his beard ragged and he looked so sick I felt sorry for him.

I said, "I would very much like to take your picture, but I can't. It's just a cheap folding camera and there's not enough light in this room, as I'm sure you appreciate."

"Lights!" he cried in that odd accent. "That's it!" You need the sun blazing. You can't take pictures

in the dark." He leaned over to me. "I can see in the
dark — it's all darkness where I come from. I hate
the dark, I've had the dark — I crawled out of it and
I'll never go back. The things I've seen would scare
the likes of you."

"It's the film," I said, and thought: What is this
embarrassing man yapping about?

"We'll find the sun," he said. "Come with me." He
turned his back on the plump woman who — almost
certainly his wife — had started to rise and restrain
him. "This is America," he said. "There's a sun here
for everyone."

He stood up. He was one of those short people who
don't gain any height by standing up. On his feet, he
looked even smaller and frailer than before.

"Where?" I said.

He said darkly, his beard jerking — and I thought:
Oh, come off it! — "Where the sun lives."

"Try the yard," said Mr. Seltzer, who had been
listening.

"The garden," said the man, touching me nervously
on my knee. "Get your camera, lass."

The woman looked worried, angry, mystified, impatient; and her seated quaking body made her seem
helpless, too. Like his mother, I thought, hopeless
and envying, as if she wanted to knock him down just
so that she could pick him up and dust him off in her
arms.

"Get your camera, Maude," said Mr. Seltzer in a
resigned way, gently trying to get me to cooperate.

"Come into the garden, Maude," said the man.
"For the black bat, night, has flown."

I got my camera from the hall table and loaded it
and thought: If that's Lord Tennyson I'm going to get
my picture in the papers. I hurried into the garden
and again saw how small he was and thin, with a
terrible cough, like a man who should be in bed. Dark
hair, dark eyes, and a pinched face and a beard that
wasn't growing right. I was afraid of him. He reminded me not of Orlando but of my desire, as if it

had jumped out of my guts and become that mangy sniffing man. To disguise my fear I showed him the camera and popped it open. It had a lid you opened that made a little shelf for the stiff bellows.

"Queer," he said, putting his nose near it.

"It won't hurt a bit," I said.

He didn't laugh. He glared at me and then looked at the garden, which was one of those narrow New York gardens surrounded by a high brick wall, with a heavy fig tree and ivy and ferns; like an aquarium without the water, so green, so full, sort of rotting and growing at the same time. The pale late-summer light hovered softly among the thick leaves and the pollen spilling from the hollyhocks and made it seem as if the marble statue of the naked woman was white flesh.

"Stand over there, please," I said.

"No."

"The light's better there."

"But you're here," he said, and his voice was small and vibrant in all those ferns.

"Excuse me, but I thought you wanted me to take your picture."

Suddenly he said in the same cross voice he had used upstairs, "Have you ever felt it?"

Felt *what?* I thought. I said, "I don't rightly know."

"You've never felt it." He sounded disgusted.

"Not necessarily. Maybe I have and maybe I haven't," I said, trying to be businesslike. "Now if you just get into position I'll snap your picture."

"You haven't," he said, "or else you'd know. You'd remember — the blood remembers. What do you call these flowers?"

"Hollyhocks," I said.

"We call them hollyhocks, too," he said, making his voice mysterious.

I said, "Everyone calls them hollyhocks."

"They're open — look how they're parted and dripping with pollen. They want the bees to enter and suck that gold on their hair. They think they're innocent, but they're begging to be entered, and gleaming. Did you ever see anything so shameless? They wink and twitch — they're sex-mad!"

He had made them seem revolting with his nasty description, and still he leered at them. There were bubbles of scum in the corners of his mouth.

I said, "I don't know who you are, but I'm sorry, I don't think they look that way at all."

"That cat is watching us," he said.

I said, "That cat is not seeing anything."

"You've got brass," he said. "You're a photographer, aren't you? You want my soul, but you won't get it. It's too dark — it won't show up!"

He took a step toward me. I hated his face.

"I know what you want," he said. He had halitosis, the vapor from his decaying lungs.

"I want to take your picture."

"No," he said, and he was beside me, not holding me, but pressing against me. It was a kind of canine hostility, like a slobbering mutt with its wet dognose smeared against my skirt. I knew he didn't like me, I could feel it like dampness. I sensed his fear — woman-hating cowardice: he was trying to make me afraid. And there was something else about him, an ugliness that might have been his shriveled size or his stinking cough on which I smelled his lungs.

"Cut it out," I said.

"You and your bloody picture-machine," he said. "What do you see? Go ahead — look! — you won't see anything, lass. You're as blind as your camera."

I said, "This camera sees a lot. It'll make those hollyhocks a damn sight prettier than you did. It will do you just as you are, and you might be surprised by what you see in your own face, mister."

He made a grab for me.

I said, "If you won't leave me alone I'll call Mister Seltzer and he'll come down here and fix your wagon."

"Seltzer's a bloody coward — they're all cowards and prostitutes. I don't belong here."

"Then why don't you just go away?"

He said grimly, "Because I want to teach you what a man is."

I thought: *Orlando!*

"And what loins are," he said.

A meaningless piece of meat shaped like a cave man's club was all I could think of, but before I could do anything he said, "Those are my loins," and bumped me, "and that's my willy," and bumped me again. "Do you feel it now?"

Willy: the word was bewitching and I almost laughed out loud. But I cannot describe the effect this had on me. I was clasped in the jaws of his skinny thighs and it was like the bite of some poisonous reptile. He was touching me, making my hands sweat on my camera — trying to violate me. Strangest of all, I had never felt so pure, and this feeling of deflecting his assault with my innocence kept strengthening me.

I thought: This is what happens when you leave home. I sensed a new refinement in my passion for Orlando, a purer urge that I could bring back to him. I understood again why he had suggested I visit New York. He wanted me to know how much he mattered.

Bump, bump. Dusty sparrows chirped on his garden wall but the sun still lit the man's coarse hair. He went a little distance and started to laugh — a cruel laugh with no pleasure in it, just an angry little bark from his dreadful lungs. His laughter choked him and he coughed — terribly, bending over and shaking, as if he were going to spit out his heart and die.

He seemed ashamed: he had betrayed his weakness to me. He walked into the tent of sunlight and turned away from me. He tried to wipe his mouth with a hanky that was stiff and wrinkled from use, but he kept on coughing, like a cat puking and retreating.

I went behind him and snapped a picture of the back of his head: a narrow hive of selfish lies.

That night I took the Long Island boat back to the Cape and Orlando, to the only person who would ever matter to me. And it seemed as if it would always be this way, everything I felt or did circumscribed by him; I could endure any assault, because I was bracketed by his love.

Frank still held the picture.

I said, "D. H. Lawrence."

He scribbled a number on it with a squeaky felt-tip pen, then he said, "The writer?"

"The sap."

"Maude," he said, cautioning me, as if I'd blasphemed.

"Phooey," I said. "He was a peckerhead."

Frank looked at the picture again and tilted it. He said, "It could be anyone from that angle."

"No," I said, "even from the back it could only be him." And it was true. That year, I was to take many more people from the back, and the name was always obvious from what you could see between the ears. The brain-case and its bumps and beneath it that expressively eroded gully I believed to be the most telling part of the anatomy, the hardest to fake. If I didn't see what I wanted on a person's face I said quickly, "Turn around!" and got him retreating.

"Amazing," said Frank, and I could see he was impressed. He treated the photo with a new reverence.

Long after that day in New York I tried to read Lawrence. I found him dull, repetitive, laboriously vile and evasive. And, as with most fiction I attempted to read, I gave up after a few pages, wondering at its importance, because it was so much less interesting than my life. I suspected that my work was touched with that same failure, for a knew I was nowhere in it.

Frank said, "How about a bite of lunch?"

[10]

Wellfleet Swells

YES, enough — away — forget the picture palace. The sight of Lawrence's tiny head had shaken a mouse out of my mind. But Frank's mention of lunch uncoiled a thrill in me that took ten spins, then jammed and made me want to jump. I got an urge — the push of the picture, the pull of the sun — to drop everything and get moving out of memory's undertow. Besides, I heard the noon siren begin to scream at the Bass River Firehouse, cutting the day in half, and that was always a shrill provocation to feed my face.

I said, "Let's go to Provincetown."

"Fine by me," said Frank.

And we were on the road, breezing along the Mid-Cape Highway. I gave Frank a friendly slap on the thigh and he caught my mood and gave me a chattering laugh.

"Funny," I said, poking my toe on the gas, "I only like Creedence Clearwater Revival when I'm doing seventy."

The radio was going *boopy-boop,* making the dashboard rattle, and I rolled down the window so I could mingle the music with the tires sucking at the road and the *whup* of passing trailer trucks. Blue skies, sakes alive! I sat back and basked in America's most underrated pleasure, the big car on a straight road with the radio on and the sun beating in and out of the trees, gold pulses between the boughs, all the light and speed

more calming than a square meal, and a kind of glory-
bounce of joy in it, too.

I liked the sky's bottom edge flat and far on the
fast-lane ahead, and just stamping the throttle into low
and letting it whine for half a minute made the car
seat vibrate with a massaging drone and drained my
ears of worry. Delicious: and I was thinking, America
even at its most grotesque is more fun than anywhere
else on earth, so who wouldn't feel like a sinner and
make guilt a duty to pay for that rumble of pleasure?
Up the pike for twenty miles I was humming and
working the power steering like the dune-buggy freaks
on Sandy Neck, with my hands crooked over the top
of the wheel and turning it with my wrists, having a
field day changing lanes and roaring past a pausing
oldster at the Harwich exit.

What is the past then, when you are cruising at
seventy in a new Chevy? It is distant and simple and
so small it barely belongs to you. One year is so much
like another; one season is ten minutes on a bike, the
next is a single swing of a sailboat's boom, another a
meal or a face. Try hard at that speed and all you
hear is the sound of the Cape in summer, which is a
screen door straining its spring and slapping shut with
a clatter of sticks and wires; the skirl of gulls, bare
knees in wet sand and Miss Dromgoole saying, "More
jam?" When I was ten I had fried clams, and that
memory of the Seltzers is just a chilly twilight and a
quick muscle of fear in my leg. Fragments and double
exposure, and not one clear picture but an endless roll
of blurs: two seconds of this year, a minute of that one
in a train, youth in small pieces, childhood dust. Perhaps there *was* nothing else?

No. Because past Orleans the highway gave out and
my memory became mobbed and I was returned. We
weren't flying anymore and the car slowing on Route
6 caused a stir in my mind. I thought: How impossible
it is to be near home and do anything and not repeat
a motion of the past. We were approaching Wellfleet,
but I might as well have been back at my house on

Grand Island and approaching a patch of familiar
wallpaper at the turning in the staircase and pausing
and going under. And just as a chance word in the
parlor I grew up in never failed to rouse a ghostly
echo, the unerasable wrinkle on the wall, touched with
the eye, toppled me headlong into my retrospective.
On that wall, in that room, a whiff of winter and how
that mirror sees outside to a whiteness in the windmill
— this is where memory lies.

There was a yellow blinker. I braked and the planet
began to stall and cloud up. Then there was that unmistakable sign that the road had narrowed for delays
ahead. The going would be heavy — there was the
proof, a wooden-roofed shed with its front flap wide
open and its counter stacked with tomatoes and spin-
dles of corn. The roadside stand, snarling traffic, and
on a grassy bank, WELCOME TO WELLFLEET, PEN-
ALTY FOR STEALING HOLLY $500 OR SIX MONTHS.

"Wellfleet," said Frank with satisfaction. "Maybe
we'll see some clamdiggers."

I wanted to punch him in the mouth. This was supposed to be my afternoon off. He snatched at the dashboard as I kicked at the brake again.

It was a Friday, years after the Lawrence episode. But
the date wasn't important: it was the sequence that
mattered.

We hadn't gone to the school in Switzerland, and it
wasn't me, it was Phoebe who had first refused, then
taken sick. She sat down pale and wouldn't budge.
Miss Dromgoole was kept on, and I was glad it had all
happened that way, because I had never wanted to
leave Orlando. "Maude can't go alone," Papa said,
and that was that. He said to Phoebe, "But if you're
too sick for Switzerland you're too sick for Florida,"
and they went to stay with a rich crazy man — his
friend Carney — who played at being Lorenzo the
Magnificent in a fake palace near Verona, on Florida's
Gulf coast. They left Phoebe and me at home with
Miss Dromgoole and Frenise, the pair of them fighting

most of the time about what we should eat: "greens," said Frenise, "stodge," said Miss Dromgoole. "People in China would be glad to have that," said Miss Dromgoole, using the hunger of these poor people to get us to eat. It was illogical and cruel: she was in fact threatening us with starvation.

Then Orlando — who was certainly at Harvard, because he had his driver's license — Orlando showed up one Friday afternoon like an angel and said he was taking us to a party. He was red and out of breath and stamping from the cold and looked snorting and healthy in his fur coat.

"The roads are bad," said Miss Dromgoole.

Orlando took no notice of her. When she repeated it he simply smiled and sort of leaned toward her like a bright light until she left the room. The next thing we knew she was shouting at Frenise, who was muttering "basset" and "bidge."

Phoebe started to cry. She said, "I wish Papa was here."

Her tears gave her color and made her look like a saintly doll with a pure face and a crumpled dress. Orlando put his arm around her and hugged her and I felt like weeping, too.

"Look," I said. "It's snowing again."

It seldom snowed hard on the Cape — a few inches, no more, was all we got. But that day it made pillows on the lawn and was piled against the house, and though I had not gone out I had spent the day photographing icicles at the window. From my room the great stiff scooped-out drifts at the windmill were like the chalky curves of sea-worn clamshells. There were dragons of ice on the drain pipes and glassy gargoyles bunched at the gutters, and white sugarloaf mounds over the flowerbeds. The property was subdued and rephrased by the snowstorm, and none of my pictures came out, which was why I remembered it so clearly. I took them from inside the house; I hated the cold — it stung my toes and froze my eyes.

Orlando said, "It's beautiful out." Now it was dark-

ening and the flakes wer shifting slowly past the parlor
window, made gold by our lights and swaying like
feathers as they fell.

"Where's the party?" asked Phoebe.

"Wellfleet," he said. "At the Overalls."

We had always known the Overalls. Like us, they
were year-round residents of the Cape, and had a
house on Chipman's Cove. My parents went to the uproar in Boston with Mr. and Mrs., and we played
with the two children. I think they looked down on us
a little because they swam in the cold water of the Bay
and we had the warm water of the Sound; the implica-
tion was that they were hardy and we were effeminate
and sissified. Standish Overall was about Orlando's
age, and Blanche was somewhere between Phoebe and
me. Papa didn't think much of Standish, and in fact
said, "He looks like a girler," which in Papa's eyes was
the worst thing you could be ("I hear this Frank
Sinatra's a fearful girler," he said some years later.
"How I wish that man would leave the building!").
Standish, who positively honked with confidence, was
good at everything, had an athlete's bounce and like
other wealthy boys I knew had begun to go bald at
twenty. Blanche was a vain prissy thing who behaved
like his wife and who had occasional fits of aggression,
like a person who knows deep down her feet stink.

Orlando said that Mr. and Mrs. Overall were away
for the weekend and that Standish — or Sandy, as he
was known — had got his hands on some bootleg liquor
and was giving a party.

"I can wear my new dress," said Phoebe.

"Miss Dromgoole's not going to like this," I said.

"I'll take care of the Ghoul," said Orlando.

"What'll you say?"

"That I can't go to a party without my sweethearts."

Phoebe smiled, but I knew what he meant.

The Ghoul raged, but off we went in the winter
dark, the three of us in Orlando's car, the snow curling
wildly in front of the headlights. And though we
weren't that young anymore, I felt we were all about

ten years old, because no matter what age you are, if you are related like that you feel truant and reckless if you're all sitting in the front seat of a car in a blinding snowstorm. Brothers and sisters never outgrow their past if it's been happy. Orlando told us about his English poetry course and how he liked Harvard, and then we sang "Clementine" and "She'll Be Coming Round the Mountain."

The Cape was empty, the fallen snow was black, the trees looked stiffer in the cold; and if I thought anything I suppose it was about having spent the day photographing snow scenes from the window and how easy and untruthful it was compared with being in it. I sang, but I stared at the low wolfish woods and the toppling flakes and heard the tire chains doing a smacking rhumba on the mudguards. At the brows of hills the snowy sky and storm clouds hung like a shroud. It was coming down hard, but it wasn't freezing — this snowfall brought a somber warmth to the road, damp and temporary — so the car cut its own track and tossed the slush aside and I could see the flying blobs sink in the banks and plow-marks at the roadside. Every so often there would be a soft thud as a mound of wet snow slid down an evergreen bough; then the bough would shake itself and spring up sighing.

Orlando said, imitating Papa, "Gawjus."

Outside Wellfleet, below the small village, the Overalls' house was twinkling on the cove. It faced the Bay, where a commotion of waves, whiter than the snow, was rising to meet the storm and traveling in to beat against the low jetty: flecks of white on the swells highlighting the turbulence, peaks subsiding and beginning, a sound at the sea-wall like icy digestion, and from the house, laughter.

There was something barbarous about all those drunken people raising hell in the house on such a beautiful night, and as soon as I saw them at the windows I wanted to go away. I said, "I hate parties."

"You might meet a nice fella," said Orlando.

"I've got a nice fella," I said. I squeezed his gloved hand. "I'm staying with you."

He said, "What about you, Phoebe?"

"You know damn well what I want," she said.

Orlando laughed, then yanked up the hand brake. The motor shuddered, coughed, spat, and died.

Inside, there were mostly youngsters, tearing around and sweating. They were ladling some sort of orange poison out of a punchbowl which had hunks of bruised grapefruit in it. It was a fairly typical get-together for those years: if people weren't drinking there was a dead silence; if they were, they were drunk. There was no in-between.

Everyone cheered, seeing Orlando, and they swept him away from Phoebe and me. For the next hour or so it was a madhouse, the noisy college crowd making a night of it, one enormous brute pounding a ukulele with his knuckles, couples canoodling on the sofa, and some out cold and making a Q-sign with their tongues hanging out of their mouths.

I was deeply shocked. It dawned on me that I was seeing another side of Orlando: this person had been hidden from me, and I wanted to take him, then and there, and go home. Boys in crimson sweaters kept coming over and asking Phoebe to dance. She said no, but at last I said, "You might as well," and she began dancing with Sandy. Then Orlando, who had not been dancing, snatched a girl's arm and whirled her around in front of Phoebe. The dancers were jumping so hard the pictures shook on the walls. I sat there with my feet together thinking: I'm a photographer.

Later, Orlando came over to me. His eyes were glazed and his other self smirked. He said, "Where's Phoebe?"

"Dancing her feet off."

He made a face. "Why aren't you?"

"No one asked me," I said. "Anyway, I don't want to."

He dragged me out of my chair and whisked me to the center of the room. Then he did a kind of monkey-shuffle; I imitated him and we were dancing. I heard someone say, "That's his sister," and I tried even harder.

Orlando knew a trick that took my breath away each time he did it. It was this: he stood in one spot, clenched his fists at his sides and did a backward somersault, landing on his feet. He had done it for us in the garden or on the beach — I had a photograph of him where he appeared as a pair of whirling trousers above an admiring Phoebe. That night dancing with me he did three of them in a row and caused such a sensation that everyone stopped to watch him. He very nearly took a spill on his last somersault — he back-flipped and I thought he was going to land on his stomach — but he came up smiling on two feet.

Phoebe said, "Stop it, Ollie, you're going to be sick."

Orlando, who was red in the face from all those jumps, said, "I'm all right — I can prove it."

"Go ahead," said Phoebe.

"Give me room."

People had gathered around to listen, and after that wild dancing and those somersaults Orlando's curly hair was damp with sweat and lying close to his head. He blazed with energy, his shirt half unbuttoned and his teeth gleaming. Someone kicked the phonograph and it stopped yakking "What'll I Do" and Orlando said in his growly voice,

They flee from me, that sometime did me seek
With naked foot, stalking in my chamber . . .

There was a hush — he had silenced them with his superb poem, one I had never heard before. And I knew why he was saying it. I was proud: he was declaring his love for me. I saw everyone watching, and even Phoebe, who had criticized him for his somer-saulting and acted as if he was showing off — I saw her rapt attention. Her dress was open at her neck and she was breathing hard, her breasts going up and down. I tried to catch her eye, but she faced Orlando, her mouth rounded as if she were saying, "Ollie."

Orlando's voice teased and swelled and dropped, became emphatic on one word and nearly sang another. Each syllable had a different weight. Now he was hunched, and seemed to be listening as he spoke.

> *When her loose gown from her shoulders did fall,*
> *And she me caught in her arms long and small,*
> *Therewith all sweetly did me kiss*
> *And softly said, "Dear heart, how like you this?"*

I heard *It was no dream*, and I knew, I remembered that summer night when I had stolen along the hall and thought the house was going to fall down, and he was in the dark waiting for me. So it had mattered to him, too, although he had been so young. What a beautiful memory he had made it in the poem. He had cast his spell over everyone, and outside the snow dust sprinkled at the window and the waves gulped as they tucked into the sea wall. He loved me. I stepped back so that no one would see my tears.

Phoebe was beside me. She said, "Don't cry."

But she was crying herself. It did not surprise me: we were sisters, and wept or laughed together.

"Let's take him home now," I said.

There was applause. Orlando had finished, but before we could get to him a boy stepped between Orlando and us and said to him, "You think you're something."

Orlando smiled at him, his bright devastating smile that shut people up.

The boy said, "I loathe the Elizabethans."

"Wyatt wasn't an Elizabethan," said Orlando. "He was dead before Shakespeare was born."

The boy spoke at large: "He's a Harvard man!"

Orlando said, "I don't think I know you."

"Charlie," said the boy, and put his hand out, and when Orlando didn't shake it he said, "It's trite and sentimental."

"I like it," said Orlando.

"*Like* it? What kind of literary judgment is that? Let's take it line by line and see if it stands up."

Orlando looked sad. I wanted that boy Charlie to stop.

Charlie said, "You don't have the slightest idea of what it means — you're just seduced by the tumpty-tumpty rhythm." He looked around for people to agree with him. "It sounds important, but underneath it's just Dorothy Parker."

"Lay off," said Orlando quietly.

"He's getting mad," said Charlie.

"Just shut up." Orlando started to walk away.

"Look at the professor now," said Charlie.

"You've had too much gin, sonny," said Sandy, trying to quiet Charlie down.

Charlie said, "It's the cadences that get me."

I knew Orlando wasn't going to say anything, because he never talked about poetry like that. He had been so happy, and now he looked as if he was going to walk into a wall.

Phoebe said, "I'll get his coat."

But Charlie said in a wuffling critic's voice, "He wanted to impress us. It sounds very sweet, but it's just artifice, low cunning, a kind of trick —"

And Orlando, who had been walking in circles, went over to him and grabbed him by the lapels and flung him across the room.

Blanche screamed.

Charlie got to his feet. Orlando hurried over to him and hit him hard in the face, and as he fell back someone opened the door and out he tumbled, doing a frantic tap dance on the steps and struggling into the snow. Orlando descended the steps, waited for him to rise, and knocked him down again.

Orlando said, "It's time to go."

Seeing that we were leaving, Charlie picked himself up and laughed — a rueful and defeated snicker. He had snow on his back and snow on his head and looked punished, like a tramp in a storm.

Orlando's was the best reply I had ever seen, and it taught me everything I needed to know about critics: a critic was someone you wanted to hit.

"I'm sorry," said Orlando, when we were in the car. He started the engine and chuckled. "No, I'm not sorry."

I had never loved him more. His poem had kindled a fire in me where there had been warm ashes. It was unlike him to fight, but it was unlike him to do somersaults in public or recite poems. He was full of surprises.

Frank said, "What's the matter?"

"Nothing," I said. "You're sure you want to go to Provincetown?"

"It was your idea."

We were now beyond Truro, the road had widened, the sky was everywhere, propped magnificently on shafts of sunlight that held the clouds high. And soon we were sailing across the dunes into Provincetown. It had saved me before; it saved me again. I'd done it.

Boogie-Men

A PLACE I had plumbed with my camera had few memories for me. The pictures were definition enough, done at so many angles that the photographs were the whole; more was presumption, mere lies. If a person said, "I've seen your pictures — now I want to go there," I knew I had failed. Only bad pictures made you look further. A great portrait to me was intimate knowledge, ample warning that there was nothing concealed, nothing more to say. I knew from *Mrs. Conklin, Frenise,* and *Slaughter* that my camera recorded surfaces, but that surfaces disclosed inner states: a person wore his history on his face, past and future, the mortal veil of lines and the skull beneath. There is a self-destruction, suicide's wince, in the eyes of my *Marilyn* and my *Hemingway,* and my *Frost* shows an utter egomaniac. I never denied the truth of the savage's complaint about photographers, that in taking their pictures we were stealing their souls.

I had always been interested in what people called savages. I thought of them as boogie-men. They bulked large in my first exhibition, which was held in a boathouse, formerly the Wharf Theater, in Provincetown. Frank wanted to see the place and hear about the show. I could tell he was rather let down by its size, the dinginess that gave it the look of a little chapel. If you didn't have the faith you wouldn't hear; you'd just find the acoustics awfully echoic and the stage too narrow and the whole building a firetrap.

Frank said, "Is this all there is to it?" I said yes, and he said, "It's just the way I imagined it."

"Sure it is."

"But I wish I'd seen Provincetown before it got commercialized."

"Bull-sugar," I said. "It was always commercialized. It's been like this for sixty years — vulgar, plastic, phony antiques, windows full of saltwater taffy, queers everywhere, and pennants saying 'Provincetown.' It was declared a national monument by President Taft, and he weighed three hundred and fifty pounds. It's been on the map ever since they started to sell egg-timers with Pilgrims painted on them and ashtrays made out of quahog shells. Don't knock it — that's its heritage."

We were on the street, walking to the Town Wharf for lunch. Frank said, "Really strange people, too. They're all on drugs."

"Nonsense."

"I blame their parents."

"Bull. They're carsick. Listen, it's a long drive."

Provincetown before my time had been an appalling fishing village of dull clapboard houses, narrow streets, creaking porches, one severe church, and sand blowing down from the dunes eroding the Puritan geometry. It had always had its Sunday painter: watercolorists change nothing. It was the poets, the queer antique dealers, the escapees, the actors and loonies and curio sellers who gave it life. The summer people in their roadsters carried frenzy here and saved the place from being just another sand dune.

Until I did it, Provincetown was portrayed as quaint and dead. The painters painted the dunes, the photographers took pictures of the wooden houses, the sculptors collected driftwood and made these warped sticks into lamps and horror-objects. The writers ignored it; they rented shacks and wrote about their terrible childhoods. But I had been born on the Cape; these houses and boats meant nothing to me, and I had seen enough fishnets and lobster pots to last me a life-

time. It was the rest that excited me — the funny little
boathouse that had once been a theater, the fairies
walking along Commercial Street with their pinky fingers linked, the visitors who stuck out a mile.
Throughout the Twenties and into the Thirties I took
pictures there. I saw a man with a perfect head and
photographed him, and later I found out he was the
poet Cummings — a wonderful memory because I
thought he was a genius before I saw a single line
he'd written: I liked his head and the way his joke-
ster's thick lips curled when he laughed. He was much
funnier than the other one, who looked ruined and
squinting, the sunlight removing half his face, O'Neill.
Pugmire and his vast collection of medicine bottles,
Bunny Wilson and his cronies, the tragic Bruno Bas-
sinet who was found floating face down in his underwear in Hatches Harbor, the get-togethers O'Neill
arranged above Peaked Hill Bar: this was my Provincetown.

And there was a direct link between Provincetown
and New York City. In the space of ten years I did
two sets of Robeson pictures, the first before the notorious hand-kissing scene in *All God's Chillun*, the
next in 1932 during the New York revival of *Show
Boat*. Robeson sang (always "Lindy") as I did him
and he had more moods than anyone I had known.

"They want me to play Othello," he said at our
first session.

"That's only natural."

"I really want to play Hamlet."

But in the event he played Emperor Jones.

He was my first boogie-man. Even as a celebrity,
Robeson was considered a savage by most people, like
the Ubangis my uncle Tod brought over from Africa,
who were paraded out as freaks on the stage of the
Old Howard in Scollay Square. "They were so sad,"
he said. He guessed they were homesick, and to cheer
them up Uncle Tod let them sit near the furnace in
the basement boiler room where they sweated until
one — the man — died; the woman was shipped back

to Africa. This story infuriated Robeson, who had the idea — mistaken, I think — that the Ubangi man was an African chief in boiler-room bondage. "But it's not your fault, honey."

Next to Orlando, Robeson was the most complete man I had ever met. He was success-conscious, impressionable, and had no political savvy, and he had a fatal gift for rhetoric; yet he had a law degree, a corrosive intelligence, an athlete's sinew, and a gentleman's charm. He was fearless, dignified, and polite, the sort of superman envious weaklings gang up to destroy. He was bowled over by my photographs. He had dressed up in fantastic costumes, like an African prince, a statesman, a revolutionary, a convict, a pirate; he got the duds out of the wardrobe of the New York theater and made the right faces for them. He told me not to tell a soul, and he bought the more outlandish pictures from me so that I couldn't exhibit them. I thought at the time that they were parts he wanted to play, because he gave little speeches for each one — jabbering like an African, orating like a president; but later it occurred to me that they were people he wanted to be, and it didn't surprise me when he went to Russia, because one of the pictures (fur hat, overcoat, and growling *minski-chinski*) foretold that.

It was Robeson who introduced me to the other blacks in New York, the *Show Boat* cast, the hangers-on, girlfriends, spivs, and bookies. "My people," he called them, "my brothers and sisters" — it was my introduction to those words used in their larger senses. Some of them were religious types, Holy Rollers and preachers and evangelists, with names like Father and Daddy; or sly fast-talking sharks with sharp teeth and an odd black puppety walk and names like Pigga and Doolum; others pretended they were real Africans, and one told me he was God. A few tried to interfere with me, but I said I would not stand for it and if they didn't cut it out they could get their picture taken elsewhere. But how they dressed! Top hats and tails, earrings, blankets and war bonnets, leopard skins, bandanas, and one in his shorts, just a pair of boxer's trunks. Strange as the others seemed, dressed up as Uncas and General Othello and Crispus Attucks and Shriners in red fezzes, it was the boxer who caused the sensation: no one had ever seen a confident muscle-bound black man before. He was a bizarre Negro who looked like a bullfrog and claimed he was an Indian and called himself Tashmoo.

"Maude's cannibals," people called them. Robeson had supplied me with New York subjects, Frenise helped me on the Cape. Many blacks lived then, as they continued to do, on Martha's Vineyard. They were servants, houseboys, cooks, sometimes gardeners, but never chauffeurs (the Irish did that, though Papa disapproved: "I would never hire a man who believed in an afterlife to do a dangerous job"). For years I traveled around the Cape and out to the Vineyard doing blacks, and when I had my first exhibition in that wharf gallery in Provincetown people were astonished — not by the blind portraits, or the perfect one of Cummings or *Clamdiggers* or the nasty one I had set up called *Eel in a Toilet,* but by the blacks, because they had never seen them before, so many of them, like human beings.

For one thing, they were not black. Instead of printing them the usual way I fuddled around a stage further and made negative prints. A few years later, even amateurs knew how to do this, reversing the order, backassward, printing a positive to get inkblot whites and illuminated shadows. But then it was considered wildly imaginative, and to use black subjects in negative prints a stroke of pure genius. They appeared lighted from within, an internal glow that livened the skin and blackened the eyes and picked out the teeth like obsidian choppers. They were incandescent golliwogs in two dimension, but it was especially creepy because my pictures showed the familiar in reverse, solarized people with white hair and white noseholes and gray fingernails and black teeth, and I must admit that the first few I did nearly scared the pants off me with their superhuman looks, right out of a rocket, as if there were a million more somewhere in the sky in the Mothership who were about to land and take over the world. And although some of the blacks were printed as usual (I didn't take any liberties with Robeson) none looked as black as those whitened negative prints or caused people to study them so closely. Thereafter, whenever I took a picture that I thought people would not look twice at — some ordinary scene I felt deserved attention — I printed it this way and never failed to drown the viewer in it. My white Negroes made the show; they were arrestingly familiar and yet had the definition of sojourners from the spirit world. Now people noticed the lipshape, the long crown, the huge noseholes, the forehead ridge, the small beautiful ears.

It was news, and everyone said what brilliant pictures they were and what a great future I had: This gal is going places, mark my word. I had to laugh. I knew that the pictures were easy and only the subjects amazing, like shots of bad weather or big game, hailstones and tigers, or our old friend "Snake Swallowing a Pig." The subject was the thing, and so my skill was praised, but I knew that there would always be someone to say I was a photographer of accomplishment if I exhibited a picture of a person with two heads, giant or dwarf, or blood-splashed murder victim. Even the Cummings one — it was his head that counted, not his name.

With Teets it was his mouth. All the blacks talked while I had done them, but Teets, whom I had met on the Vineyard, had kept up a nibbling monologue that lent a sour scavenging expression to his buffoon's mouth and gave glimpses of the roots of his teeth and the way they molded his gums, like carved wax inside the scratched tissues of his lips.

He had the liverish just-dug-up color of an earthworm, he wore a sock on his head, and he hid his intelligence in clowning. He was a reader; not a self-

improving type, but a man of restless solitude who
searched in books for his counterpart. He read everything and, like many of us, he failed to find in any
book a clue to his own world, a familiar smell or
gesture, a quality of light — that little kick in fiction
that tells the truth and makes the rest plausible. "It's
just a story," he would say, tossing a book aside: he
did not believe.

In him I saw, as I often had with Frenise, a fellow
sufferer, passion sandwiched between innocence and
duty, yearning to soar. And he even looked the part,
like a crow on a branch complaining with his beak,
"Dummies. I can't read this book. It's about dummies." Or his more solemn conclusion, "I'd rather
read your pictures Maude. They's like stories."

Teets's photograph, in stiff robes, a pharaonic profile, was praised for its weirdness — wild eyes and a
gobbling mouth full of teeth. But there was a voice,
like the "shet" and "bidge" that didn't go with
Frenise's church clothes, that insisted there was more
to Teets than his pose.

That day in the dunes above Edgartown, dressed
as an Egyptian and sitting cross-legged in the sand,
he said to the camera, "There's only one book which
is the truth, and it's the Bible."

Troof, Bahble. I thought: So it comes out at last —
he's a religious nut, a roller or a jumper.

He explained to the camera, holding his hands for-
ward, as if he expected birds to light on his wrists,
"Not the Holy Bible, but the other one, the plain old
Bible they hit you with when you're little."

"Do tell." I was winding and snapping, winding and
snapping.

"It's the truth about what people do. They cuss.
They kill their childrens. They do wrongness. They
suffer for years and years and they look around and
suffer some more. And sometimes nothing happens
for two-three hundred years but begetting."

I said, "But lots of books are about that."

"Cussing, yes, and dying, yes, but not begetting

with their own daughters and brothers and sisters. But that's the truth."

"Brothers and sisters?"

"Doing it hard," he said. "It ain't in books — it's in the Bible."

I said I wasn't happy with the pose. I told him to relax and get on his elbows and keep talking and don't mind me.

He said, "Sure it's the truth. I know someone that done it, and," he smiled, "that someone is me, baby."

"Cussed?"

"Jammed."

"With your daughter?"

"With my sister. Hard." He sucked his teeth. "Got no daughter."

I said, "I don't think you ought to be telling me this, Mister Teets."

"It's the truth, so don't get vex. The truth is the truth." He did his crow-squint, lowering his head and saying into the camera, "Know how it come about?"

I didn't know what to say. His head shook in the viewfinder and swerved at me.

"Sit still."

"I am setting still, but your camera is vex, jumping up and down, and the reason is you just heard the truth."

Troof again. "I didn't hear anything."

"Here she come then, Harry and me — Harry is my little sister, living in Oak Bluffs, where my father was stewie for the Phippses. That's where it all come about. It was maybe October, blowy, sand in the streets, all the summer people gone and only us there and a few Phippses. There were town people there, the ones you say hello and thank you to, but you couldn't do nothing with them and you couldn't touch the Phippses. We was alone, Daddy, Harry, and me, and Daddy was doing all day, which leaves Harry and me."

He had inched forward. I was on my knees — I took all my best pictures on my knees. His broad black face was not a foot from the camera. I saw a nose and two eyes, like a face pushing through a door I was trying to close.

"Think about it — no one else on the island. We're the only ones, her and me. Like in the Bible."

I noticed he was avoiding the words white and black, but I got the picture, the pair of them and their belief, a simpler version of my own family.

"Pretty soon I realize I'm a boy and Harry she's a girl, and one day in the soft barn loft I lifts up her dress and I say, 'What you got down under there?' and I reaches."

Teets licked the cracks from his lips and looked tenderly at the camera, perhaps using the lens as a mirror. I probed his perspiration.

"Harry doesn't say anything, a grunt like 'nuh,' but she reaches, too. We start reaching and reaching, and kissing so hard my teeth hurt, then she says, 'Stop nuh.' This goes on for a few days — no one there, like in the Bible, just Harry and me, boy and girl — and she keeps saying stop. But one day I'm reaching and she's reaching, and I got such a nice grip choking her tadpole she forgets to say stop and we do it, sinning and sweating like holy blazes."

He raised his speckled eyes and looked at me hiding behind my camera. A great hairy cuddly thing began to carouse in my entrails.

"She cried. I couldn't stop her. But then we knew how to do it, and we kept on, until the summer people came back. I was almost sorry when we weren't alone anymore, and I liked her better than any woman, because she was my sister. That's the truth." He thought a moment, then said, "At the end, when she wasn't afraid anymore, she kissed my snake, and I cried I was so happy and pushed her nice little thighs against me ears like I wanted to drown."

This left me shocked and full of hope. I said, "Weren't you afraid someone would catch you?"

"There wasn't no one, so it was all right," he said. For seconds he smiled beautifully, a light filling his face. He dropped his jaw to think, and darkened, and the smile was gone.

I said, "No, like you were before. Smiling."

He grinned like a jack-o'-lantern.

"Lost it," I said. "Try again. What were you thinking about?"

He said, "I loved that little girl."

The smile moved up his face, from his mouth to his eyes, creasing his forehead, making the crystal pimples of sweat meet and run, tightening the skin at his temples and drawing his scalp back, a kind of sorrowing satisfaction.

I snapped the picture and at once the expression passed, as if I had peeled it from his face.

This was my last Provincetown picture. The exhibition, my first, was held in that boathouse on the wharf and Papa and Mama drove up with Phoebe for the opening. Orlando came in the steamship from Boston. I showed them around, introduced them to the gallery owner (who was disappointed by the turnout) and felt that because of my photographs the place was mine and no one could take it away from me.

Most of all, I wanted Orlando to praise me. Although I did not examine my motives at the time I had gone to all that trouble so he would see I was worthy of him. People praised me for my negative prints of the blacks, but no one remarked on the amorous dazzle on Teets's face. There were murmurs about his perspiration. Subject was technique; outrageous truth — the luck of those unusual faces — obscured the fact that on the whole the pictures were fairly ordinary. I knew this and was desolate; and I got no comfort from Orlando.

The real pictures of Provincetown were not to be found in the exhibition at all, but rather at the Town Wharf, not far from where Frank and I had lunch.

Orlando was leaving. He said to Papa, "Well, what about it? Will you let her go?"

"It's her decision," Papa said.

I said, "I don't know what you're talking about."

"It's Phoebe," Papa said. I could see they had been making more plans. While I was going up and down the Cape and to New York, shooting pictures to get them to pay some attention to me there had been some sort of family issue that had nothing to do with me. I was hurt.

Phoebe said, "I don't care."

"That's not what you said this morning," said Mama.

"What's going on?" I said.

"The Yale game," said Orlando in the belittling tone he used when he was embarrassed.

"Some party," said Papa. "Ollie thinks it would be a good idea if Phoebe went up there. I'm against it myself. I haven't heard anything about chaperones, but you're big girls now and it's up to you whether you want to make something of yourselves or throw your lives away at parties."

I hated this talk: the hectoring demeaned us, and anyway I *was* making something of myself. We were standing there in the October wind, the gulls clawing at the updrafts, and the waves hurried at the wharf.

"Be a sport," said Orlando.

"You're more anxious than she is," said Papa.

"That's a lie," said Orlando quickly, then he apologized and said, "It's just a weekend."

Mama said, "I've heard about those weekends."

"Blanche Overall is going," said Orlando.

Phoebe said, "So I won't be needed."

Orlando felt obliged to ask Phoebe, since she didn't have any hobbies and didn't get out much, certainly not as much as I did. The photography I had taken up as a means of attracting Orlando had itself become an activity that displaced him and helped me forget the heartache I felt for him.

I said, "I hate parties and I can't stand football games, but if it'll help matters I'll go."

"What a good idea," said Papa.

"At least I can take my camera," I said.

Orlando was looking at Phoebe and Phoebe was looking at her feet. The wind blew her hair around her face like a yellow silk shawl and it lifted her skirt slightly and pressed it against her round backside and helped it between her legs.

"Maude can keep an eye on things," said Papa.

"That's right," said Phoebe suddenly and she looked up at Orlando. "We can all go together — you'd like that, wouldn't you, Ollie?"

It was as if Phoebe knew how he felt about me and was taunting him in a flirtatious way to get him to admit it. I didn't like her for it, but I was interested to see how he would respond.

He looked at the wind, distance and thought in his eyes.

Phoebe said, "I think Maude should go instead of me. She can keep an eye on Blanche."

"Maybe we should forget the whole thing," said Orlando. "I can catch up on my reading."

My heart snapped shut like a purse, with such a deliberate click I imagined everyone could hear.

Orlando pulled his cap down and tugged his coat around him. He didn't look back at me. He walked down the wharf with the gulls diving at him and screeching their blame.

Papa said, "That boy's got a lot to learn."

Mama said, "He doesn't know what he wants."

"Stop talking about him like that," Phoebe said. Her voice went shrill and broke. She stamped her foot. I looked down: her foot was perfect, and prettier than anything I knew. "It's not Ollie's fault — it's mine! Why can't you see that?"

From where we sat, Frank and I, the wharf was a bar of sunlight and seemed to stretch into infinity. I looked down and saw five regretful phantoms pacing out their departures separately, and the big clouds roaring over their heads and tearing into gray rags as they swelled. Then there were only four phantoms and a steamer's whistle, and the wind carrying apologies away and mingling them with the gulls' cries.

[12]

Cross Purposes

WE KID OURSELVES best, but just for so long, since our moods are visible in our gestures. It was not until I kicked a wastebasket and saw the dent that I knew the true width of my anger. The way I parked and braked the car — Frank let out a little cry — told me I was boiling.

Home again with Frank and the ghosts, I considered that other homecoming. My house on the Sound was at the margin of time, and I never jounced up the driveway without feeling that I was turning my back on the present and gunning my engine at the past. Orlando overshadowed everything.

My Provincetown show was a critical success, which is the worst of flops. Critics were skinflints and browsers; they praised me with their hands in their pockets; they didn't buy — but critics never do. What counted was cash on the barrelhead and a show in New York, and I was very far from that. I was looking for fame, to win Orlando's love. Yet I was unknown, and I had failed to get approval from the only person who mattered to me. In this failure — a camera to me was something to capture Orlando with — I had begun my career as a photographer; it was only failure that inspired me to continue. As long as Orlando eluded me I would work, and when I had him I would close my eyes on the world and start living.

I suppose I had started to doubt that day that I would ever have him. He had left home; his leave-taking had changed him. The rest of us had stayed the same, but he had other absorptions. He seemed different: bigger, shallowly happy, a bit of a glory-boy with a disloyal attention to strangers; it was as if he was ridding himself of his intelligence, substituting action for thought. He spoke of going to Harvard Law School, he became captain of the crew, he waltzed Mama around the parlor and made her squeal like Jocasta for my mismatched *Dancing Partners*. There was hope in his recklessness: one day he might simply jump into bed with me. But he showed no signs of doing that, and it was too late — I was too old — to pay a nighttime visit to his room on one of his infrequent weekends on Grand Island.

So the Provincetown show had gained me very little, but how to explain this to Frank, who was delighted by the day trip? He rummaged deeper into the stacks of pictures in the windmill, and he sorted them and saw my life as an orderly whole, as if, decades back, I had set out to fill his gallery, room by room, for the retrospective. He invented my past from my photographs: I did not recognize myself as the dedicated picture-taker, but what did he know of the thwarted lover?

Frank was striding up and down, rubbing his hands.

"Don't you see?" he said. "That show contained the germ of everything you did afterward."

"Germ is the word," I said. "It made me sick."

But he had found the pictures, every last one, not just the prints I remembered — boogie-men, the blind, the negative prints, the early New York excursions, my Brownie miniatures — but pictures I had no idea I had taken, which showed me experimenting with halation and flare: they were daring and now I saw new features in them, a significance I had missed before. The windmill appeared as a bulky fan in nearly every family shot; there were pictures within pictures — mirrors, windows, reflections on water tumblers; the toes of Phoebe's patent-leather shoes showed a seductress's petticoats — and had she al-

ways been a wallflower in *Dancing Partners?* The
foregrounds were dated, the shadows were eternal.
My camera had seen more than I had.

Frank said he had a great idea: "One room in the
retrospective will be your Provincetown show. I'll do
a mock-up of a wall in the boathouse — weatherbeaten boards, cracked window, a tape of the surf
going *sploosh.*"

"There was no surf."

"Gulls then, a tape of gulls — *kwah! kwah!*" — so
help me, he flapped his arms — "and fishnets. And
all your pictures, just as they were. Can you see it?"

"Delete the fishnets."

He had it all worked out: gulls, timber walls, driftwood, lengths of kelp draped like bunting, and my
pictures; a reconstruction. It seemed to me an utterly
silly idea.

I said, "I hate to say this, Frank. It wasn't like that
at all."

"But I've found all the pictures! They were in the
windmill all this time — you didn't even bother to
look."

"They're only half the truth," I said. I refrained
from going further and telling him that the least important event that year was my show.

"No, let me handle it." He wouldn't be interrupted
— wouldn't pause long enough to find out that there
might be more. For him, my pictures were my past.
"Your first real show — all those great pictures re-
hung. Why can't you see it?"

"I saw it. It didn't matter much then. It doesn't matter at all now."

"It does."

"It jolly well doesn't."

He said, "You refuse to see the integrity of your
early work."

Normally he rubbed his eye with a nervous shameful bunch of fingers when he was telling a lie, like a
child hoping he's not going to be caught. I stared at
him. He was motionless; he meant what he said.

I tapped a cigarette and lit up, puffing it reflectively to demonstrate that I was taking his suggestion seriously and to keep me from laughing in his face.

"It's all here," he said, breathing hard. He dealt the photographs importantly onto the table and paced the floor. I had never seen him so excited. His Adam's apple was plunging with certitude. "Look at these people!"

I obliged him and looked.

"You can see a terrific artistic ego in that one — typical overdressed Twenties writer," he said, pointing to one of a flounder fisherman who had insisted on wearing his Sunday best. "And this derelict," he went on, drumming his fingers on a morning-after shot of Eugene O'Neill, "you've captured all his hopelessness — the guy's a mess, he's dead, skid-row by the sea."

I didn't correct him. He believed; perhaps I should have been grateful for that, but he was believing for the wrong reasons. To me the pictures were obvious, and some were grotesque (how could I have had the nerve to do *Eel in a Toilet*?). And the surprises: I had forgotten that boogie-man on the beach, walking away from the camera, his high buttocks and bowed head and the tide wrack of straw and broken boards: all the grays; Orlando and Phoebe solarized in a sailboat, conferring silhouettes; a Cummings I thought I had jettisoned, grinning with heavy sea-slug lips — what a happy man!

Some needed cropping or touching up. I was reminded of my boast. I used to think: No one will make me change a thing; every detail is mine. "Airbrush flies, remove genitals," someone at the *National Geographic* had scribbled in green ink on my *Caged Baboon* — I had told the editor to take a flying leap. Now the imperfections, the surprises, the successes and embarrassments seemed of no importance whatever.

Still Frank raved. "You were roughing it out, setting yourself on course, looking ahead to refining the shots."

It is hard to know where true praise ends and the

critical leg-pull begins. I felt we were pretty close to the seam. But Frank yammered on without hesitating.

"It's about people — they're all foreground. That's what really knocks me over."

"I was never big on landscapes."

"And there's this insistence that's never actually stated, on the outdoors. You've exteriorized your — "

"Frank, this was well before the flash cube."

" — nature at the edges, the suggestion of surf here, the broken sapling as a frame for that, um, colored guy's despair."

Despair? It was Pigga, who ran a numbers game, doing a soft-shoe on a curb near Prospect Park after a rainstorm. The important feature of it was that he was wet — or rather that his skin was wet but that he was bone-dry. I had been fascinated by how water affected black skin. It wasn't absorbed; it stood in droplets on the oily surface, defying the porousness like a coating of pearls. Pigga's skin was jeweled with rainwater and his hair was full of whole pearls, too.

Frank had taken Prospect Park for a precinct of Provincetown. He said, "You can put the town together from all the backdrops. The lighthouse, the main street, those cars and dunes. You haven't missed anything. It's a whole world — an age! Here, this is one of the best things you've ever done."

I might have known he'd pick a fraud: Slaughter, the blind piano tuner, struggling to find a chord; his fingers spread, his bulging eyes marbled with glaucoma.

Frank was silent for a moment. Then he said, "But the thing is, they're all so sad, even the ones in fancy clothes — they look like they're pretending to be happy, putting on faces. Nobody's *doing* anything." He chewed, pursed his lips, and farted. "A kind of deep-structure of rhetorical inaction."

It was how I had felt, kind of blue. I was so young. I knew nothing of passion or deceit. I was simple, blundering, impatient. Perhaps Frank saw this strange girl's reflection in the pictures and could not convey it

in his jargon. But he didn't know what I knew, how —
far from mirroring my emotions in my pictures — I
had always chosen opposites: the old when I was
young, the blind when I'd valued my eyes, the black
and the bizarre when I'd felt white and ordinary, and
in my severest depressions the very glad. It was only
confidence and a feeling of well-being that enabled me
to do down-and-outs, and my comic shots were done
in a mood of near-hysteria.

"Maybe you're right," I said, trying to surrender. I
was touched by his piety: his version of me sounded
true. He had faith in my pictures — he was wrong, but
his faith would save him. I only hoped I had not misled him. Yet his belief in what I had abandoned called
me back. The hesitation I felt was that of the woman
who drives her lover away and sees him by chance
years later with a new woman and endures the slow
panic of regret. What if Frank was right? I had known
before that I'd only half understood my best pictures
and was humbled when, by degrees, their truth was
revealed; and that other fear — how, knowing so little
(no one has more immediate ignorance than the
picture-taker), I might never be able to repeat my
luck.

I had sworn after meeting Greene that I would
never take another picture, but here was Frank saying
without a stammer, "A kind of deep-structure of rhetorical inaction" and using words like integrity to dis-
cuss Pigga. He insisted I had captured an age in a
manner I was well aware I had renounced.

Frank, full of his discovery, somehow loomed like
the scholar-flunky he was, thinking he was making
himself small and useful. He said, "You've concretized
not only your own vision, but also the elusiveness of
the subjects. It's a triumph over technique. You built
the kind of relationship between artist and subject that
one only sees in the greatest pictures. Your Camerons,
your Bournes."

Eyewash, I thought; and if he mentions Arbus I'll

kick him in the teeth. But I lit another cigarette to
show I was listening.

"Just this picture alone" — he was holding one of
Orlando and Phoebe, picnicking with their backs to
me — "is enough. It says everything. That sky, those
lonely figures, the sea — that's the human condition."

Typical browser's praise, the skinflint critic mooch-
ing among the masterpieces: Ah, what have we got
here? Nothing less than the human condition! Very
nice, he says, jingling his bus fare in his pocket and
thinking: It ought to cost an arm and a leg. Out the
door: he's not buying today.

I was tactful: "It leaves a lot unsaid."

"No," he said. "This is it. It's got allegorical thrust,
but it can be read as straight naturalism."

Orlando and Phoebe? Allegorical thrust? But Frank
was happy. I wondered if he believed as I had believed once, and that he would have to wait as long as
I had to see the trickery. In praising me he was com-
plimenting the craft and making me doubt my decision
to mistrust my life as a sequence of photographs. I
thought: What a thing to say to an old lady who's
made up her mind!

He was saying, Wait! Look! Hold on there!

It was unnerving to hear someone speaking with
such assurance about Orlando's picture. Though I suspected Frank of having the faith of the believer, an
ignorance more unshakable than the priest's or proph-
et's; and saw myself something deeply untruthful in
the pictures — overcertain and prying and misleading;
though I doubted his barnacle's grip on my work, I
couldn't let him down. The guy sounded sincere. My
pictures mattered to him.

All this happened the day after the Provincetown
visit.

I had three days of alarm. I drank to relieve myself
of doubt, and between gulps I heard him on the phone.
At one point, pompously argufying with a caller, he
used the phrase, *My retrospective*. For a moment, I
felt like an intruder on this busy genius's routine and

then I remembered that I had allowed him to poke in my picture palace.

On the fourth morning, at breakfast, he said, "Can you give me a lift into Hyannis?"

"What's up?"

"I've got some things to do in the city." The city: so he was going to New York.

"Can't you make it some other time? Things are a bit unsettled at the moment."

Unsettled was an understatement; I was feeling so bent they could have named a pretzel after me.

Frank said, "I'll only be there a day or two. I've got to contact the designer and start budgeting for materials. The committee wants a preliminary presentation. Life goes on, Maude. I've got to prove I'm not up here on vacation."

"Frank Fusco, you're going to be the death of me!"

My old biddy act calmed him down. He liked to be joshed, and I could tell he was looking forward to a few days away from me. I had been on the sauce and behaving badly, playing the radio too loud and leaving glasses around the house. And I had spent part of each morning noisily vomiting the night's damage.

"Bus station," he said, when we were on the road.

"The plane's faster."

"I hate planes."

"Sure you do." Why is it, I wondered, that single people are more morbid than married ones? Frank was full of fears about flying, eating, smoking, muggers, riots, swimming after meals, dune-buggy gangs, getting trapped in elevators, breaking the speed limit, not using a safety belt. He read Solzhenitsyn and worried about Russians and labor camps. At the station he bought a Tootsie Roll and the paperback of *Jaws* — that would cause him a few sleepless nights — and waved out the window of the bus like a ten-year-old.

Back home I poured myself a snort, but to prevent my guzzling it too quickly went into the studio Frank had set up in his room. I decided to have a private view of my Provincetown show.

I slid open the drawers of the filing cabinet. I have always approved of the honor system — no locks, no seals — because if it becomes necessary to snoop there's no hassle. There were letters in one folder, prints in the others. I found "Provincetown" and pulled out the sheaf of enlargements: *Eel in a Toilet* on top — I threw down the pictures in disgust and read one of his mother's letters. *I would have thought if she had a heart condition she wouldn't carry on like that.* My peevishness justified my looking further. The nerve! I went through his closet and bureau drawers, and every shirt and wrinkled sock told me that I did not really know this man.

Beside the bed there was a small table: a lamp, an alarm clock, *Cancer Ward,* and some cough drops. I yanked the drawer open and under copies of *Creative Camera* and *Photography Today* found a heavy envelope. I could tell by its density that it contained photographs. Mine?

I sipped my drink, but didn't swallow. My heart went boom-boom.

Once, I had been commissioned by a magazine to do a series of erotic pictures. It was a challenge I gladly accepted: the anatomy had limits then, suggestion was everything. The idea of spread-eagling a whore on an unmade bed so a subscriber could do a drooling pelvic on her was out of the question. I did a half a dozen: a girl's face in profile licking a ripe strawberry with the fleshy spoon of her tongue; a bird's-eye view of a nude on all fours — just the cello of her topside; an angle shot in reticulation of a girl flopped forward over the hood of a car; a delighted thing squatting on a man's foot, clutching his cigar; another with one breast upturned peering at her nipple; and — my biggest coup, the one that was singled out for praise, my piece of revenge on the creeps who ran the magazine and the men who bought it — a sizzling shot of a leggy nude climbing a pole, which no one guessed was a very humid buttocky boy.

The photographs I found in Frank's drawer — and

they showed signs of handling — were something else.
My first reaction was to flick through them, then put
them away. I shuffled them quickly and saw great soft
bodies, and clearly a snail's head caught between the
stinging lips of a sea urchin; a withered rosebud; a human face with bulging cheeks, feeding; a starved an-
kle. I sat down mystified and took them one by one:
how stupid and weak naked flesh seemed! They looked
in close-up like porous giants — huge bums and
shanks and dirty toes. They were comic heaps, fooling
with punctured dolls. Then I saw their dumb agony,
the leers of pain, and I knew they showed, more
graphically than I could have imagined, people dying.

It was a dance of death performed by hairy children, only superficially ridiculous: deep down it was
intimate treachery. I was outraged and could not separate them from Frank's praise. Again and again my
gaze was drawn to the fingers and feet, the crooked
teeth. I was sparing myself the wounds. I saw anonymous flesh being pinched, a man straining over a huddled woman, strangulated faces, desire simulated as
grievous harm. Pale hairy buttocks, shadowy faces,
mortal wounds: slick injured beavers, veiny swollen
probes. Technically, the pictures were a mess. They
were to photography what grunts were to human
speech, inarticulate terror, almost unreadable cruelty,
mournful bullies in pig-like postures.

Murder: here was a woman being torn in half by a
man clumsily shovelling at her legs; and another
woman on her knees pleading with a man who held a
lethal squirt-gun against her cheek. There were stab-
bings, and there was suicide — women choking on
furious rats and stuffing themselves with sticks of dynamite. I saw varieties of cannibalism that were unknown in Borneo, people engorging one another with
mouths like vacuum cleaners or, conversely, looking
as if each person was trying to inflate his partner. I
saw simple assault: men ejaculating a kind of poisoned
oyster on women's faces and in a delirium of greed
others licking the clotted things off; urination — spat-

tering jets sliming crouched figures. The last showed a
stew of women arranged like slabs of fat, head to tail,
snuffling.

I wanted to be sad. I wasn't. I felt cheated, like a
witness to a casual massacre, too detached to mourn
the victims I knew to be anonymous. The mangled
body without a name was only a sensational casualty,
and the bodies were indistinguishable. It was the scandal of it — the scandal of lust, not the lust itself. The
wounds were their sex. And it occurred to me that
such pictures — the millions of them in the world —
showed only the same two people, over and over
again; one degraded couple who played all the parts
in every picture ever taken. Here they were again,
more vicious than the last time I had seen them, dirt-
ier, older, and a little desperate, but the same familiar
bums, leaving me shaking my head and saying gosh. I
gave them names: Kenny and Doris — they were
every fucking couple ever photographed; Kenny with
his greasy hair and his I.D. bracelet, Doris with her
cheap mascara and her appendix scar.

And they gave Frank pleasure! The man who had
praised my pictures could find room in his judgment
for this junk. Perhaps more than I, Frank had under-
estimated the power of the photograph to deceive. He
had hidden them, and what worried me most was that
he needed this squalid couple, found satisfaction in
Kenny and Doris. How then to reckon his praise of
me?

He had fooled me for a while. I didn't matter. But
he had fooled himself.

I was not confused. This confirmed what I had felt
about my life and work: they were separate, contradictory, as different as Kenny and Doris were from
any couple I had done. I had been right to chuck photography. Frank's surprise — that dirty dog — proved
I could not trust him; nor could I trust my own pictures. The ones he claimed said everything, said nothing.

"Frank! You worm — you pathetic liar. You say

you care about my pictures, but what about this garbage you keep beside your bed? You weak silly man, you think this is passion! Look at your thumbprints on them and tell me you don't peer at them when you're all alone at night — does your willy rise like a snake out of a basket? They're not even good pictures! They've got hypo stains, they're underexposed, the flesh tones are green, they need to be cropped and airbrushed, the light's all wrong, they're sixty percent shadow — trash! Put these in your gallery and worry everyone to death talking about integrity with a Tootsie Roll in your mouth. You're kidding yourself, sonny boy. And maybe you're just curious, but if these pictures are a turn-on, you're in bad trouble —"

Frank was of course in New York. I spoke to the wall.

I had barely finished congratulating myself on how pure I felt surviving these pictures. It had been quite a shock to my system, but I had understood Frank's complexity and the whole pictorial conundrum more clearly — somehow, this trash was crucial, I couldn't dismiss it. I didn't want to eat or drink — not after what I'd seen. But I was vindicated! How right I had been to doubt what Frank had said about my Provincetown pictures and photography in general. I'd had a glimpse of the underside of his enthusiasm — not a pretty sight — and had begun to pity him.

Then it became small and unimportant, kid stuff, as my memory woke and yawned, reddening its tonsils at me. I remembered my own deceit.

Charades

IT WAS the day I stopped the fracas in Boston. That gave me the courage I needed, because until then I had wobbled badly when I thought of deceiving Orlando. But I thought: It's for his own good and he'll appreciate it afterward, and better me than one of those shrill Radcliffe tramps who smoke stogies and stink of gin and use the Harvard men as dildos.

By now Miss Dromgoole was gone. Frenise was old and walked around with batter on her fingers. The day Miss Dromgoole left us we gave a family lunch party for her — Orlando came down for the day and presented her with a box of her favorite glazed fruit. Then, when she got into Mr. Wampler's taxi, we dashed into the house and tore our clothes off and ran around naked, whooping in celebration and relief, though Papa stayed in his BVDs and Mama kept her bloomers on. My *Deliverance* — half-naked folks at the windows of a white house, shot from the lawn — is a record of that day.

My parents were ailing, yet the family balance remained plumb perfect. Phoebe and I, who had stayed on the Cape to enjoy our parents' protection, now looked after them, became protectors ourselves. It happens to children who linger at home. Papa and Mama, our charges, depended on us. They denied this once a year by making a fall trip to Florida, just to show they didn't need us. But they always came back rather silent and grateful, smiling as if to say, "What would we do without you?"

At a certain age you stop being a child and start raising your parents, educating them past the age they left off learning. You overtake them, and after that everything they know, if they are still teachable, they get from you. But they are getting feebler, so your rearing only makes them younger and more dependent, until at last you have that bizarre reversal known to many spinsters, the parents turning from interesting old ruins into protesting geriatrics, with bibs on top and Chux on the bottom. The spinster coaxes her mother to eat, and the mother, objecting, bats the spoon away and slops her food and responds only to baby talk. I saw a time when I would be fussing that way, but instead of scaring me it made me feel more wifely toward Orlando.

He was away now at Harvard Law School. No one mentioned him. Certainly, Phoebe and I never discussed him as we once had. We missed him, though. I had associated him with surprises, laughter, and exciting weather. He had reminded us that our family was the world, and had had us in stitches with his imitation of Papa. "Who's this? Who's this?" he'd say, sticking his hand out so we'd let him perform. He could do Papa putting on his trousers, shaking them and wiggling his foot for balance before he stepped into them. He did Papa's Yankee accent, his saying "Let's get some color in those cheeks!" or "Abyssinia!" Orlando was also brilliant at charades and had always chosen me for his team. At night he had told us ghost stories. "Three-Fingered Billy" and the insane asylum one that ended with his scream, *Why me?* After the folks went to bed he told an elaborate story which concluded with us all going down in a plane and what we were saying one minute before the crash: Papa, with his arms folded, saying, "The country's going to the bitches — ", Mama's "I could have told you — ", Phoebe worrying about how the crash was going to spoil her new frock, and me crying, "Hold it!" taking pictures of the disaster that was shortly to overwhelm us. He also played the trombone.

There was no telling if or when he would come back, and no one was laughing.

I kept off the subject. It was clear to me that Phoebe loved Orlando as much as I did. It was her beauty. Her love for Orlando grew out of her deep distrust of the attentions of the many men — Sandy was one, a dope named Foggis another — who chased after her. I knew no such attentions and so had a hopeless and single-minded love for him, which was like an object I had treasured from my earliest youth and could not cast aside, since it had the high polish of affectionate handling. Phoebe's love was a rejection of men in general, mine the desire for one in particular. I believed mine to be the more painful, the more genuine, and I did not want to break her heart by telling her I'd have him. It would send her crazy and blind.

Seeing how I had stayed home she mistook my stubbornness for timidity and became timid herself; and indecisive, and superstitious about going away. But soon, I thought, she will realize the strength in her beauty and outgrow her love for Orlando. As yet I had only my camera, and what I knew of the world was what little of it I chose to see through the viewfinder. I made forays in New England and occasional trips to New York, where I met other photographers, notably Edward Weston and Imogen Cunningham and Weegee. But I did not care much for their work, and seeing their success only made me think that the fame I required to capture Orlando's attention would never be mine. And I hoped that Phoebe would leave Orlando to me. To show her how pretty she was — to give her confidence enough to go away — I did her repeatedly.

She had grown up. She was tall and slow. Her skin had a few glamorous moles, vivid as ladybugs, that made it seem flawless. Her breasts slooped at her slightest movement. She could not be taken in at a

single glance — she had to be studied in parts, like a
landscape. Nothing she wore, not even her winter coat,
could conceal the beautiful protrusions of her body, or
her shimmering bones, or cool hollows. She knew her
mouth was large, so she kept her lips together, wryly
kissing the air she stroked with her fingers. At night,
when she unpinned her hair and let it tumble past
her shoulders, and melted out of her silks, she looked
as if she were made of gold. Then she gathered her
hair and twisted it and chewed on it as we gabbed.
There we sat, hiding under the light, too old to be still
at home, and not admitting why we were waiting in
that house. But our parents were asleep: we could be
children again and use the house against our fears.

Phoebe took a great lazy interest in her body,
pinching and smoothing her skin, wondering at her legs
and weighing her breasts in her hands. She would press
her tits together to make a slot and then gently chafe
them. She licked her finger and used it to moisten her
elbow, holding one pink nipple in the crook of her arm
like a kitten's nose. Her body had such sweeps, such a
shine of health, such trembling ripeness, that her every
posture was a pose and even motionless, she looked as
if she were moving.

She made my pictures masterpieces. Like Marilyn
Monroe, she photographed about ten pounds lighter
than she was, and she gave me the illusion of having
unique photographic skill. But it was really very simple: she was shockingly beautiful, her angel's face had
tiger's eyes. She brought to each photograph a special
light that flattered my technique and reminded me of
how small my talent was, how insignificant my camera,
how much subject mattered. The greatest pictures are
those which for minutes make you forget who took
them: you are shot forward, the picture becomes part
of your own experience as you drown in your glad
eye. Anyone could have made a reputation doing
Phoebe.

But when I showed her the pictures, to prove she
was a woman who had power — yes, a priestess —

she mocked them. "You can see my raggedy petticoat," she said; or, "I'm all backside in that one."

What she wanted from me were pictures of Orlando. I had hundreds of them, which she sorted, choosing the ones I had done of her and Orlando together. She gave them back to me the next day cracked and curled, as if she had crushed them against her breast.

With such primitive equipment to work with, I had to depend on effects. At that time I was terribly interested in back-lighting, shooting into the sun to make the smallest object explosive with unlikely halation. I could deepen the picture with dimension, creating giant spaces, so that a crowd of people looked like an obstacle course, or I could bring that young man in the foreground close enough to kiss.

In one of Phoebe's favorites, Orlando stood soaking wet in a spring storm of rain and sun, with his white shirt open and his fountain pen bleeding in his pocket, his arm around Phoebe, who held an umbrella over her own head — a pair of rainbirds. In another, he was removing a speck from her eye, with his hands framing her face, and peering at her, his head tilted as if he was pronouncing a blessing. A third was of Orlando alone, leaning out of the windmill door, listening because he had heard a noise, which was me sneaking up on him: I took that picture hunkered under him, before he saw me, while he was still holding his breath and poised as if about to launch himself from the porch.

These pictures were better than any of the more famous ones I did at the time. The critic who had praised my Provincetown show in the *Transcript* would have keeled over if he'd seen them. But I kept them private and only showed them to Phoebe. It was her fascination for them that impelled me to act.

Her borrowing them excited me and made me jealous. Not that I was worried about her, but I knew there must be others who had their eye on him. To me the pictures were much more than souvenirs of Orlando, more than pretty relics I had hoarded. I had concentrated all the skill I had on him, so that in taking the picture of my love I had recorded a moment of communion. Though I did not appear in any picture I believed my heart's eye to be visible at a decisive moment of light. It was impossible for me to see anyone holding these pictures and not resent their intrusion, since they were using me to see him and loving him with my eyes.

The lust of the eye. The best photographs were, to me, like an experience of drowning. You were swamped and sunk and then made strangely buoyant. You floated away changed. My pictures of Orlando had this effect on Phoebe. She saw them and loved him — loved him for my pictures.

Another summer had gone, the hurricane damage was repaired and I was faintly ashamed of the pictures I had done of the storm's aftermath: ordinary pictures of sensational ruin. Surely a picture had to be more than subject? I had to get busy and do something new. This season was for action — fall was purposeful in Massachusetts.

Here, every month smelled different, and the aromas of autumn, a richness of mellow leaf-dust, the scent of bonfires and pine needles and the low haze of woodsmoke — the sea-mist in the mornings, the clear, iron-dark nights — sharpened my mind with enterprise. Those sensations and the coaly presence of trains fizzing busily at little tile-roofed stations, more particular and blacker when the trees were going bare. In those days a passenger train ran from Hyannis to South Station in Boston, taking in Sandwich and crossing the Canal at Buzzard's Bay before heading for the shoe mills of Brockton and Southie's tenements. In the late spring the train was full of lady schoolteachers and their bikes; in summer, campers and families. But after Labor Day it traveled nearly empty, a great dusty chain of coaches. It was noise, the clatter of boiler plate rattling through the low woods of the Cape leaving fragile lengths of smoke behind; and an engineer with his grinning grubby face and striped cap and blue elbow at the locomotive window.

The folks were in Florida "having a swell time."

I detached myself from Phoebe and boarded the train. I had no idea of what I was going to do, and had brought my camera in the hope of finding an extraordinary picture, the *Life* cover that would convince Orlando I was worthy of him. When the black conductor came over to punch my ticket I almost grabbed his sleeve. I could tell he was hiding uneasily under his uniform, but I wanted him to know that he had nothing to fear from me, that I was the girl who had been written up in the *Transcript* for her Provincetown pictures, that I felt forlorn and black behind my own white eyes searching for my brother's heart.

Every time I opened my mouth I knew I was talking to myself. It was to steady my own mind that I said to this black ticket-puncher, "I think the world of you people."

He flashed me a nice smile that was a little hungry and a little lonely, and afterward I wished I had taken his picture: the cracked visor and tarnished badge, shiny thick cheeks, wide hairless nostrils, and a gold tooth he let glitter for a few friendly seconds before he chewed and swallowed it. The wrinkles on his neck were rimed with sweat-froth, the fabric of his jacket sleeve was worn to a grid of threads, and his hands, which were three distinct colors, smelled of bacon. Like all missed opportunities (he was wonderfully back-lit; in tight close-up you could have jumped down his throat) it remained vivid in the picture palace of my mind.

At South Station I bumped against the world again after the rolling seclusion of the train. People were active here; the marble floor transmitted the clang of luggage carts and I had that sense I always got in railway stations, of being in a cathedral — the muffled quaking voices, the echoes of insignificant sounds made important by the hugeness of the ceiling. It was still early, hardly two o'clock, and because I had not made up my mind about what I was going to do, I decided to walk the length of Atlantic Avenue and then cut through the North End to the Charles.

I didn't take any pictures. Number one, I was walking away from the sun. The gritty light leached the brickwork and the cobbled avenue of interest; the best pictures were behind me, between me and the flaring sun. Number two, I had chosen this stroll by the wharf area for pondering my next move with Orlando. It wasn't the attraction of the wharves. Even then, the picturesque made me sick — I avoided it and hoped that people would see me in my pictures more than was there, see them as more complete than they were, as I sought the ambiguity of shape in the echo of image, so that up close what had looked most definite to the observer turned into grains of soaking light, as it might appear to someone drowning in the sea on a beautiful day.

There were fish reeks from the barrels of scraps and a whiff of horses from Haymarket Square. The air was crusted with salt and charged with cold sea smells and slime. But the harbor was hidden by the warehouses. I played with the idea, one that was to puzzle me for years, of taking a picture of this air and trying to suggest the seascape that made it so pungent, of using the light to mention the smell and that smell disclosing an enormity that could be sensed but not seen, like the harbor. The idea drove me to tinker at the margins and crop the obvious. I never considered a good portrait to be a big plain face, the nose dead center in the square, the glum puffy-faced madonna that painters favored. I was after the iridescent shadows of telling aromas, the black hand smelling of fatback bacon. I had looked hard at the work of other photographers. Stieglitz's painting-like faces were calculated to look full of the past. But I could not see the art in that — I wanted the portrait's future, too. Edward Weston, who had boasted that his eight-by-ten view camera weighed forty pounds with its tripod, said, "Miss Pratt, American faces are all landscape,"

by which he meant that if he was doing a Nebraska
farmer there would be furrows plowed across the
man's brow, and a backwoodsman would have a grizzled face, and your beachcomber would look like a
hunk of driftwood. It was cheating, matching the face
to the landscape, ignoring the Yankee who didn't have
crags and making every butcher look like a mindless
meatcutter — what if he had fine sensitive hands? I
was not interested in only telling people what they
knew, showing the past or present scribbled on a person's face. I wanted to portray the future in the depths
of his eyes, what he would become, a harassed father
in that bratty child, a bard in young Cummings, a con
man in that artist; the suicide in the actress, the bankruptcy in the tycoon, the hag that would overtake the
glamorous woman. A face was more than an inner
state — it was a history of the person's life, some of
it yet to be lived. The infant's death mask: it was the
photographer's job to reveal it, to make the future
visible, to use the camera to improve upon the eye. I
was studying the possibilities of this — light as odor,
mortal shadow as time future — when, after a few
blocks of Atlantic Avenue, I saw a spill of Italians,
and further on, dockers lounging to remind me that I
was a woman and trying to intimidate me with their
stares — challenging me to stare back, as men do in
their silly little gangs to make women feel defenseless.

I was approaching Atlantic Wharf when I heard it,
a terrible scream, like a cat's protesting yowl on a
summer night, and then the tramp of running, the
shudder of blundering boots. A little black man shot
in front of me, out of the alley, nearly knocking me
down. I was startled — fearful — before I realized
that he was harmless: he had passed his fright to me.
I still heard the feet rumbling closer and finally blaring as six sweaty men came booting out of the alley
waving gaffs, hooks, and clawhammers.

"Where'd he go?"

Like a fool, I pointed to the warehouse the little
man had beetled into. "In there."

"Out of the way, lady. After him!"

They were shouting and struggling into the warehouse. It had all happened so fast I hadn't had time to think, but at that moment I knew the man being chased was innocent and the others with their clumsy weapons were going to brain him for nothing. And now that I could no longer see him I remembered his face: it had been gray with terror.

"Wait!" I yelled. But it was too late. I could hear the grunts, the boots slam-banging on the warehouse planks, and the men barging into metal drums.

As I entered the building I saw them leaving by the sunny door at the far end, going at a good clip onto the wharf. I saw no sign of the black man. The warehouse stank of rope and tar and fish oil. I ran through to the wharf, where a ship's horn drowned the noises of the chase, the six brutes hounding the little figure along the pier.

The light made it bearable. The sun on the water shone so intensely they were diminished, half-sized, shimmering narrowly after the man who seemed no longer than an insect in that glare. It turned the brutality into play, almost a dance, the sun slowing them and making them twitch with their toy-like weapons. Light is an unintelligent pencil. It is kind or cruel; it distorts; it is seldom fair, it is never innocent. If I had not looked those men in the face I would have said they were children fooling and gone away.

But I stayed and watched them stop running. The little man was trapped at the end of the pier, dwarfed by the violent light and by the black logs that served as hitching posts for the ships' hawsers. I thought of calling a cop, but I knew that if I left that place it would be too late: the man would be in the drink or worse. And though I could hear the noises of Boston, the trains ringing down Atlantic Avenue, and even voices skimming clearly on the water from boats and other piers, there was no one around to help me stop this persecution.

I didn't want to go any nearer, but there was nothing else I could usefully do. I had given the poor man away — I had to save him. I ran to the pier and along the boards a quarter of the way, making as much noise as I could. The men's backs were turned; the little man crouched near a ladder on his last inch of safety, holding his palm up in a feeble protest. Behind him, great gulls swooped as if they thought this desperate man was flinging them crusts.

I said, "Hey!"

They didn't turn. They prolonged their menace by walking slowly toward their victim and raising their weapons.

I screamed, I fumbled for my camera, I shook it at them. And now the men did turn, as I aimed it at their heads. They covered their faces. Strange — it was as if they had never seen one before. They behaved like true savages, for whom the unknown is dangerous, cowed by the tiniest mystery. I held it at them and took a step. They reacted by staggering and twisting their faces. They dropped their arms and looked at me sideways.

One said, "Put that down!"

Another muttered, "Get him."

Him? It was the back-lighting. The sun that made them small made me big, a man, a threat.

"You just stay where you are or I'll use this," I said. "And you'll be sorry."

"It's some crazy dame."

I screamed again and made them jump. I must have looked vast, toppling at them from the dark eye of the sun, the fierce exaggeration pitching my shadow at them. Really, we were eight people on a pier, counting the victim; but the midafternoon sun of autumn lighted us differently with drama and the halation and flare put me in charge and ridiculed them; it made them cowardly and me brave, and now I saw I had them backing away.

"You better be careful with that thing," one called out.

"Stay right where you are," I hollered. "Stay put!"

They tried to shield their eyes and I knew that as long as I kept the sun behind me I was safely distorted in its dazzle.

All this took less than a minute, but with bluff only seconds are necessary. The next sound was the clack of oarlocks. The little man had scrambled down the ladder and found a dinghy under the pier. He was away, rowing like mad and bouncing his oars in the water.

"There he goes!" The men ran to the pier-head and shouted at him and I fled the way I had come and jumped on a bus. As soon as I paid my fare and found a seat I put my face in my hands and burst into tears. It was not that little man's life I had saved, but my own. The man, I knew now — and it was something that had been crucial for me to remember — looked exactly like my old subject, Teets.

In this unexpected way I came to trust my camera. It proved useful, even when I wasn't taking pictures. And there was a further reckoning to make: the light. The camera had given me courage, but the light had saved me. That peculiar angle of the sun had made me briefly a giantess and stretched my shadows all over the pier. People mattered according to the way they were lighted: I could make Orlando listen to me.

And, as frights will do, my mind had been squeezed and concentrated. There had been a sense of finality in my attempt to rescue the little black man. In my response was an ultimatum: danger had triggered inspiration, boldness had made me bolder and my sense of charade more inventive. I had my idea and I knew where to take it.

Orlando, in his second year of law school, had a tutor's suite of rooms in Adams House. As I entered Plympton Street I saw him shouldering his way through the Adams House gate. I almost called out to him, but thought better of it, and instead followed him past the Lampoon Building and down the slop-

ing streets to the river. He must have sensed my
eyes on him because at the Harvard Boat House he
turned. He was in his sculling gear — sneakers, gloves,
shorts, jersey — and he looked in the aching autumn
light like an unbuckled prince fixing to set sail, the
sun at three giving his beanie a halo. Orlando appeared to own anything he was near: the river, the
meadow, and all the maples of Back Bay. I faltered,
but instead of going down on my knees I snapped
his picture with my usual devotion.

He didn't act surprised to see me. That was Orlando, as calm as you please: he never betrayed surprise. He said, "I've been looking all over for you.
I had something to ask you."

I fell for it. "You do?"

He said, "Yes. How's your belly where the pig bit
you?"

Then he laughed and hugged me and we walked
into the Boat House hand in hand. On the ramp
he said, "You won't fit into a shell, so choose a skiff
and let's go while the sun's still shining."

He grabbed the painter of a small rowboat and
pulled it into the water. He threw off his beanie and
heaved us away. In the river we were buoyed by the
rising light, now dim, now dazzling, as the yellow
leaves from the shore wavered under the water's
mirror. The wind swept a shower of them from the
maples. They were gold foil torn from the boughs,
curling in gusts across the grass and into the river
where they magnetized their reflections, leaf to leaf,
and spun. It was like paper fire — the bright cut-out
leaves scattering down from the trees and turning the
trees dark and small — the sort of cool light I could
touch, big ragged atoms of it dancing wildly in the
wind and then becoming part of the river's surface.

Orlando began rowing. He did it easily, by
stretching his arms and drawing the oar handles
smoothly to his chest, feathering the blades, and
before they dripped slicing them into the current and
making the boat glide without a lurch. We were

headed downriver to the bridges and the basin. In mid-
stream a breeze sprang up and wrinkled the water,
puddling it with ripples.

"You warm enough?"

I nodded and said, "Ollie, I've missed you."

"How's the Cape?"

"If you came home once in a while you'd know."

"What about your pictures?" he said, still solici-
tous. "People ask me about you all the time —
you're famous, Maude. Your hurricane pictures in
the papers."

"The Boston papers."

"Boston's the world, cookie."

I said, "It isn't either."

"And you're still snapping away."

"I'm snapping."

"Maude," he said. "You look so damned sad."

"I love you, Ollie."

"I love you, too."

I started to cry. I was glad we were far from the
river banks, where no one would see us. My weeping
surprised me like a stomach cramp and I blubbered
out my pain, but after the first sobs I kept on, crying pleasurably, enjoying it. I could have stopped,
but I realized that it would make what I was going
to say more plausible. It was trickery, the tears running into my mouth.

Orlando still rowed. He said, "Look — geese."

They were flying overhead in a honking lopsided
chevron, like swimmers they moved so effortlessly,
beating the air and keeping their necks outstretched,
making for Florida. Orlando, I knew, had been trying
to distract me, but I looked up and cried all the
more when I saw the great confident letter they were
carrying across the sky.

He said, "That would make a terrific picture."

"No, no," I said. "Too much sky — they'd look like
a dish of gnats." I blew my nose and hunched up
some more sobs and said, "Have you seen Sandy?"

"Old Overalls? He's at the Business School. I see him sailing now and then. What's wrong?"

I was sniffling. "Did you ever hear of incest?"

Orlando pounced. "Sure I did! Little things, aren't they? With six legs — they climb all over you."

"Ollie!"

"Sorry," he said, and feathered his oars.

"I'm serious and you're making it awfully hard for me. Blanche told me all about it."

"Look," he said. "More geese."

I could see them, high up, like a coat hanger creeping past the corner of my eye, trailing their far-off honks. But this time I didn't look up. Orlando's head was tilted back and his eyes followed the birds with a kind of longing. When they were gone he gave his oars a splash and trudged with them. I was sorry for confronting him like this, trapping him with my tears and making him listen.

"They were lovers — Sandy and Blanche."

"Blanche?"

"Both of them."

Amazingly, he missed a stroke, raked the air with one blade. For Orlando this was like stupefaction. We started to spin like the leaves around us. He worked the oars half-heartedly and leaned forward to examine my face.

I said, "Cross my heart."

He pricked up his ears. I saw his scalp move: he was interested — more than interested — grave with scrutiny. "Blanche?"

I said, "They got it out of the Bible."

"You're a crazy thing," he said.

"Listen, Ollie, it's the truth. It was last year, when their parents were away. October, I think — he summer people had gone home. The staff was there, but you know what Blanche thinks of them, barely human. So Blanche and Sandy were all alone in the house. Alone, think about it — just the two of them, like in the Bible."

"That's not in the Bible."

"It is, because after she told me I checked." The boat slipped sideways, turning in circles down the river. "You know them — they're very close, like us, and they don't keep secrets from each other. One day Blanche was in their hay loft doing something with the bales, and she heard Sandy on the ladder. She told me she was afraid and she didn't know why. They got to fooling around and before she knew what was happening Sandy lifted up her dress and said, 'What have you got down there?' "

"He didn't!"

"He sure did. But that wasn't all. Instead of pushing him away she just laughed —"

"She never laughs."

"This was different. Sandy was reaching and kissing her so hard Blanche said her teeth hurt. She felt him pulling her bloomers. After a while she told him to stop, which he did."

"That's only right," said Orlando and thrashed with his oars.

"But neither of them —"

"There's more of this?" He lifted his oars at me.

"Neither of them was really sorry, and after a day or so they were at it again, going to town in the hay loft, just the two of them. Blanche said it was funny — she had always dreamed about it happening like that, and she had sort of rehearsed it in her mind. So, once they started, they carried on, and she couldn't stop it then even if she had wanted to, which she didn't. He had a good grip on her and she closed her eyes and they did it."

"Did what?" he said hoarsely.

"Jammed."

"Maude, I've never heard you talk like this."

"Like nobody's business," I said, nodding with approval.

"That damned girl."

"She was glad — you can't blame her," I said.

And I told him that Blanche was especially tickled that it had happened with Sandy, because love is knowledge and no one knows more than a brother and sister.

"Blanche?" he said. "Tickled?" We were under a bridge and Orlando's voice leaped at us from the granite pillars and arches in a gulping echo. We were still drifting, nudged by the eddies at the pillars and losing our spin as we cleared the bridge.

"Of course she cried, but that was sheer happiness and gratitude. She wasn't afraid anymore and she told me that as long as she lives she will never forget it and never love anyone as much as Sandy. Which I can understand. Can't you?"

"And she told you this?"

"She showed me the bites and bruises. They were beautiful, like purple pansies stamped on her skin."

He looked mystified. The oars rested limply in his hands and the blades dragged on the water.

I said, "I don't hold it against her."

"No," he said wearily, "not if she loved him."

"And I know how she feels." I was hoping to extract a response from him, but none came. I said, "Do you know how she feels?"

He faced me. His answer made his eyes blaze and heated my face and dried my tears. He said, "Yes, I do!"

"Think of it," I said. "Just the two of them together."

"There's no room for anyone else," he said, turning cautious.

"Exactly — that's the beauty of it."

"What did their parents say?"

He wanted more reassurance, but I couldn't give it. I said I didn't know, but I told him my views on that, how at a certain age your parents exhaust themselves of knowledge: you outgrow them and have to begin raising them, keeping certain things from them.

He said, "I thought you were so proper."

"Ollie, they're just like us! What is more proper than a brother and sister in bed in their own house? It fits exactly. People go through life trying to find the perfect partner and never realize that that person is back home — the one they left. It's their own flesh and blood. It's so simple I don't know why more people don't do it."

He said, "Because there's a law against it, cookie."

"The law hates lovers," I said.

"Tell that to the judge," he said. "Listen, even primitive societies are against it."

"But they're against everything that's sensible — that's why they're primitive. But there's nothing primitive about the Pratts."

He said, "I thought we were talking about the Overalls."

"We're talking about brothers and sisters," I said. "People like you and me."

He spoke to the gunwale: "I didn't think you could get away with things like that."

"So you've thought about it."

"Of course I have," he said. I thought he was going to amplify this, but all he said was, "Blanche had me fooled."

"And me. The funny thing is, ever since she told me I've liked her more. I didn't think she had it in her. You think people are different, but they're not — they're as strange as you. I know how she feels, don't you?"

He considered his thumbs. He said, "I'm glad you told me."

The wind stirred his hair, an agitation like a process of thought.

He said, "Why am I so happy all of a sudden?"

"Ollie," I said, and kissed him and took his picture: that expression of intense thought draining away and leaving his face lively and untroubled. The sun had set his hair smoldering, and I was soused with sunbeams.

He looked up and saw that we had drifted to the

Boston shore. He straightened and gripped the oars and swung the boat around smartly, then — and I could see that it had sunk in — started back to Harvard with swift decisive strokes.

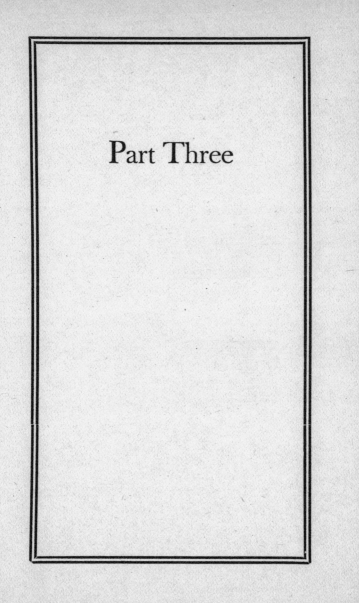

Part Three

Part Three

[14]

Fellow Travelers

HE WAS back. He returned to Grand Island in the middle of the night and used his own key to make poking clacks at the keyhole, like a burglar's tired attempt at an inside job. I opened my eyes, blinked away the rust, and rose from the luminosity and chatter of a dream to the dark stillness of the house. It disturbed me: I surfaced, I opened my mouth, the dream trembled, and everything was black.

His noises made him big and busy, a lumbering body. He snapped on lights as he moved from room to room, and then there was that sequence of sounds you only hear at night, that makes its own brief pictures. A door shut and bolted; a spattering jet of bubbles propelled into a bowl; the uncorking of a valve and a chain's releasing rattle; a collapse of water pressure in the pipes and a fugitive hiss and suck in the walls. The snap, snap, snap of light switches; the complaining stair plank; the resonant crunch of bedsprings; the latecomer's surrendering sigh in his soft bed.

I subsided into sleep myself and did not wake again until I heard a South Yarmouth lawnmower rat-tatting across the agitated blue of the Sound. It was a beautiful autumn day, a breeze making the sunlight leap from the spiky waves like fire in crystal, and all the long grasses on the dunes brushing softly against the breeze's belly. He was in and out of the windmill, in and out, the slap of feet and doors, scrabbling in the

129

picture palace. Though in bed I could believe that forty years hadn't happened — one's bed is the past — I got up on one elbow and saw him through the window, striding across the lawn with boxes of photographs, carrying my work into the house to examine. I sprang up, put on my housecoat and slippers, and shuffled downstairs into the present.

"You're at it bright and early, Frank."

He muttered something about the night bus.

I said, "You strike bottom yet?"

"There's a hell of a lot more where these came from." I saw a crude form of criticism, a kind of impatience, in the way he tossed his hair to the side, but his forelock flopped back into his eyes. "If you ask me, I don't think they've ever been touched."

"I'm counting on you to do that," I said. "For the life of me, I can't imagine how they got there."

His cheeks were dusty. Not even nine and he was already perspiring, the sweat stickling his sideburns and smearing his forearms. He looked — rolled-up sleeves, harassed face, trembling Adam's apple — like the photographer himself, hugging his property to his chest. He had an artist's preoccupied air, an artist's petulance. I was bothering him; I had no business wasting his time. He gasped to remind me that he was hard at work.

"That's a biggie."

He weighed the box and said, "Some early ones — the Thirties."

"Mind if I look?"

"I'm pretty busy, Maude. All this sorting." Gasp, gasp. "Maybe some other time."

He frowned and tried to get past me.

"What's this?"

"Trains, travelers, people at stations. I'm cataloguing them by subject matter as well as date. Topical chronology kind of thing. My faces, my occupations, my vehicles —"

I didn't mind him saying *vee-hickles,* but what was this *my?* "Trains," I said. "You come across any of

Harvard? Charles River? Fellow in a boat, full face, rowing?"

"In the windmill," he said without hesitating. It scared me a little to realize how thoroughly Frank knew my work: he knew what I had forgotten. He went on, "I'm not putting it with this batch. I'm keeping it for my vessels sequence."

"I don't know how you do it," I said.

Sweat drops flew from his chin as he spoke. "I'm working flat out. You mind moving? This thing weighs a ton."

But I stayed on the path. "Coffee?"

"Maw-odd!"

On this return trip to the windmill I stopped him again on the path and said, "The rower — get it for me, will you?"

"It's right inside the door," he said. "Didn't you see it?"

"Didn't look."

"Well, look now!" He became a hysterical bitch, jerking his sweaty head and tensing his finger bones.

"Not on your tintype," I said coldly.

"It's your thing — they're your pictures."

"I don't go in there."

"How did the pictures get inside?" he shrilled at me.

"I threw them there. Now listen, you shit-kicker, go in there and get that picture and make it snappy."

"Right under your nose," he mumbled, hurrrying inside and retrieving it. He dangled it, using his thumb and forefinger to ridicule what he would never understand.

I looked at the picture.

"And there's some more," he said. He handed over a chunk of prints.

"I forgot I took so many."

He glanced at the one on top. "It's not as busy as your best work."

"I suppose not."

He pinched the mustache of sweat from his upper

lip and said, "I'll never finish the retrospective at this rate."

I withdrew to my room, taking the pictures of Orlando. *Hold the phone,* I wanted to say. *Correction.*

The sun had not set his hair smoldering, the river was turgid, and the trees I had remembered as streaming with light were bare. Orlando was dark, hunched over the oars as if sneaking ashore for some furtive assignation. His head was tilted, his ear against his shoulder, and his face, a brown leaf, had a whisper of stealth on it, the wary listening expression of someone who has just heard an unusual sound. His jersey was full of muscular creases, but it was his hands which gave him away, his grip on the oar handles like a hawk's fists on a branch. His straining stance was more than a rower's posture: it was flight, he was leaving me.

I had been wrong to remember him gliding downriver in a halo of autumn light. There was no shower of yellow leaves. This was a determined boatman one distant afternoon, who knew it was late and wasting no time. Those shadows on his face gave him a ferocity that could have been impatient hope trying to displace sorrow, or the anger of thwarted lust. He looked heavy and grave and his back was to the riverbank that seemed a sodden frontier. There were a dozen pictures in all. In the last he faced the camera. He was so private, so engrossed in his mood, he might have been rowing alone. I barely recognized him.

The camera lied. And had I been foxed by my memory too? The past, drowned and buried by time, was unverifiable. But I had been fooled all right.

I needed a drink. I made a jug of martinis and sluiced the morning away.

At lunch, I gave the pictures to Frank and said, "These are for the shredder."

He had a sandwich in one hand. He raised the pictures, raised the sandwich, took a bite of the sandwich, and holding the pictures, chewed. Then he tucked the bite into his cheek and said, "Who's the guy?"

"Fellow I used to know."

"If they're personal we should include them. Otherwise forget it — they won't reproduce."

"Like I say, shred them." I snatched them from him and started to tear them. "Pack of lies."

"Don't do that!" he squawked, spattering me with mayonnaise. "They're primary sources. They've got to be catalogued. Nothing gets thrown away."

But I went on tearing them. "I am executing these pictures."

"Stop it!"

"Finish your lunch," I said, and dropped the pieces next to his plate.

"Look what you did," he said. But his tone was softened by gratitude. He began arranging the photograph pieces like a jigsaw, fitting them and puzzling. He smiled as he chewed. He looked eager; this was like making his own pictures — creation.

"I'll need information on these for the catalogue."

"You tell me. They're no damn good, but that's your problem. It's your retrospective, ain't it?"

He put down his bite-scalloped sandwich. He said, "I know you think I'm a fool. That's what you think, isn't it?"

"Your pictures, your everything. Who cares what I think?"

"I care," he said. "I care very, very much what you think, Maude."

"All right," I snapped. "I think you're a fool. So there."

He narrowed his eyes at me. "And this morning you called me a shit-kicker. That's the thanks I get."

"What's in it for me?" I said.

"This retrospective's going to be the biggest thing — "

"You've got to be joking," I said. "Listen, I'm seventy-one years old. I've got more money than I will ever spend and there's nothing I want in the world that I can't buy in Hyannis. I've had critics eating out of my hand for fifty years, but don't judge me by my pictures — I don't give a rat's ass for them, anyway, burn the lot of them for all I care. I don't need a retrospective — I didn't take pictures for people like you. I took them for myself, understand? I've had a long fascinating life, and I'm happy, Frank!"

"Then why do you sound so mad?"

"Because you're pissing me off something wicked, that's why."

He swallowed guiltily and looked down at his bitten sandwich.

"You," I said, wagging my finger in his face, "You say you're going to make me famous. Well, thanks very much, Frank, but I've got news for you — "

"I never said famous. I'm just trying to broaden your appeal."

"Who the fuck are you trying to impress? I know what you want to do — you want to put your own name in lights. Just like these squirts who make the celebrity scene — they get a hammerlock on the luminaries. Why? Because they want to be famous themselves, and the by-line ends up bigger than the picture. That's how it happens, you know — any jackass with a two-dollar Instamatic can get billboarded all over *Vogue* if she does the right people. And you're doing me the very same way. You're piggybacking. Deny it."

"I deny it." He shuddered and added, "Strenuously."

"You don't know the first thing about me."

"What's got into you?" he said pityingly. "You're really bitter. You've said some terrible things to me."

"Get off the bucket. If you're not interested in fame, what is it?"

"I am sincerely interested in your work. I think it represents the America of this century."

"Hogwash," I said. "It doesn't even represent my life."

"An artist's life *is* his work."

"I don't buy that," I said. My life wasn't in my work: perhaps that meant I wasn't an artist? But Frank was convinced I was, and unshakable in his conviction. I said, "I can't help thinking there must be a pile of dough in this for you."

"Money is not one of my considerations. Fortunately."

"Really? You're loaded, right?"

"I have sufficient funds," he said: the prissy verbosity of the self-righteous.

"Come off it. You think you can make a bundle. The museum pays you for all of this."

"As a matter of fact, they don't. I'm on a year's sabbatical."

"You're doing it free?" For a moment I was ashamed.

"Not exactly," he said. "I've got a Guggenheim."

My mouth went dry. "Repeat that."

"And it's renewable."

"You've got a *what?*"

"Don't tell me you never heard of the Guggenheim Foundation."

"Jumping Jesus, doesn't *that* take the cake!"

"What's wrong with a Guggenheim?"

"Everything," I said, and decided to let him have it. "Ever heard of Edward Weston?"

"The photographer?"

"No, Edward Weston the dogcatcher," I said. "Of course the photographer!"

"We had a really big Weston retrospective years ago," he said, sounding a little tired and knowing, the way the French do when you mention wine, as if nothing I said could be news to him.

But I pressed on. "Long before you were born, I met Weston in New York. He said he liked my pictures, but he was a horny devil, so when he said, 'I'd like to see a lot more of you' I figured him for a bumpincher. We had a set-to — he gave me his usual baloney about farmers with furrows on their faces and

Kentuckians with bluegrass growing out of their eyebrows. I took exception to it — I mean, what if your
farmer happens to be a little shrimp with eyeglasses
and beautiful hands? Eugene O'Neill looked like a
wino, I told him, and Lawrence had a case of
halitosis that made the shit-plant on Moon Island seem
like a rose arbor. And let's face it, most of those
black pimps and numbers runners I did in New York
looked like kings and princes of Bongo-land. But
Weston disagreed, and he wanted to prove his point."

"Artistically, Weston's Mexican — "

"Keep your shirt on, Frank. At the time — this
was 'thirty-six — he got it into his head to apply
for a Guggenheim. They were giving them to painters,
English teachers, playwrights — in fact, every filling
station attendant in the country believed that as soon
as he got a Guggenheim he'd write *Leaves of Grass*.
Weston said if those fakers got them, why not him?

" 'I'm an artist,' says Weston, and smacks his lips.

" 'Well, I'm a photographer,' I says, 'and I wouldn't
touch one of them Guggenheims with a ten-foot pole.'

"He said he needed the freedom. The money would
free him. 'How very American,' I says. Give this boy
a few bucks and suddenly he's free. I couldn't see the
point of it — still can't. How much money makes
you free? I told him he'd be de-balled by patronage
and end up being just another castrated wage slave.
The only virtue in being an artist — that was his
word — is being your own man. No masters, no enemies, no rivals, no patrons! I said he was talking a lot
of garbage — you were free until you took the money,
then you weren't free anymore, you were in the pay
of Jack Guggenheim or whoever.

"This really annoyed him. 'My equipment costs
money,' he said, 'and I want to do an epic series of
photographs of the West.' 'Get a loan,' I says, 'mort-
gage that tripod — you can repay the bank when
you're rich, but with a patron, no matter how rich you
get, you'll be in debt for the rest of your natural
life.' I told him I was from a banking family and I

knew what I was talking about. I said, 'You're a good risk for a loan — big on talent and low on overheads. After all, you can take all the pictures you want of the Grand Canyon and no one'll send you a bill.'

"He couldn't see why he should get a bank loan instead of a gift from a fame-sucker on Park Avenue — I guess he figured the bank might foreclose and repossess his genius. 'It's my mind,' he said. 'I need spiritual freedom to do anything I want' — and these are his exact words — 'from a cloud to an old shoe.'

"'To me, there's not a dime's worth of difference between a cloud and an old shoe. The sky's full of old shoes,' I says to him.

"We were getting nowhere. He said that he was going to apply for a Guggenheim just the same. And he did. And I'll be goddamned if he didn't get one. In 1937, he was the first photographer ever to get a Guggenheim, but as I said to him, 'Your camera still weighs forty pounds and if you shoot any nice pictures you'll have to go around afterward and say thank you to all the Guggenheims.' Imagine, an artist saying thank you! I didn't see much of him after that."

Frank said, "You peed on Weston, so you're peeing on me."

"On the contrary," I said. "The next thing I know I get a letter from the foundation. Do I wish to apply for a Guggenheim grant? Well, I made a big mistake. I was young, I wasn't as smart as I am now. It wasn't the money, but somehow if they gave me the money they were testifying to my art. You're an artist, here's ten bucks to prove it — that kind of thing. Was I worth it? There was a crisis in my life. I needed encouragement. That's the worst of patronage, you know, the belief that having a patron means having talent. But the answer to 'Am I an artist?' must always be no, because no artist would ask that dumb question. Right?"

"Interesting," said Frank.

"I filled out the application, in triplicate. My name,

outline of project, previous shows, sponsors. It was like a Means Test — no, it was like a Pauper's Oath. Then I waited."

"I never knew you had a Guggenheim," said Frank.

"That's the point of the story, you peckerhead. I didn't get the fucking thing!"

"I see."

"No moolah for Maude."

I fell silent. I had applied in October, this receding time of year. The leaves, the grass, the withered flowers, just like this. And the air rounded with a chill amplifying the rasps of autumn, everything that had been alive in the summer turning to confetti, smoke, dust, and haze. Even the fires dying into yellow vapor, the sunlight weakening on the Sound, somewhere a buzz saw, and hammerings from the Hyannis shore. I was parched with incomprehension; I could taste the driest disappointment, and it stifled me like defeat.

"Afterward I hated them — for making me want it, for making me need proof, and for thinking, when I didn't get it, that I wasn't worth it. But I got over it. Everyone who gets one of those things deserves it. The best never ask."

"What was your, um, project?"

"Something to do with Florida."

"But you did Florida!" said Frank. "It was your first big success!"

"So it was. If you have something to do you do it. You don't sit around on your fanny waiting for someone to put you on the payroll." But I could not remember how I had done Florida, or why I had gone.

"Some payroll," said Frank. "Subsistence — that's all I get."

"You let them buy you Tootsie Rolls, is that it? Ain't it a riot? They're paying you to study my work, but they refused to pay me to produce it. What's wrong with a Guggenheim? That's what's wrong. They don't care about the ship — all they're interested in is the goddamned barnacles."

In my anger over lunch I almost blurted out to Frank that I had seen his raunchy pictures. But I resisted: his back was to the wall — I couldn't throw that at him. And furthermore, I had not worked out in my own mind how they mattered: the mind is more fastidious than the eye. I didn't know whether to witness or judge, and had not decided if such stuff should be suppressed. The soul of art is human emotion. Although pornography depicted anonymous emotion and was crude as a cactus, the people who needed it brought imagination to it and pulped the lumps and spines into art and let this simmer in their brains. It was like making your own amorous masterpiece, the pure glory of love's double image — the classically serene embrace — out of the furious meat of Kenny and Doris. Perhaps in Doris's bivalve and Kenny's knobby anemone Frank saw a whole sea-floor of possibility, or were these fuck shots merely a sleazy detonator for his libido? "Rhetorical," he might say; but how did they refer, and to whom, and why?

It baffled me. I resolved to wait.

Quite late — I was in my room, something on my mind, an unformed consequence — Frank knocked on my door. He rapped impatiently, loudly hectoring to alert me to his anger. He burst in, heaved himself at me, then drew back.

He shook his bony fingers and glared.

"You've been in my things!"

Enraged, he had a look of starvation. I had never seen him so skinny or so pale; his eyes bulged, there was a beggar's cringe in his shoulders. But I had seen this sort of thing once before. I knew this intrusion, a particular one — which?

"You know what I'm talking about."

I smiled at him: I had heard that once, in precisely those words. "Haven't the faintest."

He said, "My personal property. Pictures."

"Describe them."

"Don't be funny — you know the ones I mean." His voice cracked and I thought he was going to burst into tears. Single people are fairly unembarrassed about crying: they practice it alone in their rooms. He sat down and took a deep breath and after exhaling it seemed much calmer. He recovered his aggrieved tone. "If there's one thing I hate it's people who don't respect private property."

"Then get your skinny ass off my chair and clear out. This is my private property, buddy."

"I want an explanation. I'm not leaving until I get it."

"I went into a room in my house, opened the drawer of a table I happen to own and found some of your pictures. I wasn't going to mention it, but since you raised the matter I can tell you I think you have rather a grim taste in anatomy. That's all there is to it."

But I didn't want him to go. I needed him to help me remember that other intrusion. His eyes were damp with anger. He had gotten even skinnier since entering my room and looked as if he might let out one maniacal honk of wind and shrivel like a bag before my very eyes.

I said, "Also, I thought I recognized the people in them."

"You're putting me on."

"Turns out it's the same couple I've been seeing for years. Kenny and Doris. They could use a vacation. I wonder what folks like that *do* on vacation. Probably tear open a six-pack and shoot the bull. Watch television. Stuff themselves with Twinkies."

"You're not even sorry."

"Sorry?" I said. "I'm appalled!"

"I want an apology."

"You came to the wrong place, buster."

He shook his head vengefully. "Know something? You're really incredible."

"Just as a point of interest," I said brightly, "how did you know I'd seen them?"

"That's my business."

"Very clever of you, I'll grant you that. Seriously, how'd you know I'd been nosing around?"

"So you admit you were nosing around!"

"Of course. I've got a right to in my own house, haven't I?"

"Not with my stuff you haven't. No one touches my stuff."

"Your 'stuff'? If us photographers said that, where would you museum people be?"

"That's got nothing to do with it."

"Listen, you peckerhead, for the past three months you've been pawing over my pictures and drooling. Have I complained? I jolly well haven't. And remember," I said, flinging a finger at him, "when they were handing out Guggenheims no one gave me one. As far as I'm concerned you're just another burglar using his Guggenheim as a license to pry, so shut up and be glad I don't report you to the police."

"That's all you have to say, is it?"

"No. I still want to know how you found out. Just curious, I guess."

"I'm not telling you."

"And the other thing. Why does a fellow who has so much regard for the integrity of the photograph waste his time with that kind of pictorial garbage? What do you see in it, huh?"

He panted crossly instead of replying.

"You're a very mysterious person, Frank."

"I just want you to know that I'm having serious doubts about this entire project. Yes, it's a great idea, but if my personal life is in jeopardy — "

"What about my personal life!" I said and noticed a scream rising in my voice.

I had been calm. I had had a vague desire to re-enter my own picture palace and examine that moment in the rowboat with Orlando. Had he really been so dark, so tense, so obviously deceived, as the picture showed? And what was the sequel to it? Frank's intrusion shattered my mood, destroyed my calm. But he had given me a notion. He had reminded me that I had endured another unexpected assault, and his heckling — all this woeful indignation — had woken a memory, not pleasant but necessary.

"I'm going," he said.

"Don't go." I needed his indignation now to stir my past and make me remember. Someone had come, just like him, and accused me.

He sat on the edge of his chair and gave his Adam's apple a workout. Plunge, plunge: it was like sarcasm.

I said, "I want you to know that I didn't take those pictures lightly. No sir. They worried me. Frank, I was shook. Now I respect you — you've always found things to admire in my work. But how do you account for *them*? What, may I ask, are they in aid of?"

"It's a different ball game altogether."

"Well said. But these horny pictures — are you doing something with them?"

"What do you mean 'doing something'?" his voice was uncertain and shameful.

"Writing a learned article, that sort of caper."

He hung his head. "Not exactly."

"Go get them. I want to look at them again."

"Never."

"Don't be ashamed of them. It's an aspect of photography that's been somewhat overlooked." Frank didn't budge. I said, "I found them rather alarming."

"So you said."

"Photography is all about secrets — the secrets in surfaces. But Kenny and Doris don't have any secrets that I can see. They're out of sync, there's no surface — technically, they're nowhere, they look like they were bled off by Dracula, so you can't use the old erotic art gambit to justify them. Or is erotic art just another way of saying tit-show? And doesn't it scare you to realize that in order to enjoy that sort of thing — Doris double-clutching, say — you have to endure the sight of Kenny's great hairy ass or his dripping tool?"

"Cut it out," said Frank.

"All right," I said. "But I find it odd to think that

you have room in your judgment for those pictures and mine. What's the connection?"

"I'd like to know why you're so disturbed by them," he said, turning on me. "That says a lot about you."

"Good point. I *was* disturbed."

"Hah!" He stood up. "See, that's the real problem, isn't it? It's you!"

"And how! But they're your pictures."

"They don't worry me a bit."

"Amazing."

He said, "There are worse. Scenes you wouldn't believe."

"What are they *for,* for heaven's sake?"

He was silent, standing like a crane.

I said, "Tell me how you knew I'd seen them."

"Leave me alone."

"I'll stop razzing you if you tell me."

He looked at the wall, making his jaw mournful. He said, "Because you messed them up."

"I did no such thing."

"Yes — you mixed them up, scrambled them out of order."

"Oh, my God."

"That's how I knew. The sequence was wrong."

"The sequence!" I started to laugh.

He had gone to the door. "And it better not happen again," he said. "There's a word for not minding your own business, for invading people's privacy and sticking your nose where it doesn't belong."

He swung open the door, but he pushed his white face at me. "Treachery, that's what it is!"

Treachery? I said, "I've heard that one before," and then, "Yes, that's it! You're absolutely right! That's just what I wanted to hear!"

But he was out of the door and down the stairs before I could thank him for his appropriate intrusion.

15

Treachery

IN MY VERY ROOM, in those very words, demanding explanations and apologies, but not satisfied with my innocence and using the occasion to be rude and hurtful. People say they want apologies but what they really want is to bite your head off and spit it into your face.

She burst in late one night, a few days after I had seen Orlando at Harvard. She was out of breath and sort of whimpering at me. My memory was of thumps in the hallway and the door to my room suddenly pushed open and her looking as if she were going to fling herself on me. She said, "You — you — you!" and carried each word a step closer to where I sat with my peepstones and a stack of pictures.

Her jump into the room, the way she swung herself at me, had lifted her hair and given her dress an updraft of coarse folds and made her coat sleeves look like beating wings. I caught her pouncing as one explosive instant, an action shot framed by the doorjamb. She seemed in that moment of agile fury — her fists near her bright slanted eyes, her knee raised, all this force balanced on one toe — as if she were about to streak forward and stamp on me. It was the picture Frank, in his indignation, had suggested. I had not wanted to remember this episode.

She had the fearsome nimbleness of the deeply wounded. In my terror I tried to freeze her. I did not see her moving continuously at me, but rather caught her in a series of still leaps, each more exalted than the last, and mounting toward me intimidatingly to howl.

I said, "Blanche, wait — "

I felt a seismic thrill, as if a picture I had been taking had swallowed me in its undertow and made me a subject, too.

"You bitch!" she said.

Profanity from someone who had never used it before, anger in someone who had always been solemn: it was truly thunder to me. And angry, she looked physically different, all sinews, teeth, and hair, like a person animated by an electric current.

"Now, now," I said, wishing to calm her.

"So help me," she said, and stepped back, not withdrawing but threatening me the more by giving me a glimpse of the whole voltage of her anger.

"Not so loud," I said, as reasonably as I could, and moved past her to shut the door. "Phoebe's asleep."

"I could kill you, Maude Pratt." She showed me her hands, which she had crooked into a strangler's claws.

I said, "Now that wouldn't do a darn bit of good, would it? Just simmer down and we'll have a nice long talk and you'll feel a whole lot better." I went on in this way, talking gently, plumping a cushion, pulling up an armchair, and easing her into it. Sort of taking the initiative.

I thought I had succeeded, but when I brushed past her to sit down myself she sucked in her breath and stiffened and said, "How could you?"

"Not sure I get your drift," I said.

"There's something wrong with you," she said. "I never would have believed it. I always thought you were so good — a little dull, but good deep down. I was glad when I heard you'd been successful with your photos and making a name for yourself. Now this!"

"Thanks very much," I said, "but I don't have the slightest idea of what's at the seat of your — "

"Don't give me that, Maude Pratt," she said, repeating my full name again in that judging way, as if to make it sound unpleasant, like that of a prisoner being sentenced. "I've heard the stories you're spreading about me."

"Stories?"

"About me and Sandy."

"Oh, that," I said. "Honestly, you wouldn't understand."

"You admit it! You're shameless."

"I've had my reasons," I said. "It wasn't supposed to get back to you, obviously. But no harm done. Drink?"

"How can you be so horrible? What have I ever done to you?"

"Why, nothing, Blanche. I think the world of you. But I'm afraid I had to make up that cock-and-bull story. It would be better all around if you just forgot it, though if you understood why I did it you'd be glad for me, you really would."

"But it's a lie," she said. "And it's filthy. How would you like it if I said that about you and Ollie?"

I laughed out loud. "Wouldn't bother me a bit!"

She sat forward on her chair and began to cry. I felt sorry for her, hunched there with her fingertips on her face and that lonesome shudder in her spine, and her toes together making a pathetic angle of her feet, and dampness on the back of her neck making her short hairs into moist spikes and foretelling a lifetime of this. She had come down with grief like an everlasting cold and was practicing a comfortable posture for her sorrow.

I touched her. She reacted as if I had left a sting in her. She straightened, smarting, and stopped weeping and said, "You have no business talking about me like that."

And I started to wonder if perhaps what I had invented about her was the plain truth and she was taking it badly because of that. Certainly, she and Sandy were capable of those feelings, and I had always suspected that it might be true; but it was my boogie-man, Teets, who had furnished the details. Blanche seemed shocked, as if she'd been found out: I had discovered her secret.

So I said, "You shouldn't take it so hard. Lots of brothers and sisters have been passionately in love with each other. It doesn't happen every day, but then great passion is a rare thing at the best of times. Only a lucky few are chosen — for all I know, you might be one of them."

"It's an insult," she said.

This annoyed me. By objecting, she was demeaning my love for Orlando and finding something weird or irregular in it, and in her stubborn way perhaps denying her own love for Sandy.

"You're confused," I said. "There are all kinds of love. Simply because you haven't felt it doesn't mean it doesn't exist. Someday — "

"You've spoiled everything," she said. "Why are you so cruel?"

"I haven't 'spoiled everything,' as you say. I told a white lie because it was necessary. Who knows about it? You, me, Orlando — I suppose he told you. He shouldn't have, but he never could keep his mouth shut."

She said, "I'm ruined."

"Don't be ridiculous. No one really gives a hoot. You're the same person you always were. I can't hurt you, but I do apologize."

"Forget it," she said. "You've destroyed me."

I thought: Yes, I put it into words and it frightens her to know that she's been found out. But she'll recover and she'll be better off for facing facts. I saw her then, for that little while, as my own sister, waking up to her love, and I felt there must be a whole sorority of us yearning for our brothers, aching for nothing more than that long summer of intimate play, rejoined to our other halves in love — the perfect fit of brother and sister that was celebrated in most families as a kind of passionate chastity.

She said, "You've snatched away my lover."

"Sandy will grow up," I said. "And when he does he'll love you and you'll never be alone again."

"No," she said. "It's Ollie." And in a small voice that was almost a squeak: "I've lost him."

This was unexpected. "Ollie?"

"And it's all your fault. We were planning to get married when he gets out of law school — "

"You and Ollie?"

" — we haven't talked about anything else all summer, how we'd live in Boston and have children. But you knew, didn't you? You knew why he didn't spend this past summer on the Cape — you knew we were in that room in Cambridge. I wanted to tell everyone, but Ollie said, 'No, if you divulge secrets, people spread them like lies.' I thought we had kept our secret. I should have known you'd come nosing around with your camera and spoil it all."

I said, "I had no idea."

And I hadn't, not the slightest.

"That's a lie," she said. "To separate us you made up that horrible story about Sandy and me. Ollie came straight to me and asked me if it was true. I almost fainted. 'How could it be?' I said. But he didn't believe me. For some reason he wanted to believe your lie. Now he's gone," she said, her voice cracking, "and I'll never have him."

I was not surprised that Blanche had loved him: I had never met anyone who was not warmed by the sight of Orlando. But I found it hard to believe that he had loved her. While he was not selfish, he was usually oblivious of the effect he had on others, and so, carefree, he seemed self-absorbed. That too was part of his beauty, for his humility was attractive — every mood he had enhanced his magic. How easy it was to think someone so happy could love you! Blanche had deceived herself.

In wishing to convince Orlando of the possibility of us consummating our love I could not have chosen a better ploy. I had, without much thought, cast Blanche and Sandy in my dramatic monologue, and I had accomplished a great deal more than I had attempted. I had rid him of her for good. It was an unexpected picture I'd made, for I had hastened to snap one, but — as with my very best — I had exposed something else and come up with a bloody masterpiece, Blanche's shadow lurking in something I had thought was all mine.

Not that I hadn't thought she'd be exposed, but that expecting one Blanche, and guessing that she mattered, I had come up with quite another Blanche, who mattered infinitely more. My best photographs happened in just that way, but I had created this symmetrical thing without touching a camera. By concentrating my attention on her and being single-minded I had caught the soul of her intention and trapped her flat. I had applied the strict rules of photography once again to my own life and discovered the great accident of form.

Blanche was still in the chair. Calmer: sobbing relaxed her. Yet I was still apprehensive. I had never believed that the loss of love was so grievous a thing. She looked ill and was doubled up, as if her heart had been torn out. My consolation was that it had been necessary, because if she hadn't been stopped in her wild presuming she might have made life hell for me and Orlando.

What was so sad was not that she looked destroyed, but that she had come to within an inch of destruction. The only life in her was the thin warmth of sadness. This in itself was frightening, for the survivor of a tragedy looks twenty times worse in a photograph than the carcass of a casualty. I was thinking that I would rather be dead than blind and crazy and twitching with grief in some stranger's house.

As if reading my thoughts, she stood up and tried to pull herself together: stretched, yawned, wrung her hands.

I said, "Are you sure you won't have that drink?"

Her eyes widened. She said, "You haven't heard the last of this."

"It's late, Blanche. We can talk about it tomorrow."

"I don't want to see you tomorrow," she said. "And if you're smart you won't want to see me — ever. I won't be responsible for what I do to you."

"There now," I said. "You shouldn't threaten me."

In a terrible voice, colder than the one she had used for *I could kill you,* she said, "I'll harm you."

"I'm going on vacation," I said, although until I heard myself saying it I had no intention of doing so.

"It better be a long one."

"Florida, actually. To do some pictures. The folks are there."

"Just keep out of my way, Maude Pratt," she said. "I'll never forgive you for this treachery."

With that, she went, sideways and silent, for she had left all her whimpers and tears and threats in my room. I looked out the window and saw her crossing the nighttime lawn. It was a picture no camera could take. There was no moon, though there was a bulge in the sky, a great pillow of lunar brightness in the heavy clouds that lit her. Seen from my upper window she appeared to be fleeing for her life, dying and disappearing as she ran, like an inkblot that was once a word. She was silver-black on the silver-black grass and the Sound was striped with wicked white froth. She had the movement of a flightless bird and I knew I was responsible for this grounded owlet careering into the dark.

I'll never forgive you is an absolutely meaningless sentence; but her threat was real. People kill for love, perhaps only for love or the loss of it. And I knew better than to press my luck. So far I had cleared my way toward Orlando, and though I was relieved that he had used my story as an occasion to dismiss Blanche — what was it she'd said? *For some reason he wanted to believe your lie* — I was hurt that he had had an affair with her in the first place.

I decided to go away for a while, as I had said. Florida was the easiest destination, since Papa and Mama were there, soaking in dejection like runaways.

I had an inkling that some great fortune awaited me there, just as I was certain that on my return to the Cape Orlando would be here with his arms folded and his hair blazing like a coronet and saying, "I've been looking all over for you!"

And yet, already, I had begun to know regret. So much had happened to me, but I had so few pictures of it. I stood on a crack that divided my life from my work, perceptible only to me. Beyond the crack everything was lighted wonderfully, behind it was the shadow in which I lived, for which I had no photograph or permanent record. I could chuck my camera away and march forward and melt into art; or I could step back from the thin line that would become an unbridgeable canyon, to give my eyes a chance, in shadow, to gladden with light. I stepped back and loaded my camera.

16

Speed Graphic

Or rather not my camera, which was why for a while I was celebrated but remained unknown.

It happened like so many of my pictorial flukes as a contrived accident shortly after I arrived in New York. My morale was high. I felt I had freed Orlando and won him back. This was twelve hours after that battle of wits on the Cape with Blanche Overall, and I had intended to keep moving and continue on a trail to Florida. Not that I was afraid of Blanche shadowing me and bashing my brains out for exposing her, but largely because I was so suffused with confidence and wanted to prove that I didn't need the Guggenheim Foundation to get me up the lower slopes of Parnassus, much less to Verona, Florida. But I missed the train, and I found to my annoyance that I would have to spend a whole weekend kicking my heels in New York.

My usual berth was still at the Seltzers', but I didn't want to answer awkward questions. I barely knew myself why I had chosen Florida. I didn't like to think that it was because Mama and Papa were there. The idea of following my parents around struck me as being uncomfortably close to a domestic form of the Guggenheim disease. I was sure that something important awaited me there: jungle, alligators, swamps, Indians, new scenes — sights for sore eyes that I could carry back to overwhelm Orlando with. It was a continuation of the courtship I had been engaged in since the day, twenty years before, when I knew I

would have him or go blind. I had turned his head
with my camera: photography worked. Now I wished
to be triumphant in it and to share my fame with him.

With this mood came a desire to travel. Travel is a
funny indulgence, the simple challenge of congenial
strangeness to animate portions of the body and soul.
Embracing the unknown to find the familiar; a way of
remembering.

This was my first taste of travel, and my best. I
knew that America had a prodigious madonna's body,
and that though our literature had only hinted at what
our photography had made explicit — that landscape
was anatomy — no country could touch us in a physical geography lavish with brains, breadbaskets, heart-
lands, a whole wilderness of visceral rivers — so
different from the ailing or infantile islands of the
world that prevented us from matching view to mood.
A country was not a country until you could lose yourself in it, camera-wise: the vagrant surrender of the
eye to something flabbergasting. What attracted me
then was that I could disappear for a few weeks in the
hot green parts that had always reminded me of America's appendix.

But Florida would have to wait until Monday. I had
missed the train. I checked into a hotel and lay down
in my dark room and became anxious. I had not given
my going a second thought, but in that square room
with its smudges of reproaching dust, its threadbare
seams of sealing wallpaper and the dead echoes of
lovers stifling their moans against the bedstead — its
history audible in cracks and stains and scorchmarks
— in that dark room, that ghost-box of crucified passion and lively sorrow, I felt I did not exist. It was a
feeling I had often sweated out: alone, I was sometimes invisible to myself; my inner eye was squeezed
shut, I'd quickened and vanished into the obscure
room's obscurer dust. It was my art's highest achievement, was it not? The solitary photographer conjuring
with her instrument and disappearing at the tippety-
top of her own Indian rope-trick?

It was not what I had wanted. It was no joke. Spirited away from all that was habitual, and hooded by the wholly strange room, I was numbed by a sense of nonbeing and needed a witness. In the usual motion of travel this was no great problem, but every room is a six-sided colony of dark rules. It took wit even to remember your name in such a place, or to dissuade yourself that you might, like any lost soul, be paying an unwelcome visit to someone else's body — a person you might yourself have invented.

Ordinarily, it was a convenient panic: it had made me a photographer. In that distant doubting frame of mind I was forced to snap pictures to prove my own existence — make a world from my eye, bring it into focus, stop it long enough to say, "I see!"

Because in my lonely love-struck way I had grafted the camera to my body. I was nothing but a two-legged prop for the winks of this Third Eye.

But on that afternoon, in the New York room where I was no more than an atom of dust in a wisp of light, I needed more immediate proof. I called Orlando.

"Adams House," came the reply.

"Hello there," I said, as to a rescuer, and instantly was calmed: here I am, alive and well. "I'd like to speak to Orlando Pratt."

"Just a sec — I'll get him."

It's me! Now you know I love you. Blanche is gone. It's all ours —

"Sorry, he's out."

"Oh."

"Who shall I say called?"

"His lover — "

Yurble went a noise in the throat of the line, an amiable chirrup of shock.

" — and I am waiting."

In the rain, as it turned out. For professional reasons, as much as to kill time, I left the room and set out to buy a new camera. The rain was a handclapping sound, like applause at my feet. I made my way to

the East Side, staggering as visitors to New York so
often do — something about those right angles.

It was a rolling city and not at all the populous and
filthy ruin of traipsing photographers who sought children, derelicts, pigeons, Gushing Hydrant in Harlem,
or that old favorite of the Guggenheim Fellow: Ragged
Beggar on Wall Street. In my pictures, New York was
an ocean liner, unsinkable and majestic, with a lovely
curvature from port to starboard, steering seaward on
the flood tide of its two rivers, New Jersey and Brooklyn the smoky headlands of friendly coasts. I envied
New Yorkers as I envied sailors, and always portrayed
them as adventurers with iron stomachs and sea legs,
who regarded their glamor with irony and treated visitors as faint-hearted passengers who'd soon disem-
bark. Today there was a gale and the decks were
awash.

Weston had recommended the shop Camera Obscura on Second Avenue. It was an uncompromisingly
dingy place that catered to what he called "real artists
like us," though I doubt that he was including me in
that description.

"I want to set a Speed Graphic, please," I said to
the clerk, who had raised his eyes to me and spread
his fingers on the counter.

He sized me up, giving me a chance to decode his
own features: polka-dot bow tie, elastic bands on the
biceps of his sleeves, restless skinny hands, Harold
Lloyd glasses, and too many teeth. His face fit his
skull tightly like a zombie's mask and chasing his
smirk was a contradiction of irregular bone.

"You don't want anything as fancy as that," he
said, and plucked from behind the counter a goggle-
eyed idiot box the size of a lobster trap. "Take this,
madam. It's so simple a child can operate it."

"Sounds just the thing for you," I said. "Now show
me the Graflex."

This annoyed him, and hoping to put me in my
place he went to the stockroom and came out carrying
an eight-by-ten monstrosity on a tripod. It was some-

thing between a whopping doodad for colonic irrigation and a kind of magician's outfit of mirrors and slots out of which rabbits, boiled eggs, and nosegays of silk flowers were produced. Dangling from its snout was a long hose with a rubber bulb.

"Course if you're really serious about photography you'll want one of these." He piled the equipment on the counter — lens hood, lenses, filters, film, plates, film holders — then pursed his lips at me in smart-alecky satisfaction.

"I said a Speed Graphic. Do I have to sing it?"

"This is the best camera we've got —"

He ignored my icy stare that was telling him, in a wintry way, to shove it.

"— get beautiful results with this little number." He grasped the rubber bulb and, leering at me, gave it a salacious squeeze. "I bet a girl like you could use something like this."

"Do I look like I need an enema?"

"Hey, watch it," he said. Anger made his face a membrane. "Ask the top photographers, if you don't believe me. Stieglitz has one. He tells all his people to buy them."

"I'm not one of his people," I said. "Anyway, it doesn't look very portable."

"You don't look like you're going very far."

I picked up a film holder, a metal sandwich with German words on the crust. "So Stieglitz has one of these, huh? I thought he was still in jail."

"That's not funny. Stieglitz isn't just a photographer. He's photography."

I stepped back unconvinced. The clerk had that sour breath I couldn't help associating with baloney, the liar's inevitable halitosis.

"If you believe that, you'd believe anything."

"Who are you?" he cried.

But I kept my temper and demanded to see the Speed Graphic, and when I found the model I wanted, I said, "Wrap it up — and I'll take a half a dozen of those," indicating the film holders.

"I've got news for you," he said nastily. "They don't fit that Graphic."

"I've got news for *you,* buster. I said I want six of them and some film, and if I get any more of your sass I'll have a word with the manager. Now start wrapping."

It had been Stieglitz who'd refused to exhibit my work in New York — the Provincetown show I had had such hopes for. It seemed to me that Stieglitz in denying me this exposure was trying to thwart me in my courtship of Orlando. Of course, he knew nothing of Orlando, but the fact remained that my sole intention in studying photography was ultimately to persuade my brother that his proper place was with me in my darkroom. Stieglitz had spurned my photographs and in so doing had belittled me as a lover.

If Stieglitz didn't like it, it wasn't photography. Though I considered him of small importance — simply a man who had bamboozled a doting group of people with his lugubrious attentions — I knew that when Stieglitz loaded his camera the world said cheese, or at least his sycophants thought so. He was enthroned in New York in An American Place, his own gallery, and no one could call himself a photographer who had not first wormed some approval from this dubious man. I supposed I could be accused of bias, but I believed the clearest example of his complete lack of judgment and taste was his failure to recognize me as an original.

This early absence of recognition — I was now thirty-one — was the mainstay of my originality. I avoided photographic circles, and while students of photography gathered in "schools," their very bowels yearning for "movements," I had grown to loathe the cliques and seen them as nests of thuggish committee men, shabby and unconfident mobsters of the art world whoring after historians and critics. I blamed Stieglitz for this. His authority had weakened photographers to the point where they hadn't the nerve to go it alone

— they were resigned to being part of his legend. The movement — so frequent in the half-arts — implies a gang mentality; it is the half-artist's response to his inadequacy, something to do with pretensions of photography, the inexact science that was sometimes an art and sometimes a craft and sometimes a rephrased cliché. The movements begged money from foundations and put themselves up for grants and awarded themselves prizes and published self-serving magazines. A racket, and poison to us originals.

What got up my nose most of all was that many photographers I respected, and some I idolized, had had their work exhibited at Stieglitz's various galleries. Even Poopy Weston had bought his forty-pound peepshow on Stieglitz's advice. Weston had shown me how to use it and had said, "You'll never get anywhere unless you meet Alfred."

"I hold the view that the work ought to precede the person."

"He's seen your work."

"And he didn't like it, so he ain't seeing me," I said. "I'm not a Fuller Brush man, Westy, and you can tell him I said so."

Pride is scar tissue. Mine made me wary of a further rebuff, another wound. Yet I was insignificant. I could turn my back on him, but who would notice? Not him. As far as I knew, his back was already turned. I would gladly have killed that man, if only to be given the chance to say why. In every murderer's mind must be the innocent hope that he will have his day in court, to say what drove him to it.

This homicidal impulse cheered me up at the hotel as I unpacked my trays and stoppered bottles of solutions. I examined my new Speed Graphic and took it apart until it lay exploded on the bed. I loaded the eight-by-ten film holders and futzed with my equipment. At last I sat motionless in the room I had deliberately darkened for my film's sake. It was still raining in that applauding way but, outside, the luminous descent of liquefied light crowded at the pinhole of the window shade and cast through this imperfection a perfect cone of calm, an image of the windowy city on the wall that I studied until the day, red as a mallard's eye, was lost in the blaring pit that sloped from evening into night.

"Ever hear of Alfred Stieglitz?" I asked a taxi driver the next day.

"Who? Look, lady —"

"Just testing," I said, and satisfied with this proof of his obscurity I gave him the Madison Avenue address of An American Place.

A Saturday: the place was jammed. Weekends are for photographers, since most photographers are amateurs who spend the rest of the week working in offices to pay for the equipment the job prevents them from using. The ones at Stieglitz's were bent nearly double with cameras around their necks, as ludicrous a sight to me as museum-goers studying paintings and sculpture with sticky brushes, mallets, and chisels. I cannot remember much about the exhibition: Imogen Cunningham's *Magnolia Blossom* must have been there — it was everywhere; some Walker Evans billboards — how that man liked a mess; a Berenice Abbott traffic jam, some of Strand's peasants, maybe Steichen's shadblow tree, an Edward Weston weather report (partly cloudy, scattered showers, bright patches later) and some of his peppers and seashells, some Käsebier dames in gowns made out of Kleenex, Oursler's *Admiral Byrd* (glacial features, ice-blue eyes), and soft-focus Stieglitzes — hairy rose petals, nipple studies, and chilly little things that could not qualify as nudes since they didn't have bellybuttons. There were some untitleds deservedly anonymous, too many fire escapes and quite a lot of photojournalism from the WPA slush-bucket (rivets, steam shovels, leaf-rakers, grease monkeys — the photographer's keen embarrassment with manual labor). And the usual photographic clichés: Abandoned Playground, Rainy Street, Lady in Funny Hat, Torso with Tits, Shoeshine Boy, Honest Face, Drunken Bum, Prostitute in Slit Skirt Standing

near *Rooms* Sign, Mr. and Mrs. Front Porch America,
Flock of Pigeons, Vista with Framing Branches, City
Snow, City Lights, Haggard Peckerwoods, Every Hair
of a Bushy Beard, Spoiled Brat, Good-Humor Ice
Cream Man, Country Road Leading to Bright Future,
Muddy Field in Europe, Lovers on a Park Bench, Pic-
nickers, House with Broken Windows, Sand Dunes,
Obviously Unemployed Man in his Undershirt, Dog
Lover, Wrinkled Eskimo, Mother and Child, Jazzman
with Shiny Instrument; in other words no Pratts.

You could see more exciting things — in its simplicity, one of the most devastating pieces of art criticism imaginable — by sticking your head out the
window.

Instead of asking for Alfred at the front desk, I
marched through the crowd of shufflers and pushed
the first door I saw marked PRIVATE. I was full of
confidence as I shoved it, as if this were one of the
last doors I'd have to open to arrive at recognition.
Room to room: in the last I would find Orlando waiting. I entered a rather gloomy back room. I was certain
from its smallness and its shadows that the people in
it were photographers.

"— smudgy life studies that are a dime a dozen,"
I heard, and saw beyond the speaker, who was a tiny
man with very red ears in immaculate overalls, and beyond a woman dressed as a man, and a man in yellow spats — beyond this bunch, Stieglitz himself at a
desk heaped with the scrolls of curled-up pictures.
He moved — not his head or the fist at his cheek, but
his black eyes. The speaker turned slightly and hooked
his thumbs in the straps of his overalls. Seeing that I
was of no importance, he made a face and went on
with his story.

Stieglitz stared at me, and before he opened his
mouth I could see what it was that gave him so much
authority. He was dark and displeased-looking, with
a millionaire's modesty, a dangerous edge to his silence, and a grim little tyrant's bite he had cut his

mustache to match, as if he had patterned a template of hair to fit his sneer.

I had seen his camera as a magic box. It suited him, for his scowl was that of a bad-tempered magician who considered no audience worthy to observe him at his tricks. But there was more to this cardsharp and rabbit-grabber than that, because in his look of unconcealed disdain there was a blink of suspicion. It emboldened me. Any sign of weakness in others made me brave. I could endure this disdain, for it was minimized by a suspicion I knew had to be fear. So this was the bluffing coward who wouldn't hang my pictures!

"Are you looking for someone?" It was the red-eared man who had been faltering in his monologue ever since I entered. He was fussed and umming.

"I want to see Mister Stieglitz."

"Out to lunch," said the man.

"I have reason to believe that he is in this very room."

"Who are you?" This was the lady in the pin-stripe suit. In her trousers and tie and slicked-down hair she looked madly attractive.

"Gosh, you wouldn't know me," I said, and thought: If they recognize me I'll tell them everything and beat it. "But I am very interested in photography and I've heard ever so much about Mister Stieglitz. Gee, he's not just a photographer — he's photography itself."

It was like smelling salts, this flattery. The dark man at the desk wrinkled his nose and tossed his head and said, "I am Stieglitz."

"Gee."

"I was telling a story," said the red-eared shrimp.

The woman lit a slender cigar; the man in spats crossed his legs and kicked.

One look from Stieglitz froze them. He snorted and they were still. In that interval I had time to look around the room. Newspaper clippings, posters of past exhibitions — Stieglitz's name on most of them — some pictures the color of turpentine of mousy Whis-

tlerish women in plumes pining at bay windows, a few
virginal girls coyly tormenting some rapist off-camera,
Steerage; and snapshots — very bad snapshots which
for all their gloss had more guts than anything else
on view. Snapshots are the only true American folk
art. I found fault with the intrusive gangway that bi-
sects *Steerage* and moved on to the mementos and
antiques, a burnt-out flash holder, a freckled daguerre-
otype, medallions of the sort I had seen on beer cans,
and a very old and beautifully made wooden camera
that looked like a Fox Talbot. Off to the right, in an
otherwise empty corner of the room, was the magic
box, an eight-by-ten plate camera on a tripod. Even
from where I stood I could see it was a banger, standing not quite straight, all chipped, with a dangling rubber bulb on a pink perishing hose.

"Gosh."

"What do you want?" said Stieglitz.

"I want to take your picture."

This brought a frank honk of derision from the lady,
and the other two were silently guffawing in that
struggling way, as if they were straining to lift something off the ground. But Stieglitz wasn't laughing and
when they saw he wasn't they stopped their nonsense.

"You forgot your camera," he said gruffly, perhaps
wondering whether his leg was being pulled.

"Left it home on purpose," I said. "But I've got
plenty of these." I showed him the loaded film holders.

"You need something to stick them in."

I gave him my sweetest smile. "I thought I might
use your camera, Mister Stieglitz."

From the expression on the others' faces you would
have thought I had asked their bishop for his jockstrap.
The very idea! they were thinking. *How could she!*

But for the first time since entering the room I saw
the traces of a smile on Stieglitz's mustache, the flattened ends rising and curling with interest, his mouth
a wrinkling phrase between reluctant but definitely
mirthful parentheses.

"That's a pretty big camera."

"I'm a pretty big gal."

He nodded and passed his hand down his mouth, restoring his mustache to its former sneering shape.

I noticed that he had ignored the other people. It occurred to me that he disliked them and was willing to demonstrate this. He got up and, one shoulder higher than the other in a resentful slouch, went over to the beat-up camera, and walked around it, eyeing it sideways, as if he were preparing to stick his hand in and pull out a bunny.

"So you're interested in photography, eh? Know anything about it?"

"Enough," I said. "I get a real kick out of it."

"Gets a kick out of it," he said to the puzzled watchers. "Hear that? It's important." He waggled the bulb at me. "Think you can handle that?"

I took it and gave it a hard squeeze and heard the shutter plop.

A sly look returned the parentheses to his mouth and he said, "All right, make it snappy."

Humoring him, I had let him think he could humor me. If I had introduced myself as Maude Pratt of the Negative Boogie-Man Prints I would have been out on my ear. But who was I? Just a plain-looking gal in a wool hat, with a handbag full of film holders, saying *gosh* and *gee*. If he had known who I was —his meticulous assassin — he would have given me the bum's rush; but as a beginner, fumbling with her sleeves, I posed no threat. And the fact that I was a woman probably had something to do with it, too: he had nothing to lose. It was the secret of our success. As woman photographers we were either ignored to the point where it did us absolute good, or else courted in that sexually testing way that turned every approach into a flirtation. The business with the rubber bulb: this simulated hand-job was supposed to make me flinch. American photography, with very few exceptions, is the story of a gal with gumption aiming her camera at a man with a reputation.

Stieglitz had caved in, but any inkling that I was

a photographer, his equal, ambitious, with nothing but contempt for his magician's bluff—the slightest hint that I was more than I seemed, and he would have kicked me into the middle of next week.

He had moved over to the wall and rocked himself back and fixed his face into that grim little look, as if he had just noticed the roof leaked, posed like Steichen's *Gordon Craig*. The dirty window filtered a lemon light across one side of his head and gave the rest of him inkstains of shadow, black arms, black coat, one black ear. He was more than ever the vain magician refusing to reveal the unsurprising object on his person. I knew as I opened the back of the camera and saw his face flickering there that this was how he wanted to look, disliking everyone and everything. It was the expression I tried to catch, his weak challenge of malice.

"It's shaky," I said, aiming the camera. "And what's this?"

"The lens," he said. "It's a Goerz Dagor. Best there is."

"It's so darn oxidized I can't read it. Gosh, this diaphragm's really illegible. I don't know how you do it —"

As I criticized his camera he forgot his face and started to think. If people aren't thinking it is impossible to get a good likeness. Now I could see, upside down on the frosted glass, uncertain thought starting to snarl his mouth, and his eyes pricked with suspicion sighting along the bridge of his nose.

I slipped the film holder in and standing next to the camera grasped the bulb and said, "Here goes," and squeezed it. I heard that curious *per-plunk* as of something caught in a small trap.

Bang, I thought, *You're dead.*

"Keep going." He did not change his posture, though with each shot he inched back until on the last one — impatient to be done and perhaps aware that he'd been jacklighted like a porcupine on a lantern — his eyes had grown much smaller, giving his head a ducking tilt varnished with the hard gleam of scorn and envy. He had been holding his breath.

"There," I said. "Now that didn't hurt a bit, did it?" I put the exposed film holders in my bag.

He sighed and sat down changed. I knew — not from anything I had seen when I had shot him, but from the way he looked now — that I had succeeded. He was crookeder and stamped with exhaustion, and instead of sneering, naked. It was as if in photographing him I had peeled a layer from his face he now realized was gone.

"If you're quite finished, young lady, you can go." His voice struck dull tricked notes.

"Thanks a million," I said, and at the door, "Would you like to see the prints?"

"I very much doubt they'll be worth looking at."

Wrong, I thought. I smiled at the people who had watched it all. I had witnesses.

And the hotel room I had fled for feeling so useless and guilty in seemed on my re-entry like an intimate corner of my soul. I screwed in my red bulbs and drew the shades and stuffed towels against the cracks of light. I padded back and forth in the rosy darkness uncorking solutions and filling the bathroom sink. Then I began that simple and pleasurable chemistry that is like laundering in reverse — producing human stains on clean sheets. I washed the negatives and dunked them in developer and agitated them until they ripened. I fixed them. The mottled result was a perfect image of Stieglitz, the layer of him I had filched, but much better than I had expected. Right between the eyes.

Sunday I spent making three sets of prints, and my only regret was that Orlando was not in the dark room to marvel at these trophies and tug me in congratulation.

Nor was he at Adams House.

"Who shall I say called?" said the voice.

"His sister," I said. "And I am still waiting."

I sent one set of prints to Stieglitz, without a note,

without a name and yet in the assured belief that my originality glittered in the work. He was vain: he would hang them.

The other set I sent to the Camera Club as my calling card. I would have more before long, and a show, and the kind of fame that would have Orlando shouting, "You've done it, cookie!"

My sense of victory was all the keener for my being truly unknown. I relished my anonymity in this triumph since I knew it could not possibly last. The celebrity's assassin, no matter how obscure, inevitably gains his victim's fame: it's part of the act. There was no magic, but dammit, I deserved that man's head.

17

Swamp Dwellers

THE PORTER, wearing a crimson pillbox, complained in dusky mutters about the number of trunks he had to carry — the peepshow that was virtually the contents of my darkroom. I couldn't blame him — he didn't know me. And I wasn't pretty enough to forgive on sight. People looked at me with unfocused eyes in a grave lopsided way, as if at a double image.

After I boarded the train no heads turned. The man leaning at the door to the next compartment, seeing me smiling at the door to mine, concentrated his disappointment on my hat and knees. The steward slopped my drink and didn't say sorry. (Now I was tippling regularly, gin for preference; I thought of it as hypo bath because it fixed me.) I could have been miserable, but — far from it — I was so convinced of my success as a photographer I felt I was traveling incognito — like the original who leaves her triumph behind and rather enjoys her fugitive's disguise, since she knows that as soon as her true identity is discovered she will be eminent. My deed was inescapable. My own secret for now, soon it would be the world's.

But I was a photographer for love. Orlando was the reason for my camera, and he would make it superfluous. I had no ambition beyond tempting him to its darkened side, and while my fame was crucial to this it struck me as foolish to pursue the lonely distraction of art beyond the room where we made a sandwich of our passion.

I was at the corner window, looking at my two faces
in the double pane. The more distant one was prettier,
like a mask behind a face.

"I love trains." It was the man from the next compartment, propped on his forearms, simpering.

I said, "I wish they went a bit faster."

"That's the beauty of them," he said. "I'm in no
hurry."

"If you're not in a hurry, what's the point in going?"

I spent most of the trip in my compartment, drinking, using my hypo to dream. It was the same dream:
my surprise. Orlando was waiting in the windmill on a
night after my return. Obeying his instinct he had kept
this vigil alone. The promise we had made in childhood had matured to a vow.

The meniscus of moon hung between the windmill's blades and bathed the earth in that exposing
dustglow and made the salt marsh and the shore and
the whole gray world, floor and ceiling, a flat-sided
chamber for this vision. We were two images stealing
together, as if we existed as fixed lovers in a field beyond the moon. Our ecstatic light-beams twisted toward earth, brother and sister, to be joined. The
crickets, the sea-splash, the tremble of wind. And I
knew he was there from the candlepower of his body
that made the windmill shimmer like a lantern.

Back from the far side of the moon I crept across
the grass and up the steps to where he lay. Somehow
I shed my clothes. He laughed softly and folded me in
his arms. He prepared me, then covered me and
pumped me with life. My chafed skin was alight.
Dreams are unspecific tumbling and heat, but I knew
what I wanted — for him to burst through my squinting iris and demolish the virgin darkness in the camera
of my flesh. Then goodbye photography! Goodbye
film! Goodbye —

"Orlando, Orlando, anyone for Orlando."

I woke and worked the shade up, and I knew from
the look of it where we were.

Florida, rinsed with green, with small sulking bushes,

and here and there palms, was a wild garden of aching ferns in a clear yellow sunrise. After the low woods came seepages, fingers of water, then an ocean of hyacinths with birds diving into it and through the tangles of wines. They were not the spindly sandpipers and clumsy gray sea birds I was used to, but ones that had flapped from the dawn of the world, with flashing tails, long beaks, and legs that swayed and folded under them taking off. The white plumes of their feathers fanned out as they spilled again. The morning was so hot there was no dew on the leaves, which made the place look, for all its greenery, very old. Rags of moss dangled from overhanging branches and what flowers I could see were lotus-like, so delicate a photo would sink them.

In places the swamp water had scummy stretches, with black saplings and bitten-off tree trunks standing in them, some like gallows and others like coatracks and drowned knees. Each dead thing had collar stripes of dark tide marks, a decoration that took the curse off them. The green lace of stagnation hit by the morning light exploded like a dish of sulphur with an afterburn of midges sifting in bunches above it. I could not imagine furry things surviving here, but only families of waterproof reptiles pushing their snouts through the warm swamp and depositing eggs.

It had a lively smell of danger and it was huge and spreading in vine-whips and fleshy shoots, sliding from stump to stump like a sponge growing in a puddle. It had gone on fattening in the ooze, but for all its density it had a limpness: the smallest movement of a bird stirred it. I had never seen anything like it. It was the earliest moment of life in America, before the canoes, and so different from what I knew on the Cape, where there were footprints in the remotest dunes. I had not known places like this existed; I could not believe my luck.

Eden was like this. Not that manicured park of fruit trees and fig leaves and trimmed hedges, the Old Testament orchard signposted with punishments for pick-

ing the fruit and walking on the grass — not that, but
this wilderness of succulence, trackless, risky, and
half-sunk in bubbly mud, sprawling sideways in an
infancy it could not outgrow — order without rules.
Here, one could imagine brother and sister bumping
like frogs in broad daylight, for in one plump tree with
its feet in ferns an orchid clung amid a bandaging of
vines, moss dripped, an upright fringe of green flames
flickered along its boughs and its own leaves were shel-
tering hands. Other identical trees embraced, wrapped
together like lovers and swelling where they touched.

One thing about photography: there are no second
chances. I tried to do this vision of Florida from the
train, but the rocking window jogged my camera.
Though I was able to shoot it later, without the
whoops-a-daisy of the train, none of the pictures
looked genuine. My best pictures saw more than my
eye and these lacked that great slap of sight.

We'll have our honeymoon here, I thought: a honeymoon in paradise.

"I hope you find something to do here," said Mama,
almost her first words to me after I arrived in Verona.
Her tone was dim and discouraging. She blinked at
me as if to say, *You shouldn't have come.*

Papa read the words written on Mama's face: "I
can't for the life of me think why you came all this
way. Furthermore, I doubt whether Carney has room
for you."

"You said there are twenty bedrooms in this house."

"Palace," said Papa. "Twenty-five. And they're
full."

"Can you beat that."

Carney's palace (we were on settees in a mammoth lounge) was an Italian-style fruitcake with a bell
tower and battlements, a courtyard filled with leering
statuary and surrounded by a blundering wall. On the
shore side a pier jutted into the Gulf of Mexico. But
the yachts at the pier impressed me less than the pelicans I could see opening like umbrellas for their

dives, and the chandelier in our lounge wasn't half as splendid as its reflecting shape, the pyramid of oranges in the crystal bowl beneath it. The place itself, with its pictures and gold pillars and baroque scrollwork and high painted ceilings, although magnificent at a distance, was up close much shabbier. It was nailed together several degrees out of kilter and thickly regilded: movie theater or opera house decor, a spectacular silliness. Here bad taste was gluttonous, size mattered more than finish, and I was sure that none of it had the grandeur of the swamp they had drained to build it on.

It distressed me to think that Mama and Papa could be happy in this monkey-house of vulgarity, and had visited year after year. But I think what worried me most was the person responsible for this mess. It was a motiveless satire of grace and art, and each smirking cherub and blistered wall showed it. It did not reduplicate the Italian original, it did not come near — it was as if the savage who made it, having failed at creation, could only mock it in debauched stucco and brass. The tropical storms had done the rest, completed the parody by pocking it with salt. A person who would do this would stop at nothing.

"Don't worry about me," I said. "Tell Carney I've got a room in a boarding house. Mrs. Fritts's. She's a nice old body."

Mama said, "Circus people stay at those places."

"She's a big girl now," said Papa. He stared hard at me. "But what about your sister? What's she supposed to do while you're gallivanting down here?"

Speak for yourself, I almost said. But I was warned by an anxious look on his face, a double image of worry in fact, since they were both tanned and wore blue and white outfits that matched. Far from home they looked startled and ashamed, as if seeing them here in Florida I had discovered them misbehaving in a state of undress and was spoiling their fun.

Papa said, "She won't sit on her hands if I know my Phoebe."

"Phoebe can look after herself," I said.

"Hasn't got a brain in her head," said Papa. "And Orlando's probably out raising hell. I tell you, Maude, if anything happens you're responsible."

"I'm not staying here long," I said. "I'll just do some pictures and go."

"Carney doesn't allow photographers on his property."

"Then he's either a fool or a criminal," I said.

"He's a Renaissance Man — American Renaissance," said Papa. "He doesn't want to be made a fool of."

"Your Mister Carney is mistaken. We interpret, Papa. We do not create."

"He's quite a patron of the arts —"

I turned to the portrait of Carney as Papa spoke. He was a red fleshy man with tiny eyes set deep in a swollen swinish head, a porker's hot face and bristly neck, hands like slabs of meat, and wisps of white hair, like smoke coming out of his earholes. He was squatting in that ornate frame over the mantelpiece as if watching us through a window with his raw rummy's face.

"— but he's a hoofer at heart," said Papa, "and he's a wonderful host. If you're smart you'll keep out of his way. And remember, no pictures — not here."

"*Who says*," I started, for Papa was talking like a patron himself, but I simmered down and said, "Who says I want to take pictures here? Why, I wouldn't give him the satisfaction."

"You can do the Indians," said Mama. "They wrestle alligators down the road. Pictures of them would be worth something."

"Sure," said Papa, "don't go back to the Cape without doing the citrus groves, or the ballpark up in Sarasota, or Millsaps Circus in its winter quarters, or the drive along the coast."

"Coral Gables is picturesque," said Mama.

"Ever see a grapefruit tree? No? Big yellow basket-

balls hanging up there? That's what I call picturesque."

"Picturesque is what I avoid," I said.

"It's what people want to see," said Papa.

"That's why I avoid it."

"Negroes," said Mama. "There are some Negroes
down in Boca Grande. You like Negroes."

"Then you can go back to the Cape," said Papa.

"We'll see you to the station," said Mama.

"What about the sourbob trees and the people crabbing and sunset on the wampum mills?" I said. "You
didn't mention them. And I couldn't come all this way
without doing the migrating chickens or the untitled
driftwood."

"Don't be funny, Maude," said Papa in his broker's
voice. "The least you could have done was tell us you
were coming."

"What would you have said if I had?"

"I would have told you not to come. You've got no
business here."

My eye is my business, I thought. I said, "This is a
fine how-do-you-do."

Mama looked at Papa slackly as if to say, *What are
we going to do with her?*

Papa said, "I don't know what you want, Maude,
but I hope to God you don't get it."

I almost went home that minute; then I saw the
shifty look on his face, worry and hope.

He said, "How you could leave Phoebe up there
alone is more than I can understand."

But I thought: He doesn't care a damn about her.
He just doesn't want me here, and I'm going to find
out why.

"I'd better be getting back to Mrs. Fritts's," I said.
"She's expecting me for dinner."

"You do that," said Papa, and led me through the
palatial house. It was empty, yet it held the evidence
of many people — the yachts at the pier, different
kinds of tobacco smoke, and something harder to ex-

plain, the immediate memory that rooms have for strangers who have passed through.

To get to the front vestibule we crossed a landing that surrounded a high wall. More paintings, more vases. Out the window I saw, enclosed by a wall, a tent being erected: roustabouts yanked on a great sail and hammered stakes into the ground.

"What's that?"

"A tent," said Mama.

"That Carney!" I said.

"Don't cast nasturtiums," said Papa. He nudged me past the window and hurried me on my way before I could take a picture.

18

Boarders

THE BUNGALOW Mrs. Fritts ran as a boarding house
was just south of Verona, behind a palm grove that
gave it the look of an oasis. In her neat garden was a
twisted tree laden with elongated seed pods; she called
it her cigar tree. The bungalow was furnished with
upholstered chairs and carpets with floral designs like
puked fricassees. On most walls were religious mottoes, THE LORD WILL PROVIDE and PUT ON THE
WHOLE ARMOR OF GOD, and on one was a coconut
carved into a monkey's face. Mrs. Fritts said there
were "scorpshuns" on the grounds. There were also
sheds of various sizes — an ostrich in one, a kangaroo
in another. These animals, and some others I knew
only as stinks and nighttime coughs, she looked after
for Millsaps Circus, which had its winter quarters in
Verona proper. She was a tidy damp-eyed little
woman, seventy-odd, who had ceased to see anything
extraordinary in either the animals or the people she
boarded, the circus's overflow.

Perhaps they weren't so odd, I decided on my third
day. They hadn't changed — my eye had. I saw them
all over the house, Mr. Biker the dwarf who played
"Daisy" on his ocarina and sat on three telephone
books to eat; Orrie, whose hands grew out of his
shoulders; the Flying Faffners, Kenny and Doris, who
cycled on the high wire — but they did no tricks
here and looked quite colorless hunched over their
checkerboards. There was a man called "Digit" Taft,

from Georgia, whose specialty was sticking his finger in the knothole of a horizontal board and kicking himself upright and balancing on that finger: he had a bird tattoo on his cheek, which flapped when he chewed gum. Harvey and Hornette were bareback riders; there were no horses in Mrs. Fritts's sheds; Harvey and Hornette read comic books. They were all very strong: Digit could tear Mr. Biker's phone books in half, and Hornette, a pretty girl of about sixteen, could get the caps off cherryade bottles with her teeth.

The group portrait I did of them, *Boarders,* was one of my best — another pictorial fluke in available light, since anyone's Aunt Fanny could have done the same with a Baby Brownie.

They are solemn, the seven of them, plus Mrs. Fritts. Orrie is old, Mrs. Fritts in her frilly church dress. They stand together: it might be a family portrait, a Sunday on a southern porch, a gathering of the clan in summer dresses and white suits.

But you miss it entirely unless you linger for a fraction of a second and having accepted it as a plain family you are shocked: the nipper is not a nipper, that old man has hands but no arms, the shadow on that other man's cheek is a bird tattoo, and those girls, Doris and Hornette, have muscular trapeze artist's shoulders. Behind Mrs. Fritts, reflected on the parlor window, is the most bizarre detail, an ostrich, but so faint you won't see it until you've seen the others. The picture celebrates the unexpected, as one person after the other is revealed. You accepted it from the first, deceived yourself into thinking you had seen it before. Yet my object was not to mock or trick the viewer, but to hasten his understanding and impel him to look for more: Digit's thick finger, Mr. Biker's kindly eyes, Hornette's shanks, the weary dignity on the face of Mrs. Fritts, maybe the ostrich. Then it's a family again. Looking at this picture ought to be like reading a book, a time exposure, a lesson in seeing. The viewer goes away instructed. Nothing looks the

same to him after that. The world hasn't changed —
he has.

I printed the picture, distributed it, and made
eight friends. "You're the best in the business," said
Hornette. And Mrs. Fritts said, "I hope you stay
here a good long time."

I told them I wasn't down for long, but that I
planned to go over to Carney's. Mrs. Fritts's face
clouded.

"No," she said. "You don't want to do that. Stay
away from there."

"I want to do the pelicans," I said.

"Ain't them pelicans something?" she said. "I came
down here in 'twenty-five and I still can't get over
them. But you do your pelicans somewhere else. That
Carney's a holy terror and his friends are worse."

I didn't say that my parents were there. I was
ashamed of myself for being ashamed of them.

"He's got a money machine up north," said Mrs.
Fritts. "But that's all he's got. Am I right, Biker?"

Mr. Biker, in his kiddie's drawers, kicking his feet
on the sofa, said in a high voice, "Something wrong
with that boy!"

"Have you been over to his house?"

"Once a year. But that ain't no house."

Orrie came into the room, his fins flapping.

Mr. Biker said, "She wants to know about Carney."

Orrie pushed his lips apart with his teeth and made
a horrible face.

"See what I mean?" said Mrs. Fritts. "Now you keep
away from there."

Warning me about my own folks. I said, "I
thought I might go down the coast to Boca Grande,
too. Take some pictures. The sourbob trees. The old
socks. The people crabbing."

"What?" said Mrs. Fritts. She opened her mouth for
my answer.

"The Indians and whatever."

"That's more like it," said Mrs. Fritts. She spoke

again to Mr. Biker: "She wants to go down to Boca Grande."

"More like it," screeched Mr. Biker. "But there ain't nothing in Boca!"

He was wrong, of course. Boca Grande was a beautiful ruined town with sand on the tufty streets and crumble-marks all over the Spanishy buildings and decayed grillwork. In front of a grand old house a boogie-man sculpted a green urn in a hedge with his clippers. There were palms and clumps of hibiscus and fruit ripening in the still sultry air, and a fish and smoke smell that I badly wanted to photograph.

"Better shake a leg," said Harvey, who had driven me down in his Nash with Hornette. "Looks like it's going to rain."

"Really?" I said, because it was sunny. But he pointed out the storm sliding darkly in from the Gulf like a blimp in a shroud. "I think I'll wait for it."

Harvey laughed and kept telling Hornette he'd never seen no photographer *wait* for no damn rainpour. When it started crackling on the tin roofs and swishing the shutters and flooding the street — so loud Harvey was hollering in my ear — I set up my Speed Graphic under a storefront's awning and did the children on the opposite veranda watching the darts come down and the electrocutions overhead.

It was gone in minutes, leaving drops still streaking in shining threads, but by then it had turned into a Walker Evans, so I suggested we move on before it became an Ansel Adams. We went to the potash depot where there were boogie-men with rags on their heads. I did them walking among the palms, their bright footprints in the sodden sand. The rain had not seeped down far and just under the dark surface it was dry where their feet pawed it into patterns. They were rather silent, these blacks, and wouldn't come near me, although they could see what I was doing.

Some of these depot pictures I planned as read-

ing pieces, time exposures with secrets. There were
bushes and trees and shadows, and I hoped they
would appear as tropical landscapes, quaintly pretty
coastal scenes. Then, only after the viewer started
reading them would he see twelve black sentinels,
some as stumps and some as trees; chickens, footprints, shacks; clutter that wasn't flowers; potash
dust, dead white, that wasn't sand. Not a statement —
no summary — but details leading onward to a jigsaw of episodes until everything that had looked
familiar was strange. I used quaint arrangements to
reveal depths of disturbance.

But I had sucked all the light out of it and after
a while could not see it to save my life. Boca Grande
didn't exist anymore: it was in my camera.

"This is for you, Maude," said Hornette as we got
into the car. She gave me a candy bar she'd bought
in town.

Harvey turned the car south, along a swampy road
where reaching vines had yanked down the Burma
Shave signs. I said, "Aren't you going to have one
yourself?"

"I got to take care of my teeth," she said. She
smiled nicely at me. "For my act. Sometimes I hang
by them, see."

She looked a bit embarrassed. It was the first ref-
erence she had made to her circus act.

Harvey said, "Circus folk got to look after their
bodies. If you don't you can get killed. It ain't easy,
down here in winter quarters. You get rusty. But
Hornette, she looks after her body, wouldn't you say?"

"Yes, sir," I said. And I noticed how at Mrs. Fritts's
they didn't smoke and drank only Doctor Pepper and
cherryade and went to bed early. "But what if you
want to have children?" I said. "What happens to your
act then?"

Hornette giggled and Harvey almost busted a gut.

"Why, this here's my little sister!" said Harvey, and
he reached under her and pinched her bum.

Hearing that, and knowing they slept in the same

room, probably the same bed — why not? — I grew
melancholy and remembered Orlando. I envied them
their happiness until I realized I was doing this for
him. At the end of all this picture-taking lay Orlando.

"Where are we headed?" I said.

"Gator farm," said Harvey. "You never seen nothing like it."

I said, "But this is all fantastic. It's wild. No one's in
charge here," and I thought: Those water lilies
aren't getting paid by Jack Guggenheim to gleam, so
why should I?

"You can show them Yankees what a wild old
place this is," said Harvey. "They won't believe their
eyes."

"It's beautiful," I said.

"Beautiful *looking*," he said, driving slowly and regarding the swamp. "But people go in there for a
weenie roast and you never see them again. It swal-
lows you up. Don't it, Hornette?"

Hornette was saying "It sure is" and "It sure
does" when I steered the conversation to Carney.
They both went quiet and sort of exchanged glances
without looking at each other.

Finally, Harvey said, "That Carney's the worst."

"That's what everyone says, but how do you know?"

"He's the shareholder. He's bigger than Millsaps
himself. But he's a whole lot meaner."

Hornette pushed her knees together and seemed
to sulk.

"He's putting up a tent," I said. "In his yard.
It's one hell of a big tent."

"That'll be for the Pig Dinner," said Harvey, but
his expression betrayed nothing. *Pig Dinner?* I
thought he might say more. He didn't. A few miles
further he pulled in beside a painted shed and said,
"Here we is."

The rain had been here and passed on leaving
puddles and damp silk over everything. A muddy
Indian — a Miccosukee of the Creek Nation —
splashed over to us and while Harvey bargained

with him I went with Hornette for a look at the alligators. Big and small, they were submerged to their nostrils in a filthy pool. They were watched over by some Indian children in rags who looked away when I did them. Harvey joined us and said, "You choose one, Maude. It's your treat. Pick a fat one."

They were well made, with thick seams and rivets and stitches and plates, and dragon spikes on their tails. I chose a likely one, and the children slipped ropes around its snout and dragged it into a shallow slimy pit where a Miccosukee stood in his underdrawers.

"What's he going to do?"

"Rassle it," said Harvey. "Look at them bubulous eyes."

The Miccosukee kicked it in the belly and danced around it in the mud until the alligator lowered his head and came at him. Dodging the jaws, the Indian got down beside it and flipped it over like a log: it resisted for a second, then trembled and clutched the Indian gently in its glove-like feet. There was no strength in its shimmying or even the flop of its fat tail. The Indian grunted and changed his grip. He was not wrestling the alligator but simply punishing it with his greater cunning, and this was what I wished to show in my picture — the unequal struggle: the crusted mud on the Indian's back making him look like a hideous reptile, and the cracked white belly-flesh of the alligator, and the loose skin at its throat, the human pouches of its defenseless underside.

If Harvey hadn't encouraged me I would not have taken the picture. But he saw it as his favor to me. I could not disappoint him. I felt terrible taking those pictures, for the Indian had seen my camera and he started overdoing it, tormenting the exhausted creature, and I thought: I didn't come all this way for people to pose for me.

The pictures were fakes, they dignified the Indian, they gave him a dragon slayer's drama. If I'd had the nerve I would have taken a picture of the alligator slithering headlong in terror back to the safety of its pool, or the Indian sticking his muddy claws out for Harvey's five bucks.

"What I'd like to see," said Harvey in the Nash again, "is some old gator eat one of them rasslers."

"That's more like it," I said. "What about Carney instead of an Indian?"

"Then we'd be out of a job," said Harvey.

"That's what I want to be," said Hornette. "Out of a job."

Harvey glared at her and said, "Shut it, honey."

"I'm told he's a patron of the arts," I said.

"If arts means hell-raising, he's a patron all right," said Harvey. He parked at a roadside stand. "Want an ice cream?"

Hornette and I stayed in the car while Harvey went for the cones. I wanted to know more, but didn't know where to begin. Like the others at Mrs. Fritts's they were not very bright, and yet their combination of good will and guilelessness made them appear more mysterious than they really were, as if they were hiding something. Simple good humor can look like the ultimate pretense.

"No one likes Carney," I said, groping for an angle.

Hornette shook her head.

"The Pig Dinner," I said. "What in hell's the Pig Dinner?"

"It's coming up."

"Ever been to it?"

"Honey," said Hornette, "we're *it!*"

"Tell me then."

"You never seen nothing like it," she said. "There ain't nothing like it."

"That's what Harvey said about the alligators, and I didn't think much of them."

"This is worse than the gators. I couldn't tell you about that Pig Dinner if I wanted to. There ain't words for it, or if there is I don't know them."

"Indescribable?"

"You said it."

"Just the thing for my friend here." I patted the Speed Graphic on my lap.

Hornette closed her eyes and said "Yipe!"

"You can help me," I said. "You will, won't you?"

But before she could reply, Harvey came back to the car with two cones. He gave one to me, and after licking the ice cream from the other he passed Hornette the empty cone to crunch.

"You go on and eat, Maude," he said. "We got to look after our bodies."

19

The Lamar Carney Pig Dinner

FLORIDA'S HOT EYE was shutting on the Gulf, confining us in a black after-image. We were on the porch, sitting together on the glider, kicking the floor. The regular swinging was like thought.

Hornette said, "You don't know what you're asking, girl."

"What am I asking? Tell me, and I won't say another word."

She gave the porch an emphatic kick. "Carney don't want you to see it."

"That's the point," I said. "That's why I want to."

Hornette considered this. She said, "I can't help you."

We rocked in blind night.

"So you do everything he says."

"I do not," she said crossly, making her eyebrows meet.

"Then help me," I said. "Get me in — or else tell me what I'm missing."

"I ain't talking," she said. She braked the glider by stomping on the porch. She looked around, then whispered, "You'll have to see for yourself. But it sure ain't going to be easy."

The next morning, Mr. Biker knocked on my darkroom door. "Maudie!"

"Don't come in — I'm processing!"

"There's someone wants you out on the porch."

I finished off the negatives (Boca Grande, alligator

184

wrestler, swamps, and a nice one of a dog in a green celluloid eyeshade being walked by a tubby man wearing the same get-up on his head). Downstairs, I saw Mama on the glider.

"Maude," she said, "who was that extraordinary man?"

"That's Mr. Biker."

"Is there something wrong with him?"

"I hadn't noticed."

"He's terribly small," she said. She frowned at the porch. "If I'd known it was like this I would have made other arrangements for you."

The voice of the patroness; but I let it pass. "I like it," I said. "I'm going to town here. I've fixed up a darkroom in the attic. Mama, why are you dressed like that?"

She wore smoked glasses, a wide-brimmed hat and gloves. Instead of her usual handbag she was carrying a wicker basket.

"This is my traveling outfit. I'm taking a trip," she said. "Coral Gables. That's why I stopped in — I thought you might want to come along."

"What about Papa?"

"He never comes."

"You've been there before?"

"Every year," she said. "Papa stays behind for the dinner."

"Why don't you go to the dinner?"

"Don't be silly." She tightened the strap on her basket. "It's all men. I wouldn't like it. It's just Carney and his men friends. Besides, we're not allowed. The Pig Dinner's famous for that."

"I've never heard of it."

"That's how special it is," said Mama proudly. "Now how about it? Coral Gables — just the two of us."

Come on, daughter, she was saying. *Put that old camera aside and start living.* But I had made my choice.

"No thanks."

After she went away Mr. Biker looked rather curious, as if he wanted to ask who she was. I wanted to be spared having to deny that she was my mother, or to explain that I had taken this trip to prove to my parents that I wasn't theirs. If he had asked, I would have said, "She's another Guggenheim." He didn't ask. He was small, but he was a real gentleman.

And he had, as I saw, other things on his mind. A change had come over the boarders. The people who had been so nice to each other, and just grand to me, got in the grip of a kind of tension. They quarreled, complained to Mrs. Fritts, slammed doors, that sort of thing. Brainless anger: they weren't smart enough to argue, so they banged. Mrs. Fritts said nothing. When there was trouble, she studied the messages on her poker-work mottoes. One lunchtime, Digit smacked a ketchup bottle so hard with the finger he used in his act it flooded his scrambled eggs in red goo. He cursed it and flung the whole plate out the window, which mercifully was open. Then he went off, banging.

"He jess thew it out the winda," said Orrie.

"Shit on him," said Mr. Biker. He picked up the ketchup bottle, and seeing that it was nearly empty, said, "We ain't got but one of these."

"Don't mind them," said Mrs. Fritts, taking her eyes from YE ARE OF MORE VALUE THAN MANY SPARROWS. She breathed at me, "It's the Pig Dinner."

Mr. Biker looked smaller, Orrie more mangled, Digit fretful and foul-mouthed. The acrobats paced back and forth and threw themselves into chairs. This was the frenzy of circus folk; I had forgotten they were performers. Under pressure they had become grotesquely grumpy; they carried violence around with them; there was a threat of danger in their silences. And they excluded me: it was like blame, as if I represented that other world, the public, and was responsible for them making fools of themselves. At night, in my darkroom, I heard shouts and the sound of crockery smashing and "I ain't doing it!" and "You gotta!" and little wails, like a child trapped in a chimney.

For my own peace of mind I printed pictures: Boca Grande, the boogie-men, the rain, *Green Eyeshades;* and when I heard the screeches I turned on the faucet hard to drown them. It was so strange: the loud footfalls in my ears and those peaceful footprints in my pictures. But that contradiction showed me how far my work had diverged from my life.

"You still serious?" said Hornette the next evening.

I said I was.

"Cause I worked it out," she said. Her voice was conspiratorial; she was secretive, with a bundle of clothes in her hands. "Try these on for size."

She gave me a man's jacket, a pair of striped trousers, a derby hat. I put them on and looked in the mirror. I was a man. She said, "That's so they don't eat you up."

"I barely recognize myself."

"It's a damn good thing you ain't pretty."

"I hope you realize I'm going to be taking pictures. And I might exhibit them later on."

"Girl," she said, "I want you to show them all over creation."

"You might get into trouble."

"Sure thing," she said. "Or Carney might. It's his show, ain't it?" And in her laugh I identified the little chimney-wail I had heard the previous night.

The Lamar Carney Pig Dinner was held in the tent I had seen being hoisted on the grounds of that so-called palace my first day in Verona. I was in my suit, but I think if I had been wearing a sandwich-board and snowshoes I would still have gone unnoticed, because the others were benumbed and rode in the back of the van like people being taken out in the dark to be shot.

I smelled cooking — an odor of woodsmoke and burned meat — as soon as we entered Carney's grounds. After we parked, I peeked through the flap

in the tent and saw them all, with red faces, shouting
and laughing and finishing their meal. There were
about a hundred of them, men in tuxedos, seated at
tables which were arranged around a circus ring. In
the center of the ring were embers in spokes, the
smoldering wheel of a log fire; and on a spit the remains of a cooked pig, hacked apart, and only its
tail and trotters intact. It was not hard to identify Carney. He had the place of honor and in front of him on
a platter was a pig's head, his spitting image, one
meathead above the other, dead eyes in the thick
folds of gleaming cheeks and that expression you see
on the faces of the very fat — dumb swollen pain, as
if the scowl has been roasted onto it.

I wanted that picture.

"You just keep out of sight," said Hornette. "But
don't worry — no one'll see you. They'll be looking
at us."

"What are you doing here?" It was Harvey.

"She came along for the ride," said Hornette.

I said, "The whole thing was my idea."

"Go on home," said Harvey.

"She can't," said Hornette, "on account of they'll
see her leaving the grounds if she does, huh."

It was true: we had passed through a number of
checkpoints on the way in and surly guards had waved
us on. Now we were in a small tent, an anteroom to
the big top in which the men were eating.

"Show starts in ten minutes," said a man dressed as
a ringmaster. He was wearing tails and a silk hat, and
he had a whip which he cracked at nothing in particular. "Positions," he said, "positions."

"That's Millsaps," said Harvey. "If he squawks I'm
not taking the blame for you."

I smelled animals, the steam of fur and feet, but it
didn't come from the cages — it was the circus folk
who had started taking off their clothes.

"Get on up there," said Hornette. She motioned to
a tower of scaffolding just inside the tent. "And don't
forget what I said — all over creation."

I slipped through the tent flap and climbed a tall
ladder to a platform, where there was a cubicle and a
rack of spotlights. I could not have been in a better
place than this crow's nest, in the darkness behind the
lights. I had a view of everything and yet was made
invisible by the lights' glare.

A moment later I was joined by the lighting engineer: baseball hat, screwdrivers tucked into the belt of
his dungarees. The canvas tent-top slumped near our
heads and the smoke and chatter rose to the height of
the poles.

The man said, "You got authorization? You can't
stay here if you ain't got authorization."

"This is my authorization," I said. "Smile."

He did, and I snapped his picture. After that he was
nice as pie. His name was Monk.

"Shift," he said and signaled for me to move. "Look
at them." He jerked the lights into position. "I wish
I had me a gun. Ain't they the limit?"

Ain't this? I thought, as Monk slashed the diners
with light. And I knew I had passed a frontier and
had left all the other practitioners behind. Where were
they, anyhow? Out goofing off, shooting sourbob trees
and dingbats, rubber tires, storefronts, cottages, snow,
Abandoned Playground, Ragged Beggar on Wall
Street, Torso with Tits: embalming quaintness for the
next generation. But this was different; it smelled
different and had art's startling flaw as its beautifying
scar. It was flesh and riotous, a cannibal feast in
tuxedos, an event which no previous photographer had
drained of its light. By a combination of luck, risk,
and gumption I was its first witness.

But I almost cried at my bravado, for down there
not ten feet from Carney, clouting his food and moving his hands to his mouth, and with an eater's squirm-
ing motion — his back turned to the world and
gobbling like the rest of them — was my original patron, my father. If he had not been there I might have
seen it as less momentous, this pattern of hogs merely

a piece of news. He made me hesitate; he made me act. What a long way I had come to catch him!

His was the first picture I took. I half expected him to keel over from the shock of it — just pitch back with his face missing and his feet sticking up. Nothing happened. But I knew I had started something: my Third Eye told me. Not skirmishing with the picturesque or tinkering with technique, but acting on the raw conviction that, alone in this tent, I was leading an attack on patronage.

They had finished eating when the band marched in, going oompah-oompah and wearing blue uniforms with gold braid. MILLSAPS was a blur on the bass drum. It was the brandy and cigars phase of the dinner, and while the music was playing — the diners banging spoons — two blacks came on and shoveled the remains of the barbecue — the burned logs, the carcass of the pig — into a barrel and carted it away. The band continued to march. And there was a new sound, a whistling and fluting — this was the steam calliope puffing on a horsedrawn wagon. It was a beautiful contraption, smoke and steam and flute notes: a man was seated at an enormous red and gold pipe organ and beating the trays of keys while the pipes shot jets of steam out as whinnying music.

But that was not my picture, for as the band took their seats under my scaffold (and now I could hear them blowing spit out of their instruments) the steam calliope turned in the ring. I could see an old man stoking a furnace at the back end of the organ, getting up the steam by heaving coal into the firebox. He was reddened by the flames and roasting on his little platform like a pig. So my *Stoker,* which everyone took for a portrait of a fireman on a train, was actually a stoker on a steam calliope, a man feeding a fire to make music: the underside of all art. I don't believe there was a photographer in America who would not have preferred the calliope player to the stoker, but I knew the fickle tyranny of patronage —

I had a point of view, and I was aware that at the top of this scaffold I was doing my *magnum o*.

"Good evening, gents!" shouted Millsaps the ring-master, strutting to the center of the ring as the calli-ope beeped away. He flourished his whip and said, "Once again, the Millsaps Circus is proud to perform for its bennyfactor, Mister Lamar Carney and his es-teemed friends. As in other years, we are privvyledged to be invited to do our stuff for the Pig Dinner —"

He went on in this vein, saying what a pleasure it was, flattering the banqueting cigar-puffers, and I saw Carney beaming with each compliment, the pig's head beneath his similarly grinning. But that was not the only resemblance. There were multiple images: Millsaps was also a version of Carney, and there was something of Stieglitz in his whip-cracking swagger — even something of Papa and the rest, gloating in their tuxes. Then and there I decided it was how Jack Guggenheim himself looked, a creature of snuffling assurance who believed moolah was power and power license — and sitting on his fat ass and trafficking in taste.

Carney grew impatient and interrupted Millsaps's arrogant fawning. He didn't shout. He sucked the cigar out of his mouth and said sharply, "Cut the crap, Milly, and start the fucking show."

"Music, maestro!" said Millsaps, and another crack of his whip brought clowns tumbling into the ring. Among them was Mr. Biker, dressed in a Lord Fauntleroy suit; Mr. Biker — the solemn little person from *Boarders,* who had been so nice to me — with his face grotesquely painted; Mr. Biker — whom I had also done on Mrs. Fritts's sofa with the big tomcat on his lap — now riding a child's tricycle, now leapfrogging the other clowns, his tiny legs work-ing like mad and tipping him from side to side when he ran. One would not know from his work that this fool was a man.

This wasn't what the men wanted. Led by Carney, they booed the clowns; they booed poor Orrie who

expertly juggled five oranges — booed so loudly Orrie
panicked and dropped them; they booed Digit, they
booed Turko the weightlifter, and they howled so
furiously at a dog act the little mutts scattered yapping
out of the ring.

All the while I was doing pictures: Carney, the pig,
the drunks in tuxedos, the catcalling. And it dawned
on me that the whole purpose of the dinner like the
purpose of patronage, was a meal ticket to mock, to
sit in judgment upon people whom money had made
into clowns. They craved a chance to boo, and I saw
Papa laughing with the rest of them. I didn't mind
doing his picture anymore, because this was the truth.
Each picture made me ever more solitary: photography was something that rid me of images by disposing
of the visible world, a lonely occupation that made me
lonelier.

It was about fifteen minutes after these acts came
on, with the band crashing and the men booing, that
the others started. There were trumpets and drum-
rolls. I saw them enter; I verified them in my viewfinder, then I looked at Monk, who was working a
spotlight at them. Monk was nibbling his lip and
though I was not in his way he was saying, "Shift,
shift."

I couldn't believe my eyes, but I believed my
camera. First, Harvey and Hornette, galloping in on
a white horse; then the Flying Faffners, Kenny and
Doris, prancing back and forth on the high wire; then
a girl named Glory, whom Millsaps introduced, as he
had the others, by screaming her name and cracking
his whip. The circus ring was in motion and up above,
Glory was swinging on a trapeze over the heads of the
men at the tables.

The men had gone silent. They craned their necks
at Glory. No boos for this; the only sounds were the
horses' hooves, the band playing "The Loveliest Time
of the Year" in a muted quickstep, and the squeak
of the trapeze ropes; and the reason was the costumes,
for they had no costumes.

They were stark bare-ass naked, Harvey and
Hornette wobbling on their horses, the Faffners upstairs on their wire — their bums shining in Monk's
spotlight — and Glory, a stripped doll on her trapeze
swooping with her legs open. The nakedness alone
didn't shock me; it was their movement — they were
endangered white figures and looked unprotected in
their skin. Glory flung herself backward, started to fall
and caught her ankles on the bar, hung briefly like a
side of meat and then came at Carney reaching and
so fast her breasts were yanked and I could hear the
wind rushing against her navel.

There were tumblers. They came in a small jalopy
and piled out, twelve of them, boys and girls, with
springy bodies, doing cartwheels and handstands —
such a splash of energy it was hard to tell they were
naked except by the tufts of hair between their legs.
They tumbled in pairs, linked in a brisk double image,
repeating around the ring, miraculously missing the
horses' hooves.

Harvey and Hornette drew level on their horses and
Harvey vaulted behind Hornette to a corn-holing posture. The watching men found their voices and rooted
loudly. At first all the mounted brother and sister did
was canter. As they rode into Monk's green light I
noticed their flesh and the horse's, the way their
straddling legs clutched the blanket-folds of his muscles
and looked so frail and damp. The cries increased, and
the band's braying; Hornette stood up and raised her
arms, and her breasts jogged as Harvey held her flanks.
He got to his feet and around they went, one behind
the other, naked on the slippery horse.

Glory had swung to a rope. There was a red
stripe on her buttocks where the trapeze bar had cut
her. She slipped one foot in a stirrup loop and upside
down scissored her legs open — and pulled a length
of magician's scarves, knotted end to end, out of her
mousehole. She arched her back, and as Monk painted
her in light she slipped the other foot in and spun herself to a blur.

The young tumblers made themselves into a pyramid. They pitched forward somersaulting and rolling in the sawdust in brief copulatory gymnastics, the girls on all fours throwing their hair from side to side as the boys rushed them from behind making little slaps as they met the squealing girls.

Body on body, naked, pairing — double exposure: two of everything. And how strange it was when they walked on their hands and showed their beaks and cracks as wrinkled fluidy faces in collars of hair between their kicking legs. But I was frightened by the roar of the men and their table-thumping; by the sight of the circus performers stripped naked, and the grunts that reached me in my cubicle; by the heat. What disturbed me most was seeing people I knew so changed — not just Papa hollering, but Harvey and Hornette belly to belly on the tramping horse.

Nakedness speaks in a way no voice can, saying fear and woe and age. But it wasn't naked anymore, nor a show of muscle and damp hair. It was a thin bruised suit, pale enough for me to photograph the stitchings of veins, and luminous in the cigar smoke and dust and paint. Their defenseless skin! Flesh has a tremble that clothes hide: everything they did looked dangerous.

Typically, the nude is shown in repose or making love. But this was against all tradition — Hornette swiveling by her teeth, the tumblers becoming bizarre people with fuzzy shrunken heads, Hornette rejoining Harvey on the horse. It was unimaginable human motion, animated by a crowd of cheering men. I would not have believed it without my camera.

What Harvey and Hornette were doing at a gallop, the Faffners did on their high wire, without a net. I could barely keep my camera steady when I saw them get down on one knee and face each other, mimic a caress eighty feet in the air, denting the wire where their knees pressed it. They remained suspended, swaying slightly, in a risky balance. Their lips touched and their shoulders met: I expected them

to be jerked to the ground and to end up in a broken
pudding of arms and legs. This danger made its
eroticism vividly blacker.

But they stayed on the wire and continued to simu-
late the sexual duet. The symmetry anchored them.
The pair of them were saved by the electric field of
their two bodies: the man and woman joined making
them a perfect magnet, incapable of coming loose.
She chased him; she sat on his face; she hung by
her knees, hinged upside down on the wire and,
crouching, he gratified her with his finger, while she
rocked back and forth in the air, her arms outspread,
like spiders at play.

Hornette was doing a headstand on Harvey's own
head, repeating his seated posture in a mirror image.
The tumblers had gone off. They were replaced by a
lion act, six growlers on red stools making mauling
motions with their paws at the naked girl with the
whip and chair. I could not bring myself to photograph
them licking her, and I looked away when she pulled
their tails. But I had six tries at them lunging through
her legs and rubbing and lifting her as they passed
sleekly under the arch of her thighs.

Flesh had never been mocked like this; bravery and
invention and skill had never looked so futile. The
laughter was a devilish whooping of encouragement.
I looked through the lighted smoke in the noisy pit and
saw degraded artists and their maniacal patrons burning with pain and pleasure.

I knew there could be nothing beyond this. My last
picture showed a row of men, Papa among them, on
their feet behind a table holding the remains of their
pig dinner, jugs, and bones; and damnation on their
faces and on the tent wall near their heads, like
smoke, the crooked shadow of Harvey skewering
Hornette. The picture was partly accidental: I was
photographing a sorry cry.

Yet I was calm. Pictures are supposed to reflect
the photographer's mood, but nothing could have been
further from my somber mood than this frenzy.

Though I had caught my breath more than once, the only sound I made was the barely audible click of my Speed Graphic's blink.

I had never felt more alone. I had found what I was looking for; and what Hornette had said was true — it was indescribable. The speaker heaves images around, his telling simplifies the truth until simplicity makes it a lie: words are toys. But my camera saw it all, and my photographs were memory. With equipment far clumsier than words, my trap for available light, I could portray what was unspeakable. And now I had the ultimate picture, a vision of hell.

I couldn't face them after that — not Papa, not any of them. It only remained for me to develop and print the pictures and hang them over my name and await celebration. I left that night, before the circus folk got back to Mrs. Fritts's: a taxi to St. Pete and the train to New York.

I spent five days and nights in my darkroom at the hotel, processing the stacks of negatives and printing them. They were even better than I expected: I had snapped a sturgeon and come out with pictures of caviar. I knew when I delivered that portfolio to the Camera Club that it would cause a sensation. Anger is a knowledge of failure; I was happy, calmer than I had ever been. My part as a photographer ended when the pictures were out of my hands — then they belonged to the world. I wanted that, but I wanted more.

20

Love's Mirror

I WAS innocent for the last time, and shivering with cold. The weather contradicted my dream: was there significance in this chilly reality? I had seen myself arriving on a hot evening in dry moonlight; a whisper of wind; a landscape banked like a room. But in my hurry to reach my brother I had boarded a night train in New York after delivering my Florida pictures to the Camera Club. The canal crossing from Onset to Bourne, a mile of metaphor, confounded me by plunging me into dark early-morning mist. The Cape was imprisoned in freezing sea-fog, and dawn was far off. The spikes of mist continued until we were halfway to Yarmouthport — Sandwich or thereabouts — where it began to lift on the crewcut marshes and revealed in flecks of escaping light nature's frostbitten eyesores.

The Cape was bare and looked assaulted. It was that naked spell in late autumn between the last fall of leaves and the first fall of snow. Damp fields in Barnstable, an exposed farm house in Cummaquid, a frail soaked landscape of harmed hills and squashed grass and sunken meadows. In this stalled season, without muffling foliage or insulating snow, the brooks were louder, the rasp of crows noisier, and the sea-moan a despairing lament some distance inland through the dripping fingers of naked trees. That amplified racket, and the excluding cold, made me a stranger.

In those years, Hyannis was one street — a white church, a post office, a filling station, ten shops. That wet morning its off-season look was gooseflesh and senility, and it wore its shreds of fog like a mad old bride in a torn veil. It jeered at my homesickness and reminded me that home is such a tragic consolation of familiar dullness — that tree, this fence, that shrinking road.

Yet I was as happy as a clam. The photographer's habitual impulse is to go on shooting, despite her incredulity. The camera — her most private room — must be used for memory. But I had taken care of that. On my Florida sojourn I had found the limits of the eye and I believed there was no more to see on earth. I had done air, earth, fire, water, and flesh, and now I could dispose of the world as I had disposed of photography and Blanche and Papa — my obsession, my rival, my patron. What I saw of Hyannis looked ridiculous and insubstantial, but with Orlando all things were possible. I was determined to begin again. It only remained for him to embrace me, for a return home was a return to childhood: a beginning.

I sat in Mr. Wampler's old taxi — a beach wagon with wood paneling on the outside — my camera in my lap, my hands over its eye. We passed CLOSED FOR SEASON and SEE YOU NEXT YEAR signs. I was lucky. I knew this: we are offered not one life but many, and if we are alert we can seize a second or third. Sorrow is for those who expect too much from one; who, having exhausted all the possibilities of a single life, turn inward and refuse to see that schizophrenia is merely a mistake in arithmetic. When I heard someone described as a split personality I thought, *Only a schizo?* Why choose two lives when so many are available in us? My life as a photographer was over — there were no more pictures to take — but I had other lives in me, and there would always be others as long as I was in love. Wasn't love the chance to lead another's life and to multiply his by your own?

With Orlando I could be anyone I wished. It was

the feeling I had known as a child, a longing but-
tressed by hope, and during that brief ride out to
Grand Island from the railway station I felt a tide
of blood batter my heart and at last a great warmth
— though the day was bleak; and a blossoming of
optimism — though the mist at the windows had
turned to pissing rain. I was drenched in a freshet of
joy as we bumped over the sand sludge that rutted the
road.

There was the letterbox stenciled PRATT and the
house snug on its own stretch of coast and surrounded
by pines. Behind it, where the bare orchard began,
was the looming windmill with its sails anchored, and
some straggly dead geraniums blowing in the window
boxes. And a maroon car parked near the house: Orlando's Hudson.

"This is far enough."

"Can't stop here," said Mr. Wampler. Mr. Wampler
had a froggy voice; a tobacco-chewer, he spat often
and inaccurately; he was known as "peculiar." He
jerked his thumb at my peepshow in the back of the
beach wagon. "Can't carry it all that way — not with
my back."

"Stop the car," I said. "I want to walk."

"Too damned much to carry —"

"Leave it here by the letter-box."

"The rain'll raise hell with it." He put on his
"peculiar" face: puzzlement, glee, incomprehension.

"I don't give a hoot about the rain. I don't need
this stuff anymore."

Mr. Wampler was still protesting as I paid him. I
heard the thud of my trunks hitting the roadside as
I made my way up the long drive toward Orlando.
Instead of using the knocker, I let myself in with my
key, and I saw my hand trembling to turn it. I pushed
the door open and waited for some responsive sound
of welcome. But there was only the grumble of the taxi
dying on the road, and the regular slap of the sea,
waves emptying on our length of beach.

My dream had been flawed. I knew even then I

had been deceived by its moony romance. I was cold. It was a weakly lighted morning, with a storm pushing at the house. My moonlit windmill was fanciful. I corrected my dream: I would find him here, in the house. And he *was* here — there was his car, parked under the leafless birch.

I stepped in and slammed the door, walked from the parlor to the kitchen. Dishes in the sink and a smell of coffee: hope. I went up the backstairs and groped down the dark hall trying the doors, opening them left and right. Then I was at the front of the house again and looking back at the hall brightened with all the doors open. Not a sign of him. The rain simpered monotonously on the windowpanes, the wind sniffed at the eaves.

Of course! He had gone out. He had risen, made his bed, had a coffee, and gone for a walk in the hope that I would be here when he returned. Orlando loved rough weather. I made my way to the parlor and laughed out loud — a great hollow yuck — when I noticed that I was still wearing my huge camera. I had grown so used to its weight and the strain of its strap I hadn't felt it. I did not unharness myself, but rather relished its tender and useless weight.

The parlor mirror showed me this businesslike person which, even as I gazed, I ceased to believe in. And it was then — my image fading almost to transparency — that I saw its reflection.

It was movement, it was white, and it appeared as a little flash in the windmill at the depths of the mirror. A swatch of hair, a hand, a face; I could not tell. But the sudden warmth of this tiny signal stirred a creature in me, and it stretched and shook itself and blinked as I brought my face close to the glass for more. My dream had made me cautious, but this was as I had imagined it: the beckoning stroke of light — he was there, he was waiting, through the looking glass, in the windmill.

I woke from this pause and ran through the house, out the back door and squelched across the grass of

the sodden lawn. But even as I ran I was holding
back. I had waited so long for this — contained my
innocence for so many years — I kept myself from
rushing to the windmill's narrow porch and bursting
in. My habit of innocence was its own restraint, and
the stinging rain from the low cloud slowed me. I was
terrified by what I knew was about to happen, as if I
were seeing a fuse sparking toward the cylinder of a
bomb and anticipating the boom in willful deafness.

And for the first time in my life I knew real fear, a
corrosion in my brain that had eaten to a core of
panic, shrieking *No! Give up! Go back!* Frightening
me with images of insane joy, drooling thunderclouds,
the flooded beach, and showing me risk in the great
high sails of the windmill — the blades shuddering
and the spit of raindrops sizzling on the windows of
the black tower. All the trees pulled at my hair and
light was bleeding from my eyes as I fought my way
to the wall.

So I did not go in, and I was weeping before I
raised myself to the spattered window and saw him.
He was on his knees, the veins standing out on his
forehead, marble and blood, in a posture of furious
pagan prayer, his mouth fixed in demand. There were
clawmarks on his shoulders. He might have been
swooning, dying in a fit, he looked so tormented.

His reflection blazed on the floor, a white shadow
struggling under him, his double heaving at him. This
was my dream exactly: the two bodies creased, light
on light. I raised my knees and clasped my ankles at
the small of his back and thrust and we were almost
there, in a spasm of completion, one body. I twined
my hands on his neck and lifted to press myself
against him and print my body on his. It was better,
wilder than I had imagined, and it refuted the conceit I had carried home about nothing more to see,
for there was more and more, a limitless vision that
mocked my certainty. The eye was a palace and the
world inexhaustibly lovely. I was humbled — terrified
— and then by an old reflex I was seeing it all

through the intense light of my Third Eye; and at last I understood that it was not me panting against him and raising my throat for him to kiss — not me, but Phoebe.

She called out and the next instant passed into him with a sob and was lost: they were one. Throughout, a clicking had sustained me. But each click was a subtraction of light and finally my feeble effort to see caused a last click and I was blind.

And yet, as if sighted, I went back to the house, to my room, and put my camera down. I hadn't stumbled. I hardly knew what had happened. Everything was in order. I heard the rain, the waves breaking on the beach, my gasps. But my doubt would not leave me — something was undone. To the mirror, then. I took four steps to the far wall and gazed. And tried again. It was hopeless. I had no face.

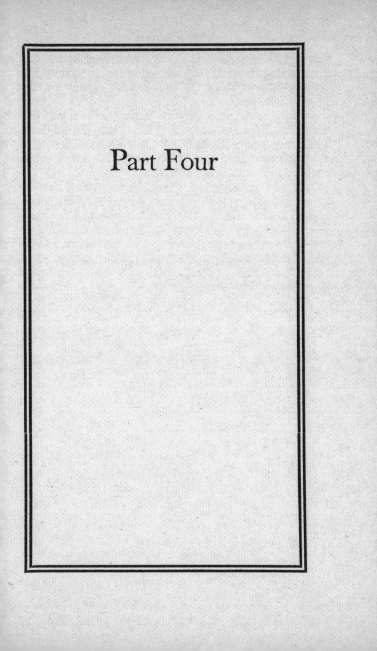

Part Four

Part Four

[21]

Blindman's Buff

THE TELEPHONE was ringing again, a clanging that caused an itch in my finger joints, the tip of my nose, my tongue. My eyes were in mourning. Blindness, the black sparks of light in its infancy, had stimulated my other senses, given me a responsive circuit of naked nerve ends to compensate for my blindfold. My scalp told me the temperature; my ears were photosensitive; I followed my nose. My retina was a blur of glaucous shoes, and beyond it, in my eye socket's depthless jelly, I swam and tried to surface. But I was slow, and though my being never ceased to throb with the slurred tattoo of time, I felt submerged and misunderstood. Imagine a lovely pellet of amber trapped in a dead fly. I was bashed with energy and suffered a continual buzz of sensation. Imagine a worm squeezed in its burrow, or a clam in a gale.

I was blind, but my body was alight.

"It's another cable from the Camera Club," said Orlando.

They had stopped delivering them; they were phoning them through. From across the room I could feel the receiver heating in Orlando's hand.

"That makes twenty," said Phoebe. "Aren't you thrilled?"

"What'll I tell them?" said Orlando.

"If it's money, say yes. If it's more congratulations, say thank you. If they haven't paid for a reply, forget it."

Phoebe said, "You're a hit, Maude! Won't Papa and Mama be pleased!"

They were still in Florida. What was keeping them? I said, "They'll die when they see me like this."

Phoebe was approaching me. I heard the crunch of her petticoat. I could practically taste her oncoming hair. She had started a warm draft that reached me when she was still ten feet away.

She said, "It's just temporary — eyestrain or something. Think of all the pictures you've taken. You'll see."

Her tone was confident. But Phoebe had bought me a pair of smoked glasses and urged me to wear them. I knew it was because she couldn't stand my staring eyes.

"Sure I will." They did not know why I was blind, what I had seen. My success had caused my breakdown: fame, overwork, exertion. It's only natural, they said. They had no idea that I had had two lives, that the one I had valued most had failed me, that it had nothing to do with my career.

"Won't she, Ollie?"

Now Orlando was approaching Phoebe. I heard his wink, like an aperture shutting; heard the skid of his cheek on hers, and their soft soap-bubble kiss, and his disguising heartiness: "You're going to be all right, cookie."

"I'm all right now," I said. "It's high tide. The gulls are sunning themselves on the roof. Scallops and mashed potatoes for lunch. And I love you in that green dress, Phoebe, with your new petticoat all stiff and crackly."

Orlando said, "How does it feel to be famous?"

I wanted to say, *Quit looking at me like that.* But I didn't want him to know that in our games of Blindman's Buff I had learned to see.

I said, "Remarkable."

Blindness was not oblivion — not here, at home. I knew every inch of the house, every chair and table, the position of the radio, the ashtrays, the clock, the nap of every carpet. Experience was the same as sight, and my blindness made the touch and smell of the house much keener. I could walk from room to room without faltering or sticking my hands out. And my blindness made me see what my pictures never had — that it was a creaking wreck of a place, with musty and moth-infested corners, a cupboard of family intimacies. Nothing had changed in the house, but I had not understood its secrets until now. In a way, I had been blind before. I ought to have seen, years ago, that Orlando and Phoebe were lovers. But, then, I'd had only my eyes.

All the pictures I had taken were diminished by what I discovered to be true. I hadn't begun to be a photographer. I had once thought, when I had done blind old Mrs. Conklin and Slaughter the piano tuner, that blindness was serene, like sleep. But it was not that at all. It was ceaseless vision, a babble of voice: the floors spoke, the walls, the potted plants, the books on their shelves, every phase of daylight — nothing was more audible than dawn, or Orlando's look of pity, or Phoebe's skin. Shouts and whispers; and each sound was a vivid picture, reminding me that I had seen nothing.

I remained shut in. I was in the ultimate darkroom, my body. It is every desperate soul's best refuge, and its darkness gave it a startling size, the dimensions of a cathedral, and the iron and stone echoes of an oubliette. So my body seemed a camera obscura conceived on a vast scale — not the hot little chamber I had sometimes dwelled in, but a great thing, with space for the most complete pictures, memory's cyclorama towering at the back of my mind. But this one had no pinhole, no meniscus lens. It was in utter darkness, a total absence of light, the original darkroom, before the slightest puncture of violation.

Sealed by this virginity I ought to have been wrapped in silence, entombed and mummified by my thwarted sensuality, and remorsefully lonesome. But I wasn't. I had remained motionless in my chair; I had heard the distant whispers saying *shock* and *breakdown*. I knew the words — they went with "nerves," they made you cry, they embarrassed your family. You were pitiful. You couldn't cope. You apologized. You said, "I don't know what's got into me." You were drowning: everything had gone black.

I shed many tears before I realized that I had been turned inside out. I was restored. This darkness revealed like light. The victim of a breakdown is speechless. The vocabulary of despair is so limited; indeed, despair is the end of language, merely sobs and babytalk. And here visions begin. The pictorial faculty, the mind's picture palace, has nothing to do with language, and in an inward way the images came so fast I could barely get a fix on them. I had been deceived by my eye; I was not deceived by my blindness. All my senses but one informed the pictures. There was in my vision a purity and sharpness found only in the symphonies of deaf composers and the eloquent monologues in the minds of dumb statesmen.

Blindness is not simply a loss of sight, a shade drawn on the world. It is a void. It makes you vanish. You are invisible to yourself. Its onset is darkness, within and without, like the start of the long swim from the womb where one's suffocated soul bawls out of terror. Much worse than the outer darkness is this inner state of gloom which seems deaf and mute and everlasting and lifeless. I couldn't reason. I had turned into a bat, and if — as I imagined — I killed myself, I would bleed spurts of ink. Blind things were blind inside and out: the clam a muscle of sand and sinew, the worm crammed with dirt.

I was sludge.

"What happened?" Orlando had said that morning. "Why are you looking like that?"

I had no reply. I lay shut and sealed on the floor like an ugly box without an opening. For that was how they found me — in my room, with rain on my face, stiff and sightless. I had just banged down and didn't care.

Then, with the first phone call from New York, I began to stir, like a bean-shaped fetus in a sac. I kicked timidly to discover I was buoyant. I rummaged in the darkness and gasped. I could make out shapes — shades of black — inviting passages, praises carrying from unexpected quarters. I risked the journey over nearly familiar paths made wonderfully dangerous and exciting by their new feel. A great river ran through me and I followed its fury to a landscape of crystalline voices raised in sweet song. It was a world of the permissible, a kingdom without demons or monsters, better than the one I had known. Children played here, the boy and girl in their nakedness; there were lambs; it was the world before the fall. It was dark, but the darkness did not threaten. I absorbed it and found it kind. I had tunneled serenely beyond fear to be reborn and to recover my innocence. My blindness had taught me to see.

It wasn't a miracle. It was another game in which, like the game of Hide and Seek that taught me to use a camera, Orlando was the principal player.

Blindman's Buff started in the simplest way, after I had sat desperately in my darkness for a sorry week or more. Then the phone rang — the Camera Club ecstatic about my Florida pictures, Orlando crying, "You've done it, cookie!" From an ounce of warm ash black light was kindled in me, enough of a clue to give me hope. By degrees I tested my space, and what I perceived mattered more to me than anything I had ever seen, because it had none of the evasions of conventional light. It was a lesson in seeing, the teaching that light misleads: light is fickle, unreliable, and lying. I came to know that I was inhabiting in my blindness a camera obscura of palatial proportions. I had not lost the visible world; I contained it.

Orlando and Phoebe's footfalls, their voices, their touches. How much more telling they were than their vagrant images in the pictures I had taken. Their voices buffeted me, but their footfalls were explanatory, passionate, apologetic; attempting to conceal, they were thorough, and the completeness of this sneaking gave them away. I listened; my senses were wide open; and so, in play, I rehearsed my body for seeing.

I had been fooled before, handicapped by my eyes and made into a vegetable — a great deluded root. But now I gloried in my rebirth, in the roaring of timbers in the house, the warping of joists which caused the woodwork to yelp. My ears were returned to other sounds: the restless grass, the passions of air, the wind's fingers at the wall, the grieving of pine needles, the sweet paradoxes of time too subtle for photography — the future kissing the past. And all around me the footfalls of Orlando and Phoebe. They had no idea of how receptive I had become, how I had heard an uncomplaining fly dying at the window, or the damp piano twisting a fraction to give his death a dirge — like the plangent chord of a plucked harp; or the folding of gulls' wings as they settled on the roof to mourn, or — at that same moment — the whisper of snow- flakes sifting like crumbs into the yard. Nothing was hidden from me. Sound was movement; sound bruised the air.

The game had begun.

"Going shopping, Maude!" Phoebe said.

Harumph, went the front door.

"I'll see to the car while she's gone," Orlando said.

Pshaw went the back door.

To a sighted person this might have been the end of it. They had said they were going: they were gone. Previously, I would have hurried to my darkroom to potter with my enlarger.

But in this darkroom there was much more. There were tramplings, the speaking feet of two people, not far away.

Seated — not moving — I followed them.

The muffled footfalls reached me as narration and I was able to recreate a picture of the breathless pair rounding the house, squelching down the muddy path, scuffing the windmill's steps. Their movements exposed not only them, but the house, the path, the garden, the sky, the sea behind them, the watchful windmill I vowed never to enter. They were the necessary figures in a landscape that made it at once complete and visible.

The bolt was shot in the door. Thuds. The scrape of clothes being removed; the sighs of discarded garments being crushed. There came a steady chafing of skin that was at first dim and scarcely audible until, like gold burnished with a velvet pad, it brightened to a spangle of sound, a chime that rang in a glittering echo. And it started murmurs, the discovery of pleasure in pain, the slow enjoying grunts of an ancient dance with a smothered drum.

Then the house trembled from the movement in the windmill, and the heat was more than I could bear. A sob of effort coaxed a cry of relief, and such a flash of light it was impossible for me to believe they had survived it.

A wing-shaped shadow passed over me and left me in a thunderous chill.

"It's only me," said Phoebe, a half hour later, pretending she had returned.

That was one instance of the game. There were others. In the house one day, hearing Orlando go upstairs, I gave him time and then followed him to his room. I knocked. He let me in, and there I felt the vibration of a third presence.

"Maude," he said.

He was in an old jacket. She was naked, lying on his bed, her knees drawn up, her breasts gathered between her arms, her hands over her face.

"Is that you, Ollie?"

"I was just reading." He reached for a book

He was standing in a screening position between me and the bed. He let me bump him to show me I could go no further.

"Read to me." But I was stalling. I had begun to doubt that she was there. That was the game: I had to find her — to establish that they were together. After that first clear impression my vision clouded and now I was not sure.

He said, "I'll be down in a minute."

His lungs were choked with apprehension. He straightened, took a step and gave her away: her fragrance tumbled past him to me.

"Mind if I sit down?"

"I'm way behind in my reading, cookie."

He was gallantly protecting her. She was lying on a thick blanket. I could sense its roughness against her skin, and more: I could feel the heat from the places his lips had reddened on her.

"Where's Phoebe?"

"Out," he said, too quickly. "I don't know."

Curled there, she was the shape of a fallen leaf.

I had won. I did not feel victorious.

Blindman's Buff: what images! But he should not have been playing — he was supposed to be at Harvard. I knew he was taking advantage of the folks' absence. He did not know how I could see. I saw them most clearly when they were naked; I could hear them embrace three rooms away; even their glances jarred the air like a jewel-flash on the cut faces of turning gems. And sometimes, sitting alone and listening to the radio, I would be warmed, as if the clouds had parted and the sun splashed my soul: I would know they were in each other's arms, the posture of rescue, the lover with his lost half.

To the stairs, softly; down the hall to the vibrant room — a winter evening, but only they were in darkness. I had moved through the house in my own daylight. Their darkness deceived them — they thought they were safe.

"Ollie?"

I stroked the silence.

"Phoebe?"

The silence purred like a cat.

I paused in the doorway. If I'd had eyes I would not have seen them. But there they were, hoping I would

go away. He lay on top of her, his mouth open on her
nipple, his tongue stiffening it. Rescue: I watched from
the shore. I was buffeted by their love and I marveled
at how perfect they were, sharing blood, bone, and
hair.

"Is there anyone here?"

Nose between paws, the silence slumbered. Yet
how clearly I could see them — her soft cheek, his
ribs, the scratches on his shoulders, their mutual grip
beneath the seam where their bodies were joined.
They were frail, falling through their darkness. Perhaps I frightened them; perhaps they took pleasure in
the game. I envied them too much to pity them.

Had I brought them together? It didn't matter —
they had delivered me from my own darkness. I was
no longer tricked by sunsets, the lowings of pine
woods, the ocean's endless march to the shore, the
beguiling drum-roll of the picturesque. I saw beyond
the sunset to the cold zone of colorless sky, and beneath the trooping ocean to its vastness and old slime;
and what astonished me was its wondrous terror, a
glissade deepening into infinity. I was ashamed of myself for having believed there could be an end to
art.

Once, when I'd had eyes, I thought there was no
more to see. Now I was atomized by sensation. Not
the pencilings of primitive sight, or the world in two-
dimensional silhouette, or the mannered smoothness of
the so-called photogram; but a hubbub of color moving like a torrent of quicksilver through me, the in-
wardness of things, the sap in trees rising toward
the chirps in their branches, tides of air mounting the
windows, the pulse fluttering in a speck of dust. At the
center of everything was turmoil, the gas of chaos giving light.

The natural world was revealed to me and all its
mysteries were as plain as day. What was most chas-
tening was that I had thought I had done it all before:
the orchard, the beach, the house, the road, Orlando
and Phoebe. No — they were newly lit to their inmost

fiber. I saw to their core, and what I had taken to be
the most placid object — a chair or a plank — was a
mass of lighted splinters in a moment of wholeness. I
was a particle of this world and matched it exactly. I
could see passion in a stone, hunger in a hose-pipe,
my own immortality in the feeblest moth.

Somewhere within me an angel knelt over a gutter-
ing candle and kissed it and gave it a flame with her
lips; and in the darkroom of my body I was ravished
by visions.

Firebug

MEANWHILE, I was a sensation. If there is anything more effective to celebrity than one's public appearance it is one's conspicuous absence. I was visible because I was missing. To know that was to know the essence of perception — photography's deepest secret. And it was part of the paradox my blindness had taught me about Orlando and Phoebe: they had been behind a smokescreen when they were nearest to me, and I hadn't had a real glimpse of their love — the fire I had set — until I was blind.

I had not shown my face in New York. On that brief stopover from Florida to the Cape, when I stayed in my hotel darkroom to process the plates, I had simply shoved my work through the Camera Club's letterbox and boarded the train. I wanted more; I got it. And after my shock and subsequent blindness I had refused to speak on the telephone. It was Orlando who had authorized my one-man show at the club. The organizers had made repeated requests for me to be there, but it had opened without me. It had caught and blazed. The reviews were full of enthusiastic flapdoodle, the newspapers asked for my picture to print beside articles about me.

No portraits of me existed. I vowed not to allow myself to be photographed. I kept that vow, and later I rationalized it as: There is not one who can do me but me. The only person who understood this was, interestingly enough, not a photographer at all, but the American sportsman and storyteller, Ernest Hemingway. He said it was a goddamned noble vow and similar to the warrior's — rather than be killed by his enemy he rushes on his own sword. Ernest blew his brains out because he said the Feds were after him. The biographers certainly were, and I think his suicide was a version of this mad, proud samurai impulse.

No one saw me, no one knew my face. That blank became an essential part of my fame. No one remembered — and I was glad — how I had wanted to set the world on fire. I had been working on that combustion for years, and now that it was nicely alight I did not go near to warm myself. I let my mystery precede me, while I stayed home and rubbed my hands. When the requests for my portrait stopped, I was asked to visit; they would hold a special ceremony for me. Where was I? Orlando relayed my answer: unobtainable.

For at that moment of fame, as my pictures were being admiringly scrutinized and I praised for my sight, I was stone blind and at my lowest point, deaf as a post and mute as well, in the first and blackest phase of my so-called breakdown.

Then I started to play, and when I emerged from this darkness by winning the games of Blindman's Buff I saw that I was whole. Though I had caught sight of Orlando, I had lost him; and yet I had found the world. And I had, myself, been discovered. Waking, I realized I was in demand. Dealers, editors, auctioneers, jobbing patrons rang at all hours to ask me to work for them. Would I go to Europe, where a war was beginning? Would I walk up and down the earth, whacking away with my camera? They offered me permission, protection: I could do anything I damn well pleased as long as they had a claim on me.

But I didn't need them. The exhibit itself was proof of that. They had only to look at my pictures to see my contempt for patrons, and how this whole Pig Dinner series constituted an attack on the pimping known as patronage. I hadn't needed them when I was unknown — how could I possibly need them now that I was on top? The naked truth was that, like all pimps, they wanted to get into my act — not to enhance my work but to justify theirs. They persisted in their requests and tried to engage me.

Nor was this all. There was a bizarre aspect to my fame as well. Although my pictures quite clearly had the liquefaction, the "drowning quotient" that made them "Pratts," I was now pestered by people who wanted me to do other things — crazy things, pointless, unworthy, demeaning, vulgar, or plain silly.

It made Jack Guggenheim seem like an angel. Every person of achievement gets these proposals: Madame Curie must have been asked a thousand times to open drugstores or lend her name to brands of aspirin, Dr. Schweitzer to endorse mosquito repellent, or William Faulkner to write the copy for bourbon ads. I know the whisky people were always after Ernest to pose with a bottle of their juice in his hand. Most people are now too young to remember how Eleanor Roosevelt promoted Blue Bonnet Margarine on television, but the Shakespearean actor who's reduced to doing a number about the Polaroid instant-print camera — photography's answer to frozen pizza — is a good example of what I mean. The worst wanted to involve me in the selling mechanism, making me a fundraiser if not an outright accomplice in extortion: take pictures of cars, women wearing false eyelashes, men in expensive pajamas, people smoking cigarettes. With my first artistic success under my belt, my genius was complimented by a manufacturer of ladies' underwear, who promised me five thousand dollars to photograph his latest range of bras and girdles.

"Never," I said.

I was offered the anonymous hackwork of photojournalism, sports and news, travel features, fashions, family portraits — Junior in his sailor-suit, Sis and her hubby, Buddy in his khakis, Mom and Dad beaming. No, thank you. One Hyannisport millionaire demanded I do his daughter's wedding pictures: he had the cash, I had the camera — what was wrong with me?

They assumed I was for hire. This intense recruitment, with its origins in patronage, is a feature of American cultural life; it is related to the grant, the fellowship, the endowment, and every other boondoggle associated with sugar-daddy creativity. It was the height of insolence, presuming on my imagination. I did not even reply to them. They didn't know who they were dealing with. Anyway, I was blind!

And nearly every day, the Camera Club in New York rang to ask when I would be free to make my visit.

"You really should go down there," said Orlando, who I knew was trying, with the best will in the world, to get rid of me.

"Like this?" I faced him and lifted off my dark glasses and showed him my blind staring eyes.

"Why not?" he said. "You could bask."

"I'd just bump into walls."

"Don't give me that," he said. "I've been watching you, cookie. You don't miss a trick."

Phoebe said, "I don't know how she does it."

Instead of replying directly, I said, "Your slip is showing, Phoebe."

I heard her tug and snap it into place.

All this happened in the misty weepy weeks of November, when Orlando should have been at Harvard. But he stayed on; Mama and Papa remained in Florida, unaware — as far as I knew — of my success; and Orlando and Phoebe made love in the windmill at least once a day. Though it excited me to be on hand, there was something distinctly melancholy about us three still inhabiting the family house, like children who couldn't outgrow their youthful ghosts. Because we hadn't left home we remained children to each other. Consequently, those phone calls from New York seemed an extraordinary intrusion. The more Orlando kidded me about the bonanza at the Camera

Club and all those requests for photojournalism
("They might send you to Mashpee!"), the more I
reminded him that he was playing hooky and might
just flunk his bar exam.

"I work better here," he said. "And don't worry —
I'm keeping up with my reading."

"I make sure he's on the ball," said Phoebe.

I said, "So I see."

And though it drizzled, and the raindrops hit the
withered grass with a sound like unvarying grief, and
the fog rolled in from the sea and cast its wet shreds
around the house and made the starlings roost and
drip — there were, suspended in this funereal curtain
of dampness, threads of brilliant light; and all around
me the magic of fresh fire.

But early one morning I was quickened by a pre-
monitory hysteria, an urgent intimation of change that
was a draft blowing across my soul. I knew when I
went down to breakfast that Orlando was no longer
with us.

As usual, I betrayed nothing of what I felt.

"You're up bright and early," I said.

Phoebe, who was at the table, had not spoken, and
she had grown so accustomed to my second sight that
she didn't even ask how I knew she was in the room.
But I knew more: she was alone, in her nightie, her
hair still braided, and she was biting on one of the
twisted ends.

"Coffee?" she said.

She had been crying. Her tears had dried, but I
could see the rags of sorrow in her, a destitution of
spirit. Beneath that svelte exterior was a waif with
goosepimples and chilblains, a poor abandoned child
shivering in the gray morning.

She tried to be bright. She said, "You're lucky you
can't see what an awful day it is."

"Not too bad," I said. "There was a snow flurry
last night. It looks pretty in the yard, like moonlight
on pelts of speckled ermine. And that frost on the
window, like ferns etched on the glass. It's a nice old

contraction, all this ice. But don't worry — it's going to be sunny. I can feel it in my bones."

She was looking at me in astonishment. "Golly," she said, "you're amazing."

She didn't mention Orlando. But her grief showed in the way she crunched her toast and had difficulty swallowing it.

At nine-fifteen the telephone rang.

"It's those people again," she said, holding the receiver against her stomach so she wouldn't be heard.

"If it's the Camera Club hand it over. Otherwise hang up."

"Just a minute," she said into the instrument. She gave it to me, wrinkling her nose. She was puzzled.

A wide-awake man at the other end said, "We were wondering if we can expect you down here anytime. We'd be delighted to — "

"Listen carefully," I said. "I'm leaving this morning for New York — "

Phoebe said, "No, Maude, you can't!"

" — and I'm staying at the Algonquin tonight. Meet me in the lobby tomorrow at nine and I'll put in an appearance at the show. No publicity, no pictures, no autographs, no speeches."

"If you gave us a little more time we could make an occasion of it."

"Save your money," I said and clapped the phone down.

Phoebe was staring fixedly at me. Knowing I was blind, she did not attempt to conceal her alarm, and this made it all the easier for me to read her face.

"Cheer up, Phoebe."

"Please don't go."

"Orlando will look after you."

Brave girl: she didn't say that he'd gone. She shut her eyes and held her breath and hurried into the kitchen with her hands over her face so I wouldn't hear her cry.

Mr. Wampler saw me to the station in his beach wagon.

And I learned something else: a pair of eyes were handy in New York City, but not essential. The departing passengers steered me out of Grand Central and I followed my nose to the street. As I didn't have much luggage —no camera, no peepshow — I decided to walk to the Algonquin.

But against my will I was seized by a jabbering taxi driver and whisked to the hotel. My secret was safe — all hotel guests are treated as if they are blind: Sign on the bottom; This way, madam, watch the step; Right in here; If there's anything we can do to make your stay more comfortable just sing out; Your light switch is here, your bathroom over there, the key's in the door.

It is the nature of rooms to retain. There is no such thing as an empty room. They have memories. I was not alone in this one; I was ducking images — the boiler noises of the traffic below, the honks and growls in the walls, the misery in the closet, the shushings of the pipes. It was more than I could bear, and I decided to leave not out of loneliness but because the room was too crowded. Outside, trying to get my bearings, I knew what all visiting strangers suspect but hesitate to put into words: that I had forgotten something. Most people, in their anxiety and confusion, reverse this. They cling to the belief that they are taking something away. But no; I knew I was leaving something irrecoverable of myself behind in the room.

The sidewalks were no challenge. They were precisely measured, and the whole city seemed as familiar as home. New York was a perfect place for a blind person, a masterpiece of right angles, all walls and squares on a grid of streets — a labyrinth without a monster. At one corner, bored by waiting for the light to change, I jaywalked. Then I was approached by a heavy man who gave me a sarcastic sigh. He paused; there was that delicious groan of twisting leather and a more severe clank of metal chains.

He said, "What are you, *new* around here?"

"Sorry, officer."

"Wait for the light, lady."

Wait for the light! Just another futile approach to the art of photography. But I didn't say that I had waited and seen the insignificance of light; that energy was elsewhere. I frowned ashamedly to incriminate myself, and when he released me with another gasp of exasperation, giving his leathers another wrench, I walked on, west, to indulge myself in the old thrill of being on an ocean liner.

It was better than I remembered. The city cruised along at a good clip, putting the gulls to flight, startling the pigeons; and watchers on the passing shore and smaller vessels signaled with toots at the stately ship trumpeting toward the sea. I strolled along the cobblestone deck, giving my brain an airing and delighting in the great swerve of the voyaging city. Behind me, among the giant funnels which were a shadowy heaviness this winter afternoon, I heard the shouts of people, and I could distinguish between the murmurs of salts for whom shipboard here was home, and the fearful squeals of her joy-riders.

The last blaze of reflected sun slipped away and, in the chill that was night falling, voices carried distress to me. Without a further sound, the ship capsized, and sank, and what mattered was not the ship anymore, but the emptiness around it. I saw what I had never seen before, columns of empty air and the tall watch-towers rising in silence. Below, the voices were whispers and the toiling cars suffocated grunts — nothing compared to the soundless heights that made every human noise a watery glug. The city was a steepness of remarkable air masses shaped by the specific columns of granite and fitted like a Jungle gym in impressive bars of voiceless smoke that had displaced the city. The city was unpeopled; it was its spaces, chutes of air, the sky snug in a mammoth mold. It is the secret of canyons, which are not solid things but occasions — amphitheaters for tremendous dramas of empty space. It vanished underfoot. It was without substance. Being alone I could subside in it, have a good night's sleep, and rebuild it to my own design after breakfast.

I was a bit sorry I hadn't brought my camera along, because the next morning I hung out the window and heard two men quarreling. I'm on the ninth floor; the street's full of traffic, the sidewalks swarming with people, and no one's paying any attention to the quarrelers down the block. One of those chance compositions: apparent order, procession of car roofs, patterns of windows and walls; solemn unity of pedestrians and shoppers undone by two men at each other's throat — and they're not going anywhere. Ideal angle: gap of Times Square, and a narrowing again, and then a chink — New Jersey — a slice of light counterbalancing the brutes at the bottom. And the slant of morning sun is a bonus, tidying the concrete and making the cars a file of cockroaches. The rest of the people are exaggerated by their carbon shadows attached to foreshortened bodies and printed diagonally in wedges and stripes up the long street.

At that very moment, some pretentious little shit was posing a noodle-naked girl in the broken window of an abandoned house, getting her tits into focus and thinking, *Study in Contrast,* click, click. *I'm a genius.*

I climbed in and closed the window and doused my swell picture, and after coffee and a bun went downstairs to wait for the man from the Camera Club. My bravado in front of Phoebe and my wish to conceal my blindness had made me say on the phone that I'd meet him in the lobby. But he had no idea what I looked like and I did not know his name. The Algonquin didn't have a real lobby even then. I took a seat behind the partition that separated the desk from the lounge area. Weeks before, I had removed the crystal from my watch. I touched the hands with my finger pads: ten to nine. I was sure that in his impatience to see me in New York, he'd be on time.

He — or rather they — were early. I heard a harsh whisper, "Wait," on the other side of the partition and the unmistakable sound of a plate being socked into a Speed Graphic.

I said loudly, "Put that thing down!"

There were mutters, a bustling, the suit-brushings and throat-clearings that precede introduction, and then: "Miss Pratt."

"I told you, no pictures."

"I wasn't going to do you." This was a different voice.

"Bunk."

"I can't tell you how pleased we are to see you," said the first man, and he sounded as if he meant it.

They introduced themselves as Randy Stranks and Fred Umlah. Randy, the one with the camera, was young; Umlah was the back number who had enthused at me over the phone. But they both did the seeing-eye dog routine, guiding me by my elbow, telling me to watch my step, indicating points of interest — this building, that bar.

"Filing cabinets," said Randy. "That's what these buildings are. Look at all those people hurrying in. There goes Urgent, and a couple of Confidentials. Him — he's Pending, definitely Pending —"

"Randy's little game," said Umlah.

But he kept it up. A person's yapping did more than make my head spin. It clouded my vision and finally blinded me and made me helpless. I thought: Perhaps everyone, not only the hotel guest, is treated as if he were blind. We let others do our seeing for us, so we never really learn to use our peepers. People were always trying to sell you their own versions of a place. If photography mattered it was only because so many people's seeing kept them in the dark. Randy's New York was not mine.

"Will you cut it out?" I finally said.

Umlah caught my tetchy tone and started to fawn. He said, "How does it feel to be famous?"

It was what Orlando had asked me. I had said, "Remarkable." But I wanted to give Umlah something to chew on, so I faced him and said, "How does it feel? Very exposed. It makes me feel incompetent and ugly — uglier than I am. It's a lesson in modesty. It's lonelier than failure. It's — say, is this city rather fraught today, or is it just my imagination?"

"Must be your imagination," said Umlah. "It's an average day in New York — frenetic, but who cares?"

"No," I said. "That sound."

"Which one!" screamed Randy, and he laughed: *Yaw! Yaw!*

"That. Sort of crackling — burning. Smell it? And those people yelling. Hear them?"

"It's just an average — "

"Wait a sec — fire engines," I said. "They're headed this way."

"What did I tell you?" said Umlah, in that nibbling and self-satisfied way that patronizing people digest their admiration. "Doesn't she have an amazing mind?"

"I'm not imagining it," I said. "I can hear them. And the fire's somewhere around here."

We were, by my reckoning, near the corner of Fifth Avenue and Forty-fifth Street, and having stopped on the sidewalk we were noticed. A crowd had begun to collect around us. I heard the mutters: *Some crazy dame, What's up?* and *Search me.*

"Shall we move on?" said Umlah in a whisper, clearly worried by the size of the crowd.

"I'm telling you, I smell smoke."

Someone said, "It's the dame with the glasses. She smells smoke."

And I heard a weird chattering in the crowd, a chuckle in one man's throat, an arsonist's lunacy: *Hoo-hoo.*

The engines were louder, but neither Umlah nor Randy — nor anyone in the crowd — appeared to hear them. I could tell they were watching me closely, as if I were going to throw a fit. I was the center of attention; no one heard or saw the confusion that was so close by.

Umlah said, "We'll be late."

But I stood my ground. My face was heating, my nose was full of greasy smoke, there were panicky screams in my ears. I whirled around and pointed: *"Fire!"*

There was a hush, a moment of curiosity — faces peering at mine — and then I heard, "There it is!" and "She's right!" and Randy said, "Hot dog!" and fumbled with his camera.

"Fire engines!" someone cried. The clanging was a block away.

Hoo-hoo.

"I've got to get a picture of this," said Randy.

"Hurry up," said Umlah.

Smoke was now pouring from the windows of the building across the street and filling the sky and turning the sun into a purple Necco wafer. I could hear glass shattering and whoops of excitement, but clearest of all was that solitary *hoo* of the goofball in the crowd. I listened and heard him sniffing and swallowing as he went *snark* and hoicked up the glue in his nose and gulped it down. Because this was so different from the cries of woe around me, it was amplified. I was able to make him out from his sinuses: the old black pea-jacket stinking of kerosene, the whiskery face, the tar on his teeth, the wild eyes goggling in thick glasses: a firebug.

"Let's go," said Umlah. "For God's sake!"

Randy was doing the arrival of the engines, the traffic jam, and now, as the ladder trucks were wheeled into position, the helmeted men in raincoats and floppy boots chopping the windows apart with axes. The jets of water had no effect on the fountains of flame — there was a splendid picture in the way the hoses seemed to feed the fire.

"There's some people up there!" said a man next to Umlah.

"Where?" said Randy, still jamming plates into his camera.

"Third floor," I said.

Still the firebug chuckled and snarked, and he

pressed forward to the rope that had been put up to contain the crowd. *Hoo-hoo*.

"Give me that thing," I said, and snatched Randy's camera.

Randy said, "I'll hold your glasses."

I had forgotten I was wearing my pair of opaque sunglasses. I pushed him aside before he could grab them. "I need them," I said. "Get out of my way." *Hoo*.

"What's she doing?" said Umlah.

Randy said, "She's shooting in the wrong direction, for one thing."

The chuckling firebug was three feet away and he was so interested in the blaze I was almost certain he had started it. He was breathing hard with pleasure; he did not see me. His mouth was open, he was thrilled, watching the action on tiptoe. I knew exactly how he felt: this, for him, was fame. He had stopped traffic and brought out five fire trucks; people were screaming and fainting; and the city was dark — he had blotted out the sun! It didn't matter to him that no one knew his name — if anything, his anonymity was part of his achievement. His face was dappled by fire, his hair was alight, and on his glasses were the reflections of crisscrossed ladders and men in rubber capes swaying on them, making their way to the flaming waffle-iron of windows. This laughing face in the grim crowd was my picture. He went *snark-snark, hoo-hoo*.

I took three shots of the firebug, and each time, the instant I clicked, I saw in a flash, literally that, the whole bright picture, in a sudden spurt, as if the irises of my dead eyes had opened and shut and admitted a jet of light that singed my mind and left a black burn-spot there. In this fleeting cusp of vision the man with the map of fire on his face, snarking. It startled me and I repeated it until three black stars danced in my eyes. It was what my sight had once been — creakily pictorial, like a child's scrawl — but so much less vivid than what my blindness had shown me, I gave it no further thought.

pressed forward to the pose that had Jeya out up to
confuse the crowd, Pino too.

"Give me that thing," I said, and snatched Randy's
camera.

Randy said, "I'll hold your glasses."

I had forgotten I had on my pair of opaque
sunglasses. I pushed them up before he could yank
them. "I need them," I said. "Get out of my way."

"What's she doing?" said Orlando.

[23]

Exposure

"YOU'RE DOING a land-office business," I said, after
we arrived at the Camera Club. There was a mob on
the stairs and more people inside, rattling their catalogues and shuffling around the room where the pictures were hung. The usual gallery phonies — horny
old men in berets hugging tragically pretty young girls
— plus students, housewives, shoppers, joy-riders,
mumblers, lens-lice. And in the air that din of appre-
ciation you hear at parties, the noise that seems a
special form of heat.

"They're all here for your show," said Umlah. "It's
been like this ever since we opened."

"Cash customers?"

"There's no entrance fee," he said.

"I mean, are they buying the pictures?"

Umlah said, "I suppose they would, if they were for
sale."

"Of course they are!" I snapped. "Don't tell me
you're not selling them."

"I had no idea," he said disgustedly, "no idea you
were doing this for the money."

"I do it for my health. It's expensive."

"I understood you enjoyed taking pictures."

"Back up," I said. "That's the oldest trick in the
book for exploiting artists — capitalizing on their
sense of fun. Anyway, what's it got to do with paying
the rent, wear and tear, overheads?"

228

Randy said, "We thought you were on a Guggen-heim."

"Fuck you, Jack — don't patronize me."

"Please," said Umlah. "What is it you want us to do?"

"You," I said, poking my finger at Randy, "you're playing with yourself. Lay off the pocket pool and go over and put price tags on them."

"I'll take care of that," said Umlah, sounding pretty shattered by my outburst.

"Yeah," said Randy. "I want to go upstairs and process these plates of the fire."

"We'd better price them together," said Umlah.

"That's easy," I said.

"There are quite a few of them."

"I always say, if you're vulgar enough to put a price on things you're vulgar enough to price them by size. Me, I do it by the inch. The eight-by-tens are a hundred apiece, anything smaller is sixty. There are a few big ones — I think we can ask a hundred and fifty for those."

Umlah's face was lit by indignation and greed, the hot twisted look of a celibate's lust: he was aroused by the money-value of my pictures. He said, "And where does that leave the club?"

"Ten percent for you."

"Twenty is standard."

"Okay, I'll split the difference — fifteen. I'm no Arab," I said. "But, my, you learn fast, Mister Umlah. I knew the minute I laid eyes on you that you were a practical man. Now let's get those prices on before everyone clears out."

"Come along with me, just to make sure I don't make any blunders," he said. "We may as well start at the beginning. Here — oh, this is a perfectly marvelous one — that porch scene."

What porch scene? I leaned forward and looked, and though I was aware of the wall returning my murmurs to me, and quite conscious of a group of admiring people nearby, I could not make out a picture for the life of me. I had had no difficulty perceiving the city, my hotel room, two men scrapping nine floors below, the fire in the building, or the arsonist. But the pictures were another story entirely: they were impossible to see. Indeed, as far as I was concerned, they were indistinguishable from the wall's featureless din.

"What do you say, Miss Pratt?"

The wall was pale green; a vein of stress ran down the plaster, splitting the paint; fingerprint whorls near the door, kickmarks on the baseboard, a horse hair prickled in an old brushstroke. But the picture? I couldn't tell whether it was big or small, dark or light. was it *Boarders*? Or Hornette on the glider at Mrs. Fritts's? Or what? I said, "Hadn't we better measure it?"

"Fred," said a man to my left, "mind if we tag along? We're doing a piece on Miss Pratt's show."

"That's up to Miss Pratt," said Umlah.

"Feel free," I said. But I was wondering how I was going to plow through the whole exhibition without revealing my blindness. So far, I had been lucky; but my pictures baffled me, and might betray me. I could not see them.

Umlah said, "I'd like you to meet Iris Clinch and Dick Shuggery. Reporters."

"Critics, actually," said Iris. "We're *Time-Life. Life*'s giving you a spread. We're going to use a whole raft of your pictures."

"First I heard of it," I said.

"Aren't you pleased?"

"Tickled pink," I said. "But there's a little question of copyright."

"We'll come to some agreement," said Shuggery, his voice all Crisco with confidence.

"Hold on — I don't do any horse-trading where my pictures are concerned. I call the shots around here, get it? If you don't see things my way" — which was ironic, because I couldn't see a blessed thing — "the deal's off."

Iris stiffened, probably thinking: The avaricious little so-and-so, ain't she ever going to be satisfied? *Life*'s giving her a spread!

She said, "We were hoping to buy some outright."

"You going into business?" I said. "Out of the question. You can buy these prints — hang them up and admire them, hide the cracks on your walls. But I keep the negatives and all reproduction rights. I've got to look after my interests, toots."

"You mean we can't use them?"

"Sure, on a one-time basis, for a fee, if you dig deep enough. But let's leave the dickering for later. We've got to get on with this pricing."

"Suit yourself," she said.

Shuggery said, "It's a truly amazing show. Something scandalous and at the same time very artistic. It's an unbeatable combination — genius vindicating the almost unlawful. The virtuosity in the outdoor shots, all those prehistoric swamps and dead trees, and the total aridity and nakedness of that banquet, sort of stylized savagery —"

"Shall we say a hundred dollars for this porch scene?" said Umlah.

"Fine," I said.

"In a sense," said Iris. "But — correct me if I'm wrong — there's something deeply European about them, old world and, oh, pagan. I'm talking about intensity, I guess — it's rare in American photography, which is so preoccupied with space, so naively naturalistic. But your landscapes have a terrific indoor quality — I mean, that foliage looks like parlor drapes and hunks of furniture and you've sort of hidden the people, haven't you? And, as Dick said, the banquet is breathtaking and, well, it's Roman — you've got a beautiful little grudge there. Maybe it's because I'm devoted to Brassai, but I never thought we could produce the same thing, the decadent skin-tones, the effect of squalid pleasure. Let's face it, Florida's not France — we can't match their old-fashioned rituals, but your photographs pass the hardest test of art —"

"Sixty?" said Umlah, moving along.

"All right by me," I said.

" — I mean, the toughest criterion. They're *news!* Dick and I think they're intimations of war."

"And sixty there," said Umlah, "and another sixty and a pair of hundreds."

"Slap on the tags," I said.

Shuggery sidled up to me. "Walker Evans was here the other day — *the* Walker Evans. Know what he said? Tell her, Iris."

Iris said, "You."

"He said, 'These are classics. I don't care who took them or how it happened, but this is art — it is experience. This photographer has broken the code and instead of simplifying it has translated the message into the calligraphy of art. Shapes, and beneath the shapes an intelligent pattern, and beneath that, flesh and blood — and behind it all, truth. It is pictorial language, the mirror we all have to pass through to see the world as it is. I will walk out of here a different man. Everyone who sees this will be affected. It is the highest art — the kind that changes your life. Nothing will look the same after this — the world will have a light in it that wasn't there before. A light, and of course a shadow. It helps me to understand religious art, it makes me want to get down on my knees.' That's what he said. Walker Evans."

Music to my ears, exactly what I had intended, if a bit florid in the retelling. But all I said was, "Sounds to me like he was having an art attack."

Umlah said, "A hundred apiece for these four?"

"You bet." And to Shuggery: "I think Walker was pulling your leg."

"She thinks Walker was pulling my leg," he said.

"All those arts. Arts and flowers. Art strings. Art and soul. Bleeding art. He gave you the business. The world's the same, more or less," I said. "Ain't it? Besides, Walker Evans is employed by the Farm Security Administration. They pay him to say things like that."

Umlah said, "From here to the fire alarm on that wall, all sixties."

"You're the boss," I said. I heard him hungrily licking the labels and I thought: I'll never take another picture in this condition — it's money in the bank.

"They're as timeless as paintings," said Iris. "That's what he was really saying."

"Shit and derision," I said. "That's a silly comparison. People are always saying that, but what's so great about paintings? Paintings look so confounded *wet* to me, as if you'd get sticky stuff on your fingers if you touched them — ketchup, axle grease, marmalade and jam. I'm not talking about your Van Goghs and your Rembrandts, though some of those Van Goghs drip like crazy and I've seen Rembrandts that look like melted cheese on burned toast. But this modern junk! Rotting candy, discombobulated people, Cubists with rulers! They're decorations, aren't they? They're supposed to match the color scheme in your breakfast nook. Don't talk to me about Steichen — I know he's a painter, too, but if his house caught fire you can bet your bottom dollar he'd come rushing out with an armload of his own negatives. Look, paintings are for museums — museums are just churches, all that tiptoeing around, everyone whispering. Or the decoration angle — 'Let's brighten up that corner with a nice blue Winslow Homer' — that sort of thing."

"Who's pulling whose leg now?" said Shuggery.

"Get off the bucket, I'm serious," I said. "Oh, sure, museums are harmless enough if you happen to admire that kind of taxidermy, but if anyone put my photographs in a museum I'd shoot myself. You call these decorations? Like hell. You can roll them up, wrap fish in them, put them in your pocket, lay them out flat, then dive in and paddle around. Don't let me catch you admiring them — you don't admire blizzards or swamps or circuses, do you? Or that jaybird on the trapeze? They move too much for you to sit there and gawk at them. I could barely get clothespins on them they were leaping around so much! This here ain't art, it's life. Hey, them are windows!"

Someone — Iris perhaps — was writing all this down. I could hear the pen nib scratching and sputtering on the pad.

" — and a hundred and a hundred and a hundred," said Umlah, who was far enough ahead not to hear my impromptu lecture. "Nearly done."

"Do you have any idea of the impact these pictures have made?" said Iris.

"I won't know that until I see my accountant," I said.

But she soldiered on: "The French think they're French, the Germans think they're German. The Communist Party in New York thinks you're a reformer and the *Daily Worker* wants to interview you. But don't laugh yet — you've made quite a splash with the decadents, too. Naked lion-tamers, tight-rope walkers in the altogether and your Lady Godiva? You've got the collectors running a temperature. The Christians think you're a moralist, and the bohemian crowd takes you for a fellow pagan."

"Let's call that sixty and that a hundred," said Umlah.

"Okay," I said. "What you're saying is, everyone likes my work."

"For different reasons,'" said Iris. "I can't explain it."

I was going to mention my "drowning quotient," but I felt I had said enough, and anyway Shuggery interrupted.

He said, "But there's some people who won't like it."

"I wonder who?" I said.

"The people in the pictures."

"I'm on their side. The people who perform in circuses are always hungrier than the spectators, but it's the spectators who eat well — the performers get rotten meals. So you get the weak performing for the strong, people doing handstands on an empty stomach. That's the point about the nakedness."

"I was talking about the spectators," said Shuggery.

Umlah said, "And a hundred and fifty for that last one. Stieglitz. That about wraps it up."

Iris said, "Mind answering a few personal questions?"

"All questions are personal," I said.

"What sort of a family do you come from?"

"Leave them out of this."

"She doesn't want to talk," said Shuggery.

"If I knew how to talk — or do anything else — do you think I'd waste my time taking pictures? This is all I have to say," I said, gesturing at what I hoped were the pictures on the gallery walls. "Why is it that people expect photographers to be talkers? Photography is the most inarticulate of the arts — it's probably not even an art."

"All photography?"

"Look, most photographs are works of subversion."

"Too hard to talk about them. That it?" said Iris.

I shook my head. "Too easy. Talking always simplifies things. And anyway, who cares?"

"You ought to. They're your pictures."

"Ah-hah! There's where you're wrong."

"But you took them."

"I happened to be there when they were," I said. "It could have been you. Ubiquity — that's what photography's all about. Locomotion. Not thought — action. Know how I got interested in photography? A friend of Mama's bought me a camera because she thought I wasn't getting enough fresh air."

Shuggery said, "She's joshing."

"I was lucky," I said.

"But you created these pictures."

"Don't be a sap. I found them."

"She *found* them!" Scratch, scratch: someone was copying down my words. And I could tell that a sizable crowd had gathered to listen to me. But I was tired. I wanted to sit down. I was about to tell them all to clear out, when I heard a commotion.

"Sure, I found them," I said. "No one was looking, so I took them."

Umlah said, "Here's Randy."

"Miss Pratt," said Randy excitedly. "I've got your pictures."

"Keep them — they're yours," I said. "It was your camera."

Randy said, "No. Now I know what true genius is. We were both there. It was my camera — my chances should have been the same as yours. But look what happened!"

He rattled the pictures and pressed them into my hand. People were breathing down my neck and there were murmurs of interest.

"Very attractive," I said. They were still limp from the processing. I tried to hand them back.

"What do you make of this one?" he asked, pushing closer to me.

"I don't make anything of that," I said, which was the truth: I saw nothing. "Excuse me, I must sit down. My dogs are barking."

"The face," he said. "That man."

I held a picture up: blackness. It might have been blank. "Oh, yes, found him," I said. "Firebug. I heard him clearing his throat, and that's when I whipped around and did him — wrist-action, very important. Nifty, huh? He liked the fire — you can see it on his face. Frankly, I think he started it."

"Who started it?" said Iris.

"Him," I said. I peeled off the picture and showed her.

"I don't see anyone," she said. "All I see is a fire truck."

"That's mine," said Randy.

"I meant this one," I said, and peeled off another. It had to be there somewhere. "This man — look how crazed he is. He loves fires, that one. A real goofball."

"That's a burning building," said Iris.

Now they were all nudging me. And they weren't looking at the pictures anymore — they were looking at me, probably wondering why I was wearing dark glasses indoors. Their eyes were boring holes in my face.

"This," said Iris, and took another of the pictures. "Is this yours?"

"I'm not absolutely sure."

"The rather mad features with the firelight reflected on the face — the hair all askew — yes?"

"That's it," I said.

"Now take your glasses off."

"No." I tried to pull away, but the people were crowding in on me and I was bumped back into Iris's cunning grip.

"That's not the picture," she said. She was really enjoying this. Her patronizing remarks hadn't got her anywhere with me; she obviously felt rebuffed and thought she'd take me down a peg or two. I could have throttled her. "Take a good look."

"Go scratch," I said.

Umlah said, "What seems to be the problem?"

"She's being evasive again," said Iris.

"Evasive!" I yelled. "Look at this show — is that evasion? Open your eyes!"

"I'm not talking about the show," she said. "I'm talking about you."

"Never mind about me — I don't matter. And I didn't come down here to get the third degree. Don't you people ever learn?"

I dropped the pictures and tried to get away. I was lumbering and heavy, stung like a stupid baited bear. I heard people hissing, and in my distraction I could not make them out, only the odor of stale cigarettes and the drizzling light of the gallery, and the itchy wool of winter coats. I caught an elbow in my ribs and bringing up my hand to steady my glasses I was too quick — I knocked them off. When I bent to retrieve them I heard someone step on them ("Whoops" and "Uh-oh"), a chewing crunch like ice breaking under skates, but with a shattering finality that only broken glass conveys. "Out of my way!"

"You shouldn't have done that, Iris."

I attempted to hide my staring eyes with my arm.

There was a muttering and a whispering. I stuck out my free arm and blundered forward.

"Miss Pratt?"

"No more questions," I said. But I wasn't getting anywhere. I smacked into a wall, dislodging a picture.

"Please," said Mr. Umlah.

"Can't you see I want to get out of here!"

They made way, they cleared a path for me. The floor was at once echoic. But this was worse: the room tilted oddly. I inched forward foolishly in blackness, using my hands like a swimmer. I should never have come, I thought. Why had I? There I was, in the middle of this crowd, a jackass, exposed. There was a hush in the room.

No, someone said.

"I'll be all right in a minute," I said. "I just need some elbow room."

Oh, God.

"Let me give you a hand," said Mr. Umlah.

Do something.

"Go away," I said. But I was off balance and started to teeter. The deck bucked and nearly toppled me. I heard surf, a heavy sea — this was a gale. I struggled on.

Very distinctly, one of the fretting voices — but this was both a whisper and a shout — said, *She's blind!*

It is a terrible word. It stopped me in my tracks. They were bellowing at me. Most people think that if you're blind you're deaf as well (and kind and forgiving and charitable and not interested in money). They screeched and rushed forward to help me, and of course, being gallery buffs, they all had cameras. I heard film being wound, dust caps removed, the ratchetings of lenses being focused.

"No pictures!" I said. "Put those things down!"

And they obeyed, they gave me room. But I'd had enough. The sob started in my chest; I fought it, and then let go, and in front of all those people I turned on the waterworks.

24

Buffaloed

PHOEBE said, "It's another cable."

"Don't!" I blocked my ears. I'd had just about enough of apologies and people weeping over me. The pity was much worse than the praise. It was hard being famous; it was unbearable being a freak. My photographs, which I had found in a mood of adventure and exuberance — the greatest joy I had ever known — were prophetic in a grotesquely wounding way: I was now like one of the wilder-looking members of Millsaps Circus, being celebrated for my deformity.

It was no use explaining that I had been fine when I'd taken the pictures in Florida. I was assumed to be a champion of the afflicted. No one knew the true source of my special sort of blindness, and I wouldn't quote anyone my favorite line from Orlando's poetry book: "I Tiresias, though blind, throbbing between two lives." ("He was a Harvard man," said Orlando when, to educate me, he read these poems.) For the camera crowd I had become my own pictures. Americans adore a handicap in a celebrity. I had been revealed as The Blind Photographer of the Cape. The attention exhausted me. It was the tyranny of admiration. So I had fled and I wanted nothing more than to curl up and make myself as small as a comma or the tadpole it resembled and just wriggle away.

"Listen," said Phoebe, and even with my fingers stuck in my ears I heard her. "It's from Papa. They're on their way home, they're —" She stopped and took a deep breath.

"What's wrong?" I looked closely at her. She was squinting hard at the cable, her face twitching in hesitation, her eyes darting as she reread the message.

"Nothing."

"Read it."

Her voice went flat as she read, *"Leaving today."*

"There's more."

"No."

Tumblers gulped in her little locked heart as they fell into place.

"Read the rest of it, Phoebe."

"How do you know so darned much!" she said, and went on reading in a dull defeated voice, *"Leaving today, thanks to you. Papa."*

" 'Thanks to you,' " I repeated. "Does that mean me?"

"Us, apparently. There's no name."

"Sounds like sarcasm, don't it?"

She was shaking her head and her mouth was set in a rueful little pucker. "It beats me."

I said, "He's burned up."

"I can't see why. Can you?"

"Sounds as if something's seriously wrong."

She turned on me with surprising heat. "You're crazy! Why, there's nothing wrong. He's just being funny — that's his idea of a joke."

She was embattled, and she had her reasons. She knew she had nothing to fear from me, but we had neighbors and they had eyes. Suppose one of these local infidels had an inkling of what was going on here between her and Orlando — seen them somehow from a dinghy? Or, ignoring the NO TRESPASSING signs and cutting through the yard — as they often did to go clamming — had a glimpse? If they had seen, and alerted Papa (it was possible: they were a contrary bunch) there would be hell to pay.

I said, "Maybe not seriously wrong — maybe just a little peculiar."

"Peculiar?"

"Unusual," I said, but I regretted that word.

"What do you know?" she said. "You act so high and mighty, but you can't see your hand in front of your face. You go creeping around the house pretending you're normal and barging in where you don't belong — don't think I haven't noticed — but that doesn't mean you can see. This is the thanks I get for reading to you and making sure your seams are straight —accusations and blame!"

"No one's blaming you, Phoebe," I said calmly.

"You're a fine one to talk!" she said. "You're the unusual one around here. You're downright peculiar. Yes, Maude, I think there's something strange with you upstairs — I'm sorry, but I really do."

Something strange with me upstairs — look who's talking! But I held my tongue.

"This isn't getting us anywhere," I said. "The fact is, the folks are on their way home. And something's — well, something's up. We'd better get the place shipshape."

"The place *is* shipshape," she said, still smarting. "If you weren't blind you could see that."

"It's dusty," I said. "It hasn't been cleaned since Orlando went back to Harvard. Dishes in the sink, crumbs on the carpet. If Papa walked in now he'd have kittens."

Phoebe, in a voice I did not recognize as hers, said, "I can't face him."

"Sure you can. We'll get it spick-and-span in no time."

But Phoebe had gotten up from her chair. She walked halfway across the parlor and stopped and looked through the window to the Sound. And I knew what she was thinking: If he knows, it's the end, I'm done for. More than anything, she dreaded being found out. And I suppose she was afraid of what Orlando's reaction would be — defiance. Her fear was also compounded by the memory of what she'd done, for in retrospect, and in Papa's eyes, her sleeping with

Orlando was a kind of insanity. *What's got into you?*
Papa would say; and she'd cry. Love was the explanation, but that was no explanation at all, since to the
observer love looked selfish, a kind of stupor and loss
of control. People saw in lovers what they saw in glut-
tons—a shameless and faintly absurd expression of
appetite, a habit, an addiction that had no rational explanation. No matter how Phoebe tried to defend
herself Papa would stoop and say, *You what?*

Off and on, for the next two days, Papa's question
seemed to occur to her. She brought it up like wind, a
burp she suppressed with a wince.

I hoped she would fight for Orlando. But she fell
silent; she was spiritless; she was drowning. And her
descent — like people's experience of my photographs,
that surrender to memory — was a solitary plunge
from the shoals of the present to the deeps where her
love lay like a sunken ship, broken on the bottom, all
its treasure fuzzed with tufts of sea moss, and rapid
fish flashing through the wavering grasses and splayed
barrel staves. But there was a difference between her
and my fans: it was as if she wanted to stay there and
not surface, to die a watery death in that dark and be
along the split-open casks of her love until her white
body was bones and turned to coral.

She didn't reply when I said, "Phoebe?"

She was reflective; and fear, making her thoughtful, gave her a look of weary intelligence. The strain
of fright had dimmed her sparkle and made her seem
wiser than she was. I had regarded her as rather frivo-
lous — a flibbertigibbet, in fact. But this look of piety
and panic in her scared me. She had been quick to
shift the blame onto me ("You're the unusual one
around here"), but that was momentary; now she ignored me. She mooned around, taking walks on the
lonely beach to Gammon Point, as if trying to decide
whether to take the plunge. And if she did do herself
in we'd all be at fault, for suicide is usually just another way of having the last word, inevitably, *Take
that!*

She could not see that what she had done with Orlando was pure genius, love's perfect fit. But I could, and I vowed to defend her. Several times, shadowing her on the beach, I came within an ace of rushing up to her and crying, *I know all about it! Don't give him up! I'm on your side!*

Because, of course, I was grateful to her. If I couldn't have him, it was only right that she should. She was my double and so I throbbed for her, I shared their passion, hidden like a photographer. My sight had originated with their love. Then, I saw what my life had been and what my work must be. My photographs expressed nothing of this; they told no story. There had been no link between what I was and what I saw. In a picture I never took, called *Portrait of the Artist,* a grizzled prospector squats in a gully sluicing sand, a cadaverous geezer panning for gold. There is a shadow on his face, but in his rusty skittle there is a knuckle-sized nugget gleaming among the dull pebbles and grit. He might be on the point of snatching it up, or else he could be preparing to dump it back into the gully. But you see it: you are the artist. I described this picture to Phoebe to tell her how much I needed her.

She would not be drawn. I hoped when the day came that she would say *So what?* and go on loving.

She stared at the December sea, that plowed field of fugitive furrows under a mammoth sky.

Papa arrived without warning one frosty afternoon just before Christmas. We heard Mr. Wampler's beach wagon in the drive, then saw Papa — tanned the hue of varnish and in his long fur-collared coat — striding up the front walk. Behind him, Mama supervised the unloading of the suitcases. Mama looked uneasy, Papa resolute, in his brisk brass-tacks mood, spanking his hands for warmth.

Phoebe said, "Damn that Ollie. He said he'd be here."

"He'll come," I said. "He'll stick up for you."

Though this was incautious (I had nearly given myself away), she nodded. But she was trembling and looked terribly worried.

"Well, well, speak of the devil," he said in the front hall, shrugging out of his coat. "Didn't think you'd have the guts to face me."

But he went right past us, through the house, shuffled his mail, and did not say another word until about six o'clock, when he had changed his clothes and set the logs alight in the fireplace. One thing about Papa: he had a sense of occasion. He stood there in his black tuxedo, his back to the fire, a stiff drink in one hand and a big cigar in the other, as if he'd just been elected mayor.

We took our seats — Phoebe and I sat on the sofa, Mama in her wing-chair.

Papa said, "Too bright in here for you, Maudie?"

"It's just fine," I said.

"I was referring to your goggles. Mind taking them off? They're distracting me."

"I'm sorry," I said, "but I'd rather keep them on."

"May I ask why?"

"Phoebe bought them for me. She says they suit me."

"Just because Phoebe has a crazy notion," he said, "it don't mean it's right."

Phoebe groaned, dreading what was to come.

Mama said, "They make you look awful funny."

"Let's drop it," said Papa. "I've got a question to ask and I want a straight answer. Have I done right by you — ever let you down or given you any reason to complain?"

"No, sir," I said.

"Phoebe?"

She shook her head guiltily. "Course not."

"Look at me, both of you. What do you see?"

"Papa!" said Phoebe, and she was on the verge of blubbering.

I said, "There's something wrong, isn't there?"

"You bet your boots there is! If you'd take those goggles off you'd see it."

"I don't want to hear this," said Phoebe, but I propped her up and kept her on the sofa. I couldn't face this alone.

Papa said, "No, it's not your father you're seeing. Know what it is?" He bared his teeth. "It's a jackass."

"Don't be silly," I said.

"How can a jackass help looking silly?" he said. "Know what I was asking myself all the way home from Florida? Why — I was asking — why does a daughter of mine, whom I've loved and respected ever since she was yay high, go out of her way to make a jackass of me?" And as if calling a witness he said, "Mother?"

Mama was looking at Phoebe and me. She said, "You'll never know."

This got us nowhere. It was theater. When your back is to the wall, the people you love most, believing themselves to have been deceived, take their time and enumerate their grumbles instead of rushing in for the kill. They make it a production. They toy with you, taunt, reminisce, and destroy you, not with one clean thrust through your heart but by slapping one petty grievance after another into your face. What makes it so painful and peculiarly nasty is that only they know your weaknesses. Other people can hurt you, but only those you love can make you suffer.

"God," Papa wheezed, striding up and down before the fire — there was an actor in this man, "I recall when it was all different. You girls were pipsqueaks. Your mother and I would take you out in the boat —"

I suffered for Phoebe. She was there beside me, petrifying with shame, dying a slow death, sinking. And I was getting angrier. How dare he? I thought. But he wouldn't wind it up.

"— never thought any daughter of mine would go out of her way to humiliate me. It's not natural!"

Phoebe just sat there, and because she was stone she didn't tremble, she didn't move. The tears were rolling down her cheeks and the tearstains gleamed in the firelight.

"— given you a good home and I've had no regrets. I've always had reason to be proud of you. I've given you a lot of freedom, but you've abused it."

Papa, for all his puffing and blowing, seemed curiously happy. Banality followed banality, and I thought: Yes, this is his satisfaction. His discovery of what Orlando and Phoebe had done had wounded him, but he was taking pleasure in roasting her slowly by the fireside, pacing in front of the flames and letting his vengeful shadow jump all over the walls.

"— it's pretty painful to think of yourself as a man for sixty-two years and then wake up one morning and discover that everyone's laughing at you."

I said, "No one's laughing, Papa."

He smiled. Mama was somber, Phoebe still weeping softly, and I suppose my own face looked fairly grim behind my dark glasses.

"Listen," he whispered and cocked his head to the side and let the cigar smoke trail around his face. "If you listen hard you can hear them. Laughing to beat the band. Hear it? 'Pratt's daughter's gone and made a jackass of him!' Oh, sure, they'll forgive the daughter, but old men get no mercy."

I said, "I don't hear a blessed thing."

"You ain't listening hard enough," he said. "Because if you were you'd hear each particular voice. 'Kick the jackass,' they're saying. Hee-haw, hee-haw. There's a lot of people who wanted to see me down. And I fought them. Mother?"

"You fought them."

"I never fought dirty, I never broke the rules — didn't have to. I fought fair. I had friends then. But I never thought I'd get my rump kicked, and so hard, by my very own daughter." He tapped an inch of cigar ash into the fire and repeated, "By my very own daughter."

I knew then that Phoebe was lost. She had given in, she wouldn't defend herself or Orlando. She'd let this nagging old comedian bully and bluster her into a full confession. I said, "Hold on, Papa."

For it was my crisis, too. I never could take another picture without bluffing, as I had fluked *Firebug*. Though blindness was no handicap to perceiving the world around me, I was incapable of seeing pictures — my own or anyone else's. I could not read or write. So my career was at an end, and good riddance. But I positively would not be denied the satisfaction of witnessing Phoebe completing what I could not in loving Orlando. If you have no life, I thought, the next best thing is to be near someone else's. Obviously my blindness was a reaction. It was simple shock — it was resignation. If I couldn't have Orlando, then I didn't want any other lover. But they had taught me to see love and that was reason enough to live.

"Aren't you interested," I said, "in Phoebe's side of the story?"

"I know what Phoebe will say — that's why I don't want to hear it."

"Give me a chance, then."

"Pipe down," he said, and he began to chuckle, a kind of ominous mirth. He was performing, taking his time. I had never seen him so jolly or known such desperate gaiety in his speechifying. There was something final about this comic effort, the flourish of a farewell, his last bow.

Mama said, "Phoebe's crying," but Papa ignored this remark.

"Bet you think I'm going to a party," he said, giving his cummerbund a jaunty tug. "Am I going to have a high old time in this monkey suit? No, I ain't. Know why? Cause there ain't going to be no more parties. This whisky," he said, swishing his glass, twirling it to his lips, and sipping. "Best bottle there is in the house, pre-war — I didn't even drink it during Prohibition. Know why I'm drinking it now? No? Cause there ain't going to be no more whisky. No sir." He straightened and raised his cigar to admire it. "What have we got here? Not a five-cent El Ropo from the candy store in

Hyannis — this here is a Havana, like the King of England used to smoke. Aromatic, no veins on the wrapper, you want to keep the fumes up your nose until you bust. One puff and you're in Congress, two puffs and you're President. When I lit it up an hour ago it was a foot long. Want to know why I'm smoking this here big cigar?"

"Cause there ain't going to be no more big cigars," I said. "I get the message."

He came close to me and said, "Or nothing else. The party's over. Understand?"

I said, "Say something, Phoebe. For pity's sake, don't just sit there like a bump on a log."

"She's too ashamed and I don't blame her. I'm ashamed myself, aren't you, mother?"

Mama said, "I'm sick."

"Back in 'twenty-nine, they were dropping like flies," said Papa. "Foreclosures, liquidations, bankruptcies, hell and high water. Times were bad, the market had a hernia, the country went to the bitches. People with college degrees selling apples. But not me —"

This was a familiar speech: the Depression, Roosevelt, shanty Irish with their hands in the till, people pissing their money away; and the last ringing phrases about loyalty and friendship.

He poured himself a slug, the last of the whisky, and said, "Now I ain't got a friend. My name is mud."

I said, "Why?"

He tried to laugh, but his voice had grown hoarse and strangely hollow. He wasn't acting anymore. He said, "Girls, this is it. You're looking at a carcass. You did what Wall Street and Congress and every Irishman in the state couldn't do. And that's the last of that" — chucking the cigar butt into the fire — "and that" — draining the whisky and gasping — "I'm ruined, thanks to you. And all I can say is, how do you like them apples?"

I said, "I find it hard to believe."

"Mother?"

"He's telling the truth," she said. "We got the bad news in Florida. All his clients closed their accounts, emptied out their portfolios, or whatever the expression is. He'll never work again, at least not as a broker."

"Sure," he said with rueful reasonableness, "it doesn't prevent me from starting up a chicken farm or selling greeting cards door to door."

"I don't see why," I said.

"I'm a leper, that's why! No one wants a leper." Then he raised himself and as he towered over us he bellowed, "And what I want to know is, what in the name of God got into you, sister!"

At this, Phoebe collapsed. She was in an agony of regret; she choked, and throwing herself at Papa's feet, and in a beseeching voice, she sobbed, "We didn't mean it, we didn't know you'd find out, we'll never do it again —"

"Stop!" I said and tried to shut her up. I glared at Papa. "There. Are you happy now? See what you've done?"

Papa was confused. I helped Phoebe back to the sofa and he said, "I knew she'd stick up for you, but I'm not going to listen to her. I'm not talking to her — I'm talking to you, Maude. You're the one who ruined me, damn your eyes."

And in one of those exalted moments of lucid guilt I understood everything. I could think of nothing to say.

"Those pictures! How could you do it to me? And not only me, but all the others at that dinner. You ruined a lot of good men, sister. You'll never know how many people you put in the poorhouse. Carney's fit to be tied. He drove us out — I won't repeat what he said. Mother?"

"He drove us out, bag and baggage," she said. "There were words."

Phoebe stirred beside me, revived. Her crisis had passed — she had come close to destruction, but she was reprieved and she said coolly, "Maude's pictures? Is that what's wrong?"

"Didn't think I'd find out, did you? You ought to be horsewhipped," he said, his red face an inch from mine. "But it's going to be worse than that. You thought you brought me down, but you'll see — we're all going down together."

"Maude isn't down," said Phoebe. "Why, she's famous. She gets telephone calls from New York City."

"I take it you stopped there," I said.

"I didn't stop in New York. They would have torn my head off. Carney's people got the news. And I only hope you made a little money out of it, sister, because you're going to need it."

Phoebe said, "Maude didn't mean to do it, isn't that right?"

I looked hard at her and said, "I did mean to do it. I took those pictures on purpose. I'm sorry it turned out this way, but maybe there was no other way it could turn out."

"She doesn't know what she's saying," Phoebe said. "She hasn't been right since she came back."

Papa said, "She never was right."

"I'm right! I know what I'm saying. I wanted those pictures. It was too bad Papa was involved, but what was he doing there anyway?"

"Not a word of apology," he said.

I said — but I was still looking at Phoebe — "No one has to apologize for doing what they have to do."

"Hear that, mother? Just doing her duty."

"My own duty," I said. 'I'm not ashamed of it."

"Then keep on doing it," he said. "Everyone thinks you're so great. But no one knows what you put me through so you could get there. You can show them, can't you?"

"I don't follow."

"You took pictures of me at Carney's Pig Dinner, when I was watching those people disport themselves. Hadn't you ought to show the sequel to that innocent stag party — what you just found, a broken-up old man with his fire all burned down, and no whisky and no cigars and no life? Now you go on and get your camera and snap my picture. I want the world to know what you did to me."

Phoebe said, "Don't, Papa."

"What's wrong?" he said, his voice shrill with sarcasm. "No more film? All used up in Florida? Not enough money in it for you? Ain't I horrible enough?"

"Maude doesn't take pictures anymore," said Phoebe.

"That's real shame," he said. "But she's going to take this one."

Mama said, "That's what he was saying on the train, over and over."

"I'll do it," I said, and went upstairs to get my camera. I could do him — I'd done *Firebug* blind: I had my own way of seeing. I loaded the camera and thought: I owe him this much at least. And I kept thinking what a fine picture it would be, found in the last of the firelight, the craggy old man casting a broken shadow, doom in a dinner jacket, the melodrama of near-extinction. His face, and the room, had the funereal dignity of light and shadow that I had only seen before in a Cameron.

But when I got back to the parlor the mood had changed. Mama was crying, Phoebe was sniffling, and Papa, though abject, was himself again. He rounded on me.

"You let me go on," he said. "You should have stopped me. Why didn't you tell me?"

It was a picture I did not take. If I had I would have called it *Buffaloed,* though it was not half as good as the one I had prepared myself for, *Doom in a Dinner Jacket.*

Orlando came home on Christmas Eve and got the story from Phoebe. It was a sad holiday, a few presents — very expensive ("Cause there aren't going to be no more parties!") and the last of Papa's good wine was drunk. Mama cried a lot, but Papa was spent. I was given the invalid routine: I was blind, I was incapable, they confined me to a chair. Phoebe and Orlando took long walks together. It was very much a family affair.

25

Life Study

WITH THOSE NOISY EXCHANGES, that skirmishing —
my father finding an enemy in his own camp — the
year closed, and there was no more talk. The new
year moved swiftly toward Orlando's graduation from
law school. Then the decade ended, the half-baked
monochrome of the Thirties which left everyone with
a grudge. Time sprinted, but without an event to give
it shape the days were interminable. It is time's con-
founding perversity. I lived in a torpor of suspense in
which I heard every tick of the clock. But suspense is
empty: because nothing happened, the months seemed
in retrospect little more than one dull afternoon.

The eventful life has dates; it swells and pauses
like a plot. But this was an unbroken length of time,
like an endless and perfectly plaited rope. I knew
each fiber of it, but it passed without a knot, and I
was tempted out of boredom to make it into a noose.
I had shot to fame in a matter of weeks: from my
portrait of Stieglitz to my showdown with Papa took
just two months.

Then there was nothing, I entered a void, the void
was in me. My work was done, my life was over. Yet
I think I can rightly say that the following four years
or so — the war — during which I took no pictures
whatever and only moped and listened to the radio
and endorsed checks and darned socks and lost all
track of what was going on in the world of photography — pretending to be older than I was and doing

absolutely nothing of value — that barren inactive period was the high point of my career as a photographer.

My pictures, the same pictures, appeared everywhere. The show traveled, the photographs were reproduced in magazines, my early work was rediscovered and promoted. I was seen to have been an important Twenties pathfinder, one of the few American photographers who had not gone to Europe. (I hadn't thought to do so, but I would not have gone for anything, since Europe — the cheap franc, the cliquey artists, the crowd-pleasers and posturers — represented to me the most hideous kind of patronage.) Blacks were in fashion and of course I'd done them by the bushel basket. At the dreariest time of my life I'd done my funniest and most hopeful pictures; at my most hopeful I had done desperately tormented shots. When I had sought work I had been ignored, and when I was no longer looking for it I was courted. Now my fame was consolidated. I must have seemed to many people incredibly busy with all this exposure. I wasn't. Papa did all the paperwork. I didn't lift a finger.

And, as often happens, my fame became an aspect of others' — the general public confused me with other woman photographers of my own vintage: Margaret Bourke-White, Imogen Cunningham, Ann Brigman, Berenice Abbott, Dorothea Lange, and even older ones like Gertrude Käsebier.

I was too detached to be offended. I regarded this woman, Maude Coffin Pratt, with a mixture of awe, scepticism and amusement. What an engine of creation she was! What depth of field! What a glad eye! I could never live up to her achievement (her pictures *were* rather good), so I didn't try. I still got many requests to do pictures — it was an effect of the war in Europe, the urgency that the present must be caught on film, a kind of souvenir-hunting, since the world would change out of recognition. It was the superstitious deception of the photograph as a historical record, the snapshot for posterity, as a photograph of the Chinese wedding is as much a part of the ceremony as the tea-drinking. Or the other sort of picture, the view-camera taxidermy of buildings soon to be bombed, the portraits of crooked political bosses who expect to be voted out of office or jailed for fraud. But I did none of these pictures, and gradually the message got across: I wasn't faking, I was truly blind; and though I was still a young woman people began to think of me as very old and venerable, a kind of sage, reclusive and cantankerous. Soon they would be saying, "Maude Pratt? Gosh, I thought she died years ago!"

Perhaps I had. I certainly didn't see as well as I used to. Papa, who was home all the time now, took charge of me, treated me as an invalid, and insisted I never be left alone.

"Move over," he said. He was my seeing-eye dog; he held my hand and jerked me this way and that, warning me of obstacles, and sometimes woofed about the weather to cheer me up. "Another glorious day — I wish you could see the crocuses." Once, years before, he had been funny, speaking of going to the "orifice" or the "uproar," saying "Pass the mouseturd" or "Abyssinia." Now he had no jokes. He often mentioned dying: "Yep," he said, "I'm going to be leaving the building pretty soon."

"Will you look at that!" he wheezed and dragged me to a halt. I saw nothing. His company was oppressive and his constant fussings of attention, instead of helping me, only reduced my vision. He contradicted me, he slowed me up, he got in the way and made me stumble. It was only when I was alone, in concentrated solitude, that I could see clearly; but I was so seldom alone I began to lose my ability to sniff out images. The dazzle I had known was reduced to a wan play of shadows. My uncertainty made me falter and I grew to depend on Papa the more for guidance while at the same time realizing that his intimidating concern was weakening me. He demoralized me with charity.

"Let me do that," he said. And I did. It was easier for me to be supported by him, less trouble for me to turn over the remainder of my life to him than to live it myself. The patron of the arts! It was a repetition of what I knew to be the oldest folly of dependency. I was in chains, a child again. He was almighty in his paternal role and he was vindicated. Each time I accepted the favor of his help, his warm hairy hand tugging mine, I lost another battle in my war on patronage. He had enfeebled my attacks, advanced on me, cut off my retreat, invaded and taken over and occupied me. He was my mad dictator, with designs on the world, and it got so that I could not do without him. He had proved me wrong. I stopped fighting; I regarded his damaging incursions on my freedom as protection, and at last it was as if he had plucked out my eyes, for it was much worse than being returned to the early days of my blindness: I was nothing, no one, I had no name.

He took me to Boston to see a specialist. The quack examined me but addressed all his remarks to Papa, referring to me in the third person, "If she'll just look this way" and "She should try to relax."

"I can't find anything wrong with her vision," he said at last. "Retina's not detached, and there's a pretty healthy contraction in those irises. Let me put it this way — the eye's like a camera — "

"Maybe there's no film in mine," I said.

"So her eyes are perfectly all right," said Papa, "except she can't see."

"Could be she doesn't want to," said the quack. "The mind's a funny thing — "

A funny thing? That was the arrogant carelessness of a sighted person.

I wasn't treated: there was nothing wrong with my eyes, nothing to treat. I think Papa was relieved, though he went through the motions of finding me a Christian Science "healer" who drove over from Osterville and intoned long passages of *Science and Health* and finally, exasperated, said, "You're just not trying!"

I could not see, nor was I in any fit state to be seen. I had stayed away from Orlando's graduation. Orlando and Phoebe cooperated with Papa in treating me as an invalid. Was this exaggerated attention their way of keeping their own secret dark? I didn't think so. I didn't believe they had a secret. In my new obscurity — obscurer than I had ever known — I had started to doubt that they had been lovers. I had imagined it all to give myself an excuse for abandoning photography. I had been ashamed of doing the Florida pictures; I'd overstepped myself and had used that morning at the windmill to punish myself. What greater punishment for a photographer than to put out her own eyes? I had brought this upon myself, guiltily. Everyone else was blameless — I had wronged them, ruined Papa, and because I had been thwarted by Orlando I had made the innocent love he had for Phoebe into a secretive fling at incest. In my rage I had imagined them hiding from me. I had made it all up and it was impossible in this cavernous darkness to remember what I had seen. The lights were out. I had been misled and crazy and sorry and created a fantasy from the ambiguous noises in the household. I had no proof, no pictures. I had wangled the Florida shots and menaced everyone with my pretense of art, and now — and because Phoebe was no rival — I hankered after Orlando.

I deserved what followed. He failed the Massachusetts Bar Exam and got a job teaching high school in Woonsocket. It was not the bold move I had expected him to make. It seemed provisional, a kind of indecision — he was not near enough to make it worthwhile coming home every day, nor was it far enough to give him drama and look like a break with us. It wasn't letter-writing distance and yet it wasn't so close that he could easily drop in on us. It merely put him out of focus: he was a blur, quite different from the vivid face he once was. He seemed to be marking time. But then, we all were. The war had started crepitating across Europe and we were anxious, like people who hear the house next door being burgled.

Phoebe got a job, too. On the strength of some of my early pictures of her — and now they were circulating widely — Phoebe was asked to model for *Vogue*. I knew this was partly due to my staying out of the public eye, my refusal to allow anyone to take my picture. (It surprised me that any model willingly submitted to a photographer. Immortality? But who wanted to spend eternity dressed like *that?*) In a very important sense, Phoebe was my double. Much of the attention that was directed toward me was deflected to her. I didn't mind her cashing in on this, since she was so pretty and full of fun. People believed me to be as clever and attractive as Phoebe, and since I was camera-shy, unobtainable and difficult, it was considered quite a coup to have her model the slouch hats and big-shouldered coats that were so popular. She became the public side of my personality and moved my career along when I was doing nothing.

There was a further irony: Papa became my agent. At first he managed my affairs to keep himself busy in his enforced bankruptcy, and then he did it for profit — he was on to a good thing. He displaced me, kept people away from me, vetted contracts, did the accounts, and stopped talking about leaving the building. He approved the exhibitions, saw editors, conferred with curators, and generally made a going concern of what I had abandoned. It was as if he was charging admission to see the ruins. If it mattered to him that some of my photographs which he handled pictured him chewing a fat cigar at the Carney Pig Dinner and honking while naked trapeze artists cavorted above him, he never mentioned it. This was strictly business and I was glad that, just as Phoebe had found work because of me, Papa was also profitably occupied on my behalf. And both were doing my reputation an immense amount of good.

This reputation. It seemed something separate from

me, a little bubble I had blown that had drifted into the gaze of others, who valued it more than I. It had on its own swelled to quite a size, and Papa did much to call attention to it. But because it was out of my hands and in motion — I had no control over it — I could never take it seriously. And it was a bubble, no more, sailing on puffs of hot air, prismatic and flattering; peered through, it altered everything around it. People saw what they wished to see in it, yet it was no crystal ball. It was a wobbling globe of spittle which, if pricked, would so easily pop open and become vapor and vanish.

Papa, whom I had wrecked with my pictures, who was rising again by promoting those same pictures, turning the tables on me by cashing in on his own disgrace — Papa, flushed with the new success he had brought me and, for what he imagined to be his great enterprise, taking far more than a fair commission as his paternal right — Papa, now patron, benefactor, agent, salesman, spokesman, marauder, holding me captive for my own good — Papa saw that the demand for my pictures outstripped the supply and began rummaging all over the house for more than he could offer as original Pratts. The son-of-a-bitch toiled at this before my very eyes.

At one time, they had been spread all over the house, framed, stuck in albums, stacked in dresser drawers. He had appropriated these loose ones, assessed their value and put them up for sale. And from these pictures he fabricated a career for me. He fastened dates and colorful incidents to them — nearly all of them apocryphal — and reinvented me as a dedicated photographer who in her hooking bore little resemblance to what I was or had ever been. He even gave the impression, using this raft of old pictures, that I was still at it, producing the occasional perfect shot in spite of my blindness.

I did not discourage him in this. The Maude Pratt whose work was being lapped up meant nothing to me.

She was just another double, rather more industrious and pushy in her public image as artist-adventuress than I was in my darkroom, but nevertheless bearing traces of the real McCoy. She was the first of many different and sometimes contradictory females who over the years were wrongly identified with my name and pictures.

But supplies were stretched. I became aware of this in an annoying way. Although I had allowed Papa every freedom, I had cherished my privacy — specifically, my room. "Find your nitch," Papa used to say. I had found it and it was just that, a sort of corner shelf to prop my heart on. It was small, orderly, with trunks and camera equipment, chintz curtains, and my own odor. It was my retreat and my consolation; it had no other occupant. I could think here, and in a sense I had allowed Papa to reassert his hold over me in order to retain possession of it. I escaped there to mull things over. It was part of my brainpan, all that remained of my territory. I could not convert this small space to a greater freedom or use it to wage war on Papa, but it was a place in which I could be happy. As long as it was not violated I could maintain the illusion that I was free. My attachment to my room was profound, as tenacious and animal as patriotism. If it was a cage at least it was my cage. I was the lioness who, even in close captivity, is safe behind her own twitching whiskers and confident claws — it was not I who was locked in but they who were locked out. The war image is apt. I had been captured; if I were to be destroyed there would be no point in Papa's occupation. In the refuge of my room I still had a perspective on the enemy's outrages and a surviving sense of my own danger.

I must have been left with a remnant of instinct: how else could I have smelled the rat? I heard him from my armchair in the parlor, where he had ordered me to relax (relax! the Germans had invaded France and were killing Jews and robbing churches and melting down gold crucifixes!). In preparation for yet another trip to New York he had invaded my room to loot it. I felt his foraging hands as keenly as if he had been performing primitive surgery on me without an anesthetic. I bounded from my chair, hurried upstairs, and made a lunge for the door.

"Maude. What are you doing here? Go downstairs."

Sprong! He snipped the twine on a bundle of prints.

"Leave those pictures alone," I said. I may have been wrong, but I had no hint of disorder in the room. It appeared he had just started his search. I stepped over and slammed the lid of the trunk, and how I missed guillotining his fingertips I'll never know.

"There's more," he said, with puzzled pride. "Why didn't you tell me? This is just the sort of thing they want — there's a whole exhibition here."

"It's junk," I said, "and it's private, so stop scavenging."

"I want to help you, Maude. I was just having a gander."

"Pilfering."

"There's a whole cartload of stuff here — I'll bet you'd forgotten all about it."

"My eye I have." But of course by then I had been taking pictures for over twenty years. The accumulation was vast and unsorted. One of the first jobs I had given myself in the first illumination of my blindness — when I had regretted all the pictures I'd taken — — was to tie them into bundles with strong twine and stack them like bricks in my trunk. I thought I had buried them, but apparently I had not buried them deep enough, for here was Papa coveting them for their resale value.

"Do you know," he said with some of his old broker's fire, "that there are enough of your pictures here to set up a company? 'Maude Pratt Inc.' How does it sound? This could keep us all busy for the next five years. It'd give Ollie and Phoebe something to do, too. I'd be willing to bet dollars to doughnuts that there's some rare old things in this pile."

How like Papa to make an industry of it, with Orlando and Phoebe working like beavers in the picture factory he envisioned.

"It's no concern of yours," I said. "You've got plenty. Now go away — and if I catch you in here again you'll be sorry."

But I posed no threat. I suppose it was my defenselessness that shamed him into going away.

"That's gratitude," he said at the door. "You could make a fortune with all these pictures. But you never did have much business sense."

"That's my problem."

"Your problem, sister," he said in the breezy manner he affected when his pride was hurt, "is that ever since you've been blind you've been very shortsighted."

And he left me to my room. My next project was to buy the biggest padlock I could find, but before I used it I ferreted out all the plates and rolls of film I could find, emptied my camera ("I'll be damned," I muttered, pulling a used roll out of my Speed Graphic) and developed them. I relearned the washerwoman's knack, and in my darkroom, — working before the cheerful splash of the faucet in the sink, and calm enough to concentrate on my motions, I sensed a lifting of my blindness. Left alone and with the door shut and the lights off, I perceived a froth of shapes, the glow at the business end of my enlarger, and in the gleam of thickened chemical slime, which was a series of images on a strip of film, I could just make out on the negative innocent people frolicking up to their necks in molasses. There was no sharpness in any of this, nothing defined for me with any certitude, only a rather lively pictorial stew, or else a haunch of meat hanging in just enough light to show the striations of its sinews; a rose arbor; a toadstool; a helmeted tower; a swatch of hair that might well have been a tussock of grass.

I took some cheer from this and from that moment nursed the hope that I might get my sight back. Then I dumped these prints in my trunk and secured it with

the padlock against all future intruders who might want
to stick their noses into my business.

There was an intruder a year or so later. Mama was
in town, Phoebe doing a *Vogue* cover, Orlando in
Woonsocket, Papa somewhere blowing at my bubble
reputation. "Hold the fort," he had said.

It was December, but sunny and dry, the air splintery, knifed apart by the wind. I found a sheltered
place on the porch. I pulled my wool hat down over
my eyes and, rocking there in my heavy coat, half dozing, like a parody of the old woman I had become,
listened to the Sound. The idiotic heaving of the sea
doing its rhythmic spew on the beach below, every
third or fourth wave a real upchuck slobbering along
the sand and turning the coastline into pudding.

"Excuse me, I happened to be passing and —"

I shook myself awake, made a pretense of peering
through my dark glasses and said, "How'd you get in
here?"

"I climbed the fence."

"Why?"

"The gate was locked."

"You can just climb out again. This is private property."

I thought I detected a gulp of fear. It was a woman,
youngish, and I heard her narrow boot-heels sink
through the ice crust on the snow a few feet away.

She said, "They told me you would say that. I have
a small request. I was hoping you'd at least listen."

"Don't see how I can stop you."

"I want you to take a picture."

"You call that a small request?"

"Of me," she added quickly. "Not a portrait or anything fancy. More like a study. Well, you know."

"You're wasting your time. I don't take pictures anymore."

"That's what they said, but —"

"You should have listened to them. You could have
saved yourself a lot of trouble."

"I wanted to hear it from you."

"You just heard it. The answer's no."

"It wouldn't take long," she said, persisting so sweetly I found myself weakening, almost wishing I could take her goddamned picture, so she'd leave me in peace. "If we could step inside the house it would be over in a jiffy."

This seemed rather a liberty. I said, "Inside the house?"

"It's warmer in there for, um, what I had in mind. The light is good today. Near the window, I was thinking, on a sofa, but one that won't date too much."

"You've worked it out. You don't need me."

"But I do," she said. "You have no idea how highly I regard your work."

I said, "My camera's broken. Peepstones ain't working. So, good day to you."

"I have one with me," she said and put it in my hands. A pretty tinkle in her voice told me she was attractive. "I bought it specially for this."

"Never seen one of these before."

"It's Japanese."

"Do tell," I said. "Okay, say cheese."

I clicked, and in a split second of light actually saw her. She wasn't more than five feet high, in a dark coat and a beret, and she had a broad face. She was an Oriental, in fact; like the camera, she might well have been Japanese.

"No," she said. "Not here. Inside."

"Off limits," I said.

"You don't understand. I want you to do me in the nude."

"Hold the phone," I said. "Why didn't you say so before? You want a life study — the original birthday suit? Sorry, I'm in retirement. No pictures."

"I'll pay you."

"I wouldn't do it for half a million dollars. I don't know whether they told you, but I'm blind, sweetie. As a bat. Don't tell me how awful it makes you feel — I'm not looking for sympathy."

She said softly, "You're the only person who can help me."

"I can't even help myself."

She said, "I'm not married. I am very shy. I have never shown my body to anyone. It is not ugly — and that is why I am here. I am still attractive and young. I want a picture of what I am now, before it is too late. In a few years I will be old, I will have nothing."

I was touched by the poignancy of this. It was the saddest request I had ever heard. And yet her story was not so strange: she craved a little immortality for her beauty, a souvenir to return her to this day and year. It would be proof, testifying that she had once been lovely. The photo would be ageless and plump with light long after she had become a dry old stick. Photographic truth was as ineradicable and unique as a thumbprint. But there was something melancholy about it, as if the photograph she requested were like a summer flower, plucked before it withered, and pressed between the leaves of a book for another season.

"Please, will you do it for me?"

She was afraid; something was ending; she feared destruction. Why now?

"There are lots of photographers around," I said. "How did you happen to pick me?"

"You are a great photographer."

"Every photographer's great. Who can tell them apart? Not me. It's like saying someone's a great leaf-raker — look, either you make a pile or you don't, and if you don't you're not a leaf-raker. There's no two ways about it."

She had been trying to interrupt me. When I stopped talking she said, "But you're the only blind one."

So that was it! She wanted it all. *I have never shown my body to anyone:* even at her most exposed she would be able to keep her secret. How thoroughly Oriental.

"Get off my property," I said. "You don't want a

photographer — you want a lover. Don't be a coward, find a man, give yourself to him — "

As I was speaking in that heated way I heard her footsteps retreat across the frozen yard. Then nothing, no reply, no farewell. Had I imagined it?

It was another picture not taken, a superb prophetic one. And it was maddening — because I hadn't taken it, I doubted that she existed. Whether it was hallucinated fear or not, I never found out; but shortly afterward I understood. So this is how it starts, I thought, and I was sorry, because if I'd had half the imagination people claimed I have I could have told them the Japanese were planning to cook our goose. Not two weeks later Pearl Harbor was attacked. I wished I had taken the picture. We entered the war, and nothing was ever the same again.

26

The Halls of Dawn

GREAT CALAMITIES of a public nature cause people's lives to become similar. It is the fellowship of catastrophe. And it was a comfort for me to know that I was not alone in the dark — the lights had gone out for everyone. It was much more than the radio, the saving of bacon fat and peachstones, the war effort — the firehouse siren simulating an attack on the Cape, and air raid wardens pacing the peaceful streets of Hyannis and South Yarmouth. It was a shared tedium of suspense: we were all on our backsides, breathing the same darkness, waiting for the all-clear and hoping when it was over that there wouldn't be a grinning little oriental or some beefy kraut at the door about to quick-march us into the light of day.

It convinced me that Europe was a snakepit, a feudal quagmire of greasers, winos, swordsmen, and slap-happy aristocrats. Europe was corrupt, at best a brothel, at worst a rotting museum, backward looking, sneaky, self-regarding, priest-ridden, ungovernable, held together by sheer bluff and a jealous hatred of America. Its hand-me-down culture was simply patronage in rags. It had disemboweled or driven out its geniuses and made its lunatics dictators. I had never been able to understand the pro-European bias of American writers and artists. It seemed to arise from a deep sense of inferiority and a mistrust of our own free-wheeling vulgarity. Europe was a cheap meal, an easy lay, a place where you could make ends meet.

Never mind that they persecuted Jews and starved intellectuals and mortgaged artists to the hilt and walled themselves in on every national frontier — think of all that history!

But history — why didn't they know this? — is the very thing the artist must ignore. I was delighted when we declared war. They started it; we'd finish it, in Europe and the Pacific — and England was worth saving. No sooner had we begun bulldozing through battle than I felt a buoyancy in my innermost being. Light! This was my war: it was the struggle I had been losing against Papa. A year before I had identified a Hitlerian streak in Papa and seen him as a destroyer of freedom. Now the enemy was larger and particular, but so was I — I had a whole army behind me. Papa's tyranny was mellowed by the war. He sided with me more and more; he loosened his grip and stopped treating me like a blind person. Though I did not regain my eyesight I got back my second sight, that visionary sense his domination had suspended in me. I could breathe again.

Orlando joined the Marines. I was able to see that he looked swell in his uniform. His last words to me were, "When I get back things are going to be different. I'm going to open your eyes."

He gave me hope. I had been mistaken in thinking he was Phoebe's. He could be mine, and when he was, I could see. He wrote long funny letters from boot camp, and more from California, and then he disappeared into the Pacific, at which point the letters ceased. But I had no fears for his safety. He would be back.

Whenever I thought of the war, I remembered a certain evening, the radio playing a *"Shadow"* serial, Mama whipping up a batch of magarine in the mixing bowl, and Papa saying, "Look at them. They just sit there like a pair of widows."

Orlando was away: he belonged to us both. I dreamed of him often and recovered my old love for him, a rainbow of physical longing. I lay awake at night thinking of him. I imagined him touching my eyes and peeling my blindness away.

The other Maude Pratt continued to be celebrated in magazines and exhibitions, while I rocked on the porch in South Yarmouth. My inactivity, I'm sure, helped my fame, since any more of my pictures would have confused the critics and might have made a hash of their theories about me. I watched Maude Pratt become a figure of eminence: she was the bedrock of American photography, and because she produced no new work she was not reappraised. As for me, I did not feel burdened by the desire to take any pictures. I was intensely, unfashionably happy.

Phoebe was glum. She who had been so lively, who had been revealed to me as subtle and capable of a sadness that gave her a look of intelligence — then eclipsed — then the toast of *Vogue* — now seemed more mysterious than ever. She was over thirty — no more modeling. She spoke — as models often did — of going into dress-designing or becoming a buyer of some equally pointless duds. But she did nothing, and though her inaction was a suitable reproach to my own idleness there was something in it of the abandoned lover. It was the woe I had seen in her after we got the ambiguous telegram from Florida — when she was on the point of total surrender and toying with suicide. Now I could almost believe, such was the depth of her sadness, that they had been lovers and that she feared they might never be again. She could not confide her secret: no one must know; it was for them love or death.

This was guesswork on my part. For myself, I hoped to have Orlando back and my sight restored. I kept up to date on the war. My interest was the opposite of ghoulish — each success encouraged me, things got rolling in North Africa, we invaded Italy, Pacific islands were recaptured, and as we won battles my mood improved. I knew joy by the way it became a refinement of light, as in the greatest pictures; ecstasy's candle was not far off.

I had proof of this gladdening of my eye. One day in the spring of 1943 Mama decided to have the piano tuned. The man she hired was Mr. Slaughter, whose picture I had done in the Twenties and who was much in demand on the Cape as a piano tuner because of that picture. He was blind. I had been uneasy about his visit and rather dreaded his gratitude. But I stayed in and waited with Phoebe. The folks were in town and, mistrusting our ability to solve the simplest problem, they had left us with an envelope of instructions and a few dollars.

Mr. Slaughter arrived on the dot of three, in Mr. Wampler's beach wagon. He tapped his cane on the porch.

"Hi, there."

"That you, Maude?"

Then he was in the house and stooping and grunting over his satchel.

"Piano's in here," I said.

"Hate to bother you, but would you mind taking another picture of me? The last one was fine, but I was wearing my old suit. I got a new tie and a haircut today. Here, I brought this camera in my bag. It's all loaded. All you have to do is pull the trigger."

"I can't."

"Why not? It's a Brownie. Always in focus."

"Phoebe can do it."

"Won't be the same thing." He fingered a dollar bill. "I'll pay you cash."

Oh, hell, I thought. "Stand by the window."

"Just fix this here tie — "

I aimed at his voice and clicked. "Mister Slaughter, I — " But I couldn't say it, I hardly believed it — I could see him!

He looked much older, twisting a cloth cap in his hands, with a white cane and a satchel at his feet, and fish-faced, his mouth puckered, as if he were sniffing at something. And whether it was the grayness of the afternoon or his obstruction of the window, I didn't know, but I was deeply disappointed by what I saw:

the gruesome parlor, the stacks of newspapers, the paintings on the wall so much less lively, a tomb-like quality in the room, his worn shoes on the worn carpet. Everything was aged, reduced in size, very plain. If I was shocked it was not because of the miraculous suddenness of my vision, but because of what I saw — no thrill, only a pale light, a blind man in a shabby room.

"It's right over here, Mister Slaughter," said Phoebe, entering from the kitchen. "What are you two doing?"

As I looked up from the camera, the shade of my eyelids was drawn on Mister Slaughter, who had looked as white and as fragile as ash.

He said, "This war. Maybe it's a blessing we can't see what's going on. All the fighting. Still, I hope the picture comes out."

When he left he took the light with him. I had not liked what I had seen. Perhaps it was a true wartime event, a vision of failure and desolation in victory; it made me wary of more victories of that kind.

But secretly I started experimenting with my own Speed Graphic, and I found that if I was calm, and holding the instrument a certain way — and provided I was alone — I could, for the second it took the shutter to open and close, see a whole still picture, which remained printed in my retina like a photograph in a rectangle of light.

I did not tell a soul. This was not vision in the ordinary sense, but it gave me hope for something better. I knew it would take more than a camera to get my sight back.

Soldiers — the earliest ones to enlist — began arriving home in their khakis. In June 1944, we had a phone call, collect, from California: Orlando was on his way back. The next few days were a torment and every time the phone rang there were screams of "I'll get it!" But it was a full week before we saw him, and he was not alone.

He had brought his "buddy" with him. All soldiers

had buddies then. This fellow, a rawboned individual whose name was Woodrow Leathers, was from Stillwater, Maine. Orlando had promised him a ride there in his car after his own homecoming on the Cape.

"Cookie," said Orlando as he kissed me in his old tender way, lingering a fraction on my lips, promising more with that pressure. Phoebe he treated strangely, with a distancing formality, nipping her on the cheek and then drawing Leathers to the window to point out the windmill in the far garden, which he affectionately ridiculed. I suspected that things had changed between them, if indeed anything had ever existed.

Leathers — or "Woody" as Orlando called him — made a beeline for Phoebe. "You married?" he said, not mincing his words. Clearly encouraged by her reply, he went on, "I wouldn't mind settling down once this war's over."

"Make yourself at home," she said. "I'll show you our beach."

This left Orlando to me. He was just what I needed. He had been my ailment, he could speed my recovery, for love is both a sickness and a cure. I remembered his promise: *I'm going to open your eyes.* Well, here he was. We walked along the beach, he skimmed stones into the Sound and said, "I dreamed about this." Up ahead, I could hear Phoebe flirting with Woody.

At dinner, Papa said, "This calls for a celebration."

"It's real nice of you folks," said Woody.

Mama had roasted a turkey, Papa uncorked his New York chablis. Woody sat next to Phoebe, and I had Orlando.

"It's a bit flinty in taste," said Papa, sipping the wine, then pouring. "I hope it doesn't destroy your palate, Woody."

"Tastes real good to me," said Woody, and after two glasses his manner changed. He steadied his elbows on the table and guffawed and told us about the gooney birds on Midway Island: "I see this son-of-a-

whore in a chair looking at the birds and I says, 'What
do you do all day?' And he says, 'This.' *This!* Looking
at the fucken birds!" He became expansive about the
assault they had made in the Marshall Islands: "The
Christly landing-craft fucken nearly capsized and we
could see the little bastards scattering on the beach.
But I just waded in and let them have it with my
Jesus carbine and brought them down like fucken par-
tridges. Eh, Ollie?"

The folks took this remarkably well. He was for-
given: it was war.

Orlando said, "Woody's quite a shot."

"You're no slouch," said Woody. "Anyway, the
fucken old man was bullshit, but after we took the
Marshalls we both got a stripe."

"You must be glad to be out," said Mama.

"Out?" said Woody. "We ain't out. We're just on
furlough."

"Ollie?" said Papa.

Orlando said, "He's right. We've got a month."

Mama said, "I don't want you to go back. I won't
let you."

"Don't spoil it, Mother," said Papa. "We're giving
Woody a bad impression."

"Fucken okay with me, sir. But where would the
Corps be without me and Ollie? They'd be grabbing
hind tit, sir. We're going to sink Japan — I don't want
to miss that."

"Can't you quit?" said Phoebe.

"If you want me to, I will!" said Woody. "Naw.
Hey, it's not bad. We get better chow than this, believe
it or not."

There was a silence, then a cricket's mad chirp.

Woody said, "I always say the wrong thing."

Papa said, "We know what you mean, son. We want
you to feel right at home."

"I'm having a real nice time," said Woody, and the
table was jolted as he nudged Phoebe.

"I'll bet you're a much better shot than my brother,"
said Phoebe.

"Maybe I got a better weapon," said Woody.

Orlando ignored them. He hugged me and said, "You look great, cookie. I really missed you."

And when he touched me I felt a current run through a glorious circuit in my body.

"We're going to hit the hay," Papa said later, in the parlor, setting down his brandy glass. "Plenty of time to talk tomorrow. You youngsters should turn in, too." And he led Mama away.

"Tell me," said Phoebe to Woody, and shining with flirty curiosity, "what was the scariest thing that happened to you?"

"Scariest? Gee, I don't know. Maybe that landing in the Marshalls. I mean, I could have gotten killed. I was in the first wave, see, and we were under fire from the Jap positions. But I didn't care!" He let out a huge reckless laugh. From the way he talked I could tell he wore white gym socks and loafers, had red ears and spiky hair and spaces between his teeth. I could not understand what Phoebe saw in him.

"Ollie was with you, though?" she said.

"No, he was way the fuck back. The photographers were the last ones on the beach."

"Photographers?" said Phoebe.

Orlando said, "When they heard my name was Pratt, they gave me a camera."

"I don't think much of that," said Phoebe, and to Woody she said, "You're kind of cute."

Orlando said, "You saved my life, cookie. Everything's going to be all right. You'll see."

"Is that a promise?"

"You bet it is." He stood up and yawned. "It's late. Past our bedtimes. Let's go, Woody — lights out. I'll show you to the spare room."

"Don't go away," said Phoebe. "You don't have to listen to him."

Woody said, "I'm having a real good time. I want you to know that. It means a lot to a guy."

Phoebe said, "Sleep tight, soldier. Night, Ollie."

When they had gone I said to Phoebe, "Shame on you. I think you got a crush on him."

"Who?"

I had always known that only Orlando could save me. Giving the house an hour to settle down, waiting for the pipes and floors to be still, I lay in my bed and thought how simple my art had been, compared to the endless complexity of my life. My photographs were at the windless center of the storm, the eye of the hurricane. I was celebrated but unknown — the curse of art, for the storm was too great and contradictory a thing to compress in one picture or a thousand. Anyway, one word was worth a thousand pictures.

My vision was partial. That was as much as I could manage alone. I needed Orlando's help, his love, for my eyes. Love was sight, and lovelessness made creased bats of us all, suspended in hiding folds in the daytime, and jarring at night. I had willfully blinded myself and given up. But he made me believe; he wanted me: *You'll see.*

Already I saw — my bed, my room, the padlocked trunk. I put on my robe and the darkness was not within me, it was merely the hour — veiled moonless midnight in early summer. My movements were brisk with hope. I knew where I was going, and I swept from my room and down the corridor as confidently as if the whole house were lighted. I was not nervous, and yet before I had gone ten steps I was out of breath. My heart pounded with joy; a numbness in my fingers and a great cracking in my skull bringing me a deranged lucidity in which the walls and floor seemed to be moving past me, carrying me to Orlando's room.

Long before, on younger legs, I had made other forays and surprised him. But now, like an adult shadowing a bold child, keeping a few paces behind to protect her, I was guided by her. I overtook this ghostly figure at the door, where she paused. Inside the room I unfurled my robe and threw it on the floor.

He was asleep, but no sooner had I slipped into his

bed than he was awake, embracing me, dragging my nightgown up, kneeling above me and kissing and biting me. All this was new and nearly brutal, and for the first minute or so — before I felt the whole of his weight — I thought, *No, I can't* and wanted him to stop. I was being manhandled, pushed roughly to the edge of a precipice. But I was helpless in his rolling hands and his determination overcame me. He forced my legs apart fiercely, like someone tunneling, fighting for air, planting a candle of explosive in me to blow me to bits, so he could struggle past me. He was huge and impatient, and I wasn't ready. Sooner than I wanted, the pain began, and the pain was, intensely, its own anesthetic.

It was like no picture I had ever seen, the palatial halls of dawn, a blood-red dome of sun piercing the distant sea and boiling there in a corona of its own flames and sending light all the way to the shore along the yellow furrows, until the tiniest wavelet of sea-changed surf jumping limply to the sand was drenched with heat.

My heart stopped. His face was on mine, but I felt only that star rising in me and scorching the backs of my eyes and making me bleed tears. I was confined within my own body and yet freed of it, as if I had been flayed alive and covered with gore. I cried out — not knowing whether I wanted him to stop or continue. He took my screech for encouragement and worked harder. The pain passed through me and left me in pieces, in a deliquescence of light that was like a happy death. I was perfectly still; I wanted more, I dreaded more. Now the light leaked to a pinprick, just that, as if he had caught me in my fluttering and fixed me with a pin in my tenderest spot.

He never spoke a word. He slipped beside me sighing and I realized that though my eyes blazed they were tightly shut.

I woke in my own room. It was my first sunrise. It was inaudible. I gave it time — still, it was something of a

letdown. Each twiggy tree and tremulous bud, the
wallpaper florets, the candlewick bedspread, that smug
trunk. I appreciated the detail, but the scale alarmed
me: had the room always been that small? The whites
so tinged with gray? I opened my eyes on a tinier,
shabbier world that seemed at once temporary and
perpetual, and on the Sound a sailboat blowing this
way and that like a mad hanky.

A cramp was twisted in my abdomen, the ache of a
wound between my legs. My bruised flesh was fragile
and then I saw the beetles of crimson-black blood on
my thighs and I ran to the bathroom.

"Scrambled eggs," said Phoebe, busy catching the tin
doors of the old-fashioned toaster. "Papa's making
them for everybody."

I said, "Just what I feel like."

Woody was sprawled at the table with his hands behind his head. His face was a muffin, puffy with sleep-
lessness. He yawned and didn't cover his mouth. He
wallowed in his yawn, showing his gappy teeth, and
said, "I don't care if I ever go back."

Papa said, "Give Maude a hand, will you?"

"I can manage," I said. I was still wearing my dark
glasses, partly because I didn't want to shock anyone
so early in the morning and partly because they had
the effect of diminishing the light, which I found oppressive. I had emerged from a darkroom. This brightness had an intolerable voltage, and yet, for all its
luminosity, it revealed nothing new to me.

Mama said, "Someone ought to call Orlando."

She was little and brown and looked fussed and
feathery like a guinea hen.

"Ollie!" yelled Papa, carrying the pan of eggs to the
foot of the hall stairs. "Probably dead to the world.
He'll be here in a minute."

But he did not come.

Phoebe said, "We can start without him." She looked
tired and tarnished and had lost the winking flirta-
tiousness of the previous night. It was not lassitude but

repose: she had a secret. I wondered if she had
gotten up to something with Woody in the night. He
certainly looked as if he was luxuriating in slyness,
enjoying a kind of love's heartburn.

"You look real nice today," he said, touching the
frilly cuff of Phoebe's calico frock.

"Thanks," she said, and jerked her arm away.

Mama handed Woody a mug of coffee. "No sign of
our son."

I could not take my eyes from the window, the prospect of garden and sea which on this cool morning had
a sodden cardboard truth — damp and downright and
weatherbeaten.

Then it leaped away: Orlando appeared between
a pair of lilacs, treading the dewy frost-blue grass in
his bare feet, a muscular sprite with his hair keenly
bleached and his khaki shirttails out. He was brisk and
sheepish, a shoe in each hand.

"Why, there he is," I said. I stood up while he
paused at the kitchen window. He waved one shoe at
us and made a face.

I waved back and did not notice the silence until I
had sat down. Everyone was looking at my eyes.

Papa said, "Maude!"

And Mama started to cry.

"Sorry I'm late," said Orlando. "I was sleeping in
the windmill."

"Good idea," Papa grunted. He had set down his
coffee and was rounding the table toward me. He said,
"Look at me, honey."

Orlando said, "I dreamed about it while I was over-
seas. That's all I thought about. Spending a night there,
bunked down on the floor, and — hey, what's everybody — ?"

"Maudie," said Papa, making the victory sign with
his fingers. "How many digits have I got here? Take
your time."

"Two — a dozen — what does it matter?" I said. I
was looking at Woody, his shaven head and puffy
pockmarked face, the way he grinned greedily at

Phoebe. And she was looking with love upon Orlando, who was still lamely explaining his night out to the folks. The windmill! Finally, everyone agreed: it was just like Orlando.

But I was the center of attention and, though housebound with them for years, was treated as if I had returned after a long absence. In their scramble to find out my new impressions of them, no one asked how the miracle had happened.

Orlando put his betrayer's hand on my shoulder and said, "It's like old times."

He took Woody to Maine. Phoebe waited; I no longer wondered at her patience — I knew what she was waiting for.

27

Abroad

HEARTBROKEN, I did the only thing I could, dusted down my peepstones and picked up where I had left off. Instead of hanging myself I took the sunniest pictures I could find, *Twenty-two White Horses, Graduation: Woonsocket High School,* and *Vineyard Homecoming.* I was out of love; I was miserably free. Woody hadn't left me pregnant — he had pierced my blind body and violated my darkness with light. Virginity had been my windowless room. And I did *Mother and Child,* the breast-feeding shot in which the head of the suckling infant looks like a two-hundred watt bulb — the picture itself was often referred to as "The Yarmouth Madonna."

In this phase of my career I was drawn to writers. The first of them, the biggest son-of-a-bitch I was ever to photograph, was the poet Frost. I had met him at Edmund Wilson's house up in Wellfleet (Bunny owned several of my pictures and was partial to my rear view of Lawrence's head, which hung in his study). Frost spent the entire evening monologuing to a group of admirers, a whopping earache of complaints against his family — I had never heard anyone belittle his children like that man. It was hard to reconcile the hayseed and cracker-barrel image and *Farmer's Almanac* verse — the counterpart in poetry of Sam Chamberlain at his birchiest, but with a muddy witch riding in on her broom — hard to see a rustic in this gravelly-voiced grump downing whiskies and damning the human race. He looked the part, with his baggy pants and his thumbs hooked on his galluses, but if there was a nastier and more tight-fisted self-promoter in the business I never met him.

"I wonder if Mister Frost would mind being photographed," I said.

"Mind?" said Bunny in a shrill jeer that was so unlike the growl of his prose. He threw his head back and shrieked, "He won't leave you alone until you do! But don't expect him to thank you."

At the time I was making preparations to go abroad, where I hoped to do our victory. But Wilson, a great arranger of things, gave my name to the editor of a now defunct family magazine and I was sent to Amherst to do Frost. I knew that if I alerted Frost to my intention he would insist on posing for me. I checked into the Lord Jeff and took my time. I bought the newest edition of his *Collected Poems* and read it and thought hard about him. The picture: I wanted him at the local food store buying a quart of milk and a can of ready-made spaghetti. But though I watched him closely, his daily walk — along the Common, scaring birds — took him always to the Jones Library where he had a friend.

It was there that I confronted him. I had heard his loud aggrieved voice as soon as I entered the building. He was upstairs, snorting and driveling, and seeing me he turned away.

"Mister Frost?" I said. I held out his book.

"Why do you pursue me!" He lifted his elbows and flattened himself against the book stacks. "Go away!"

The other man, frightened into politeness by Frost's outburst, interposed himself and said softly, "I think she wants you to sign the book, sir."

"I just signed five hundred of those in New York and they're selling for six dollars apiece."

"I'd be really pleased — "

"She wants — "

"I know what she wants," said Frost, and then, "Oh, all right, give me the book. What's your name?"

In large shaky upright script he wrote _Robert Frost to Maude Pratt, 1944_. Before he handed it back, he flipped a few pages, a verifying caress, like a father scratching his child's head. I had never known an author not to give his book this squinting second glance at signature time, but Frost paused longer than most.

"There was one other thing," I said. "I wondered if you'd let me take your picture."

"Who sent you?"

I told him.

"What's your usual fee?"

"Fifty dollars and a year's subscription."

"Stand back," he said to the cringing man, and gave me a side view. He knew he had a good profile, but his noggin was narrow as a hatchet and I wanted him head-on, with his close-set eyes and unmown hair and frown-marks on his forehead, all his suspicion and vanity apparent on the blade of his face, the trough of his mouth. I wanted a glimpse of his canvas shoes and the complicated apparatus holding up his pants — galluses and leather belt — and his big freckled hands clenched on his own book.

"Must be something wrong," I said. "I can't see you."

Naturally, he turned, and just as he said, "Goddammit" I clicked and got the curmudgeon I wanted. He returned his head to show me his profile and I did a dozen more, but I knew that the first one was the best.

I thanked him for his autograph and apologized for bothering him.

He said sourly, "When do I get my fifty dollars?"

There was a further delay to my European jaunt, an assignment that took me to California. I had been asked to do some pictures about morale-boosting movies that were being made in Hollywood, such as _Air Force_ and _Bomber Command_. I felt I owed it to Orlando to cooperate — he had returned to active duty and the last I had heard he was in the Philippines. The movies were fairly dreadful, but no one seemed to mind except the talented authors whose artless chore it was to work on them. The word was that John Steinbeck had written a script for a Hitchcock war-effort called *Lifeboat* and that he was distressed by the hash that had been made of it. It was my favorite theme — the good novelist in the meat-grinder of patronage and reduced to hamburg. But the cutting-edges of this meat-grinder were worth examining: patriotism, vanity, debt, greed, and warfare. I wanted Hitchcock and Steinbeck together, fat and skinny on the back lot, the most unliterary picture possible.

Steinbeck wasn't around, and no one knew where he was — some said New York, some said Mexico. All that was certain was that he had gone through the roof.

I kept busy. Hollywood was full of geniuses — inverted alchemists, as Huxley called them, who had been hired to change gold into lead. Going from studio to studio I found actors who were only too glad to make faces for me. And I did my second set of boogie-man pictures. A black bit-part player remembered my Camera Club show. The shock on people's faces when he took me in his arms and gave me a bear-hug! He was fifty or so and had aged the way blacks do, with a dull grayness on his skin and dark circles around his red eyes, his hands scaly and almost reptilian. He was wearing a U.S. Army uniform.

"Let's have a salute," I said.

He refused. "I ain't a soldier and this ain't a war. This is just a white man's movie."

The uniform, he said, had been issued by the wardrobe department of Universal Studios. As I did him he reminisced and said how glad he had been to see his "people" in my exhibitions, referring to my portraits of Robeson and the negative prints of Doolum, Pigga, and Teets and *Negro Swimming to a Raft*. He began to cry, and crying revealed everything of himself. The tears splashed down the cheeks of this troubled sentimental soul. Actors are unembarrassed and can cry facing the camera, but crying is impossible to control once the first blubs have started — it is as unselective and telling as anger or lust.

It gave me a good idea. After he introduced me to other actors — who readily agreed to be photographed — I asked them to cry for me at the end of the session. Alan Ladd, Loretta Young, Charles Laughton, Henry Fonda: I had people crying for me, and with greater effect, long before Philippe Halsman had them jumping. Bogart was the one man who refused to cry for me, but I knew that if he had there would have been no stopping him. All he said was, "Get her out of here."

Raymond Chandler said something similar, but he had more reason. I had been taken out to eat by Aldous Huxley, whom I had visited in connection with an assignment I'd asked for, a *Saturday Evening Post* photo-essay about Huxley's *The Art of Seeing,* which had come out two years before. The book had been severely criticized and even ridiculed, but I was in a good position to judge it and I believed much of it to be true. Huxley was interested that I had done D. H. Lawrence and said that he was still in touch with the throbbing turnip, Frieda. At the Mexican restaurant, Huxley read the menu with his cheek against it, looking sideways at it with one swiveled eye.

"Pass the salt, please," he said, after we were served our enchiladas.

I deliberately handed him the pepper. He did not detect this until he shook it. He sniffed and put it down and said, "That is pepper. I'd hate to think you did that on purpose."

"Gosh, no."

One eye squinting, one bulging, and both clouded and misshapen with a kind of gruesome tissue, he described the Bates Method of seeing. He said, "The eye must be re-educated. I want you to look behind me and tell me what you see."

"A man — tiny, tweedy, and drunk — with a little old lady. He's dapper, fifty-odd — but, Christ, that woman is seventy-five if she's a day. She's walking very upright, as if she's afraid her wig is going to fall off. Now they're sitting down and the man's snapping his fingers at the waiter."

Huxley hadn't turned. He said, "That's Chandler."

"So you have eyes in the back of your head. The Bates Method sure is something!"

Huxley laughed. I excused myself and, taking my camera and pretending to head for the ladies' room, I looked for a vantage point to shoot this mismatched couple. I saw concealment between a pillar and palm not far from the Chandlers' table and did a few preliminary shots. Screwing on my flash attachment I marched up to them. In situations that called for quick timing I always made a prior adjustment, setting the focus for six feet, since it is an easy distance to gauge — focusing is impossible in an emergency.

"Applesauce!" I yelled. They looked up and froze, as people do when surprised by a camera, and I snapped. Chandler, bug-eyed in the light, had the gape of a man in a mug shot. His wife, Cissy, being elderly, was slow to react. Her face had been plaster, but the flesh whitened it further: she had no lips, no shadows, only the faintest dusted lines of panic, like cracks in a porcelain monkey. Then the light abated, her face slackened, and she looked a hundred years older, as stale and ruined as yesterday's oatmeal.

"Jesus, who do you think you are!" Chandler snarled.

"Sorry," I said. "My mistake. I took out for Jiggs and Maggie."

Cissy, who was rigid, touched at her face as if to make sure it was still there, and she began to whimper. Chandler cursed me and put his arm around her. She inched over into a swoon, a richly grotesque *pietà* I could not resist snapping.

"Waiter!"

Already I regretted the pictures. They were perhaps the cruellest ones I had ever done, taken in the most hammer-hearted way — faultless timing, nastily motivated.

"Meet you outside," I said to Huxley, and dashed out of the restaurant.

"What was that kerfuffle all about?" he asked in the taxi, undermining my respect for his treatise on the Bates Method.

"A case of mistaken identity," I said. I looked out the window and seeing that we were on Hollywood Boulevard I said, "Mind if we stop?"

"Not at all." Huxley loved the sleazy glamor of Hollywood. As an intellectual he could have it both ways, be mocking about the cheap glitter, and blamelessly wallow in it because he knew it was cheap. His streak of vulgarity was a mile wide in any case: he secretly lusted after a huge whorish success, since having it was the only convincing way of despising it. But success, even vulgar success, is denied to those who belittle it as they drool.

We got out of the taxi and I did my Huxley pictures there on the sidewalk, using available glare — Huxley sticking out like a sore thumb among the bellowing movie marquees, the clip joints and dives and neon curlicues. This pecker-up Englishman in his wrinkled suit and shapeless wool tie, with his hair raked back Russian-style and his ears sticking out and in the glare a dozen blurred criminal faces: he looked owlish and prim. It was how he wanted to be photographed, yet another slumming foreigner who thought he was a real devil. But how was he to know that his eyes would appear as two useless polyps, and that he would look — smiling there on Hollywood Boulevard — like a blind man who had lost his way and wandered into a flesh-pot and praised it because it sounded jolly. The title was *Huxley*, but I thought of it as *Eyeless in Gaza*.

He had convinced himself that he could see and persuaded others of his belief. I think myself that he was partially sighted and that the rest, like much of his writing, was sheer nonsense. It was not the Bates Method, but drugs, will power, brains, and bullshit, and if my picture of him showed anything it was a man kidding himself.

"You should stop awhile in Los Angeles," he said. "This is one of the great cities of the world, a mixture of Babylon, Vienna, and — "

"Cleveland?"

"I was going to say Chichén—Itzá, but have it your way."

"I have to go to Europe."

"Europe is here," he said. "The thinkers, I mean, and they're the only ones who matter. But not only them — Schönberg, Einstein — "

"He's in New Jersey."

"Thomas Mann."

"He's here? I'd love to do him."

"You'll need an introduction," said Huxley. "But I might be able to help you."

Two days later my taxi was bowling along San Remo Drive, Mann's street in Pacific Palisades. I fought my way through the palms in the front yard and rang the bell.

"He is expecting you," said the German girl at the door. "He will be down presently."

It was one of those reverently old-world households in which one detected a great hidden presence. The German girl had whispered; another tiptoed in and smiled at me. The house was private, and dense with bourgeois upholstery and family intimacy, sanctified with feather dusters and furniture polish. Somewhere, in a room I could not see, a concentrating man was preparing his entrance.

But when it happened the spell was broken. He shuffled into the room, a stooping mustached man of about seventy, his face creased into thoughtful planes. He had a storekeeper's kindliness, he could have been a haberdasher.

"Delighted," he said. He shook my hand, then looked at his pocket watch.

"Let me do you holding that pen."

He showed me the object between his fingers and transformed it into an unlit cigar: magic. He smiled and lit it lovingly. Coffee and chocolate cakes were brought and we were joined, one by one, by people: wife, children, young men and women who weren't introduced. They watched him attentively and leaned forward when he spoke.

I said, "You must be happy here. Huxley says it's like Vienna."

"I wonder if he knows Vienna," said Mann. "It is various in this city. Plastic. But I make no such comparisons."

"I'm going to Europe pretty soon."

His gaze deepened with thought. He said, "The cockpit." Then, "What of your family?"

Before I knew it (perhaps because he was so correct and cultured and I was, in my own defense, trying hard to please) I was telling him how my parents had taken me to the opera and encouraged us to be music lovers. I ransacked my memory for episodes and, relating them, saw that he was particularly struck by the one in which Orlando and I had gone out to the fire escape during the concert at Symphony Hall; and how the man passing below had looked up at us and joined us in some mystical way, not as brother and sister, but more profoundly marrying our souls.

"I suppose you could say it was a blessing" — what was I saying? I thought I had been talking about music! — "the way this stranger looked up and smiled at the two of us."

"I know that young man," he said. "I could tell you his name."

More magic. Did he wink? It certainly looked that way.

Of course, I had no idea what he was talking about, but I was reassured, for just as Huxley had been charmed by my memory of Lawrence, Mann responded to this childhood incident. I was glad that I remembered enough of my past to interest my subjects.

"If you just stay put," I said, "the others can sort of group around you."

I saw a nice courtly picture, with the friends and

relations standing around the great man. But he wouldn't have it. He insisted on standing, half turned, with one hand in his jacket pocket and the cigar in his other hand and the folks extended between two fringed floor lamps against the drapes — a very corny arrangement, as if they were all waiting for a bus.

"Erika is in London," he said, when I was done. "You will send some reproductions for her?"

I promised I would and he took out his pocket watch: time to go.

There was only one more picture to do. I had been asked by *Life* to update their files. Their picture of William Faulkner was a studio shot that had obviously been retouched to make him look like a confederate colonel. "Get him looking human," the picture editor said. I remembered that Orlando had mentioned him and admired several of his books, one apparently dealing with Harvard, which he had started to read to me during my early blind period and then stopped, saying, "This wouldn't make any sense to you" — I suspected that he gave it to Phoebe to read, because for the next few days, engrossed in the book, she flicked pages and her body purred.

Faulkner, I learned, was staying at the Highland Hotel in Hollywood, a semirespectable residential hotel done up in a kind of ulcerated stucco. There was no one at the front desk the day I visited, so — seeing his name and room number on the key board — I went directly to his room. I knocked and waited, and getting no response I tried the door.

It was unlocked: I stole in. The curtain was half open and through the French windows I could see a bright balcony and an armchair. On a table near me were crumpled pages of typescript, an old newspaper, and two copies of *God Is My Co-Pilot*. In the air was a sweet rotten-walnut stink of bourbon whisky, but apart from the sound of traffic and the sizzle of California sunlight the room was quiet. I peeked into the next room — an empty unmade bed — and I was about to leave when I saw a half-filled glass next to the telephone and a bottle and ice bucket. It looked like an interrupted boozing session, as if he had just stepped out. The room had the lived-in appearance of a warm mangled nest, the disorder of anticipation, a certain nervous premonition.

I considered photographing the room — *Whose Room?*, another series: identify the inhabitant from the dents in the chairs and the dirty glasses and ashtrays and books. I had taken off my dust-cap to act on this impulse, and then I saw him.

He was lying face up on the floor, one hand across his chest, the other pillowing his head; and his legs were poised in a twinkle-toes angle, as if he had died in a dance-step. My first thought was that he was dead — he had busted a gut or had been robbed and killed. But there was no blood anywhere. I went closer and heard him breathe. A moment ago I hadn't heard it; now his snores filled the room with the ripsawing of his drunken doze. As he lay there on the cool floor I could see how small he was — tiny feet, tiny mustache, pretty hands, and in his shorts his hairy little legs. He had a typist's powerful shoulders and though he was flat on his back and unconscious he had a victim's innocent dignity.

This supine man in a bleak Hollywood hotel room would, I knew, be fixed in my mind as emblematic of art. I could not hear the word "literature" without thinking of Lawrence's halitosis or O'Neill's dandruff, or the word "photography" without remembering pictures I had never taken, such as our windmill in the rain. People pretended that art was complete, but it had another side that was hidden and human and wept and stank and snored and died; and I wondered whether it was not perhaps truer than creation.

If Faulkner had been dead I would have done him. But he was only drunk, poor man, and I guessed why. I went away and locked the door and never regretted not taking that picture. Indeed, I was glad it was I who found Faulkner that day, and not another photographer out to make a name for herself.

Before I sailed for Europe I stopped at Grand Island, but I warned them that I wasn't going to stay for long. I had one detail to attend to. My darkroom had to be emptied and all the paraphernalia of my peepshow secured.

"What's that?" asked Phoebe, who looked more than ever the war-bride.

"Guard this with your life," I said. It was the trunk, a so-called steamer trunk, with brass fittings and decayed labels. There was a padlock on the outside and the shots I wanted suppressed — bad ones, amateur ones, the pictures I had found in my camera and processed blind — on the inside. I had not had eyes to see many of these pictures, and now that I had eyes I didn't have the heart. They were blind pictures, they belonged in darkness, and because I had no intention of every looking at them I put this trunk in the windmill, a memory I vowed never to re-enter. I left my own room empty. It was my way of telling everyone that I was out for good, but all I said was, "I might be away for some time."

I meant it ominously: I had no plans to come back. I had my photography and I was free of all desires. It was a useful rootless trade, and if one took the Eisenstadt view one could roam the world like a gypsy, tinkering and pushing on. I had my skill, I had proven my ability to come up with the goods, and I was at last the equal in reputation, if not in accomplishment, of the people I photographed — perhaps the most crucial factor in photography, since subject is everything and technique only something to conceal.

Papa said, "Say, that reminds me. Our friend Woody is dead. He was killed in Leyte in October."

No one understood why at that moment I burst into tears.

"But Ollie's fine," Mama said. "They put him in charge of all the combat photographers. He's going to be all right. Tell us about California."

"Ollie raved about it," said Phoebe.

Papa nudged me and said, "She misses her brother."

"And how," said Mama.

Phoebe shook her head and sighed; but there was a storm in that sigh.

A week later, Papa and Mama saw me aboard the *Georges Clemenceau,* looking tiny and old as people do in their helpless farewells, already receding even as they waved. The *Clemenceau* was a French ship which had come in convoy across the Atlantic and now in safer seas was making a solitary voyage back with a cargo of wheat and about a hundred passengers, nearly all accredited journalists and photographers hoping to report the last act. I kept to myself, avoided their parties, and developed a fear of drowning. I could not sleep in my stifling cabin, so I snoozed in a deck chair during the day and stayed awake at night, roaming the ship. It was on that voyage, on moony nights, that I did my *Ghost Ship* sequence, the empty vessel awash on rough seas. Was it a fear of drowning or a desire for it? All my life I had lived next to the ocean, and it seemed always to be impatiently smacking the shore to remind me how easily I might enter and disappear. Death by drowning was not death at all, but a surrender to the immortality of a watery afterlife in the chambers of the sea.

We docked at Southampton in late March 1945. I went straight to London, where morale was high. It was my first glimpse of the disaster-prone British, obsessed with their own fortitude, making a virtue of the national vice — their love of a plucky defeat. London looked raped, as if the enemy had plundered it and gone, and yet even in bombed disrepair it wasn't beaten. I tried to show this in my pictures — not the city but the weary whistling-in-the-dark triumph in people's faces, the strain of war, the threadbare frugality. To do them complete justice and make the pictures timeless I cropped them closely from chin to forehead. There are no hats or hairstyles or neckties or ears in my *English Faces* — they are people peer-

ing through the wrong side of a picket fence — and
though there is a bishop, a lord, at least one millionaire, as well as a Bayswater prostitute, a flower-seller,
and any number of tramps and tea-ladies, I believed
they were impossible to tell apart.

Through Miss Dromgoole, whom I visited and photographed (how strange it seemed that this dull old
lady had educated Phoebe and me), I got a bedsitter
in the Star and Garter Mansion in Putney, right on
the river. It was, with the assignments I was offered,
all I needed: darkroom, bedroom, parlor, and at twilight the complete camera obscura, with the rowers
shimmering on the wall. I lived there happily, room
within room, in the Chinese box of my body, feeding
shillings into the meter and toasting crumpets on the
gas-fire. London made me feel elderly and genteel,
like some brave old dear in bombazine, secure in
what seemed an eternal old age. That was how I lived,
alone and unpestered, among dog-lovers.

My work was something else. Just after V-E Day,
I took the train to Paris and did Georgie Patton. I
think one can see the regret on his face, deflated aggression wrinkled up; his war was over, and he died
that same year, not performing one of the daredevil
stunts everyone associated with him, but in a fairly
unspectacular car crash. He was, like many fanatics
I have known, rather shy in close-up, and he talked
nervously throughout the session, swearing and excus-
ing himself, telling me the Fokker-Messerschmitt joke,
and finally saying, "You get the pistols? People say
they're pearl-handled — well, that's a goddamned lie.
They're ivory. From an elephant. You can tell them
that. From an elephant."

My portrait of Gertrude Stein looking like a saloon-
keeper ("I won't let you do Pussy," she said, wagging
her crewcut at the wretched Miss Toklas) was also
done on this visit, but I left Paris soon after. I did not
want to be tempted into any damp Cartier-Bresson
shots of lovers and bores in berets and courageous
floozies in teddy-back chemises.

On my return to London I toyed with the idea of writing a biography of Julia Margaret Cameron, the first female of my species. I thought that by writing about her I could divest myself of my own experience and my general feelings about photography. In some ways our lives were similar and we were both makers of icons — in her case "the Dirty Monk," in mine "the Amherst Grump." I could be oblique and remain truthful, even anonymous, by attributing my feelings to Mrs. Cameron, identifying myself with her in the way chicken-hearted biographers did with their subjects. I wanted to get it off my chest and leave myself with the imaginative novel-writer's satisfaction of having done us both by swapping my life for hers. But though I spent some days in the British Museum and even wrote a few opening pages about her originality, I abandoned the project. Morgan Forster, whom I did in Cambridge (I had met him through the dog-lover Joe Ackerley, a fellow Star and Garter resident) encouraged me to continue. I told him I'd given up writing. Forster said, "That makes two of us. Isn't it a muddle?"

It was Ackerley who fixed up my meeting with Evelyn Waugh at the Dorchester. I wrote Waugh a letter; he wrote back to "Mr. Pratt" and then I descended on him. He had just come back from Yugoslavia, rosy-cheeked and full of cherubic colic. I got off to a bad start by mentioning Bunny Wilson, whom he apparently loathed — though Bunny had always spoken highly of him — and then by telling him I lived close by, in Putney.

"Putney is not anywhere near Park Lane," he said.

"Not far, by American standards."

"You Americans and your standards," he said. "Besides, no one lives in Putney."

He was wearing a checkered suit and smoking a big cigar. As I set up my equipment he said, "Is your husband aware that you importune strange men in hotel rooms?"

"I told you I don't have a husband," I said. I did

about eight seated pictures and then saw a good angle at the window, Hyde Park in the afternoon sun. "Could we have a few by the window, Mister Waugh?"

"My name is not Wuff," he said.

"I'm sorry, but I said Waugh."

"I distinctly heard you say Wuff."

"Hey — "

"Please leave this instant or I shall ring for the hall porter. You might have some explaining to do. In any event, I think he'll want a substantial tip for showing you in. Isn't that customary for a woman in your position?"

Ackerley told me not to take this personally — it was Mr. Waugh's usual brush-off. And I still had a good set of pictures.

Remembering the Faulkner picture I had been too tactful to take, and the idea for the series *Whose Room?*, I set off and did a number of authors' rooms. I did the parlor at 23 Tedworth Square where Sam Clemens had written one of his travel books, James's study at Lamb House, Stephen Crane's hospital room, and Hemingway's expensive hotel room. I didn't dare to do Hemingway in the flesh, though I had a good look at him. He was accredited to *Collier's* and for some reason wore a Royal Air Force uniform: he had a broad rich-kid's face and a big mustache and square teeth. There was flint and hurt in his eyes. I was terrified of him. A noisy family lived in the room Ezra Pound had occupied, but it retained a great deal of Ezra's residue. And I did, without divulging it in the caption, my own room at the Star and Garter Mansion — the closest I had ever come to doing a self-portrait. The titles of these pictures were no more than street addresses; some critics called them my most haunting pictures. A room is like a cast-off shoe, which holds the shape of its owner's unique foot. The rooms of these expatriates, with their poignantly printed shadows framed by foreign carpentry, were even more telling than shoes. In Pound's, rectangles on the wall spoke of paintings that had been removed. I believed that it would be possible for a photograph of, say, an uncleared breakfast table or an unmade bed to tell a whole plotty story of a marriage.

There was enough of America in London for me to be happy there ("I don't mind Americans," one of the British jokes went, "but it's those white chaps they brought with them"). I stayed on long after the Anglophiles had left in disenchantment; I saw no point in leaving. Work had displaced my life, and I was well known to the wire services and the picture agencies. I continued to accept assignments which didn't compromise my idea of pictures needing a "drowning quotient." There were some jobs which anyone could have done, and there were others I could make into "Pratts": a Pratt was indistinguishable from the truth and contained both time past and time future. I had my room in Putney, my career, and my contacts. My work gave me access and so I lived what must have looked from the outside like a life. But it was nothing of the kind.

For my *Whose Room?* series I decided to do T. S. Eliot. I wrote a letter to him at Faber's explaining my plan and introducing myself. His reply was formal but hospitable: *I am charmed by your idea, but I cannot conceal my keen disappointment that you intend to exclude me from your portrait of my room.*

When I got to his house (it was a drizzly Sunday afternoon) he said, "Shall I leave now? I feel I am quite superfluous to your intention."

"I'll deal with you later," I said.

But he was showing me into his study and saying, "It's quite a proper little room — too proper do you think? It would be vastly enhanced by a provocative mess in that corner, or a book out of place, or perhaps a constellation of bloodstains on the wall. But I'm in the way. Please go on. Do your stuff and then we'll have tea."

This mock-serious patter surprised me. He produced it the way a whimsical uncle takes out a water pistol, and wonders at it, and then squirts you in the eye. And the fact that he pretended to be a stuffed shirt only made him funnier.

The desk held writing tools and a blank blue pad and a book in a foreign language that might have been Latin or Greek. On the mantelpiece was a chunk of marble, a photograph of Yeats, and on the wall a small aqueous Turner and a junky impressionist painting of some solidified beef stroganoff. The room was like him and yet had none of his humor.

"I greatly fear I am casting a shadow over your picture."

"Don't move," I said. It was true: his shadow in the gray autumn light rose from the foreground and leaned across the room and broke sadly on the bookshelves. A perfect picture of a writer's room and deepened by telling details — the paper-knife, the mirror reflecting the coatrack in the hall with its bowler hat and the urn full of walking sticks, the impatient clock and the vase of white roses. I made one alteration. I went over and thumped the stand that held the vase and knocked a shower of rose petals to the carpet.

"Yes," he said. "It needed that touch."

I shot until I was satisfied that I had the picture I wanted, one a person could browse upon for an hour or so, and then I said, "If you stand by the fireplace I'll do one for your scrapbook."

Standing, not sitting — I wanted his hunch in the picture, the bent back of responsibility. At first he refused, but he allowed himself to be bullied. He gave me his hunch in profile; his face froze in stern reflection at the fallen rose petals. It was a pinched beaky face fitted into a solemn sloping head, with thin slicked-down hair and a tight starched collar and a grim one-syllable mouth, very statesmanly and imperious, but at the same time like a man trying to determine the price of a coffin. He breathed shallowly so as not to disturb his expression, and without batting an eyelash he said, "How do I look?"

"Like a cheese-parer."

He almost smiled, but he kept it down until his eyes grew damp with concentration. Still staring gloomily at the rose petals, he said, "Mrs. Quormby — she does for me — was scouting for cheeses yesterday at the market. I like a ripe Stilton and I don't think I would live in a country where I couldn't get Double Gloucester. The mature cheddars are lovely at their yellowest, but the young ones are so insipid. Cheshire when it's crumbly, Caerphilly when it's wet, or any old Wensleydale. I don't like a soft cheese unless it's a Brie or a Camembert — we'll be seeing a lot more of them now that the war's over. The Leicesters are best when they're ruddy. One used to buy them by the wheel — do you know that locution? One has been eating the mousetrap variety for so long one has begun to feel rather like a mouse. I say, am I putting you off?"

He pondered with his pale clerical face, seeming to look into infinity, but he continued chirping about cheeses until I ran out of film.

Over tea, I felt enough at ease with him to say, "By the way, I like *The Waste Land*."

"No one," he said, "has put it to me quite like that before. I am very flattered."

That was how it went my whole time in London. I took pictures and if no one had a prior claim on them I hoarded them. In the winter of 1946 I held a hugely successful exhibition in a Mayfair gallery. I was well established in Putney and full of plans. Papa wrote and said that Orlando, who had been home for a year, had passed the Massachusetts Bar and was practicing law in Hyannis. I replied that I was about to set off on a trip: India was about to become independent and I longed to do a series of updated Bourne and Shepherd shots of the empire that was about to close up shop. *Life* had promised me first refusal but said that Margaret Bourke-White was next in line. I would not stop in India, I thought; I'd go on and do a *Whose Room?* at Mrs. Cameron's in Ceylon, and Burma, and the aftermath in Japan. And I could travel forever, for I had found that any room was home if it was quiet enough and had the consolation of shadows.

I had rid myself of my life; I had only my work. I did not dine out on my pictures, nor did I seek to be entertained. I made a practice of avoiding friendship with anyone whose picture I had taken: regrets to Eliot, apologies to Forster, so sorry to Bill Astor. Planning the trip, buying an outfit for the tropics, getting a mildew-proof case made for my Speed Graphic — all this kept me occupied in London. When I was lonely I sat down and thought of a likely subject and went out and did him. I could cheer myself up with a general, a great poet, a surgeon, or simply a fellow sufferer — I did my Edward Steichen, my Angus McBean, and my Cecil Beaton at this time.

It was my way of getting grace — by dispensing it; for though I always did the picture I wanted I often consented to do the picture the subject wanted, and I was deft enough to make fools look wise or the plainest meatball endlessly interesting. At the end of a session with an actor, I usually said, "Now let's have some tears."

After a tour of the East I would find an obscure room in Mexico or California, or elsewhere. Orlando and Phoebe were no longer part of my life, though they often swam into my thoughts like sudden frogs one mounted on the other's back, with their legs out, and I looked closer and saw them fucking. The years would roll on and erode my life, but my work if it was any good would exist outside time. I lived timelessly in my work, where disappointments could be reshot, mistakes rectified, errors cropped. It was a world of my own making — a wonderful place. I could not praise too highly the satisfactions of the craft I had compared to raking leaves. It was noiseless, it was not difficult, I could do it drunk or dead tired and it never showed. Within the limits I had set for myself I could do whatever I wished.

I had not earned any of it. I dreaded, as all lucky people do, that I would be handed a bill and have to pay up.

My luck was an ocean mirroring the sky and stretching to that theshold on the horizon beyond which, so the lover believes, there is more ocean. I was buoyant enough and, at forty, was shot of all desires and entanglements. Once, in blind seclusion, I had been older than this and had enjoyed it. I looked forward to the day when I would be leathery and have a mustache and could fart and burp and say any fool thing that came into my head; I would have the authority that went with white hair and deafness.

I indulged myself in the Star and Garter Mansion in the Mitty-dream I had seen in so many people of accomplishment — that feeling that underneath the glamor and achievement one was a very simple soul, saying "Golly" and "Darn it" and doting on cheese and biscuits. I didn't create pictures — I found them. What luck! But anyone with a good camera and a free afternoon could have done the same or better. I called them "Pratts" because the critics did, but "Pratts" were only the world in focus, the few feet of it I could manage with my peepstones. I could go to India or wherever and do the same.

I was setting out to do that very thing when the cable came.

I almost chucked it away without reading it. I'd had enough cables to last me a lifetime and I assumed it was just another one promising me the moon or saying I was swell. But thinking it might be an update on the India jaunt I ripped it open.

The message, in strips of tape, was brief and brutally glued to the flimsy paper. I did not understand it until I had read it three times and could separate the words, and give them the right emphasis. Even then, I could barely translate the words: there had been a boating accident, Orlando and Phoebe had drowned, I was to go home immediately — *boating accident? drowned?* I had questions, but a cable has no nuances; it is a foreign language, cryptic at its baldest.

The paper I held in my hand was stupid, innocent, not comprehending its terrible news. Already I was looking around the room for support and in my hysteria saw the tiny curled squares of newly printed pictures — so trivial and mocking I screamed at them. My voice terrified me. It seemed to come from outside my room, where I had left my life, and its echo was a succession of other sounds, like the harsh gasp of a cat when it sneezes.

Part Five

Part Five

28

Spitting Image

"ALL MANIACS have a spitting image," I was saying to Frank. "And listen — not only maniacs!"

Our Guggenheim Fellow was still rifling the windmill. Though I had kept pace with him in recalling the circumstances of the pictures he had progressively unearthed, I had paused so often to frame these strange events in my mind that my own retrospective lagged behind the pictorial one he was assembling. I was like a child being led away, but delayed on her journey because she keeps glancing back to remember. Mentally, I was in London, reading the terrible telegram: I had no picture of that. What happened next? I was stuck in grief, and Frank had skipped ahead ten years or more, sorting pictures of yet another European visit. In his hand was the portrait of Ezra Pound which, a moment before, occasioned my remark about maniacs.

It was the crazy-haired old man portrait showing Ezra the ham-bone singing loony tunes with his eyes shut. *Ro-hoses are bloo-hooming, Te-hell troo-hoo.*

"What I don't get," said Frank, rattling the picture — he had more under his arm, the morning's harvest — "is why didn't you have a retrospective ten years ago?"

"Because it would have meant," I said, and I stopped. I looked at his silly searching face: if I told him some I'd have to tell him all. I said, "I didn't go into the windmill ten years ago."

"You don't go in there now."

"Troo-hoo," I said, glancing at Ezra. Or twenty, when I did this European batch; or thirty, when I arrived after the long flight from London — too late to go to Orlando and Phoebe's funeral. What was the point in my delving? The windmill, however palatial a structure — raised up on our Cape Cod lawn like a Dutch forgery — had become an anteroom of my memory, a catchbasin for my pictures, an attic, a shrine. It was to my work what a corresponding piece of my bunched-up brain was to my life, another set of crenelations and ramparts, containing the past. As a picture-taker I had ruled like a queen, but in this retrospective I wished to be a subject.

I had always been orderly: I threw nothing away. The windmill held my photos and the picture palace of my imagination another set, a different version of the past. I had thought that someday I would chance the windmill — I'd go in and have a good look. But I had not dared: ghosts thrashed on the floor, the double image of lovers who had not known what I had seen in those blinding seconds before the war. It had never been mine, not any more than Orlando had been mine. I could use it like an attic, but like an attic it was not a place I could live in. I would not deceive myself further or disturb those ghosts.

All Papa had said was, *They went out too far.* Of course: it was why they had been so happy and why they died. I accepted the explanation, and I wasn't desolated, because a person's death is easier to take if he had known a great passion. Only the death of children, of the ignorant and inexperienced, is truly tragic, the loss of people who die never having lived. I could not but feel that, out too far and knowing the risks, Orlando and Phoebe had capsized and danced on the waves for a while in each other's arms. Celebrating their secret, they had known ecstasy.

It had nothing to do with me. They had lived without me and loved and died; and neither had seen me. It had made me solitary, which is the first condi-

tion of a photographer. I was, as I had always been,
alone, just a peeping picture-taker. Don't mind me —
pretend I'm not here. And the windmill with its stilled
sails, once alight with their love, was all that remained.
I might stick my head in and leave my pictures behind,
but I had no right to linger there. They had conse-
crated every corner. It was a shrine: I left my pictures
as offerings.

Knowing what I knew, it was almost amusing to
hear Frank ask me why I had never rifled the windmill myself and assembled a retrospective. Ignora-
muses pose the hardest questions!

But I could not be angry with Frank. He was doing
the spadework. Interested in my pictures he had interested me in my life, and his sifting and sorting had
made it possible for me to re-enter the past without
going into the windmill. He preceded me, cued me,
triggered my memory; he was the mechanical
medium by which I could examine my picture palace.
But my work — as I had told him — was the least
important thing about my life; and the rest, which had
always been separate and impermanent, a source of
ceaseless wonder.

The fellow knew nothing. He did not even know
Orlando's name. For Frank, I was my work, and short
of autobiography there seemed no way of proving to
him that my story was not in my pictures. It was all
off-camera, in the pitch of my blind body's witness.
And yet I needed Frank to remind me of that contradiction.

"I've always liked this one," he said, still looking
admiringly upon the squinched face of Ezra Pound,
that crumpled rubber road map.

"That's just what I mean," I said, following my own
train of thought. I wondered if I should let him in on
the secret. "There's quite a story behind that picture."

He became attentive in the cringing way that is
characteristic of fellowshippers who are fearful, hearing a secret revealed, that their reaction might be
wrong: they might laugh too hard or too soon or not

at all, the cash a dead weight on their sense of spontaneity. "I've got work to do," Frank was always saying — but if I found it hard to take my own work seriously, how could I keep a straight face about his?

"I remember when this baby appeared," he said, holding Ezra up, sort of mounting him in the air. "It caused a sensation."

"A certain flurry," I said, and looked at Frank. Over several months, while I had been preoccupied with my life and Frank with my work, he had changed his image. Some wild access of confidence? The Guggenheim money? He had let his hair grow over his ears, he wore bell-bottom trousers with three-inch cuffs, and russet clodhoppers with four-inch heels. His pink shirt was open to the navel, so I could see on his skinny curator's chest two strings of beads. Beads! They matched the beaded bracelet where his watch had been. Very stylish, but he could not quite bring it off. He looked uneasy in the clothes, like a damned fool in fact, who had gone too far and suspected that I might mock him. But I only found the clothes discouraging. As soon as I saw those beads and platform shoes I knew I could not possibly depend on him.

"Wasn't it the first picture of Pound to appear after he was let out of the funny farm?"

I said, "One day I was in a magazine office in New York and the editor says, 'Have a look at this — ever see anything like it?' It was a picture of a turkey buzzard pouncing on a snake — three pictures, actually, the approach, the snatch, and the getaway. 'Amazing, isn't it?' he says. I agreed. But it was too amazing — so perfect I didn't believe it. Anyway, wildlife photography seems as silly to me as talking animals. I says, 'There's something about that snake. Doesn't it seem rather limp to you?' He was annoyed. 'You think it's a fake?' 'Just dead,' I says. He tried to defend the picture. 'But it's a fine turkey buzzard!' he says. 'What turkey buzzard,' I says, 'would want to eat a dead snake?' We looked at the turkey buzzard, a rigged-up bird with crooked wings. I says, 'Stuffed.

And the mountain looks pretty suspicious, too.' I thought that man was going to cry."

"Wait a minute," said Frank. "Does that have anything to do with this picture of Pound?"

"Everything," I said. "It's a turkey, isn't it?"

Frank said, "You're always so critical of your work."

"You'd be critical too, if you were in my shoes."

"They're great pictures."

"They're stiffs," I said. "They don't matter. If you had any sense you'd see that."

"You know," he said, fingering the beads around his neck, "I'm glad I'm doing this retrospective. The way I see it, I'm kind of saving you from yourself."

"Listen, buster. I took that picture in Italy around 'fifty-nine or so. I'd been sent to do a photographic essay on Cocteau and Picasso, but Venice wasn't far from Cannes and my editor was screaming for a glimpse of Pound, who'd just been let out of his rubber room. The only thing was, he refused to see me. His wop servant slammed the door in my face. 'We don't want any!' T. S. Eliot gives me a pep talk and two cups of tea, and Pound won't even give me the right time. Anyway, a few days later, I'm on the coast in Rimini having some spaghetti and I look up and who do I see walking by the restaurant? Ezra! I whistled down my noodles and rushed off in hot pursuit. Ezra's just strolling along, tapping his walking stick and singing. It was unmistakably him, whiskery and old, in a floppy hat and jacket. 'Wait a sec,' I said, 'aren't you Ezra Pound?' He sort of grins and says, 'Waal, bless my buttons,' and shows me his fangy teeth. We start talking about poetry — Eliot, Cummings, Frost, whoever. He names someone and I say, 'I've done him.' 'How about a cup of tea at my place?' he says, and I can't believe my luck. My picture's as good as in the bag.

"Up the road we enter the courtyard of a run-down palazzo. He takes me into the study, a funny little room — there's a small bookshelf with only three books on it. 'The greatest books ever written,' he says. *Gone With The Wind, The Pisan Cantos,* and *Picture Palace,* by a man called R. G. Perdew. 'I've heard of the first two, and I love the title of the third one,' I said, 'but who's this R. G. Perdew?' He said, 'Why, that's me!' 'You're not Ezra Pound?' I asked. 'Occasionally,' he said.

"Occasionally? It turns out that this guy's pretending to be Pound — wants people to take him for the poet, even writes letters to him. 'Do me a favor,' I says. 'Ask your friend Pound if he'll let me do him. I can't go home until I get a picture of that man.' Perdew gave me a very Pound-like whinny and leered crazily at me. 'Looks like you ain't going home, dearie,' he says. 'Ezra don't pose for pictures.' 'Crap,' I said. 'Picasso jumped at the chance up in Cap Ferrat.' 'Ezra don't jump no more. And the fact is,' said this Mister Perdew, 'even if you did do him, no one would recognize him. They wouldn't believe you. He don't look like Ezra Pound. He's all scrawny and shriveled up with bug juice. Looks like some derelict. I know cause I've seen him. He used to look like me, this little bushy beard and sombrero. But now he don't.' So I said, 'All righty then, I'll do you.' And I did. He was so pleased he started singing a song. Later on he showed me his pictures. They were a damn sight better than Ezra's poems and so was my portrait."

Frank said, "You mean it's not Pound?"

"No, but it's a dead-ringer. Now do you still think you're throwing me a rope?" I let this sink in, then said, "My pictures are worthless, Frank. But there's a moral. Every maniac has a spitting image. Whose double-ganger are you?"

"Maybe yours."

"Don't make me laugh. I'm an original." Or was he? Was this barnacle my Third Eye, the camera I had renounced? Perhaps even in his necklace and funny shoes he was necessary to me.

"Your Picasso — is it faked?"

One might have thought it was a bit of trick photography, the famous googly-eyed head printed on a naked body. But, "Nope. That's the real McCoy. He loved posing bare-ass."

"This one of Somerset Maugham is terrific."

"The Empress Dowager — he had more wrinkles than Auden, that other amazing raisin. Poor old Willie. He was on the Riviera then, too. The English are so portable. I caught him on a bad day. He was brooding over a case of constipation, but as soon as I did him I knew people would look at him and think he was speculating on the future of mankind. Ain't it always the way?"

"And that's when you did your Cocteau?"

"Correct. Looks like a sardine, don't he? He says to me, 'Ja swee san doot le poet le plew incanoe et le plew celebra.' I says, 'May oon poet — say la shows important.' 'Incanoe,' he says, full of that weepy French dignity. 'May commie foe,' I says, and when he starts in again I says, 'Murd de shovel,' and keeps on clicking."

"I love these Fifties shots," said Frank. "All those faces."

"I couldn't stand the landscapes. Venice was water-logged, the canals full of minestrone. And the south of France, which is supposed to be Shangri-La, just looked like one of the crummier Miami suburbs, except that there was no place to park. You can have all that vulgarity at a third of the price anywhere on Cape Cod. I hated it. What is Europe, anyway? Museums, greasers, winos, toy cars, churches, bum-pinchers, ruins, worthless money — no wonder they're uncreative. History and religion. Boring? You have no idea. I used to look at Europe and think, *Do me a favor!*"

"Now I understand why you liked Cuba."

"Loved it, loved the revolution — that was a real kick in the slats," I said. "I turned down the José Marti scholarship, but went anyhow, and appeared on TV with Ché Guevara and some American college kids. All those beards! A week or so later I did Hemingway. During the war I had been scared of him — wouldn't go near him. In Cuba he was just another fisherman,

but a damned spooky one. He wanted me to make him
look athletic. I made him look like Joe Palooka.
He lapped it up. Between him and the Guevara boom
in the Sixties I think you could say I got a lot of mile-
age out of that trip."

"I'd better get back to work," said Frank.

"You don't have far to go," I said. "I didn't do
much in the Sixties. A couple of weeks in Vietnam doing refugees, a stopover in Hong Kong. Some group
shots. Keep an eye out for them — they're to go with
my Woonsocket graduation. The whole John Hancock
insurance company, every single employee standing in
Copley Plaza — I shot it from the roof of the Boston
Public Library. I did a lot of other crowds, too —
there's one of Red Sox fans on the bleachers of Fen-
way Park. They're beautiful, three thousand faces —
you could spend a week with that picture and not get
bored."

"I'll put them aside."

"I can't believe you're nearly done."

"It's shaping up. The show has to open in a month,
Maude."

"But there must be lots more that you haven't
shown me." And I tried to think what I had not seen
— the ones I had done for the *National Geographic*,
the nudes in which I had slipped the back view of a
buttocky boy, some of the steamier Pig Dinner ones.

Frank said, "I haven't hidden anything."

"I didn't say you had."

He looked offended — more than offended:
wounded by my simple statement, and desperate, as if
I had found him finagling.

"Everything's in order," he said, jerking his head at
the windmill. "Go see for yourself."

"Not on your tintype."

He said — and I couldn't help but feel he was deliberately changing the subject — "Are you going to
write something personal for the catalogue?"

"I'm thinking about it."

"Only a paragraph or so."

"Who do you take me for — Ralph Eugene Meat-yard? The unspeakable Stieglitz? Cecil Beaton? I'm no writer."

"It would interest people."

"There's only one way to interest people. Something really sensational. Do an Arbus. Take a lot of mad crazy Weegee pictures of people you hate, and then swallow rat poison. Then they'd come flocking. Suicide explains everything."

"Poor Diane," he said (I loved his use of first names: Alfred, Yousuf, Maggie, Jill, Nancy — I could hear him in New York saying, "Maude — "), but he looked like a clown grieving in those bizarre clothes, like my picture of Emmett Kelly, the sad face beneath the greasepaint. Frank twirled one of his string of beads. "If you're having trouble writing you could do what I do when I get stuck. I tack sheets of paper on the walls around my room, then whenever I get an idea I just scribble it down — a word, a phrase, anything. I get a body of thought here, a body of thought there. I put them all together and hammer out my piece."

"It sounds a bit" — I wanted to say "stupid."

"Sure, it's complicated. But it loosens the thought processes."

"I think I'll wing it," I said. "In the meantime, keep digging, Frank, and if you come up with anything un-usual, let me know."

In the succeeding days the pictures he brought me reminded me of the many magazines that had paid my way and finally crashed — dear old *Collier's*, the win-ning *Saturday Evening Post*, the all-purpose *Look*, and vividly illiterate *Life*. I had always liked the big-format family magazine in which a two-page picture could be bled at the margins, and the photograph it-self wrapped around your face, your nose in the staple where it belonged. When television sent those maga-zines into liquidation, photographs were reduced in size. They either had news value or they didn't count, and ambitious pictures like my group portraits *John Hancock* and *Red Sox Fans* became unthinkable.

It was about then, with the folding of *Life,* that I abandoned my idea for the panning shot with which I had hoped to fill an entire issue: a sequence of pictures taken from South Yarmouth, Massachusetts, to San Diego, California. *Cross Country* I had planned to call it, every inch of it in tiny pictures. And if that worked I'd do the ultimate panning shot, around the world in a zillion frames.

I stopped working for magazines. I could not bring myself to do the ghoulish photojournalism that was so much in demand — two children falling ten storys from a burning balcony, the seconds-before-death pictures of executions and ambushes and train wrecks: snuff shots, as they were called. Several publishers offered me contracts to collaborate on picture books, with texts by famous writers, as Agee and Evans had done on the peckerwoods. I probably would have done it if it had meant only pictures, but I could not see how forty pages of tortured prose like Jim Agee's would have helped my pictures. He wanted to make the reader see the pictures, so he described them, every blessed detail, but before I knew it I was in the dark, stumbling among the subordinate clauses and tripping over semicolons, each word calling to mind a thousand pictures, as I was fond of saying.

The beauty of photographs, I told those publishers, was that they required no imagination. They took your breath away, dragged you under and kept you there. The written word was a distraction, and anyone who wrote about pictures was just showing off. No one got fat reading about food — he just got hungry. On the other hand, my *Cheeseburger* was as good as a meal. Many people burped after they looked at it.

"Nearly done," said Frank, some days after the Pound business. He showed me an interior shot of my own house.

"Whose Room?" I said.

"That's what I was going to say."

"It's a sequence," I said. "Objects have memories. Rooms are psychic."

"I'd love to hear all about it," he said. "But I have to go down to New York to check the audio for the show."

"Audio? I thought this was a picture show?"

"The tapes I was telling you about. Sea gulls and waves. Traffic. It's a new concept I'm working on — atmosphere."

"If you're catching the bus to New York, Fusco," I said, and looked at his beads and those high-heeled shoes, "you'd better go fluff up."

He left me with the picture. A parlor; but come a bit closer. Look at the cigar butt in the ashtray, the knitting on the stool, the dents and worn places in the chairs, Papa's reading glasses, Mama's handbag — she never went anywhere without it. And more: two flower stalks in a vase, with their petals missing, and out the window a fisherman, obviously a trespasser, making his way to the beach: low tide. It is a poem. Two people have just left that picture.

He died first, of a coronary that killed him by pinching one pipe, then another, until finally all his systems failed. It was not the departure he had wished, "leaving the building" on a moment's notice. He was kept waiting, and he hated that. When we were together, Mama and I were strangers to each other; and she knew it was her turn. She broke her hip, caught pneumonia and finally let go. Her last words: "Pull up the shades."

The deaths of Orlando and Phoebe, the loss of my parents, only hurt me on cold rainy days, like a football injury, a bad knee.

Though I still took pictures, and was visited by youngsters — every two years or so there was a photography epidemic and I was rediscovered — I did nothing of any importance. The great picture magazines were gone, the galleries were full of conceptual junk (*Six Bricks, Doris's Tit, Untitled #82*) and minimals and people doing it with mirrors. I began to doubt that photography was an art. It was a way of life, the best vocation for a single gal to get out and meet people, find a husband, make a few bucks. "I want to be a photographer" was a plea for love.

I could not be too cynical. Photography had taught me to see. It was harmless enough, but it was only a beginning; blindness had taught me much more about vision. My life had been interesting, I had been lucky, and until Frank arrived that summer I believed that I had been mostly happy and had never hurt anyone.

Something short and personal, he had said, after I had returned from London in the summer, when I faced the fact that pictures lied like damnation, and my heart seizure — so like Papa's — needled home the fear that I might not have much time left to tell the truth.

And even then, after so long, I did not know what the truth was.

29

Bodies of Thought

THERE MUST BE more, but where? Frank was not around to answer the question. And I was glum, the Cape was deserted, the tourists had gone: WINTER RATES said one sign, SEE YOU NEXT YEAR another, and CLOSED FOR SEASON on Kopper Krafts, Pilgrim Laundromat, and the Leaning Tower of Pizza; empty beaches, clear water, hordes of tiny fiddler crabs, and every motel reflecting my depression in its pitiful motto, VACANCY. There is no wasteland like an abandoned resort, no more melancholy sight than drizzle and wind tearing at cheap plastic.

I remembered phrases; I hadn't seen the pictures that fit them. The captions had stayed, the pictures were gone, so the captions were meaningless. The baboon I had done — under protest — for the *National Geographic* remained in my mind as "Airbrush flies, remove genitals." The Marilyn Monroe pictures I had refused to retrieve from the windmill even after the editor had moaned, "Mailer needs them for his book." The annual winter swim of the L-Street Brownies. The ones I had done of gawkers at the Family of Man exhibition, of Walker in Connecticut, of the shopping mall on Route 28, of the pretty policewoman with the pistol and nightstick in Hyannis (called *Move Along*); the medium close-up of the elderly bag-carriers at Angelo's Supermarket in South Yarmouth — "They thought I was going to seed," one retired soap-powder salesman had said, heaving my groceries into the back of my Chevy and wiping his hands on his apron: I remember that, but where was the picture? Frank had not shown me that one, or the others.

Was I only imagining that I had done *Mailman's Shoes*, *Butcher's Apron*, and *Harry Truman*? I had always believed that I had been fascinated by double images. I had seen a few — but the rest? The Gay Head Indians on the Vineyard? Kennedy on his sunfish? Or the busing pictures I took only a year before in South Boston (negative prints with a difference: the shanty Irish showed up as black monkeys gibbering at white mothers)? Gone.

And where were those so-called erotic pictures I had done for the skin magazine? I was ashamed of them, but I knew that if I had a chance to look closely at them I would remember the weather, the light, the circumstances, an incident, a syllable to grasp, so I could tug memory from its dark hole.

The pictures I had taken were not the ones I studied, not the foreground figures — everything but. Oh, this was curious. My eye tracked around them to slightly-out-of-focus fences and buildings, or to little people far-off watching me work. I found a new alignment in these shots, a back-to-front reality as I traveled deeper into the picture, sometimes surprising myself by seeing new lisps and stammers. Someone watching from a window, laundry blowing from a line I had taken to be empty, or the man in the *Ghost Ship* sequence — had he been there at the time, or sneaked in at a later date? Boats appeared on seas that had been featureless when I'd photographed them; faces where there had been only shadows; buds had burst into flower and leaf and, over the years, some of the trees I'd shot had died. Most of my subjects' expressions had changed, grins to frowns, dimples subsided, eyes had grown shiftier, and people who had looked wise had become wicked or smug.

Perhaps there were no more pictures, none with secrets, only fixed images with nothing in front, nothing behind, the flat surface absolute as a mirror of ice re-

flecting my face in a certain light and forestalling my
drowning. Perhaps it didn't matter. I had remembered
the important things — my girlhood, my love, my
blindness, and the few adventures which, until I examined them, had seemed uncomplicated pleasures.

And yet, since the war, when I had felt like a failure, as if I had seen nothing and what I had done had
been strictly private — no one paying any attention
— and sensing in my loneliness the selfish widowing of
wasted time and trying not to care where my life had
gone — at these times, someone, usually a gal, always
carrying a camera, would show up and remind me that
I had been original or witty, that she had seen something I had done, and I would rejoice and want to
stick fifty dollars into her hand.

Though I satirized him for being a barnacle, I felt
that way about Frank. I could not mock him without
mocking myself. Secretly, holding my breath, I valued
him: I needed his esteem. He was the young brash
confidence I'd once had, single-minded, bossy, without
any misgivings, convinced that photography mattered.
I had become his subject: he was doing me.

Frank had my crotchets, my spinster's secrecies. He
was wary of intrusions and kept his privacy private.
He didn't know me; I didn't know much about him,
but what I knew of him resembled the part of myself
that I was determined to hide. I needed his esteem,
but more, I needed his silly questions. Without him, I
would have assumed the myth that others had created
around me, and when it came time to reassemble the
past, that would have been the version I'd have put
forth. But the truth was elsewhere, and in retrospect I
saw that the life I had taken to be so happy was incom-
plete and contradictory. Frank had helped me to see
that, because his ignorant curiosity caused him to
fling himself on me. He was still a barnacle, but he
was plugging a leak, keeping me afloat. Now he was
away. I missed the little bastard.

When I had challenged him about photography —
the pictures I no longer trusted — I wanted him to

fight back. He usually had, and I was grateful. I needed him around to verify that the person he imagined was really me. I wanted to ask him if he was disappointed in me, if there was something I had missed, and today I wanted to ask him what happened to those pictures. Were they fantasy? If so, how else had I deceived myself?

I looked out the parlor window and saw the plumed arms of cedar bushes work their elbows in and let the sea breeze bustle past. A row of dry flowers nodded, a ripple ran through the uncut lawn. And a light came on in the Sound, a bright medallion that surfaced and just as quickly sank. It was like that other time, after Mama died, when I had stood in the same parlor and found the picture of the old folks' chairs, and took it. And in removing that picture I had deleted one more vision from my world.

I was alone. I didn't like it. Frank's absence had left my life ajar. I was overdue for a gal with a camera to make her way to the front door. "Excuse me, are you Maude Pratt?" They always asked: no one knew my face. But she would remind me of a picture I had forgotten and bring me a flattering remembrance of the fact that I had lived.

At the window this fall day I experienced a great emptiness, the yawn of familiar sky and old repeating weather. Wind was wind, sky sky, drizzle drizzle: my pictures not mine. *Look out your window*, the photography manuals said. *There is your picture. In the place you least expected it. Waiting to be taken.* That was a lie only beginners believed.

I saw the windmill and said sharply, "Fusco! What have you gone and done with my pictures?"

The memory of my blindness had always kept me out of the windmill. But today, desperate for a clue, I braved the path and walked to the narrow window. On tiptoe I looked in; and I was astonished by its neatness. It had been swept bare — smooth benches on a floor of planks, a gaping trunk, the thick vertical screw and cogwheels of the vane's machinery: like

the stalled flywheel of the narrative in my mind. I
peered, as if into my empty head. Frank had been
thorough. He had done his work well. Seeing this
conical room so stripped it was as if every picture I'd
taken had been imaginary.

The past — that darkroom — was illusion. It was
possible for me to believe that because it had so completely vanished it had never existed. I was a particle
of light streaking through space, leaving no light in my
track. In removing my pictures, Frank had taken
away my past and tidied the evidence away. I had no
life — perhaps I had never had one. The feeling I got
in strange hotel rooms, that I didn't exist, came upon
me here on the broad lawn.

He had detached my pictures from me. With the
pictures I was two people, the photographer, the person. Without them, I was no one.

Panic sent me back to the house — that sense of
exposure woken by the hoot *You!*, that seeks the re-
assuring noises of habitation, the clunk of floors and
hubbub in pipes. I did not pause. I went straight to his
room.

Months before, I had been bored and curious and
had poked in his room and felt justified. Wasn't he
doing the very same thing to me? Today I sought
refuge there. I wanted to see — what? — another of
his mother's letters; read my name, satisfy myself that
I was real. And my excuse, and part of my intention,
was that there were pictures I had not seen, incidents
bleached on the tide-wrack of memory, years I could
not account for. The pictures must have been somewhere: *Marilyn, Move Along, Mailman's Shoes,* and
more — if I saw them I would be able to continue.

The door was open. After my first intrusion, his
threats, my promises, he trusted me. Thank God for
that. If he hadn't trusted me I would not have been
able to betray his trust. But what betrayal? My bed,
my bureau, my table and lamp, his shoes in my closet,
his comb on my dresser, his fusty bachelor smell in the
drawers, his calendars —

No, not calendars, but sheets of paper tacked to the wall, just as he had explained to me, his method of writing. Six of them worked over with a felt-tip, "bodies of thought."

"If people aren't thinking it's impossible to get a good likeness."

Maude says every picture contains its complete history, past and future. "The majestic echo of image."

Tape, lettering guides, bird calls, hooks, wallets, stiff cardboard. Extruded mountings. Bus ticket, bank, P.O., Bufferin.

First with golf-ball grain, high contrast, halation, negative prints, available light, etc. Abandoned them when others used them.

"The Bible is in error—in the beginning was the picture or Image." Photography: "Matter over mind."

In fifty years of photography, no self-portrait. Why?

Seeing these notations and mottos made me feel better, though I was tempted to pick up the pen and scribble additions to these bodies of thought, meddle with posterity. I resisted. I went over and sat on our friend's bed — my bed — and felt a queer sensation in my body, the bed's memory of its occupant's restless sleep. A residue of heat, his sad story seeping through the blankets. He was weak and lonely, stifled by his own grim company.

The bedside table stood handily by. I recalled my first excursion here, the pictures of Kenny and Doris. Oh, well. Let's bring ourselves up to date. Did pornography freaks outgrow their infatuation with one sequence of sticky pictures, get tired of leering at the

same set of views and move on to fresh batches, as
philanderers sought new conquests?

The drawer was shallow. A few photography magazines as before, and seeing them reminded me how for
years it was the photography magazines which had
printed the nudie shots, all the solemn camera jargon
(*1/10th, f-8, slight haze*) under a pair of tits or a
dimpled bum. At the back of the drawer was a chunk
of prints with nicked edges: Doris kneeling, twatty;
Kenny plugged into Doris; Doris in boots; Doris looking for something on her person; Doris with a grip on
Kenny's joystick; Kenny nibbling; Doris tooting his
clarinet; Kenny straining; Doris going woof-woof;
Kenny riding Doris; Doris athwart Kenny; Kenny bug-
eyed; Doris bespattered. Yuck.

And *Marilyn,* and two Pig Dinners, and my half-
dozen erotic ones, done — I now remembered — not
for a "man's magazine" but for a photography annual
which, because it was for professionals, could get
away with murder: strawberry licker, cello torso,
sprawler, squatter, nipple examiner, and the leggy
nude climbing a pole — the buttocky boy.

There was one more picture, of two people, neither
Kenny nor Doris. Nor was it deliberately erotic. I tried
to put it away. I brought it near my face, and it
brimmed like a rising tide of light.

He was on his knees, the veins standing out on his
forehead, marble and blood, in a posture of furious
pagan prayer, his mouth fixed in demand. There were
clawmarks on his shoulders. He might have been
swooning, dying in a fit, he looked so tormented. His
reflection blazed on the floor, a white shadow struggling under him, his double heaving at him. It was a
dream I had dreamed: the two bodies creased, light on
light, in a spasm of completion, nearly one.

The photograph matched my memory perfectly,
but how had it occurred?

The day was not so dark through the far window,
though the room was small and that flywheel like the
intimation of eclipse. God, they looked so young!

Hurry was implied on their faces, but they were caught in a penetrating embrace, eternally coupled in thought and body, like a pair of lovers on the weedy sea-floor where they had fallen.

No, I gulped. But I had started to go under.

30

Drowning

AFTER the first shock of bright airless matter slapped my mouth and masked my eyes and flushed me in sudden liquid, I stopped fighting for breath and bobbed like a cork. Then I fell again. I plummeted through a pipe of watery laughter and as I sank became lighter and the curvature around me more luminous and expressive. I was clearly drowning.

As I surrendered to this silly descent I slowed down. It was easy for me to see the jets of turbulent zeros bubbling past my face. This clouded cream-soda gave way to foam, to parcels of color, green and yellow-blue, like silks tossing a little way off, striping me as they moved. I made a fishy motion and the formless pressure of the fountain wrung me apart scale by scale, and I glittered, sifting down in pieces like sequins from a torn gown.

If I had not known better I should have said I was flying. But I had been here before, drowning in the wayward magic of the eye, stricken by glory — long ago, when I had still believed in the power of the photograph to drag the victim into its depths. Now I was ashamed of my helplessness at having pitched forward into one of my own photographs. I plunged toward a whimper of light.

It was a drunken experience of dying — separation and the sucked-down sensation of finality — like someone stretching me out of my tights. Shapes were clarifying below me, but I was conscious that the vision that was animating me would destroy me — I was being tickled to death. I knew that it was too late to do anything but endure it. I would not have a second chance.

The photograph (once through the floodgate I scarcely remembered what it was) had worked. It had defied and drowned me, and for those first instants upside down I thought *damn,* because I was learning the hard way what I had always known. And the deeper I went the more convinced I was that beyond this fatal blinding light there was only darkness and no one to tell.

My ears roared with the racketing laughter of the torrential water. This decreased in volume, but I was still aware of sound — of sound fading — as if I were being deafened by it. Then the silence was perfect. There was a room down here, and bodies, and voices — marine whispers.

— *I was supposed to guard it with my life.*

— *She's in London. She'll never know.*

I tried to reply, but nothing happened. I wasn't there — my body wasn't. I had shrunk to a vivid speck suspended in circular time.

— *Look at all the pretty pictures.* Lengthened voices, ribbons of them repeating *ictures, ictures.* The conical echo of that room.

— *I've seen them all before.*

— *Cookie saved everything. That's a sign of loneliness.*

— *Put them away.*

— *No. There you are. Your white dress. Your hat.*

— *And you showing off.*

— *There's Papa.*

— *That's all.*

— *Wait. Her boogie-men. And this must be Florida.*

They were children in danger. I wanted them to stop, to go away, for their own good. But they were stubbornly playing, toying with risk. I thought: The past is not illusion — it is ignorance, it is all needless danger; inaction saves us. But they would not go away. They continued to sift through the trunk of pictures, compelled by their curiosity and the love that made them foolishly bold.

— *Oh, God. Look.*

In that moment they were lost. The water surrounding me rubbed their moans in my ears.

— *How could she?*

— *It can't be us.*

— *It is. I won't look at it.*

— *We'll have to do something.*

— *Put it away. Pretend we didn't see it.*

— *It's too late. She knows. She always knew.*

— *Put it back!*

— *She wanted us to see it.*

The speck I inhabited trembled tamely touching bottom.

— *We're sunk.*

— *I won't give you up.*

— *It's impossible.*

— *I don't care if they find out.*

— *They've found out.*

— *They'll have to forgive us.*

— *No. There's only one way they'll understand.*

— *Tell me.*

— *Don't make me say it.*

A chance current disturbed the ribbed sea-floor and took their voices away. I was still listening, but their voices were gone. *Ploop, ploop* — a fish tank's murmur. There was a shadow, time turning blue; day, night; light, dark; the light changed, nothing else did.

— *You're wrong. It's not a choice. It's the only thing left.*

— *But so soon. You!*

— *Don't cry.*

But they were both crying and I knew that this sea I was lost in and had no hope of leaving was made immense by their tears. In this moonstruck tide I was pushed by their sorrow.

— *I can't live without you. So I'm not afraid to die.*

— *What they know won't die.*

— *I want them to know everything.*
— *Then we'll leave the picture and go.*
— *I'll go anywhere with you.*
— *There's only one place for us. There.*

Now a small flare of heat in that ocean of tears,
the winking deception of this depth in which nothing
solid moved — only the light invading from above
and losing itself at this motionless limit. I had died.
I knew what they didn't. But I couldn't save them.
His courage was partly pretense — he had gone too
far to deny it. And she who had been quick to love
was impatient to die, recklessly believing her passion
to be reason enough.

— *People kill themselves for less.*
— *Maybe they only kill themselves for less.*

Not even worms lived here. The dust-motes and
droplets of color simulated life among the shell splinters, stirred like me in the shallow troughs of the sea-
bed. Did they know that beneath the erupting waves
the sinking light was pulverized to dust and darkness?

— *We'll show them.*

And they showed me I deserved this death for my
blind treachery. They were whispering, excited, full
of plans, setting sail. Soon they were tacking toward
the open sea. In all that buffeting they were silent
and the voyage out was over before they knew it —
too soon. Already he was dragging the sail down,
paying out the sea anchor, comforting her as they
bobbed madly in the little boat, prolonging the moment.

— *Let's wait till it gets dark.*
— *Then I won't be able to see you. I want to hold
you. Will it hurt?*
— *Not if you keep swallowing.*
— *I'm afraid. I want it to happen, but I'm afraid.
Help me.*
— *I love you.*
— *Yes, yes.*
— *What's wrong?*

— I just thought of Maude.
— Poor cookie.
— Poor everyone.

A boom ran through the sea, causing a swell, lifting the boat, tipping it and rattling the lines. The shoreline, lightly penciled on the horizon, was indifferent. Neither earth nor sky mattered. So they kissed, their feet already in the water.

— It's cold!
— Easy does it.

They slipped through the window of this great silent palace and were happy again paddling upright and awkwardly until they grew tired and leaned back. Gulping, they ducked under and did not begin to struggle until it was too late. They ceased to move their arms or legs.

They fell slowly, wrapped together and dropping like a harmless spider on a strand of tiny bubbles. Though I passed within inches of them — and now I was rising: their dying had released me from the scrub of purification — they did not see me with their white eyes. Not a look, not one more word. They were below me, simplified to a blur, a pool of lowering light. The moment they were lost I broke clean through the surface.

[31]

Preview

New York, a wet November evening. I was walking by the museum when I saw the posters, printed on six square feet of the beatific breast-feeding shot, *The South Yarmouth Madonna.*

MAUDE COFFIN PRATT

RETROSPECTIVE

FIFTY YEARS

I was out of habit of seeing my name written so large. It stopped me. Passersby were slowing up near the posters to look. I got a kick out of my anonymity, reading over their shoulders and hearing their grunts of approval: know-it-alls boasted to their dates that they knew my work. I lingered long enough to watch some invited people go in to the preview dressed in fancy clothes, animal pelts on their shoulders, diamonds around their necks, gold on their wrists, — wearing their wealth like the rankest trophy-hunting savages. But they were hopeful, squealing in anticipation, with that just-washed look of partygoers. And they were so intent on making a graceful entrance they were unaware that on the sidewalk, in the lights of the museum marquee, I stood with my face hanging out.

I slipped in by the side entrance so that no one would see me; no one did.

The party was in progress on a second-floor landing.

To call it a landing was not to do it justice. It had an immense stone rail on one side which overlooked the staircase, and on the other side an entire wall of glass gave a grand view of the garden courtyard with its floodlit mobiles and imprisoned statuary. On the stairs to the landing people were propped, as if they owned the place, and braying.

"I am perfectly capable of finding it myself," I had said to Frank over the phone, a week before this preview. I looked for him — we had agreed to meet at the show's entrance — but if he was there I didn't see him. I assumed he was lost in the same crowd that had swallowed me.

The poster — the one I had seen out front — was plastered on the landing, rising from floor to ceiling, repeating my name and the picture, so big and numerous, was no longer mine. This was someone else's red-letter day.

"You made it! Aren't you thrilled?" screamed a woman with an animal pelt on her head. Thinking that she might be addressing me I smiled. Then she walked past me. *Oughtists,* she said in that New Yorker way to a beaming midget, *ought and ought-ists.*

"Where's Maude?" said the midget, looking directly at me. The woman didn't know. They went on talking about my works of ought.

I had stiffened to prepare myself for their rushing over and saying, "Where have you been hiding?" But no one asked the question, and I would not introduce myself. I rather enjoyed my anonymity in here, as I had outside. I could mooch around, eavesdrop, examine faces and reactions, and not be required to say a single thing. Praise can only be answered with humility or thanks; I didn't feel modest or grateful.

I was a stranger. It was the funereal feeling I had had earlier in the summer, on my return from London. But this was a joyous occasion, people saying Maude this and Maude that. I had every reason to believe that I had lived through a death by drowning. The death had shown me what I was, what I had done: it was just as well that no one recognized me.

Having entered the museum so obliquely from below I'd had to work my way up the stairs, through the throngs of people who were swigging and yelling. I had counted on seeing Frank on the landing and I winced when I gained it, expecting his shout, *Here's the star of the show!* or something equally foolish. I fought forward to the exhibit's entrance, for the party was outside the gallery proper. ENTER HERE, said a placard, but the mob I had assumed to be lining up for a look was simply gathered there blocking the way.

My impatience tired me. After fifteen minutes I was winded and wanted to sit down, or for someone— where was the peckerhead? — to rescue me. Some people stared at me and I grinned back, assuming they had recognized me. They looked away. I could not explain it, but then, I didn't recognize any of them either.

A few years before, a place like this would have been full of people I knew — Imogen, Minor, Ed Weston, Walker, Weegee — and I searched the faces for moments before I realized that they were as dead as Mrs. Cameron. In this room was the new generation of photographers and art patrons. I could spot them: that long-legged blonde in the cape, that other ingratiating gal with the sunglasses perched on her hairdo, a pair of black simpering queens, and another black looking toothy and hostile, as if he were going to shriek at me in Swahili. Most of the photographer types were wearing leather jackets, combat boots, itchy shirts — advertising themselves as toughies, men of action. Even the gals looked the bushwhacking sort. The marauders and fuck-you-Jacks of a profession that was a magnet for neurotics, they were deluded by the fear of competition and all wearing their light meters as pendants around their necks. If it was an art, it was the only one in which the

artist actually wore something that made him visibly
a practitioner.

And there were others, pairs of people, slightly
mismatched, whom I took to be photographers hand-
in-hand with their subjects. That anorexic gal and her
friend, whose face I recognized from a drugstore paperback — surely she aimed to be a credit line on his
book jacket? This dapper little man and the wheez-
ing old dame: it could only have been a relationship
that started with a studio session ("Look straight at
me, dear, and forget your hands for a minute"); the
boogie-man and the blonde with her tough twinkle —
it wasn't too far-fetched to imagine that they had
launched their romance with a camera and for all I
knew kept it airborne the same way (his brutally honest chronicling of ghetto life, her cooperation amount-
ing to human sacrifice). The bearded lout and that
girl-child; the virago and her soul-mate into, as they
would say, the woman's thing. I could identify the me-
diocrities by their catch phrases: the prancing Mini-
malists, the Deeply Committed crowd, the Really
Strange bunch, the Terribly Exciting ones, the Intos,
the Far-outs, the Flakys.

These were cannibals' success stories. But what the
hell — they were having a swell time. Photography
didn't matter: they had each other. That was the
whole purpose of taking pictures — it won you
friends, it got you fame and fresh air. "I'm working on
a new concept," said the bearded lout, and I knew
that if he hadn't been a photographer in the pay of
Jack Guggenheim he'd have gotten twenty years as a
sex offender for some outrage upon that girl-child's
person. The work was an excuse; the idea was to involve yourself with people, which was giving photography a bad name.

My anonymity made me cynical. Perhaps I was
being unfair. It was possible that they had taken pictures and developed them and, like me, at some later
date, had drowned in them, and known the terror of
what they had done.

"He's into some very exciting things."

"He hasn't had a show for years."

"I consider this an event. He's a very private person."

"He's supposed to be here somewhere."

This "he" I kept hearing about was certainly not me. I had stopped basking. My fatigue turned complacent and then panicky. I had not introduced myself, so I was temporarily forgotten. They would be justified in thinking that I was spying on them. They might round on me and say, "At least you could have had the courtesy of telling us who you were!"

But no one in that jammed room asked.

"Isn't that him?"

More than that ("Excuse me, lady," a man said, yanking a tray of drinks out of my reach), I noticed a distinct irritation when my glance met one of these wild-eyed talkers, as if I were a gate-crasher who had no right to listen. I could have put up with being ignored; I could not bear being strenuously shunned. I was in the way! And there was a lot of shoving when the real celebrities showed up, various people I had seen on television talk shows, mainly hideous novelists who had written frank autobiographical books about their unnatural acts.

"Mind moving?" This from one of our photographer friends with a chunk of expensive apparatus in her mitts, a motor-driven Voigtländer aimed at my earhole.

Someone famous had just entered. Who it was, I could not say. But there was movement, a prelude to stampede, people beating their elbows to get past me.

"Pardon me."

A man's hand squeezed my shoulder. About time. I turned and smiled.

"Are you Lillian Hellman by any chance?" The man bowed to hear my reply.

"Sorry, buster. I'm her mother."

But though I was furious for being mistaken for Lily (is there any old lady on earth who is flattered by the suggestion that she resembles another old lady?), I hoped the man would pause long enough for me to tell him who I really was. Rebuffed, he fled sideways into the mob.

Already I was sick of the party. The people had stopped talking about me and on their third or fourth drink were just whooping it up, paying no attention to the posters with my name on them.

"He's done it as a multi-media event. I'm going in as soon as they shut this wine off."

I had no business here. This was a spectacle of the kind I had avoided for thirty years. There was no reason why anyone should have recognized my face: professionally I had no face. I was for most only a name and *Twenty-two White Horses* and celebrated for a period of blindness when I had done *Firebug*. For one person I was the Cuba pictures, for another the Pig Dinner sequence; blacks knew me as the creater of *Boogie-Men*, New Englanders for *The South Yarmouth Madonna*, Californians knew only my Hollywood work, the British were aware of my London phase but nothing more, literary people my *Faces of Fiction*, and for some camera buffs I was the young gal who had done Stieglitz with his own peepstones.

To be famous is to be fixed — a picture, a date, an event, a specific and singular effort. To be fixed is to be dead, and so fame is a version of obscurity. One appeared at one's own party only to haunt it. If Frank had been around he would have steered me into the crowd and made the usual introductions, as the custodian of my reputation. But I did not see him.

Nor did I see the show. There was still a mob at ENTER HERE and it was the same bunch I had seen earlier, a bit rowdier and more drunken than before. They had found a cozy place to gather and were ignoring the exhibition — plenty of time for that when the drink ran out. The party was the thing. Yet it burned me up to think that they had come here to see each other and were not paying the blindest bit of attention to my pictures.

I wondered if I should throw a fit — wave my arms and bellow at them, maybe embarrass them with a hysterical monologue about the meaning of art; or do something shocking, make a scene that they would talk about for years afterward.

Bump.

"I'm awfully sorry." The jerk who had taken me for Lillian Hellman rushed away. The party was starting to repeat, to replay its earlier episodes in tipsy parody.

Several people, assuming my black dress to be a uniform, demanded drinks from me. They howled when they saw their mistake, but it inspired me. I found a tray of drinks and began to make my way through the room, handing them out and sort of curtseying and taking orders, saying "Sir" and "Madam" and "I'm doing the best I can."

All my photographer friends who in other times would have been here — dead. The people I had photographed: Mr. Slaughter, Huxley, Eliot, Teets, R. G. Perdew, Lawrence, Marilyn, Harvey and Hornette — dead. Editors and journalists and gallery-owners — dead. Orlando and Phoebe: now I knew I had driven them into the sea. I had killed them with a picture. I deserved this contempt — the people shunning me or treating me like a waitress; I deserved worse — to be treated like a criminal bitch who had hounded my brother and sister to death. I put the tray down and lurked in the crowd like the murderess I was.

Scuffing paper underfoot I bent to pick it up, although my first thought was to leave it so that one of these party-goers would trip and break his neck. It was the catalogue, a thickish manual with my name on the front just above Frank's, and a different picture (*Negro Swimming to a Raft* — but "Negro" had been changed to "Person," making nonsense of the picture). I had refused to write the personal statement Frank had requested and had told him that I would have nothing to do with the rest of the cata-

logue either. I should have gone further and said that
I wouldn't be at the preview party. I felt ridiculous —
guilty, stupid, ashamed — having come so far on
false pretenses. I belonged in jail.

I had made a virtue of being anonymous. I had
abided by it; and why not? Anonymity had done for
me what a lifetime of self-promotion had done for
other photographers. It was too late to reveal myself,
for there was a point in obscurity beyond which exposure meant only the severest humiliation. It was
better to continue anonymously and finally vanish into
silence. I had spent my life in shadows as dense as
those that hid me at this party. I had entered this
room as a stranger — I had to leave as one. If the
place had not been so impossibly crowded I would
have done that very thing.

Acknowledgments, I read, opening the catalogue.
There followed a list of money-machines, not only
the John Simon Guggenheim Foundation, but the National Endowment for the Arts and five others, including the Melvin Shohat Photographic Trust. If
Frank didn't make a go of his curatorship there was
always room for such a financial genius in the Inter-
national Monetary Fund.

My career, spent in attacking patronage, ended
with these cash-disbursing bodies footing the bill. But
I had forfeited the right to object. I was dead. They
were all dancing the light fantastic on my grave.

Maude Coffin Pratt, Frank's Preface began, *is
probably one of the most distinguished American photographers of our time —*

"Probably"? "One of"? "Our time"? He was pulling his punches. Quite right: I had blood on my
hands.

But there was, after all, a message from me, titled
Statement from the Artist:

The Bible says, "In the beginning was the Word."
The Bible is in error. In the beginning was the

Image. The eye knew before the mouth uttered a syllable; thought is pictorial.

Photographic truth, which I think of as the majestic echo of image, originated in the magic room known as the *camera obscura*. This admitted the world through a pinhole. Man learned to fix that image and photography was born with a bang. Painting never recovered from the blow. It began to belittle truth and, faking the evidence, became destructive.

One knows a bad picture immediately. All you can do with bad pictures is look at them. The good ones invite you to explore; the best drown you and keep you under until you think you will never return. But you do. I have had this experience myself.

Photography is interested solely in what is. *What am I?* you may ask. I can answer that question. You are a "Pratt."

On a more personal note, I was born in 1906, in Massachusetts.

Frank's work, the catalogue shorthand that left my life in the dark and my crime unstated.

"There he is," said a man next to me to his lady friend. They nearly knocked me down as they moved past me.

I got behind them and followed them across the room and saw, at the center of the largest huddle of people, the Veronica Lake hairstyle, the white fretful face, the string of beads. He wore a torn denim shirt and under it a T-shirt saying *It's Only Rock and Roll*; and bright green bell-bottoms and, I knew — though I could not see them — his platform clodhoppers. He had come a long way since the day he had turned up in a barnacle-blue three-piece suit on my Grand Island piazza. "I'd be deeply grateful if you'd allow me to examine your archives." And I had thrown the picture palace open to him.

Edging forward, I caught some of the chatter. The people surrounding Frank were talking in low voices, trying to lend sincerity to their guff by whispering it.

"It's perfectly marvelous, Frank, every last bit of it. It's got density, it's got life, and it's just about the most exciting thing I've seen for ages." This from a purring pin-striped heel, obviously a foundation man.

Frank said, "I couldn't have done it without your support. It was a long haul, but I think you'll find that your money's been well spent."

"The whole committee's here to give you a good send-off."

"It was a risk, of course, but from my point of view" — Frank made howdying haymakers with his free hand — "Hi, Tom. Hello there, Charlie. George. Norman, good to see you. Susan, glad you could make it — a risk worth taking."

His face's fretfulness had a pinch of pride. He wore a tight little smile, as if he were sucking a cough drop. His eyes were vacant with self-love.

"It must have been quite a summer up there on the Cape."

"Pretty unbelievable," said the peckerhead. "But I feel we've broken new ground."

"It's certainly a great coup for the museum."

Frank said, "The work was crying out to be seen. She had no idea."

"The presentation —"

"Presentation is incredibly important," said Frank. "I knew the minute I saw the pictures that I was on to something very big and very exciting." Saying this, he shook his head, rattling his beads, and took a tango-step forward to plant a kiss on an admiring hag.

"Frank's an amazing guy," said a young man on my right.

"Don't I know it," I said.

"He'll make a fortune out of this, but you've got to hand it to him."

"Sure do."

"Hassles? He's been getting a hand-job all summer from our friend whatsit."

"Jack Guggenheim?"

"No, um, the one who took the pictures. Pratt."

"Don't be silly," I said. "Frank's the one who took the pictures."

"Yeah."

The party had thinned out. The remaining people gravitated over to the crowd around Frank, where I was lost. Two of the photographers I had spotted earlier were snapping pictures, and Frank's face was briefly incandescent as he said, "I just hope people pick up on it in the right way."

He loved every minute of it and seemed so engrossed that he surprised me a moment later by saying, "Hey, has anyone seen Maude?"

"No," I said, and I meant it. No one heard me — they were also saying no. I crept across the room to the retrospective.

Retrospective

I WASN'T HERE, either. The place was empty, a vestibule with a stack of catalogues, more posters, a passageway like a funhouse labyrinth, and beckoning sounds: Twenties music, surf, gulls, traffic, clangs; and the sharp smell of strong light on fresh paint. No people. I looked for myself among the pictures.

The first room was book-shaped, my early shots pasted on the walls as if into an album. They were family scenes, done long ago, the boat, the beach, the house — full of wonder which, because it was innocent, looked clumsy and appealing. Not here.

A trolley bell gonged in the next room; city noises, voices half smothered in traffic. NEW YORK, *1923,* said Frank's sign, and there was *Lawrence Retreating, Mott Street, The Battery, Broadway, Chinese Grocery, Wolfpits Furriers,* and my Grand Central sequence.

The surf I had heard on entering the show was now so loud it seemed to be pounding on the adjoining wall. I walked in expecting to be dragged away by the undertow, but it was a mock-up of my Provincetown exhibition — Mrs. Conklin, *Clamdiggers: Wellfleet, O'Neill at Peaked Hill,* and the fifty or so negative prints I had called *Boogie-Men*: Teets, Doolum, Pigga, Frenise, and more.

The sea-sounds poured isolation upon me. I could not hear the party. I had entered my own world, but I felt ghostly in it — I did not exist there among *Stieglitz, Boarders, Stoker, Alligator Wrestler, Thunder*

over Boca Grande. An entire art-deco room was given
over to the Pig Dinner. There was Papa and Mr.
Carney, Harvey and Hornette, Mrs. Fritts, Mr. Biker,
'Digit' Taft, and Glory. They were slightly smoked
and blurred, as they were in my memory, and yet they
were less than I remembered. I was touched by their
trapped faces, by the naked ones' nakedness. And I
knew what was coming.

A blind wall, nothing, then *Firebug.* I did not go
close. I feared entering any of these pictures and being
submerged to suffer them again. I strolled, keeping my
distance, and saw *Frost,* the Hollywood pictures of
Huxley and Mann and Alan Ladd crying, the creepy
pietà of Ray and Cissy Chandler, the other actors in
tears. Stiffs.

The *Whose Room?* shots Frank had retitled *London
Interiors,* rather spoiling the point. But what a rogues'
gallery it was! The rooms and then the faces: Eliot,
Ackerley, Waugh, Forster, and further on Patton, G.
Stein, Cocteau, Maugham, Picasso They were not
looking at me — not surprising: the subject does not
see the photographer, only the peepstones of her Third
Eye.

I was not here, not here, nowhere, and yet I knew
that I had entered the picture palace of my own memory. I regretted my absence, but I was astonished by
how much there was here — all the forgotten pictures
Frank had not troubled himself to show me: *Apple-
Seller, The Sneeze, Junk Shop Window, Phil Rizzuto,
Mailman's Shoes, Orthodox Jewish Boys,* the impov-
erished glamor girls series, scores of blind people, and
the picture that had been inspired by an old cartoon,
Man Eating Peas with a Knife. Splendid stuff, but
where was I? Not in the group photos — *Graduation:
Woonsocket High School* blown up across one whole
wall, *John Hancock* across another — and not in
*Dancing Partners, Deliverance, Busing, Refugees,
Butcher's Apron, Move Along, Baggers,* or the twelve
pictures of Vietnamese refugees hurrying toward the
door. I looked for more and saw EXIT.

But I didn't want to leave. I headed back through the exhibit and it occurred to me how many were missing. Although to the casual viewer it was complete, an entire life, I knew there were gaps — years and years missing. Frank had left out my six erotic pictures, *Eel in a Toilet,* the ones of my family that I knew best (vivid in my mind because they were snapshots, set for infinity). Was he trying to save my reputation because he found them amateurish, or prettify his own because he thought they were vulgar?

And the murderous one of Orlando and Phoebe naked in the windmill — the only one in fifty years that truly mattered: suppressed! How like a masturbator to hide his imagery in shame.

"What retrospective?" I said aloud. To see this show, one would have thought, as I so often had, that my life had been rich and happy, full of travel and excitement, fifty years of achievement. No failures, no tears. But this was the lie of perfection imperfectly concealing that it was mostly failure. And it was hardly surprising that no one at the party had recognized me. I was not one of my pictures, or even the sum of them.

I wandered back to the Provincetown room. Frank had mounted a slide projector behind a wall, and as the sorrowing gulls cried and the waves sloshed the timbers of an invisible jetty (and was that a whiff of saltwater taffy in the air?), the pictures changed: *Dunes, Clamdiggers, Cummings, Pigga, Sunday Bonnets, Hurricane Damage.* Not mine — they were the world's property and the experience of whoever cast a glance at them. But no life was this neat.

Footsteps in the vestibule. I listened hard. One pair of clodhoppers.

"Maude!"

I turned and tried to smile.

"So this is where you've been hiding. I've been looking all over —"

"Dry up," I said.

Yet I wanted to reassure him, to hug him and say, *Forget it — it's all yours! You're welcome to it!* Then

I saw his smugly patronizing face and cough-drop sucker's mouth. I had the impression he wanted to kiss me.

I said, "I'd like to be alone."

"You've been drinking again."

To spite him, I burped, bringing the gas up from the depths of my gut. Then, pleased with this piece of theater, I wanted to go.

"Come on out and take a bow."

"No. It's time I went home."

He looked relieved. He cleared his throat. "Say, what do you think of the show?"

"Very nice, but it ain't mine. Anyway, there's one missing."

He blushed and touched at his face and left a chalk-white fingerprint of pressure on his cheek. His eyes were glazed with shame. He said, "Give it to me. I'll make room for it."

"Get a job, Frank!" I said, and couldn't help laughing. I started to walk away — and my mind raced ahead of my feet: I was home, in my room, drinking alone in my nightie and reflecting that if the pictures were his so was the guilt; and I was at last free.

"Which one?" he asked, but he didn't want to hear.

"You wouldn't know," I said. "Besides, I haven't done it yet."

I chose to leave by passing once again through the exhibition. And it struck me that the pictures told me more about Frank than about myself, for the mind was revealed by the way it distorted, or suppressed, or seized upon a particularly telling travesty. Literally that: a man in a dress spoke volumes, while a woman with a camera seemed to have few secrets. I was merely a spectator, stinking of chemicals. I had to be seen to be believed.